SALVATION

SALVATION

QUINCY HARKER, DEMON HUNTER YEAR FOUR

JOHN G. HARTNESS

Copyright © 2019 by John G Hartness

All rights reserved.

No part of this book may be reproduced in any form or by any electronic or mechanical means, including information storage and retrieval systems, without written permission from the author, except for the use of brief quotations in a book review.

For Suzy - you save me

PROLOGUE

Salvation is the collected edition of Year Four of the Quincy Harker, Demon Hunter Series, and the conclusion of the two-year Quest For Glory storyline. It is highly recommended that you read *Damnation: Quincy Harker, Demon Hunter Year Three* before reading this collection.

But you do you, boo-boo. I'm not gonna tell you how to live your life.

-JGH

I

SHE TALKS TO ANGELS

1

"Not a good time, Harker," I said into my cell phone as I put the Toaster in park. My beat up old Honda Element isn't sexy, but it's paid for and has all the cargo room I need for my day job. That day job at the moment had me stashing my panty-dropping grocery grabber at the far end of a parking lot across from The Last Ride, a biker bar on the outskirts of St. Louis. The preferred modes of transportation for the occupants of the bar apparently had at least one, usually two fewer wheels than my Element, but there were a couple of old Detroit-made penis compensation methods in the gravel lot as well. Still, I thought I'd be better off leaving my sensible sport utility vehicle parked away from all the testosterone. By the looks of the place, my car would get chlamydia if it got too close.

"I don't really care, Gabby. This is important," the self-important prick known as Quincy Harker said from my phone. I don't like Harker. I don't like the fact that he lied to me to get me to help him on our first case together (admittedly I mean more "not shoot him" than actually help). I don't like the fact that he spends the majority of his time with Dracula, the monster my great-grandfather famously hunted and thought he killed. I don't like that he seems to know a lot more about Grandpa Abe than I do, having actually met the old man when he was a little kid. And I really don't like that he and his little merry band of assholes called The Shadow Council keep talking me into doing shit that goes directly against my best interests, like getting in the middle of a goddamned demon invasion in Georgia, of all godforsaken places.

Fuck Georgia. I'm a Midwest girl, through and through. I like St. Louis. I like Chicago. I even like Detroit, and *nobody* likes Detroit. So even six months later, I was still irritated at Harker for getting me wrapped up in some bullshit save the world scheme in Atlanta last year.

"So is me getting paid, Harker. Some of us have jobs, remember? We can't all live off the riches our parasitic uncles have stashed all over the world."

"You know there's a stipend available for all Council members, right?"

I felt my eyes widen at his slightly distorted words. I took the phone off speaker and brought it to my ear. "No. That wasn't part of the friggin' welcome packet, you prick." Did this asshole mean to tell me that I'd been living on ramen and shitty bail jumper gigs for almost two years since he fucked my deal with Homeland Security?

"Oh, sorry about that. Must have slipped my mind. We can have all your back pay deposited into your account this afternoon. Now can I tell you about Lucifer?"

"No," I said. "We are not done with me bitching at you yet. You think you can just kill my contact at Homeland Security, get my monster-hunting contract with the government cancelled, and I'll forgive you just because you wave a fistful of singles under my nose like I'm some dancer at your favorite topless bar?"

"One, I don't go to strip clubs anymore. My fiancée doesn't approve. Two, you didn't even know Smith *was* your contact until he was dead and your contract got cancelled. And three, the stipend is a little more than a fistful of singles." Harker named a figure, and I got quiet. That was a *big* fistful of money.

"Is that the two years I'm owed in back pay?" I asked, swallowing hard.

"No, Gabriella, that is your annual stipend. So you're owed double that. Like I said, I'll have Dennis deposit the money this afternoon. Now can I get you to focus on the important things, like saving the world?"

I put the phone back on speaker and set it in the cupholder. I leaned back, keeping an eye on the front door of the bar. My intel said that the skip was inside and unlikely to leave until daylight, so I wasn't in much of a rush. "Got ahead, Harker. Spill it. What's so damned important? I thought we were just hunting down your hottie angel's wings."

"Yeah, it got more complicated," he said. "Lucifer is involved, and he's taken Uriel, one of the other Archangels, to Hell. If he kills Uriel while they're on a divine plane, he can take up Uriel's mantle and become an Archangel again. Then Lucifer will be able to get back into Heaven at will. I'm guessing you can see how that ends poorly for most of the known universe."

"Yeah, that doesn't sound good. So are we off of Operation Wingy-Dingy now and back on the Save the World train?" I asked.

"Not yet. We need to figure out how to get to Hell—"

"I've told you to go to hell a lot. You should have listened."

"Funny. Anyway, Luke and Dennis, along with Sealtiel, are trying to figure out how to get us across the planar divide without the requisite dying. Until they get that figured out, we're still working on the idea that the more Archangels we have at our side when we storm the Gates of Hell, the better."

"Makes sense. I'll get right on finding Ragu as soon as I'm done here."

"Raguel," Harker corrected.

"*Gesundheit.*" I hung up the phone, laughing. It was petty, and I knew it, but he was just an infuriating son of a bitch. He had it all—looks, sexy British accent, and a girlfriend that I would just love to get alone for an hour or ten. I shoved the thoughts of Harker and his hottie aside and refocused on the target at hand.

I swiped and tapped at my phone for a couple seconds, and a picture appeared. James Monroe "Blackheart" Burris was a big guy, six-three according to his mug shot, with a dark ponytail showing a little gray and a salt-and-pepper goatee. Tattoos all over his arms and creeping up from under his shirt to peek out under the neck of his t-shirt. According to my surveillance, he favored black t-shirts, often with a Harley logo, jeans, engineer boots, a chain wallet, and a leather jacket with his Sons of Hell cut on the back of it.

You know, just the kind of guy you want to take home to mama. If mama was a psychopath. I swiped across the screen, and my motivation for this job popped up on the screen. Taneisha Cooper Burris, estranged wife of the asshole currently sitting in a biker bar with his hand on a twenty-year-old waitress's ass while Taneisha sat home worrying about losing her condo if this dickhole failed to appear in court in three days. In Chicago. In Illinois, where Blackheart Burris was supposed to remain until such time as he faced trial for armed robbery according to the terms of his bail.

So while his wife worked two jobs to keep his four-year-old daughter clothed and fed, Blackheart yukked it up across state lines with some of his Sons of Hell buddies from another chapter. He'd been hanging around St. Louis for about a week before I caught wind of him, and I'd had eyes on the clubhouse for a couple days now. It was your typical biker bar—dingy, well-armed, shitload of David Allen Coe on the jukebox, and next to no police presence in the surrounding blocks.

I got out of the Toaster and walked around to the back doors. Pulling them open, I flipped the back seats down, yanked the headrests off, and lifted the inside edge of each seat, then hooked it to the wall. That turned the back of the Element into essentially a small panel van. I opened the tool box I had bolted to the floor and took out my Sig Sauer P320. I clipped the holster to the inside of my jeans and slipped the pistol home in the front of my jeans. I pulled on a loose black hoodie, dropped the front of the sweatshirt down over the butt of the gun, and grabbed two pair of zip cuffs out of the box. Not for the first time, I wondered how badly my little toy box would be received in a traffic stop and vowed to obey more speed limits and road signs in the future.

I closed the doors of the Toaster, took my hair down out of the ponytail I usually wore, and used my reflection in the rear windows of the car to slut up my lipstick and poof my hair a little. I thanked Eema for the thick black hair her Romany heritage blessed me with and put a lot more strut into my walk than normal, then headed toward the front door of the club.

I was halfway there when I realized I'd left my phone sitting in the cupholder. Oh well, it's not like there was anybody I could call to bail my ass out if I got in over my head anyway. Just another day in the glamorous life of Gabriella Van Helsing, great-granddaughter of the most famous vampire hunter in history, now reduced to chasing down bail jumpers in shitty bars in Missouri. But hey, on my off days, I got to save the world with a bunch of weirdos and monsters. Yay.

The no-neck imbecile at the door didn't even pat me down, just looked down my hoodie at the cleavage on display and waved me in. It's not even like I was wearing anything sexy, just a scoop-neck t-shirt. But men are stupid. I might as well use that stupid to my advantage.

Aforementioned stupid was on display at its finest in the bar, which boasted not only dim lights, thick smoke, and loud music, but also a pair of behemoths arm-wrestling, two stick-thin girls weaving between pinching fingers to deliver drinks, and a giant bald guy behind the bar glaring at everyone and everything. Why is the guy behind the bar always pissed off? It's not like he gets hit in the inevitable fights, he's got bar to hide behind. I sauntered over to the bar, making sure to get my hips rocking from side to side as I strutted across the sticky floor, and I leaned my hoodie-clad elbows on the damp wood.

"How about a shot?" I asked, giving him my best "come hither" look.

He responded with a scowl. "What you want?"

"Let's try something fun. How about a red-headed slut?" I gave him a smile usually guaranteed to get me at least a couple of phone numbers, if not a free drink or three.

He didn't return the smile. If anything, his scowl deepened. "All our sluts are brunettes. You want Jack or Jim?" He jerked a thumb over his shoulder at the limited booze selection.

"How about Wild Turkey? I'm feeling like bourbon. Wanna feel?"

Still nothing. Not even a crack of a smile. Damn, that one even gets me a laugh at gay bars where all the boys are prettier than me, but this guy was not interested. He poured me a shot of bourbon, and I knocked it back, feeling the brown liquor burn all the way down. I turned the glass upside down on the bar and looked at CueBall. "Another. This one on the rocks."

Then I turned around and looked around the rest of the bar, trying to zero in on my quarry. I found him easy enough, sitting at a table with his back to a wall and a blond piece of jailbait on his lap. The remains of most of a case of beer littered the floor around his table, and he and a pair of other goons passed a joint around the table right under a No Smoking sign. Everything pointed to a pretty rocking poker game in progress, and every time Burris dragged a pile of chips back to his side of the table, he slipped one into the brassiere of the girl on this lap. After a run of particularly good hands, the married bail jumper whose wife was about to lose her house because of his unauthorized travel plans spun the girl on his lap around and spent a good minute and a half using his tongue to check the health of her tonsils.

Yeah, this guy was going to get an ass-kicking. I sipped my bourbon and watched my quarry until I was down to ice cubes, then I reached behind me to set my glass down and go get my jumper. That's when the bartender grabbed my wrist and leaned over. "You're about to make a big mistake, little girl."

I really hate being called "girl." Shit was about to get real.

2

I turned to the man behind the bar and gave him my best steely glare. My glare is pretty good, but it looks a lot better when I aim it down the barrel of my Sig. CueBall took a step back, revealing the sawed-off shotgun he had aimed at my gut under the level of the bar.

"Go for it. I've been shot before. Have you?"

"I have. Not fun, but I lived through the first one. I'm willing to take my chances." I was so full of shit I squished when I walked. I'd never been shot, despite my poor choice in traveling companions and risky career decisions. But Eema taught me to bluff before I learned to drive, so I held my glare on the bartender and tried not to sweat the rest of the bikers around me.

"Put the gun down," CueBall said, making no moves to lower his own weapon.

"You first."

"My bar. You first."

Okay, that was fair. I had to give him that one. I lowered the pistol, and he stepped forward. A second later, I heard the *thunk* as he set the shotgun back under the bar. I slipped my gun back under my hoodie and leaned on the bar. "Now that we've decided not to shoot each other, what was with grabbing me?"

He grinned a little and poured me another drink. "I haven't decided I'm not shooting you yet. But if you go interrupt Blackheart while he's winning, I won't have to. He'll do it for me."

"What if I just wanted to play a few hands?" I put on my best innocent face. "I've seen poker on TV. It looks fun. But I can never remember which is better, a straight or a flush?"

Apparently my innocent face wasn't worth a shit. "Yeah, whatever. Look, I don't know what you want with Burris, and I don't really give a shit. But you bust up my place, break a bunch of furniture, and that costs me money. Then I give a shit."

"What makes you think I even know who you're talking about?" I asked.

"I'm a bartender, sweetie. I watch people for a living. You've been bird-dogging Blackheart since the second you spotted him, and that's even with the three bigger bounties in the room. So you're a bounty hunter, and not a very good one."

Three? Shit. I thought I recognized one other guy from checking out open warrants, but *three*? "Maybe I just think he's cute." That sounded lame even to me, and the snort I got from CueBall said he felt the same way.

"Okay," I admitted. "Yeah, I'm here for Burris. I don't give a shit about the other guys here, so if they're your buddies, or top customers, or whatever, I'm not gonna fuck with them. But Burris has to come back to Chicago with me, or his wife loses her house. His *wife* who isn't the slut sitting on his lap."

"That slut is my niece." I stared at him. No smile. The odds that he was yanking my chain were pretty slim. The odds that I'd just insulted his niece? Better than fifty-fifty.

"Then I'm sorry."

"Don't apologize. She is a slut. But I still don't want her getting hurt. So let me make sure she's out of the way before you go over there trying to jiggle Blackheart into leaving with you."

"Come on, dick. What makes you think I'm going to try and use my boobs to—"

"Maybe the fact that you just shoved them up into your bra and unzipped your hoodie before you got ready to walk over there." He was sharp. Maybe I could...

"No," he said as I opened my mouth.

"What? I didn't even say anything!" I protested.

"You were about to ask me to help you, probably give me some bullshit story about his evicted wife to make me think I care, and appeal to my softer side to help you get Blackheart out of here without a fuss. Well, I don't *have* a softer side, and if you want your money for bringing Burris in, you're gonna have to earn it." He folded his arms across his chest and stared at me until I turned back around and rested my elbows on the bar, staring at the poker game in the corner.

"Hey! Uncle Irving! How about another round?" the niece yelled at CueBall.

I looked over my shoulder. "Irving?"

"I go by EightBall. She only calls me Irving to cockblock me. She thinks I'm trying to pick you up."

"EightBall? I get it. It's ironic because you're like the whitest guy in Missouri. That's a high bar, by the way."

"Ha ha."

I couldn't quite see his face, but I didn't get the impression he was laughing. "You couldn't, by the way."

"Couldn't what?"

"Pick me up. I'm out of your league. Now give me their round, and I'll make sure your niece doesn't get hurt in the crossfire."

He slid five longneck Buds across the bar to me, and I twitched my way across the scuffed wooden floor to where Niece and the boys sat around a battered, felt-covered table. "Somebody need a drink?" I asked, setting the bottles down on the table, right in the middle of a hand of poker. I made sure to bend at the waist, so Burris got a good look down my shirt as he reached for his beer.

"Thanks, babe," he said, taking a long drink.

Niece reached over to take a bottle, but I slapped her hand and picked up the beer instead. I knocked it back, downing the whole thing in one long pull, letting just a little bit run down my chin and dampen my t-shirt. The bikers never took their eyes off me.

Men are so easy.

I tossed the bottle over my shoulder, hearing it shatter on the floor, and I pulled up a chair from a nearby table. "Is this a private game, or can anybody play?" I asked, sitting.

One of the other men looked across at me and said, "If you can afford the stakes, you can play. Show me the color of your money."

I pulled some cash out of my pocket and dropped it in the middle of the table. "What does two hundred bucks buy me?" I asked.

"It sure as hell gets you into this piddly-ass game," the man to my left said, scooting his chair over. "You sit right here, sweetie."

He reached over and patted my thigh, a *lot* higher up than was allowed by most social norms. I laughed, a high, girlish giggle that bore no resemblance to what my actual laugh sounds like, and patted his hand. Then I grabbed his pinkie and bent it back almost to the point of breaking. He sucked in a loud breath and swung his head around to me, the stupid grin completely gone from his round face. I plastered on my sweetest smile and said, "If you ever touch me without my explicit goddamn invitation again, I'm going to rip this finger off and shove it so far up your ass you'll be shitting fingernails for a month. You got it?"

He nodded, and I let go of his hand. He removed the offending appendage from my thigh, and I turned back to the game. "Okay, boys. Deal me in."

They played Texas Hold'em, and they played it poorly. With no antes and blinds low enough to mostly ignore, I just peeked at my cards from time to time and folded almost every hand. Finally the bets came around to me in the cutoff, one seat behind the rotating dealer button, and I looked down at a pair of red jacks.

I'm no Johnny Fucking Chan, but I've played a little poker. And growing up with a family of, shall we say, questionable employment history, I learned how to gamble and how to read my marks early. All that said, every poker player in the world hates jacks. They're too high to throw away, and too low to feel safe betting hard. I tossed in a ten-dollar raise and got called by the dealer and the big blind. Not the worst place to be, with a decent hand and position on one of the two players left.

The flop came down king-nine-eight, all diamonds. Not the worst flop in the world, but bad enough that my jacks were quite likely no longer the best hand at the table. I had a pair, a backdoor flush draw, and a shitty straight draw, but I needed runner-runner to get there and might still be drawing dead. I was dead to a made flush, and way behind any random king the big blind may have had. The big blind checked, and I tossed out twenty bucks into the thirty-odd dollars in the pot.

That little continuation bet got a flat call from the button, and the big blind looked at us both with disgust written all over his face before he called. He either had some shit hand like king-ten with one diamond, or he had the nut flush made and was Hollywooding like some TV asshole. I wouldn't be surprised if he pulled out a hoodie and sunglasses for the river.

The turn was a black queen, helping my straight, but making my jacks look worse and worse. I checked behind the big blind, planning to make a move on the button's bet, but he surprised me and checked it to the river. *That wasn't my plan, asshole.* I'm sure my annoyance was written all over my face.

The river came down with the ten of diamonds, giving me the third-best flush and making my straight. This was not a hand I wanted to show down, so when the big blind tossed fifty bucks on top of the hundred dollars already on the table, I just tossed in the rest of my cash. "A little over one-fifty," I said. "I can count it if you want."

"No need," said the button as he folded.

I looked at the big blind, who smiled across the table at me. "Yeah, no need to count."

I nodded at him and reached out to scoop in my money, and he made a clucking noise in his throat. "No need to count, unless you can beat the nut flush, bay-bee!" He cackled with laughter as he flipped over the ace of diamonds and four of clubs. The bastard rivered a better flush to beat me with ace-fucking-four. I sighed and leaned back in my chair, tossing my cards facedown to the dealer.

"You got it," I grumbled, watching my money slide across the table to the fat loser, who looked like he had to replace the shocks on his bike every month thanks to the abuse he was heaping on the poor machine.

"Looks like you need a reload, sweetie," Blackheart said, giving me a smile that didn't reach his eyes. It was time to get out of there before I lost everything I was supposed to make bringing this douche back for his trial.

"Yeah, I guess I do," I said. I reached into my pocket and pulled out my wallet, letting it flip open to the Homeland Security badge "accidentally." I looked up at the group of wide-eyed bikers, and said in my best innocent voice, "Oops. I forgot. My bankroll isn't in there."

Then I stood up and drew my Sig from under my hoodie. "It's right here. Let's go, Blackheart. You're needed for a very important meeting in Chicago tomorrow." I looked around the table. "Nobody sticks their nose in, nobody gets hurt. I'm only here for Burris."

The dipshit who rivered the flush to take my money stood up, toppling his chair in the process. "Feds!" he shouted, turning to run for the door but ending up falling over his chair and crashing to the ground in a tangle of wood and idiot. I sighed. First I lose at poker, now I start a goddamn riot. This was going sideways fast. Story of my life.

3

One of the many downsides to drawing a gun in the middle of a bar known to harbor fugitives is that most of the other people in the bar will also have guns, and a pretty well-documented willingness to use them. That's how I found myself at the center of a room full of firepower in St. Louis, Missouri, when it was supposed to be a simple bail jumper gig. Of course, when you hang out with people like Quincy Harker and make your living hunting down bad guys of the human and supernatural variety, nothing is ever simple.

"I'm just here for Burris," I repeated, my voice echoing in the sudden quiet of the bar. The music coming through the speakers was gone, CueBall having decided that my debacle of a collar needed to be seen and heard by everyone. The pool sharks in the back leaned on their cues, staring at me, and the other players in the poker game all kept their hands conspicuously visible atop the table.

"Blackheart, stand up and walk to the door," I said, taking two steps back to move me out of arm's reach. No one in the room was close enough to actually lay a hand on me now, but I was definitely within range for any of the pistol-packing bikers to reach out and touch me with a lead caress, if they were feeling particularly noir.

"No." My quarry didn't move. He didn't even look particularly concerned with thinking about moving.

I wasn't sure I heard him right. "What?"

"I said no." This time he spoke very slowly, as though speaking to someone hearing-impaired or stupid. I might have been either one or both.

"What do you mean, no? Get up, or I'll shoot your ass." I wiggled the Sig, which was getting heavy after holding it out in front of me all that time. That's one of the things nobody shows you on TV—a fully-loaded pistol has some serious heft to it. A fully-loaded pistol weighs a good couple of pounds, even when we're talking about a smaller gun like the carry version. And I'm no wilting lily, but I'm not a power-lifter, either. So the barrel was starting to wobble more and more the longer I stood there yammering at Burris.

"No you won't," the man who called himself Blackheart replied. He looked cool as a cucumber, like having a gun pointed at him was an everyday occurrence. Admittedly, I never really asked too many questions about what he was going on trial for, so it might actually have been an everyday occurrence for him. "You need me alive, and mostly unharmed, so I can stand trial. I need to not go to prison. So you're not going to shoot me."

"I'm not going to kill you," I said. "There's a lot of room in your giant carcass to put a bullet where it won't kill you."

He stood up and stretched his arms out to the sides, then turned, his movements slow and deliberate, to face the wall. "Okay," he said, turning his face to talk over his shoulder. "Shoot me. Shoot an unarmed man in the back. Go for it. Let's see how that plays with your boss. Or the prosecutor. Hell, just shoot me in the leg, then you can drag me out to your car and haul me back to Chicago. Just don't hit an artery, or I won't make it to your car, much less Illinois."

I hate bad guys that know anatomy. Good for me I had a taser in the pocket of my hoodie. I pulled it out with my left hand, swapped hands between the taser and the pistol, took a step forward, and shot Blackheart right in his blackhearted ass.

He fell to the ground, twitching and swearing as I holstered my pistol. I moved around the table, pulling flex cuffs from my other pocket as I did. I dropped to a knee beside the twitching man and yanked first one wrist, then the other, behind his back and secured him with the heavy-duty plastic cuffs. I stood up, yanking on the cuffs, but Burris stayed down.

"Get up, asshole, or I'll dislocate your shoulders. I don't need you able to scratch your ass to collect on you," I said, giving him another yank.

"Fuck you, bitch," he growled. I kicked his feet apart and gave him a swift kick in the crotch. He curled up in a ball, and every guy in the place winced.

"Call me bitch again, asshole," I growled. "Now get up." This time when I yanked on his cuffs, he struggled to his feet. Between his bound hands and throbbing nuts, standing didn't seem to be the easiest task for him. I braced myself to help him stand, hoping he wasn't faking just to get me close enough for something painful.

So, of course, he was just faking to get me close, and as soon as both feet were solidly under him, he threw all his weight backward onto me, slamming me onto, then through, the poker table, with all three hundred pounds of his giant smelly body squeezing the air from my lungs.

I wriggled around until I got out from under him and punched him in the side of the head. I'm pretty sure I did more damage to my fist than I did to his head, but I at least got a grunt out of him. This time I wrapped his ponytail around my fist and hauled him to his feet by his hair. He was a lot more compliant feeling his hair get yanked out by the roots than he was when I was pulling him around by his shoulders. I started steering him toward the door, and the gathered bikers, card players, and fugitives parted like the Red Sea.

"Stop her, you assholes," Burris grunted. "She gets me turned in, you know she's gonna come back for the rest of you. Come on, Spider, what's the bounty on you up to? A hundred grand?"

A Latino man standing with a pool cue in his hand held up two fingers. "Two hundred."

"You think this bitch is going to leave two hundred large just laying on the table? You either have to take her out, or never come back here," Burris pleaded.

I slammed his face into a table as I steered him toward the door. "I told you not to call me bitch." I hauled him back upright on wobbly feet, then stopped as the stocky Latino guy moved in front of me.

"I wasn't BSing you," I said. "I only want Burris. The rest of you can go back to playing pool, feeling up underage servers, or cheating at poker. I don't give a shit. But this douche has a wife at home who put her house up as security for his bail, and if he's not back in Chicago within forty-eight hours, she's out on the street. Come on, you're not going to let his woman suffer for his bullshit, are you?"

I hoped I could appeal both to whatever moral code these criminals lived by and his inherent machismo to play the woman card and get Spider to step aside.

I vastly overestimated the moral code of the modern criminal. He pulled a very large, very shiny pistol from the small of his back and pressed it against my nose. "You gotta let him go, *chica*. I can't let you come in here, where I like to relax, and start shit with my boys. Even with dickheads like this guy."

"So you admit that he's a dickhead?" I asked, my eyes flicking from side to side.

"Oh yeah, he's a real prick. But that don't matter. I can't be letting people just waltz in here with guns and think they run the place."

"It's not my gun that makes me think I run the place," I said.

He laughed. "Yeah, I know that. You don't run shit right now, *chica*. Now let Blackheart go, and you can go back to Chicago and apologize to his old lady."

I nodded. I could tell when I was beaten. "Okay." I let go of Burris's cuffs. He staggered forward, his weight taking him almost right into the Latino. The stocky man took the pistol off my forehead, and I kicked Burris in the back of his left knee. His knee buckled, and he toppled to the side, taking the Latino man to the ground with him.

I reached into my pocket and pulled out my last surprise. If this didn't work, I was probably going to die horribly. The only saving grace to that was that if I died, I didn't have to deal with Harker and his crazy angel-chasing bullshit.

I held the metal pineapple high over my head, pulled the pin from the grenade, and tossed the little metal pineapple over the bartender's head. I raised my voice over the cursing from the floor above me and said, "Now cut the shit or I'll blow us all to Kingdom Come."

Everyone in the place froze. Burris, the Latino, CueBall, CueBall's slutty niece, then fat idiot on the floor tangled up in his chair, all the other criminals and lowlifes—they all stopped cold and stared at the grenade in my hand.

"Now that I've got your attention, I'm going to take Mr. Burris out to my car. If anyone objects, I'll drop this grenade like a hot potato, and we can argue about this shit in the afterlife. I've got stuff to do, and I'm tired of fucking around with you morons. Is that clear?"

The Latino man on the floor opened his mouth, but I held up a finger for silence. "Don't speak. Don't even breathe loudly. Just stay exactly where you are, don't interfere with me getting this dipshit out the door, and nobody dies today. Keep sticking your little willies into my business, and everybody goes home in a pizza box."

I reached down and snatched Burris back to his feet by his ponytail. It was awfully considerate of him to give me such a useful handle to steer him by, I thought as I pointed him toward the door. "Hey, CueBall, how about you open the door for a lady?" I asked.

The bartender glared at me. "If I do, will you leave?"

"And never come back," I promised. He hustled out from behind the bar and held open the door for me. I shoved Blackheart through it and took a firm hold on his flex cuffs, steering him across the parking lot as CueBall went back inside and closed the door to the bar. I thought I heard a deadbolt as I walked away, but I wasn't sure.

"That was pretty ballsy," Burris said as I perp-walked him across the parking lot.

"Thank you," I said, looking from hand to hand and trying to figure out how I was going to deal with the crook in one hand and the grenade in the other when I needed to unlock my car. Obviously I hadn't thought this quite all the way through.

"Yeah, not many people can stare down a bar full of stone killers with a fake grenade. I'm impressed."

"Fake grenade?" I asked. "You think this is fake?"

He chuckled. "Of course it's fake. No way in hell would you try that shit with a live grenade."

I shoved him against the Toaster and turned back to the bar. No one had come out yet, so the parking lot was deserted, just a bunch of motorcycles lined up in front of the building, all leaning on their kickstands and gleaming in the afternoon sun. I laughed and pitched the grenade across the parking lot, watching it roll under the third bike from the front door. "Yeah, you're right," I said. "That would be crazy."

I had just enough time to get the driver's door open and duck behind it before the grenade exploded, sending shrapnel and hunks of twisted metal into the sky as a dozen Harleys went to motorcycle heaven all at once. Burris didn't even speak the whole way back to Chicago.

4

"Okay, Harker, what's the deal?" I asked, walking around my apartment/office the next day.

"It's like I said, Lucifer is in the game now, so everything has changed. Are you wearing pants?" he asked, his normally unflappable face showing his confusion.

I looked down. Sure enough, that was a pair of bare legs coming out of the leg holes of my teal Hanes Her Way panties. "Nope," I said.

"I thought you were at your office."

"Office is such a restrictive word," I said, looking up at the TV hooked up to my webcam.

"And Gabby is not about the restrictions of civility," chimed in Renee, my best friend/assistant/bookkeeper/tech wizard/whatever else I couldn't handle at any given moment, said from the couch. "You're lucky she's wearing a shirt." And I was, albeit a tattered *Texas Chainsaw Massacre* t-shirt I picked up at a horror con several years ago. But it was still more shirt than holes, so it counted.

"What's wrong, Harker?" I asked, needling the wizard. Harker prided himself on being able to handle anything the world threw at him, and I had a lot of fun testing that point of pride. Plus, it's always fun to fuck with the sensibilities of a real-live Victorian Englishman.

"Can't focus with my gorgeous gams on display?" I looked down. My legs did look good. The high-cut leg on this pair of underwear made them look longer and highlighted the muscles in my thighs. And I didn't even pick up any new bruises in the fight yesterday, so they were flesh-toned for once instead of spectacular shades of purple, yellow, and green.

"No, I just thought you might not want everyone to see you walk around in your underwear. But I obviously overestimated your modesty." He zoomed his camera out to show me that he was in the war room at his place, with about half a dozen other people walking around the room or working on other projects behind him. I saw Luke, Jo Henry, an older African-American woman who I assumed was Jo's mother Cassandra, Adam, and a couple of other people that I assumed were random Archangels Harker just kept lying around in his apartment in case he needed some divine intervention.

"Harker, most of the people in your room are either women, or they aren't even people. If I'm showing off anything they haven't seen before, then the problem isn't on my end," I said. I was pissed that he one-upped my exhibitionist trick, but damned if I was going to let him see it.

"Hey kids, as entertaining as this is, I've got billing to do if we want to keep this lovely 'office' open," Renee said. "So can you get on with it?"

Harker's face looked confused. "What is she talking about? Dennis, didn't you make Gabby's deposit?"

A unicorn face with a multi-colored mane appeared in a picture-in-picture box on the screen. "Yeah, I did." He turned to me. "You should be pretty flush, Gabby."

I looked over my shoulder to Renee, who was staring daggers at me. "I'm guessing by that look I forgot to mention that Harker deposited my Shadow Council back pay and salary into my account yesterday."

"Yeah, you might have left that detail out when you were asking me to scrub any video surveillance of you on the east side of St. Louis and make sure that you weren't connected in any way to an explosion outside a biker bar," Renee said. She tapped a few keys on her laptop, clicked the mouse a few times, then drew in a deep breath. "Holy shit."

"So the deposit hit?" Harker asked.

I turned around and got up on my knees, leaning over the back of the couch. Renee's face was pale, but not like I killed something and it made a really big mess pale, or I blew up the wrong person's car and now we're going to prison for a very long time pale. This was a new kind of pale, and when she peeled her eyes off the screen to look at me, I realized that I'd never seen it before.

"Nay-Nay, are you alright?" I asked. I was a little concerned. Renee has been my best friend since college, when I punched out a drunken frat boy who got a little handsy, then I got a little handsy with her myself later on that night. I've seen her pissed off, heartbroken, happy, horny, and pants-pissing terrified, but I'd never seen that look before.

"Oh yeah, I'm alright. I'm better than alright. Jesus, Gabby, we're *rich*! Do you have any idea how much money that crazy bastard just paid you?"

"A lot," I said. "But we're not *rich*. We won't have to eat Top Ramen next week, but we're not rich by a long shot."

"We're a lot damn closer to rich than we were fifteen minutes ago, when I was wondering if the landlord was still willing to let you pay the rent in boudoir photos."

"Still not happening. He's a sleaze," I said. "But we're good, right? We can pay the rent?"

"Pay the rent?" Renee asked, looking at me like I was either insane or a special kind of stupid. "No, we can't pay rent. We can buy the damn building, Ri!"

"Ri?" Dennis's voice came from behind me.

I turned to face the monitor. "She gets to call me anything she wants. She puts up with my shit. You fuckers can call me Gabby, or Gabriella, or Hey Bitch."

"How about Cheeks? Can I call you Cheeks?" Dennis asked.

I was confused for a few seconds, then I noticed my own ass out of the corner of my eye. Turning around on the couch like I did basically mooned the entire Shadow Council by video. I turned around and sat down, getting a cartoon unicorn sad face for my troubles.

"You can call me whatever you like, Dennis. You just put a ridiculous amount of money in my bank account," I said.

"Hey, I told him to pay you," Harker protested.

"It was Luke's money, and Dennis handled the transaction. Plus, he doesn't have a body for me to beat the shit out of, so I can't really do anything to him. You don't get the same leeway, Harker," I said, flipping him the bird.

"She's got you there, Q," a gorgeous blonde said as she pulled a chair up beside Harker.

"Hey, Glory," I said.

She gave me a little wave. "Hey, Gabby."

"How's humanity going?" Glory had been Harker's guardian angel, a job that should have come with heavenly hazard pay. In a big world-saving demon fight last year, she sacrificed her wings to save his life. And the lives of pretty much everybody else on the planet. But now she was human.

"Sucks. I have to pee, like *all* the time. And pooping? Jeez, you guys deal with some nasty shit. No pun intended."

I laughed. "Just wait, darling. It gets better and better."

"The only saving grace in this whole mess is I still don't have a reproductive system, so no periods."

I was confused. "How the hell does that work? I thought you were human?"

"Not exactly," the formerly divine being replied. "As far as I can figure out, and it's not like there's much in the way of research or case studies on this, I still have my divine body. It's just been made more corporeal by the loss of my divinity. I can't reproduce, but my body now has to sustain itself like a human's. So I have to eat, and everything that goes along with that. But since I'm not human, God, or whoever is watching over shit while He's on walkabout, doesn't want me making any more sorta-angels. So no internal girl parts."

I tried to wrap my head around that, but it got very metaphysical very quickly, and all I did was get confused. After pondering it for almost a full minute, I shook my head and gave up. "Fuck it, I don't need to know if ex-angels menstruate. Where do I find Ragu and what do I do with him when I find him?"

Harker sighed. "Raguel. That angel's name is Raguel. He's sometimes also called Metatron."

"Isn't that the dude on *Supernatural* that looks like Booger?" I asked.

Renee came over to sit next to me on the couch, most of her shock at suddenly not being impoverished having worn off. "Sweetie," she said, patting my leg. "The guy who played Metatron on *Supernatural* is also the guy who played Booger in *Revenge of the Nerds*."

"Oh," I said. "Okay, so we're looking for Angel Booger. Got it."

Harker slumped his head down to thump into the surface of the table in front of him. "Bollocks, woman, are you purposefully obtuse? You have to be." He rolled his head to the side, addressing Glory. "She has to be, doesn't she? Nobody this stupid could live this long. Or be this goddamned effective."

I held out my hand to Renee. "Pay up."

"Right now?" Her face turned red all the way up to the tips of her pink-and-green streaked hair.

"Right now, bitch." My tone was stern, but my face was all smiles as Renee wriggled around, pulled one arm inside the lavender tank top she wore, unfastened her lacy pink bra, and pulled it out the other arm hole of her shirt. She shoved her arm through the hole and leaned back on the couch, her heavy breasts bouncing with her motion.

"Yay! Boobies!" I shouted, shoving her bra under the couch cushion in front of me.

"What the hell was that about?" Harker asked.

"I bet Renee that I could make you say 'bollocks' in the first five minutes of our call," I said. "I won, so now the office is a bra-free zone for the week."

"I will never understand Americans," Harker muttered. "Now that you're presumably finished flirting with your…girlfriend, I suppose, can we get back to business?"

"One, girlfriend is fine, if a little limiting," Renee said. "Second, yes. Tell us what you know about Raguel and where we are most likely to find him."

"Please tell me he's in Chicago. Or at least close. I hate flying," I said.

"You hate airport security," Renee corrected.

"If somebody is going to feel me up, I at least want them to buy me a drink first. Or I want a chance to reciprocate," I explained.

"Seems fair," Renee said with a nod. "So, Harker. Where is this angel?"

"The good news is that Raguel seems to be relatively nearby. The bad news is that we don't know exactly which one of three likely suspects is your angel."

"Want to define 'relatively nearby' for me, Harker?" I asked.

"Well, you know the way there, at least."

I groaned. "You gotta be kidding me." I knew what he was going to say before he said it.

"Nope."

"St. Louis?"

"St. Louis."

"You know I was literally there yesterday, right?"

"I also know that you had to come home or let your bounty go, so I decided to let you sleep in your own bed. And shower away any trace explosive residue before you returned to Missouri."

"Silly Quincy," Renee said. "Grenades don't leave residue. That's probably the only piece of evidence I didn't spend half the night scrubbing out of existence, but I didn't have to worry about that one."

"Well, regardless, there are three men in the greater St. Louis area that may actually be Archangel Raguel. Dennis has sent their information to your email, and you should be able to find at least the first one of them fairly easily."

"So I'm going back to St. Louis?" I groaned. The drive between Chicago and St. Louis is *boooooring*. I don't do well with boring.

"You're going back to St. Louis," Harker confirmed.

"Fine," I said. "But I'll leave tomorrow. I'm spending the rest of today day drinking and making bad decisions."

"Must be Tuesday," Renee said with a grin, clicking the remote off and plunging Harker into darkness.

5

So three days later, I pulled the Toaster up in front of the Four Seasons Hotel in St. Louis and tossed the keys to a valet, who looked at my dirty, battered Honda, then back to me, decked out in a very nice little outfit I'd picked up in Chicago before I left home. Dennis's deposit had gone in, and I'd gone shopping. I paired my Jovani top and flared-leg pants ensemble with a nice Prada chunky heel boot that managed to both give me enough of a platform to stand on and still add a few inches to my height. I had a long silk wrap over my shoulders, with steel bearings sewn into the hem of the wrap to make it useful as a weapon and restraint if I couldn't convince Ragu the Angel to come with me of his own accord.

From talking with Harker and the angels he'd assembled, I couldn't quite get a handle on whether or not they were interested in sex, but I bought new underwear and a push-up bra just in case. If it didn't attract any divinity, it was fine, but the whole ensemble certainly made me look heavenly. My clutch was too small to carry my favorite 1911 pistols, Thelma and Louise, but I was still pretty well-armed. I had a stun gun tucked away in my purse, a pair of brass knuckles in the top of one boot, and a picture of the guys I was looking for on the home screen of my phone. In short, I was ready to hunt.

I walked up to the ballroom entrance, taking note of four visible security guards. Two flanked the door, one with an iPad in his hand checking names off a list while the other one looked over the guests for weapons as they passed. He was good, non-invasive, but I watched his eyes as they scanned over every inch of each guest, male and female alike. The other two stood farther out from the entrance, their eyes scanning the hotel lobby and hallways for threats or paparazzi, of which no small number congregated by the front doors of the hotel.

"Name," the tuxedoed guard said as I walked up.

"Gabriella Van Hels," I replied. The shortened last name cut down on vampire jokes at restaurants.

He looked at the tablet in his hand, tapped the screen a couple of times, then nodded. "This says you have a plus one coming...?" He raised an eyebrow, making his question clear without actually asking anything. *Ex-cop*, I mused. He certainly had the whole "ask without asking" thing down.

"Upset tummy," I said. "I'm flying solo tonight..." I let my answer trail off into a question.

He didn't leave me hanging. They never do. "Mario," he said, with a smile that cracked through his stern demeanor and stretch all the way around to the edges of his gleaming bald pate.

I held out a hand, and Mario shook it. "Well, Mario, I'm Gabriella. If you get a break later, find me for a dance."

He shook his head, smiling. "Can't, ma'am. That would be a serious breach of protocol."

"Too bad," I said, patting him on the chest and moving into the ballroom. "Your loss."

"No doubt," he said to my back.

I stepped through the double doors, looking left and right to assess the rest of the security in the room. Mario had on a shoulder holster. I'd felt it when I patted him on the shoulder. The tux did a good job of hiding the weapon, even as close as I was, so it was a low-profile piece, probably not a high-capacity pistol. Or maybe Mario was just a very good shot and didn't need as many bullets. Either way, security at this shindig was no joke. I really hoped I didn't end up in a fight. There wasn't room in my purse for lipstick and a grenade.

I counted at least a dozen security personnel around the room, and half again as many waiters moving through the crowd with concealed weapons in their waistbands. This was starting to feel more like an NRA rally than a hospital fundraiser, until I looked to the stage at the end of the room and saw the banners with the Governor of Missouri's face flanking the podium. *Well, shit. No wonder it feels like a damned political rally. It may as well be.*

I slinked off to find a bathroom and tucked myself into the last stall. I pulled out my phone and tapped the screen to wake it up. "Dennis, are you there?" I asked without making a call.

The familiar unicorn face popped onto my screen, Dennis's preferred disembodied form. "Hey, sweet cheeks, what's up?"

"Sweet cheeks? Seriously?"

"I'm trying it out. So far it annoys the shit out of Harker, Luke, and Flynn. Adam doesn't dignify me with a reply, and Jo thinks it's adorable."

"Add me to the annoyed column," I said.

"Excellent. That's another vote in the keep column. So, what's up? I saw you get past security, now what?"

"Why didn't you tell me this was a huge political thing? How the hell am I supposed to get this guy out of here in front of all these people?"

"Whoa, whoa, whoa," Dennis protested, holding up two white hooves. "I never said anything about taking him from *there*. That would be a terrible idea. You're just there to recon. We don't even know if Dr. Harmon is the guy. I think he's the least likely of our candidates, myself, but Harker and Luke think he might be the guy."

"Fuck. So this might be just a waste of time?"

"You knew that going in. We talked about it, remember?"

"No, you and Harker talked. I kinda zoned out on all that stuff."

"Why do I bother?" The unicorn head on my screen was now beating its head against a cartoon brick wall. "Why do I even deal with you humans?"

"Because you can only stand to watch so many episodes of Real Housewives of Every Damn Where, and we're really entertaining."

"Sometimes," he grumbled. "Okay, let's go over this again. Try to pay attention. I'll use small words. Dr. Ronald Harman is a respected neurosurgeon and philanthropist. He's a huge influencer in the community, but his digital footprint doesn't exist before 1980."

"How old is he?" I asked. It was odd for a surgeon to be quiet about their youth, or about anything, really, but maybe this guy was just the exception.

"He's fifty-seven. Born in 1960. So where was he for the first twenty years of his life?" Dennis asked.

"I don't know. Isn't that your thing?"

"Exactly," the head replied. "And I can't find him. So Harker thinks this might just be a new identity for an immortal."

"Like an angel," I said.

"Like an angel," Dennis agreed.

"How am I supposed to prove that he is or isn't an angel?" I asked. "I can't exactly walk up to him and ask."

"From what we've seen, he probably doesn't even know," Dennis said. "I don't know. Just…watch him. Maybe he'll do something all divine."

"I think our best case is the canapés will be divine," I said.

"I miss food." The unicorn's face went mopey, and I had a pang of sympathy for the guy. I never knew Dennis before his soul got trapped in the internet, but that had to suck.

"I'll have an extra dessert in your honor," I said, then swiped my finger across the screen to end the call. I stepped out of the stall and walked over to the sink. I pulled a lipstick out of my purse, then looked at the absolute lack of any makeup on my face and decided not to bother with the façade. I dropped the plastic tube back into my purse unopened, right next to my wallet and stun gun, and walked out to join the fray.

And fray it was. The ballroom was packed, with more millionaires per square foot than I'd certainly ever been around. Everywhere I turned were bespoke suits, handcrafted Italian loafers, and gowns that made my very nice outfit look like something from a mosh pit. It didn't take me long to wish for a good mosh pit and some good head banging music because I'd barely made it ten feet closer to the stage before I ran into a wall of humanity, all chatting inanely about the atrocities of Obamacare and the performance of their favorite mutual funds.

I spun left and made a beeline for a small satellite bar stationed at the midpoint of the room. Leaning on the bar making small talk with the bartender was the youngest non-employee guy I'd seen all night. He smiled as I walked up, perfect teeth shining above an adorably dimpled chin, and he gestured to the bar with a grandiose wave.

"Please, milady, step forward and sup from the nectar of the gods," he said, bowing a little at the waist.

"As long as the nectar of the gods looks like a double bourbon, neat, we're good," I said, nodding to the bartender. He picked up a bottle of Jim Beam, and I gave a little shake of my head. "Sweetie, I didn't put on this dress to drink frat party bourbon."

The bartender laughed and picked up a bottle of Knob Creek. "Will this do? I couldn't get any Pappy Van Winkle for tonight."

"That'll be fine," I said, reaching for my purse.

"Please, let me," Dimples said, stepping forward. "Kyle, why don't you pour two of those, and I'll take care of the young lady."

"You know it's an open bar, right?" Kyle the bartender said, smiling at Dimples.

"I did, but she might not have. Now I'll just have to tip you too much so the lady can see how generous I am." Dimples dropped a twenty in the tip jar and picked up the glasses. "Now, my lady, may I escort you to a table?"

"I don't have a table," I said, reaching for my glass.

"Then let me escort you to mine," he said, waving the glass through the air to avoid my grasp.

I laughed and followed as he moved effortlessly through the crowd, keeping to the far wall and slipping through the mass of humanity with nary a stumble. I silently wished for a fraction of his grace, as he navigated the throng without spilling a drop of our whiskey. After a couple of minutes of meandering through the crowd, he set our glasses down on a table right by the stage marked with a big sign saying "RESERVED."

"Are we supposed to be here?" I asked, sitting in the chair he pulled out for me.

"Probably not, but it was nice of them to reserve it for us, wasn't it?"

I decided I liked Dimples. Not enough to go to bed with him just for the price of one double bourbon, but enough to let him keep buying me bourbon to see exactly how much whiskey it would take. "You're funny. What's your name?"

"Jake. What about you?"

"Gabriella. My friends call me Gabby." I extended my hand, and he took it.

"Please to meet you, Gabriella," he said.

"You don't think we're friends?" I asked, enjoying the game.

"You didn't tell me what dashing men who buy you drinks should call you. Are we friends, Gabriella?"

"I think we're working on it, Jacob," I replied. "So what's a nice guy like you doing in a stuffed shirt party like this?" I waved my hand around at the crowd. "You've got the threads," I waved at his tux, easily as nice as anything else in the room. "But you seem to be missing the attitude."

He laughed, and it was the kind of laugh that made me think we were definitely going to be friends. Or at least have benefits. He threw his head back and just cut loose, an open laugh that didn't just reach his eyes, it went all the way to his ears.

"That's hilarious," he said. "Let's just say that I'm the black sheep of my family, and I'm here to make up to my dad for some tiny fraction of my misspent youth."

"Oh boy, do I know the feeling," I said.

"Family drama?" he said.

"You better believe it," I replied. "And it doesn't get any better when the family you're trying to live up to is more generations removed. Trust me." I smiled at the thought of Great-Grandpa Abraham looking down on me hunting an angel in this high-tone party. Well, he'd certainly like it better than me blowing up biker bars.

Just then my attention was drawn to a trim middle-aged man who stopped right over my shoulder. "Jake, so glad you could make it. Who's your friend?"

"Dad," Jake said. "This is Gabriella. We just met at the bar. I'm working on the friend part."

The older man moved around to stand in front of me and held out his hand. "Gabriella, it's lovely to meet you."

I looked up into his brown eyes and froze. I knew that face. I knew it because it had been staring back at me from my phone for three days. Jake's dad was the guest of honor tonight, Dr. Ronald Harman, my potential Archangel.

Shit.

6

I reached forward, almost knocking my whiskey over before managing to grab it and take big sip to hopefully cover how rattled the realization that the guy I was there to maybe hunt was also the father of the guy I was trying to pick up. *Just my luck. One cute guy here under fifty, and he might be part angel. Although that might be interesting...*

I diverted my mind from that particular gutter and stood, taking Dr. Harman's hand. "Pleased to meet you, Dr. Harman. This is some party you've got here."

He chuckled, a warm, lower version of Jake's ringing laugh. "Well, when you're trying to separate the one percent from their hard-inherited lucre, you have to use all the tools at your disposal."

"Well, you certainly trotted out all the show ponies tonight," I said. "You've got the governor, the mayor, and more guys with bad toupees than I've seen in years."

"Then you should get out more," Jake said, laughing. "Or maybe you should just get out with me more. I see these same toupees every weekend, it seems." He grinned and slipped into an awful Bogart impression. "Stick with me, kid. I'll keep you out of the clutches of these old leches."

"Who's going to keep me out of *your* clutches?" I asked with a grin of my own.

"Ha! She's got you there, son!" Dr. Harman reached out for a fist bump.

I gave it to him, then said, "You two don't seem like all these other rich assholes. What gives?"

Dr. Harman's face flashed sober for half a second, barely long enough to register, unless you were looking for it. But I was, so I caught it. I'd struck a nerve. "I was born broke in the middle of the worst neighborhood in St. Louis. I caught some lucky breaks, worked my ass off, and earned what I have. And I mean really earned it, not earned it by keeping my parents happy long enough to come into my inheritance, like most of my peers."

"And I grew up listening to Pop rage against the super-rich and their shitty treatment of everybody around them. I don't actually have any money. I have one nice suit, one good pair of shoes, and a loft in a neighborhood that is just safe enough to be trendy, but still affordable."

"So you're not a doctor?" I asked. "I thought that was the rule, that doctor's kids had to go into the family business."

Both men laughed, and Jake said, "Not so much for the studying. I'm a dancer. Not a very good one, but just coordinated enough not to fall into the orchestra pit, and just strong enough to lift all the pretty swans."

"Jake's a choreographer," his father chimed in, to Jake's obvious embarrassment.

"I'm trying to be a choreographer," Jake corrected. "I've assisted on some pieces for the ballet and done a couple of modern shows of my own."

"His stuff is really good," Dr. Harman said, pride in his son shining on his face. "I mean, that's what my friends who know anything about dance tell me. It all looks like running and jumping to me, and I got enough calisthenics in the Marines."

"You were a Marine?" I asked.

"Force Recon." He nodded. "That was before med school. Another lifetime."

Jake reached out and touched my arm. I didn't break his nose for touching me when I didn't expect it. That's how I knew I kinda liked him. "Dad doesn't talk about his military time much."

"I see too many men trading on their past service like it earns them some kind of respect today. I had a job, I did it. Some of it involved bad people, doing bad things, in bad places. I helped stop them. That was my job, and I was very good at it. I like what I do now much better."

"I'd guess there are a lot fewer people trying to kill you in the ER." I finished off my drink and set the empty glass on the table.

"Most days," Harman said with another one of those rich laughs.

"Let me get you another," Jake said. "Same thing?" He stood and picked up my glass. "Dad?"

"I'll have whatever you kids are drinking," he said with a smile. I nodded to Jake, and he headed off to the bar. His father watched him walk away, then turned back to me. "Now that Jake's gone, you want to tell me what you're doing here?"

"Excuse me?" I tried to put on an affronted face, but I don't do affronted well. I'm usually the one affronting, so I have limited experience being on the receiving end.

"You're carrying a weapon in one of your boots, and your eyes haven't lingered on anything in the room for more than five seconds in the time I've been sitting here. It might have been more than thirty years ago, but I still remember what a predator looks like. And you, young lady, are a lion in a roomful of gazelles." Every hint of the kindly doctor was gone, his affable demeanor replaced by the eyes of a killer. This was someone who had walked through some shit and come out the other side. I knew that look. I wore that look a lot of days.

I took my phone out of my purse and set it on the table in front of me. I tapped the screen and Dennis's image appeared. He was at least still, so I just looked like whatever the female word for a brony is, instead of someone with a unicorn trapped in their phone.

"Where were you born?" I asked.

"Are you with the press?" he countered.

"No."

"The government?"

"Nope."

"The police? I've done nothing wrong."

I laughed. "One—no. I'm about the furthest thing from the police. Two—bullshit. You might not have done anything recently, or in St. Louis, but I can read your eyes like a fucking headline. You've got blood on your hands from way back."

He started to protest, but I held up a hand. "I don't care. I'm looking for someone in St. Louis, and you're the first, albeit least likely, name on my list. You don't exist before 1980, and that sent up a flag with the people I work for."

"Which is who exactly?" the good doctor asked.

"You wouldn't believe me if I told you," I said, half groaning. "Hell, I don't believe my life most days. Just tell me who you were when you were born and why you became Dr. Ronald Harman in 1980, and I'll go away. I might borrow your kid for a few hours, though. I promise to bring him back mostly unharmed."

He smiled at that. "Jake is a grown man, perfectly capable of making his own mistakes. I get the impression that while you might not be what the police consider one of the good guys, you walk on the side of the angels. Most of the time, at least."

I just shook my head. "You have no idea the irony of that sentence. Now please, just tell me why you've lived for nearly forty years under an assumed name, so I can go back to getting your son drunk and trying to seduce him?"

"I can't." He looked genuinely regretful, then I caught him looking over my shoulder and shaking his head at someone behind me.

"Who did you just wave off?" I slid my hand inside my purse and wrapped my fingers around the stun gun there.

"Jake," he said. "He went to get drinks because I used our code word."

"Calisthenics?" I guessed.

He nodded. "Not something I can work into every conversation, but Jake knows that when I mention that and my past, that I'm suspicious about whoever I'm talking to. I just gave him the signal that you're not a danger, but that I need a little more time to chat with you. That wasn't a lie, was it?"

"I don't mean you any harm, Dr. Harman. Even if you were the person I'm looking for, I wouldn't mean you harm. As it is, I just need to check you off a list. Now, back to the point. Who are you, really?"

"Is it enough to just say that since 1980 I've been Ron Harman, a man who tries to help people as much as he can, and tonight I'm trying to raise money for a new children's wing of the local hospital?"

"I wish it was," I said. "I also wish you'd let Jake bring the drinks back. I'm getting thirsty."

"Who are you looking for? Maybe I can tell you something to prove that I'm not him, then my son can come back and we can move on with our evening."

At his words, the unicorn head on my phone started to blink, and a text message appeared. HE'S NOT OUR GUY blinked three times, then Dennis's face reappeared.

I tapped the screen. "How do you know?"

Dennis popped into view, his picture showing his human face instead of the talking unicorn I was used to. In this form, Dennis looked like the twenty-something computer nerd he'd been before Harker got him killed. "Dr. Harman, is your son adopted?"

The doc looked startled, then said, "Have you been recording me?"

"Not exactly. This is Dennis. He works with me. He kinda listens in whenever my phone is on."

"And whenever you don't have me snuggled up to a stun gun, which pulses even when you're not pressing the button, by the way. Plays hell with my reception," Dennis grumbled.

"Get to the point, Dennis," I growled.

"If that's his real son, then he's not our guy. Angels are neuter, even in human form…oops." Dennis blushed, then my phone's screen went dark.

"Angels?" Dr. Harman looked at me, but it wasn't the "this chick is batshit crazy" look I was expecting. It was more of a "this chick knows shit she isn't supposed to know" look, and that made me nervous.

"Is Jake your son? Biologically?"

"Yes, he's my son. Yes, he was made the old-fashioned way, from a man and a woman, having sex, which divine beings cannot do. I am curious, however, as to why you thought I might be an angel. Not to mention why you're looking for an angel in the first place." He made a "come here" gesture over my shoulder, I assumed to Jake, and leaned back in his chair, arms folded over his chest.

Jake joined us a few seconds later, a concerned look on his face. "Is everything okay?" he asked.

"We shall see," his father replied. "Your friend Gabriella was about to explain why she is hunting angels in Missouri, and why she thought I was one of the Host."

Jake laughed, pulling out his chair and sitting down. "You? An angel? Oh, that's a good one. This, I gotta hear." He leaned forward, his elbows on the table and look of anticipation on his face.

I looked back and forth from father to son and back again, getting the distinct feeling that everyone at the table knew a lot more about this supernatural shit than I did. I get that feeling a lot around Harker and Luke, and it never fails to make me stabby.

Then one of the security guards from the entrance flew the length of the room and crashed into the podium in a bloody heap, and my night *really* went to shit.

7

I saw Jake's eyes widen, and I turned to watch the body fly through the air. The big man hit the podium with a splintering crash and lay unmoving in the wreckage. All three of us stood and turned to the door, where a seven-foot-tall beast with red skin and hooves stood in the doorway. His left hand held another guard high in the air by the throat, and his right was wrapped around the face of a third guard, bashing his face into the door.

"Well, that's not good," I said, reaching for my purse. I stopped with my hand just over the black bag, remembering there was no pistol in it, then just tossed the long strap over my head and ran toward the fallen guard.

"Where are you going?" I heard Jake ask from behind me.

"Get these people out of here!" I shouted back. It took me extra seconds to get to the stage as people started to shove chairs back and look around for someone to tell them where to run. I heard Jake start barking orders as I knelt by the guard's body. I didn't bother feeling for a pulse. This guy was deader than the vamps I used to hunt. Sometimes it's hard to tell if an injured person is dead or just really badly hurt. But when their skull looks like a dropped cantaloupe, you can pretty much count on them being dead. On the plus side, people who get killed by having their brains pulped don't come back to life as zombies. Take your small victories where you can find them.

I felt around the guard's chest until I located his shoulder holster and pulled a pistol from it. Nice, a Beretta. *Don't see too many of those nowadays.* I grabbed a pair of extra magazines from under his other arm, checked the chamber, and flipped off the safety.

A quick glance down reminded me that evening gowns don't come with pockets, so I ripped the neck of the dress and shoved the spare magazines into my bra. The metal dug into my boobs, but after some wiggling and twisting, I managed to secure the extra ammo in a way that I didn't think was going to cut me or tear the cup. *I bet Harker never has to worry about where to put extra clips*, I thought as I moved to the far side of the room and started toward the doors.

Of the dozen security guards I'd logged when I entered the room, four of them were already down, most likely dead. I caught sight of another four surrounding the governor and his wife and rushing them out a side door. One was standing in front of the demon, a pistol in his hands. Not shooting, not running, just standing there watching death stomp toward him on minotaur legs.

The demon strode toward the man, picked him up by his shirt front, and bellowed, "WHERE IS THE ANGEL?"

Well, shit. He's not here for the open bar after all. I knelt by one of the round tables, steadied my arm on the back of a chair, and sighted down the barrel of the pistol. I lined up my shot, squeezed the trigger, and fired.

Right into the back of the guard's left leg. He screamed, and the demon dropped him in a heap on the floor. I wanted the demon to put him down, so I guess I achieved my objective, but shooting the hostage wasn't exactly what I had in mind. Hoping I didn't hurt the guard too badly, I shifted my aim and fired four shots at the demon's chest. I saw him jerk back from one, then two impacts, then he turned his attention to me.

He was big, and ugly, which in my experience was kinda universal among demons. Seven feet tall, with short horns curling out from his forehead, crimson red skin, and a jutting lower jaw that had a pair of fangs sticking up out of his closed mouth, giving him a permanent snarl. Not a bad look for a demon, honestly. He pointed at me with a long arm, ending in a gnarled finger with a hooked claw at the tip. A horrifying grin split his ugly face, and my blood ran cold.

"You! Where is the angel?" He started walking toward me, tossing tables to the side, an implacable beast striding through the wreckage of the ballroom. Glassware and chairs flew in all directions as he came toward me, and I felt my heart pounding in my ears.

I fired again, then again and again until the Beretta's slide locked back and the gun clicked empty. I yanked another magazine from my bra, the metal tearing painful scratches into my skin as I tried to get it free. I finally got the clip free and ejected the spent magazine, slamming the replacement into the pistol's grip. I pulled the trigger, but nothing happened. Everything slowed down as I pulled the trigger again and again, nothing happening but the demon stalking ever closer. Finally I remembered to rack the slide and chamber a round, then just as I pointed the gun back at the creature, a string of flat *crack-crack-crack* sounds came from my right, and half a dozen holes appeared in the demon's chest.

I looked over and saw the remaining three security guards advancing on the monster, shoulders tight as they moved forward in a triangular phalanx. The trio of men all had their guns out, and they moved in unison, firing with every step. They moved in a gliding gait, their aim never wavering, and every shot hitting the demon square in its chest.

And every shot did nothing more than annoy the big red son of a bitch. It looked down at the holes in its chest, then sneered at the men as the expended bullets welled up to the surface of its skin and fell to the carpet, harmless.

The guards still advanced, but as they passed my spot, the one on the left side looked over at me and shouted, "Get out of here! Let us take care of this thing!"

There was absolutely zero chance they could "take care" of this thing. I recognized it as some lesser version of the Torment Demons I'd run into in Atlanta with Harker. This one wasn't as invulnerable, since the bullets at least penetrated its flesh, if they didn't seem to do much, or really any damage.

The guard turned his attention back to the demon, and I watched as they pumped round after round into the beast. At least they distracted it. For now.

I took advantage of their diversion. I figured they were probably all going to die, and it was almost certainly going to hurt. A lot. But if that was the case, then I owed it to them to make the demon pay for their lives. I left the useless Beretta lying on the floor and crept along the wall to the front of the room. Gunfire rattled through the room almost constantly as I looped around trying to get behind the big monster.

As I snuck forward, the demon closed on the guards. They kept firing, then when the monster was on them, they fought as well as humans could against a seven-foot tall creature straight from Hell. Which is to say, not very well. One guard went low, wrapping his arms around a leg and trying to lift. The demon punched straight down with his hand open, his claws punching straight through the man's chest. I watched, trying to hold my lunch in place as the beast pulled its hand back, picking the man up by his spine and shaking him like a broken toy. He tossed the dead guard into one of his friends and turned his attention to the last man standing.

This guy looked like a serious badass. Over six feet tall, shaved head, goatee, muscles stacked on top of his muscles. It didn't matter. The demon slammed an open palm down on the man's head, then took one claw on its other hand and slit the guard open from his neck to his navel. Blood and viscera poured out onto the floor, and the demon stood there laughing as he pulled the man's guts out and tossed them in his dying face.

That's when I made my move. I reached down and tore my dress up to the knees, then pulled off the strips of athletic tape holding my blades to my thighs. "I really hoped I wasn't going to have to use these tonight."

I love my knives. They're Gil Hibben Silver Shadows, over a foot long with gleaming stainless blades. Walking around with them taped to my legs all night hadn't been fun, but right that moment, I was damn glad I had them. We were about to see if the modifications I'd made to them since tangling with Reaver Demons in downtown

Atlanta were enough to save my ass. I settled the wire-wrapped hilts in my palms, took a deep breath, and sprinted toward the demon's back. About five feet from the creature's broad back, I hopped up onto an abandoned chair and vaulted into the air.

I slammed into the demon's back with my legs wrapped around its chest, and I drove my daggers into the sides of its neck all the way to the hilt. All seven inches of blade buried itself into each side of the monster's throat, and its bellow of triumph cut off in a bloody gurgle. It flailed around, trying to figure out where this new attacker came from, and I started sawing at its throat with everything I had.

This was a shit situation. I had almost no chance of killing this demon, but if I didn't do something, and fast, it was going to kill anybody left in the ballroom, then move on to the rest of the hotel, then downtown St. Louis. If I couldn't cut this thing's head off right now, I was probably lucky I wouldn't be around to watch it turn the Gateway to the West into an abattoir.

So, I jabbed my knives into the thing's neck so deep I felt the blades scrape each other when they met at the spine, and I started pulling back, trying to decapitate the demon before it did the same to me. I felt the flesh part beneath my blades, the razor-sharp steel parting the flesh, spilling acrid demon blood to sizzle on the carpet. I made progress, cutting through the demon's neck in seconds, and for at least half a second, I thought I had a chance.

Then I saw how fast it was healing. I couldn't cut fast enough. The thing's flesh mended almost as fast as I sliced through it. It wasn't going to work. *Fuck.* I yanked the knives free, and as I threw my arms wide, hoping to drive them into the monster's brain through its ears, the demon apparently decided it was done fucking around with me.

It reached over its head with one impossibly long arm, clamped down on my shoulder, and yanked me up and over to fly through the air like a well-dressed but horribly non-aerodynamic missile. I slammed into a table, which collapsed under the impact, and I understood why that was a finishing move in so many pro wrestling matches. Getting put through a table *hurts*.

"That hurt, human. For that, I kill you slow. But first, where is the angel?" The demon stalked over to me and stood there, dripping blood and demon sweat down onto me where I lay in a pool of shredded dress, shattered table, and really tasteless unsweetened iced tea. I was pretty sure I felt the centerpiece lodged way farther up my ass than was comfortable and hated that I was going to die on my back, and not with a hot girl on top of me. Or a hot guy. Either one would be better than having shards of glass in my butt and a butter dish on my head.

"I don't know where the angel is, but here's a bird for you, asshole," I said, extending my middle finger to the demon. That's me, going out with pure class.

The demon roared and stepped forward, reaching down for me with both clawed hands. I scrambled back, trying to pull myself to my feet, but it wasn't happening. My everything hurt, and I was pretty sure I'd sprained things I couldn't pronounce, so I just readied the one dagger I still had a grip on and vowed to at least take one of this bastard's eyes with me. The demon swiped at me, opening up four parallel slices in my dress, and my belly. Fire blossomed across my skin as my flesh parted and blood started to flow. It didn't cut deep, but it hurt like hell just the same.

"I'm going to make this last, human. You'll beg for death before I'm done. But first, let's see that finger again." Its hand shot out and latched on to my middle finger, pulling me all the way up off my feet by that single digit. If you've never had your entire body weight suspended from one finger, I don't recommend it. The demon held me up by my finger, then grabbed my wrist with its other hand. It bent my middle finger back almost to the breaking point, then a *crack* split the air as it went even further.

I screamed, flailing against the monster's iron grip, and jabbed my knife into the bulging forearm that held me fast. The demon just grinned at me and bent my finger back even further, threatening to rip the broken digit out by the root. I saw black spots dance in my vision, then the creature froze, its eyes wide, and it slowly, ever so slowly, relaxed its grip.

I dropped to my feet, clutching my broken hand to my chest, and watched in amazement as the demon toppled slowly to the ground. It fell both right *and* left as it collapsed to the carpet, sliced neatly into two halves. As the demon fell, it revealed the form of Dr. Ronald Harman, standing behind the demon holding a broadsword outlined in flame of shimmering black light.

Harman the kindly doctor was gone, replaced by a man-shaped being with blue-black skin, jet black curly hair, pointed ears, and narrow features culminating in a mouth studded with fangs. A long tail tipped with a triangular point waved in the air behind him, almost as if it was keeping an eye out for more danger.

"What the fuck?" I whispered.

"I told you I'm no angel," the demon doctor said.

That's when I passed out.

8

came to slowly. Oh, I popped awake, I just took my time opening my eyes. No sense in committing all at once to something that would probably suck, after all. I let the rest of my senses fully wake before I opened my eyes, mostly because my head hurt and I figured any light was going to make it worse. I was lying on something soft, probably a bed, and I was…okay, I wasn't naked, but I wasn't wearing my dress anymore, either. I also wasn't wearing a bra, which while way more pleasant than wearing a bra, was a little discomfiting nonetheless.

I heard someone moving in the room with me, which fit with what I remembered from before I passed out. I was in a fight, trying not to get dead against a demon. I was failing, and I was wondering if I could haunt Harker from Missouri, then the demon was dead, and I saw who had saved me…

That's when my eyes sprang open and I shot bolt upright. Turns out I was on a couch under a blanket, and when I popped up, I also overbalanced, so I tumbled to the floor and landed on my knees and my elbows, ass to the sky. I landed on the blanket, which somewhat cushioned my fall, but also meant I was mostly naked with my black

49

satin-clad butt in the air. Oh well, I always did know how to make an entrance.

I scrambled to my feet, looking around for threats and weapons. Jake stood in a doorway off to my left, holding a whiskey bottle and two glasses. His father sat in a chair in front of me, a coffee table between us. He sat with one leg crossed over the other, perfectly calm, as if naked women sprang off his sofas all the time and immediately went into fight or flight mode.

Which, hell, they might have, for all I knew. Because Dr. Ronald Harman was unquestionably a demon. He still wore his blue-black skin, and his tail lay on his right shoulder, twitching a little. He held a whiskey glass of his own, and I could see the claws against the glass. He watched me look around the room for a second, then he opened his mouth, revealing the row of sharp teeth I remembered from the ballroom.

"Your knives are on the dresser in the bedroom." He pointed toward a doorway on the opposite side of the room from where Jake stood. "There is a suitcase on the bed that has a pair of pajamas in it. They are clean, but I think they will be quite a bit too large for you. I would have dressed you while you slept, but I wanted to make sure the cuts on your abdomen were at least bandaged enough not to ruin my silk nightclothes."

I looked down, and sure enough, there was a wide white bandage across my middle, right where the demon had clawed me open. I peeled back a corner of the tape and saw that my wounds had been cleaned and a few butterfly bandages applied to the deepest points. Made sense, he *was* a doctor, no matter what else he was. I looked at Harman, then at Jake, who just held up the booze as a sort of peace offering. I noticed that unlike the bartender downstairs, he did have a bottle of Pappy Van Winkle.

I turned and stomped into the bedroom, spotting my blades on the dresser, just like the demon said. Nice of him to grab the one I dropped. I unzipped the suitcase and rummaged through it until I found a plain white t-shirt and the promised pajama bottoms and slipped them on. Judging by the layout of the room and the shitty art on the walls, I was in their suite at the hotel. A little surprised they were allowed to stay in the building after the demon attack and mass murder, I went into the bathroom and looked at myself in the mirror.

Wow, that was a mistake. I looked like ten miles of bad road. Correction, I looked like something that had been tied behind a semi and dragged down ten miles of bad road. My hair stuck out in all directions, my normally untamed dark brown curls now a wild nest that not even rats would deign to live in. The entire left side of my jaw was a dark blue bruise, and there were more butterfly bandages over my right eye where apparently something had busted me open. My face was mostly clean, but there were still traces of blood and demon ick around my temples, and God Herself only knew what the goop in my ears was. As soon as I got home, I was going to take a shower that lasted at least a day, then I was going to sleep for a week. Maybe a month, depending on where else I found bruises.

I walked back out into the den after a quick rinse of my face and a futile attempt to at least tame my hair into something resembling human. I sat back down on the couch, taking the end far away from where Jake now sat on the arm, and I put my knives on the coffee table. Not exactly in easy reach, especially given how much it hurt to bend over, but they made a statement.

"I assume you have questions," the demon formerly known as Dr. Harman said.

"You assume damned straight I have questions," I replied. I held out a hand to Jake, who looked at me for a second, then nodded and put a glass full of bourbon in it. I knocked back a good healthy swallow of Pappy, letting the warm taste of ridiculously overpriced whiskey fill me to my toes.

"Be careful with that," Jake warned. "Dad gave you some pretty hefty pain meds to make you able to function."

"Toradol isn't an opiate, so you shouldn't see much reduction in your faculties, but it should help keep the swelling down and dull the pain of your injuries," Demon Doc said.

"If it's not at least Oxy, I'll be fine," I said, finishing off my drink and holding out my glass for a refill. "Now talk."

"As you might have guessed, my name is not Ronald Harman. Or at least, I was not born with the name Ronald Harman, although that is my name now, both legally and by my own usage."

"Why don't you tell me what name you started off with, then you can tell me what the fuck you're doing masquerading as a medical doctor in Missouri," I said. This time I sipped the bourbon. I really wanted to get drunk, but even though I didn't feel loopy from the drugs and the booze, I didn't want to dull any semblance of an edge I still had.

"My real name, believe it or not, is Faustus."

I was a little confused. I knew the name, and I thought I knew the story, but this wasn't how it went in my head. "I thought Faustus was the doctor that got tempted by a demon, not the demon."

"Some things get lost in the retelling," the midnight-hued demon said, his voice placid as a midnight lake as he sipped his drink and watched me. I made a "go on" motion with my hand, and he smiled. "You want more? Of course. It has been some time since I told my story, and I suppose it will do you no harm to hear it."

"The tales are true. There was a man in the fifteenth century names Johannes Georg Ferstus. He was a swindler and a 'magician,' going from town to town barely staying one step ahead of angry fathers and swindled merchants. He claimed to have a tincture that warded off demons if smeared above a home's doors, and to drive out angry spirits if ingested. In reality, he sold creek water tinted with wine and ink to give it a purple color. It was largely harmless, but it did sometimes make the buyer piss vibrant colors for a few days."

"Old Johann came to my attention when fleeing Heidelberg near the turn of the century, pursued by an angry mob accusing him of deflowering their daughters and bilking them with his useless snake oil. They were right, of course. Johann was a libidinous scoundrel, and an inveterate liar to boot, both traits I found quite amusing. When cornered in an abandoned church, of all unlikely places for him to be found, Ferstus blamed all his misbehavior on being corrupted by a devil, who branded him for all time with, of all things, his name."

"Huh?" I wasn't sure I was following.

"He claimed that a demon named him Faustus, and by forcing that name upon him, bound him to do the evil creature's bidding. I'm quite certain that he had no idea there really was a demon named Faustus because when I appeared behind him on the altar of the church, he quite literally shat himself, then fainted dead away."

I didn't want to laugh. All I knew about demons was that they were really hard to kill and had a lot of juice. All I knew about this particular demon was that he'd saved my life by killing a seriously badass other demon, so he wouldn't have any trouble slicing me into a dozen pieces. But I had to admit, he was a charming bastard. That was most of what worried me—his charm. That and the fact that I still kinda wanted to bang his son.

"Then what?" I asked.

"Well, I called a few little fireworks down upon the gathered villagers, incinerated one or two of the more persistent ones, and the rest took the hint and ran away. I waited until Johann woke up and had a little chat with him about using names if he didn't know who or what was attached to them. Names have power, you see, and the church Johann took refuge in sat in a place of some power, so the walls between worlds were thinner there. When he called my name several times, I heard it, got curious, and answered. I showed him the piles of ash where some of his attackers once stood to drive home the point that me answering might not have ended as well for him as it did had I not been amused by his antics and in a forgiving mood."

"So then what? You traveled the countryside with this guy Ferstus for a while until Goethe wrote an opera about you?" I asked.

"You have absolutely no concept of history, do you?" He didn't ask it to be a dick; it was more out of pity.

I still blushed because he was right. "Let's assume that's a no."

"I was quite busy in that century impressing upon a monk named John Cor the importance of aging his whiskey at least three years, preferably more, before unleashing his firewater on the world. So I didn't have time to escort a charlatan around the Black Forest keeping him out of trouble. Or more realistically, I would have insured that he at least got into interesting trouble. But in either case, I left Johann to his own devices. It wasn't until much later that I learned that his legend grew into that of a philosopher tempted by the devil into turning away from God. But things really got interesting some seventy years later, when Kit Marlowe became involved. That's when I took serious note of what was being said about me and decided to turn this silly story into something useful."

"You knew Christopher Marlowe?" I asked. This time I thought, *fuck it*, and tossed back the rest of my whiskey. I turned to Jake and said, "You can switch to the cheap stuff now. No sense wasting three-thousand-dollar bourbon on me after the second glass."

He nodded and passed me a bottle of Knob Creek. I spun the cap off onto the floor and knocked back a healthy slug. The warm brown liquor made me tingle all the way to my toes, and as I enjoyed the burn of the booze, I looked over at the demon named Faustus and said, "Okay, buddy. Tell me all about Christopher Marlowe."

9

Marlowe was a fine little fellow. A little pure for my tastes, but talented, and as soon as I met him, I set to work on the purity issue. He was in his late teens when I met him, about a year after he arrived in Cambridge. He was working diligently on his studies, and I found him scurrying along back to his rooms after leaving the library late one night. I had a running bet back in those days with a lesser Pit Lord named Calipzibar to see who could find the most nebbishy, boring, socially inept student each semester and turn them into a rousing drunkard and ladies' man in the shortest time.

When I spotted Kit skittering along the deserted streets, I was on a losing streak. Cal had bested me three semesters running, largely on the basis that while I made my subjects more popular and more certainly destined for damnation, he started with more pious and boring victims, so by the arcane scoring system we set up back in Alexandria when we started the game, he outscored me every time, despite the fact that one of his subjects went on to become a Cardinal.

Now that I think about it, that may have actually tipped the scales in his favor. I'll have to ask Cal about that if I ever run into him again.

Unlikely, since I plan to never return to the Pits, but still worth remembering.

So I saw Kit, his hair a rat's nest, his clothes abominably out of fashion, and every single thing about him screaming 'Virgin!' from the very rooftops of Cambridge, and I knew that if I could even get him to touch a woman under her skirts, I would win this semester's wager. If I managed to somehow get the little shit laid, I would have credit going into next year.

I garbed myself in the semblance of a fellow student, an upper-classman of means, and conjured up a bottle of spirits to share with the new friend I was about to make. I positioned myself adjacent to his path, pretending to piss against a wall, and when Kit hastened past the darkened maw of the alley, I staggered out, pretending to stumble into him."

"Oh my goodness," I said, looking down at the scrawny man lying on the ground in a tumble of books and papers, his inkwell lying atop his breast and rapidly turning his clothes a lovely splotchy black. "How clumsy of me, fellow. Here, let me help you up."

Of course, as "drunk" as I was, when I reached down to him, I stretched out the hand holding my jug, and as befuddled as he was to be suddenly tackled by a stranger, he simply reached up and took it.

"Oh, are we just going to sit down and have a drink?" I asked, sitting down cross-legged beside him. "That's fine, too. My legs don't seem to work as they should this evening." I held out a hand. "Thaddeus Cooperson, at your service."

"Christopher Marlowe," he said, shaking my hand. He looked back and forth from me, to the jug, to the scattered papers and ink, to me as if waiting for someone to tell him how to behave in this odd situation. So I did.

"Well, don't just hog all the liquor, son. Drink up!" I tapped the jug, and he made is if to hand it back to me. "Don't be silly, boy. You wanted to drink. So let's drink! We'll finish off that jug and go off in search of another. Or maybe we'll find something better to wrap our lips around. I know a house not far from here with women that'll drain your vessel just fine, if you know what I mean."

From the look on his face, I wasn't sure that he had any idea what I was talking about, but he took a drink. He probably drank more to shut me up than anything else, but he drank. And after he took one sip, he took another. And before he knew it, we'd sat there on the sidewalk three hours drinking liquor and singing bawdy songs, all of which I had to teach him, but he sang them nonetheless. And my seduction of Kit Marlowe was well and truly begun.

Marlowe and I were inseparable for the next few weeks. He was like a babe in the woods, all wide-eyed sincerity and shock as I introduced him to the true meaning of college—wenching and wine. It was tough sledding at first, breaking down the walls of a truly isolated upbringing, but I persisted, and before long, Marlowe was far more in his element in a brothel than in a classroom. After some initial hesitation, he took to debauchery like a fish to water, and soon came close to outpacing even me. I'm sure were I working with normal human reserves of stamina and tolerance, he would have left me face down in a ditch more than once. It was almost as if he was trying very hard to make up for lost time.

After working with Kit for months, I uncovered his greatest desire, the one thing I could leverage against him to not only corrupt him and drag him into an interesting life, which would almost certainly damn him, but get him to sign away his soul. I learned that Kit Marlowe wanted to be a playwright. But not just any playwright, he wanted to become the greatest playwright of his age. Now this was something I could work with.

So, one night after a spectacularly awful performance of one of Marlowe's plays, in which the ingenue was forced to leave the company after sustaining a concussion from being struck with unripe fruit from the groundlings, Marlowe finally said the words I had longed to hear from the first time he dragged me one of his godawful productions.

"I would do anything to be a successful playwright, Tad," Kit moaned as we meandered through the streets from bar to bar, trying diligently to avoid any establishment frequented by theatergoers or the poor actors who suffered the indignity of Marlowe's dialogue.

"Anything, Kit?" I asked, a smile creeping across my face.

"Absolutely anything," he said, stopping in the middle of the street and turning to face me. He swayed on his feet, a natural reaction to the amount of whiskey I had poured down his gullet over the course of the evening. I was striving mightily to get him to pass out so that I could visit another one of my "projects" in Cambridge, a young man named Godwin who wished for prosperity and fame for his heirs, a desire that I would grant, but a request that didn't come without some challenges for his great-great-multiple times grandson William Godwin, and would be visited even more strongly on William's daughter Mary some three hundred years later.

But, as so often happens, I digress. I focused all my attention on the distraught and drunken Marlowe, who looked at me with teary, bleary eyes and said those beautiful words that I hear all too infrequently these days. "I'd sell my soul just to write one great play."

That was my cue. I looked at Kit, drunk as a lord in the middle of the street, and decided that it was time to seal the deal, as it were. I snapped my fingers and shed my mortal disguise, appearing just as you see me now, except in Elizabethan streetwear, which is much less comfortable. I snapped my fingers again and magicked Kit sober in an instant. Okay, in an instant and a fit of horrific vomiting, but poison has to be expelled one way or the other, and that was the direction I chose.

I drew one fingertip across my palm, slicing it open to allow my ichor to seep out of a narrow wound. Then I took Kit's right hand and did the same. As our blood pooled in our hands, I looked at the now-terrified young man and said, "Do you really want it, Kit? I can make it happen. I can give you what you need to write one great play. And all it costs is something you'll never miss. You can't feel it; you won't even know it's gone. Will you really sell your soul to me to be the greatest playwright of your generation?"

There was a moment when I thought he was going to pull his hand away. I thought for an instant that I'd overplayed my hand by showing my true face. I had to sober him up—Lucifer didn't allow us to take the souls of the insensible. But he didn't have to see me to agree. I could have gotten his contract in my human form. I chose to go for the dramatic flourish, and in those few seconds, I thought it had cost me a soul.

Then Kit reached out and shook my hand. He clasped our palms together, mingling his blood with mine, and said, "Yes. I trade my soul to be the greatest playwright of my time." And that's how I bought the soul of Christopher Marlowe, who adapted the story of Johann Georg Ferstus into the play *The Tragical History of the Life and Death of Doctor Faustus*, which at the time of its first performance was considered the greatest play of its time. Of course, Marlowe never got to see it performed in his lifetime, but that wasn't part of our deal. I made him a great playwright. I even let him write one of the great plays in English history. But I never once told him he would get to see it on stage.

I am, after all, a demon. It's not like I'm one of the good guys.

Faustus/Dr. Harman leaned back and crossed one leg over the other, looking at me with a steady gaze. "Now, how do you feel about that?" he asked.

"You said something very interesting there at the end, Doc," I replied, setting my glass down on a side table and preparing to try to run if he reacted poorly to what I was about to say. "You said you weren't one of the good guys. But you've been a doctor for almost forty years, and that's just in this disguise. You saved me from a demon, at the risk of your identity, and with nothing to gain. So if you're not one of the good guys, you're damn sure a pretty shitty bad guy."

Taunting demons is not something I do sober. Let's face it, there's not that much I try to do sober. But taunting demons definitely isn't on the list. So I'm blaming everything after that moment on the bourbon.

Faustus looked at me, surprise on his ebon features, then broke out into a laugh. "Oh, Gabby, you are a delight. You got me. I haven't had any dealings with Hell in centuries. Not since that little shithead Marlowe managed to weasel out of our bargain for his soul. I lost all taste for soul-hunting after that and have spent the last several hundred years just living my life the best I can. I'm not trying to get into Heaven. I'm Pit-Born, not Fallen. There's no place for me among the divine. But I also don't have any interest in dancing on lakes of fire and flaying sinners for millennia, either. I just want to have nice things, enjoy my life with my son, and drink a good bourbon whenever I feel like it."

"So why save me?" I asked. "If you're just having a good time drinking your whiskey and chilling with your boy here, why step in and murder that demon?"

"Jake would be upset if you died," he said. "And I found you interesting. So I intervened. Besides, it's been a long time since I killed anything, and I kinda got itchy with all that blood flying around." He licked his lips, and the sight of those fangs reminded me to watch my step with this guy, both literally and figuratively.

"How much more help are you willing to give me?" I asked. "I could use someone with knowledge of the city, and maybe a little extra muscle wouldn't hurt, either."

He grinned, brilliant white teeth splitting that blue-black face. "I'm sure we can come to some type of mutually-beneficial arrangement."

1 O

―――

Three hours later, I was dressed in a set of street clothes I retrieved from the car and walking out the front of the hotel with Jake and his dad in tow. Faustus was back in his human skin suit, and as an added bonus, conjured himself a pair of jeans and a Cardinals t-shirt. Jake had to actually change clothes. I guess being half-demon doesn't come with all the cool perks of being born in a lake of fire. But he also didn't have fangs or a spiked tail, so I was counting the overall package as a winner.

The valet brought my Toaster around, and Jake and his dad both stared at the battered Honda. "What?" I asked. "You don't like my car?"

"That's a car?" Faustus asked. "I mean, I've seen them, of course, but I thought they were mainly delivery vehicles."

"Just for that, you're riding in the back seat." Then I remembered that the back seats were still tied to the walls in their cargo position from hauling around a fugitive the day before. I walked around to the back of the Element, opened the tailgate, and spent about a minute on my knees in the back of the vehicle resetting the back seats into their passenger configuration. Once I got the headrests re-installed, I scooted back out of the car, only to bump into Jake standing there.

I grinned up at him. "You checking out my ass, Harman?"

He grinned right back, and I felt a flutter somewhere below my ribs but above my kneecaps. "If I admit it, am I ever going to get the chance again?" he asked.

"If you lie about it, you sure as hell won't," I jabbed back.

"Then I was definitely checking out your ass." He put a hand on my hip, but I moved it aside and pushed past him toward the driver's door.

"Later, big guy," I said. *Definitely later*, I thought as I opened the driver's door and hopped up into the seat. I pulled my phone out of my clutch and slipped it into a holder mounted to the center console. I swiped a finger across the screen as Jake and Faustus got settled in and put their seatbelts on. Well, Jake did, anyway. His demon dad was either flaunting the law or just invulnerable, as he didn't bother with a belt.

"Okay, Dennis. Dr. Harman wasn't our angel, so who's next on the list?" I asked, holding a thumb over the phone's camera.

"You know that I can still see you, right?" Dennis's unicorn face asked from the screen. I've never understood how he manages to make a unicorn look disdainful, but the guy's got skills. And a lot of time on his hands.

"I don't know what you're talking about," I protested. "Maybe the camera got busted in my demon fight last night. I won, by the way."

"*You* won?"

"I'm still here, right? So I must have won."

"That's true, but I think you might be leaving out some credit on the part of your passenger," Dennis said. I sighed and took my thumb off the camera. The unicorn head nodded toward the back seat, then at Jake. "Doctor, Mr. Harman. Good to meet you both. I'm Dennis, and I'll be your disembodied voice of assistance on this adventure. Please continue to make sure that Miss Van Helsing comes through this safe and sound. The Shadow Council appreciates your help."

I couldn't see Faustus, but I didn't miss the sharp intake of breath. "The Council is involved in this matter?" he asked.

"Did I forget to mention that?" I kept my voice light, remembering that there was a demon very close to me, definitely within arm's reach. "Yeah, I'm a member of this super-secret band of magic nerds and oddball creatures, with a couple of humans thrown into the mix as diversity hires I guess. They call us the Shadow Council."

I saw Jake's head sag a little out of the corner of my eye. "Stay cool, Dad," he said.

It sounded a lot like Faustus was working really hard to keep his shit together behind me, and I appreciated the effort, since all I had in reach was a .357 revolver in the console of the car, and I knew that wasn't going to do shit against a pissed-off demon. "You have a beef with the Council?" I asked, trying to keep my tone light. "Because you've been cool to me, especially considering the whole demon thing."

"I have had my issues with Count Vlad in the past. It is usually considered safest for everyone if we aren't close. Like the same continent." Faustus's voice was almost a growl, and I was starting to rethink not yanking out the revolver and at least making a go of it, when a familiar voice came on the line, all cultured European aristocracy.

"Good morning, Dr. Harman. I am known in this time as Lucas Card. You may call me Luke if you prefer." Every head in the car snapped toward the phone as Luke's face appeared. Dennis's unicorn head shrank down to a little picture-in-picture thing that I didn't even know my phone could do. Of course, with Dennis around, certain upgrades might have been performed that even the factory didn't know about.

"Hello...Luke," Faustus grumbled from the back seat. "Are we to resume our games?" There was a lot hiding behind that question, and I was pretty sure it had a subtext of ripping out my spleen buried in there somewhere.

"No," Luke replied, and I saw tension flow out of Jake in the passenger seat. Me too, since it was most likely my spleen that was in imminent danger. Luke went on, "We are both different...men than we were in our past meetings, with different goals. All I desire right now is for Gabriella to receive all possible assistance in chasing down this missing Archangel and his Implement and bringing them both to me."

"What do you want with angels, Luke?" Faustus said from over my right shoulder. "You've always tried to steer clear of the divine before."

"Lucifer has stirred," Luke said. "He has stepped onto this plane, and I believe he intends to restart his War on Heaven. He must be stopped, if he can be."

"That may be the first time in the six hundred years I've known you that I agree with something you've said," Faustus said, leaning back in his seat. I relaxed a hair, glad to no longer have his breath tickling my neck and giving me goosebumps, and not in a good way. "Why in all the Pits would he want to do that?"

"If I'm right, he thinks he can win this time."

"He can't even get to the Gates, much less ascend to the Throne," Faustus said. "He can barely escape Hell for an hour without torment."

"If he ascends, he can go anywhere he likes." Luke's voice was calm, but his eyes gave away a hint of the fear he felt.

Faustus laughed. "He can't ascend! None of the Fallen can. They were cast out, Luke. Only the Father can remove their banishment. He would have to take on the mantle of…oh, fuck."

I turned to see Faustus sitting back against the seat with his mouth hanging open. "Dr. Harman?" I asked. "Are you alright?" I reached out to shake his knee, and he jolted back to the present.

"Tepes, are you telling me that Lucifer has an Implement? In Hell?"

"And an Archangel," Luke replied. "He has Uriel."

"Fuck me," Faustus said. "Fuck all of us, more likely." He shook himself. "What are you going to do about this? Is this what you sent this girl, this *human* to try and stop?" He looked at me, and my expression must have been a little insulted. Probably because I *was* insulted. "No offense," the demon doctor said.

I turned to Jake. "You ever notice that the only time anybody ever says 'no offense' is either right before or right after they offend the fuck out of you?"

He chuckled. "Yeah, I have." He turned back to his father. "What's going on, Dad? What's the deal?"

"The deal is that we have to find this Archangel, and fast. If Luke and his band of merry idiots are going to have any hope of keeping Lucifer from storming the Gates of Heaven, they're going to need all the high-powered magic they can find, and angelic Implements are among the most powerful in the world. Horsehead-boy, where do we go?"

"Does that mean you'll help Gabriella locate the Archangel Raguel and his Implement?" Luke asked.

"Yes, you ambulatory lamprey, I will help your human find Raguel. But you and I are owed a reckoning, and if the world still stands when this is over, we may well have to settle our issues soon."

"Thank you for your assistance, and I will await your arrival with bated breath," Luke said, vanishing from the screen.

I turned back to the demon in my car. "What the abject hell was that about?"

"Let's just say that there are stranger things on Heaven and Earth than are dreamt of in your philosophy, dear Gabriella. Luke and I have crossed paths many times over the centuries, not only in his work with the creation of the Council, but also when working with other shadowy groups of humans and non-humans. Sometimes we have stood on the same side, but most often we find ourselves in opposition. This appears to be one of the rarer times when we can actually work together for the betterment of humanity, inasmuch as humanity deserves any betterment."

"Yeah, I can see where you and Luke have spent some time together. Trying to have a conversation with either one of you is about as much fun as flying through a fog bank. Are you still helping me, or not?"

"I am more inclined than ever to lend my aid. If what Vlad says is true, and while he is many things, he is not often a liar, then the world is in grave danger. Lucifer means to restart his War on Heaven, and I, for one, would rather not see that happen."

"Why is that?" I asked. When his eyebrows went up, I clarified. "You've been pretty clear that you aren't a 'good guy,' so why do you give a shit what happens to the world?"

"Oh, I don't," he said, and this time when he smiled, I saw just the slightest hint of fang. "I could care less what happens to you hairless apes. But if Lucifer goes to war, he's going to expect every single one of Hell's soldiers to charge right in there with him. No matter how long we've lived on Earth, or how little we give a shit about his petty battles. He'll conscript every demon in Hell or above to his side, and I am unfortunately one of those numbers."

"So there's no charity in your desire to help out. You just don't want to be a grunt in Lucifer's demon army," I said.

"Precisely," Faustus agreed.

"I can get behind that," I said, turning back around. "Just don't screw me over, demon. I don't have anything to threaten you with, but I'd really like to sleep with your son, and I'm not going to be able to do that if you get me killed."

"That sounds like a perfectly admirable reason to keep you alive, don't you agree, Jake?" Faustus looked at his son expectantly, but Jake just sat there, stunned into silence. I guess he doesn't get a lot of forward women in his life. After a moment's pause, Faustus waved to the steering wheel. "Now, don't you have somewhere to be, an angel to find?"

I tapped the screen of my phone, called up some tunes, and plugged the audio cable into the bottom of the black rectangle. Kendrick Lamar blasted through the speakers, Dennis re-appeared on the screen as a unicorn in a Black Panther costume, and navigation appeared to send us to the next possible angel sighting.

A woman, a demon, his son, and a disembodied unicorn roll out to save the world. Sounds like the beginning of a really mediocre joke, right? Nope. For me, it was just a Sunday morning.

I knew something was wrong when we pulled up in front of the suburban ranch-style home and the door was standing wide open. See, I once had lunch with a guy whose great-grandfather was the guy who hung out with Sherlock Holmes, so I've got these mad detective skills. I pulled the Toaster into the drive and got out of the car, walking around to the back of the car to dig around in my overnight bag.

"My dear, I believe we should be moving toward the house, not away from it," Faustus said as he slid out of the back seat. I noticed him rubbing a knee and almost felt bad about jamming my seat all the way back, then I remembered the whole demon thing and got over it.

"Don't worry," I said, grabbing my Sig and clipping the holster to my hip. "I'm heading into the house, but I don't think the open door is an invitation, so I figured I'd at least go in ready for surprises."

"Got another one of those?" Jake asked, joining me at the rear of the car.

"Open the center console," I said.

He went back around, opened the passenger door, and leaned in to reach the compartment between the seats. "Jesus Christ!" he exclaimed. "You really think you need this hand cannon?"

"It's just a .357," I said. "I know a guy down in Georgia who carries really big guns, if that's what you're into. I don't have a holster for that one, so just shove it in your pants and let's go."

He looked at me between the front seats and gave me a saucy grin. "What if there's not room for the barrel?"

"Then you've got some serious problems, sweetie, because I assumed you'd put it in the back waistband so as not to shoot your dick off." I grinned back at him and closed the hatchback.

"If you children are finished flirting, I think you should come up here," Faustus called from the porch. "This looks like someone broke in," he said as we joined him on the small landing in front of the remains of the door.

"What gave it away?" I asked. "The splintered wood, the door hanging off the frame, or the blood in the foyer?"

"Pick one," he said, stepping through the open doorway. "What do you know about the person, or angel, that lives here?"

"Sheelagh McCourt," I replied. "Thirty-five, social worker, active in her church, volunteers for a ton of local charities, no spouse, no kids, and no records of her existing prior to twenty-five years ago. She just appeared in St. Louis and started a life. No prior driver's license, college transcript, bank records, medical records, nothing."

"That does sound suspicious," the demon in doctor's clothing said, moving farther into the house. "Well, who or whatever she was, she put up quite the struggle."

I moved through the foyer into the living room and had to agree with him. The place looked like somebody threw a wrestling match in the suburbs and forgot to move the furniture first. The coffee table was shattered, the couch was flipped, an end table lay on the hearth before the gas logs, and the tv was hanging from the wall by its cable cord.

There wasn't much blood, but a few drops here and there. "Do you get any sense that there was an angel or a demon here?" I asked Faustus.

"What do I look like, a bloodhound?" he asked, but closed his eyes and turned slowly in a circle. "No. If there were demons here, they were masked, as I am now, in human guise. The same goes for angels.

There's no sense of divine magic here, nothing that trips my alarms at any rate."

"Speaking of tripping alarms," Dennis's voice came from my phone. "It looks like you guys did just that. The police are on the way."

"Shit," I said. "We need more time to look around, see if we can pick up any clues. Dennis, can you re-route the call? Send them to the wrong address?"

"I can try, but if they're close, it's going to be tough."

"Do what you can," I said. I looked at Jake and Faustus. "We need to split up and cover the whole house in the next couple of minutes. Doc, you handle the front room and kitchen. Jake, you get the guest rooms." I pointed to a hallway leading off to the left. "I'll get the master bedroom and bath." I moved off toward a door that stood open to a ransacked master bedroom off to the right of the room. Jake started down the hall, but his father didn't move.

"Is there a problem?" I asked.

"I've stayed out of this shit for decades. I swore I was through with magical power struggles. Now you're trying to drag me back in. I don't like it." His face looked drawn, almost sorrowful, and for a second, I felt bad about yanking him into my mess. Then I remembered the whole demon thing and I gave a lot less of a shit.

"Sorry, pal. But your life here is fucked whether you help me or not. They kinda shot up your fundraiser last night, and somebody's going to have a lot of questions about that. So you might as well help me out before you blow town. Do some good for once."

"Because that's what demons are known for," he said. "Doing good and leaving primroses and daisies in our wake. Why don't I just burn the entire city to ash and scrawl my name in the scorched earth instead? That would at least be interesting."

I froze for a second, not sure how serious, or capable, he was. I took a deep breath. "Well, could you at least help me finish my part of the job before you nuke the city back to the stone age? Because I don't want to listen to Luke bitching if I come back empty-handed."

The mention of Luke jarred him into action. "Yes, Vlad. It would twist a knife in his undead gut to get help, even indirectly, from me. That's a little entertainment while I set up a new life. Very well, I'll help you search." He reached down with one hand and flipped the couch back upright like it was a pillow.

I moved into the master bedroom, shaking my head. My life started off weird and just kept going further and further off the rails. I had made it through the drawers on the bedside table before I heard a car pull into the driveway.

"Shit," I muttered. I pulled my phone from my pocket and pressed the center button. "What the fuck, Dennis? I thought you were going to buy me some time?"

"I can only do so much, Gabby." The unicorn wore a sad face and a single animated tear ran down its cheek. "Whoever this is, the computer in their car is hardened as fuck, and I couldn't get into their system fast enough."

"So this isn't the cops?" I asked.

The unicorn vanished, replaced by Dennis's human face. He looked scared, something I'd never seen before. "I don't know who this is, Gabby. I can't get any kind of digital signature off them. Nothing. It's like they know to shield against me specifically. Be careful." His face blinked out, and I drew my pistol.

"Guys, we've got company!" I shouted. "Dennis can't tell me who they are, so be careful."

"That doesn't mean kill them, Dad," Jake called from the back of the house.

"Who the hell raised you to be such a spoilsport?" Faustus shouted back. I stepped through the door of the bedroom and shot him a dirty look, and he snapped his fingers. I gasped a little as he vanished in a puff of smoke, leaving a hint of sulfur in the air. All that was missing was a *bamf* sound.

Just then, a pair of big men in tactical gear rushed into the room, rifles pressed to their shoulders and helmets and goggles obscuring their faces. They split as they came through the foyer, one dropping to a knee and aiming his gun down the hall to where Jake searched, and the other pressing his shoulder tight to a wall and pointing his rifle right at me. The barrel of his gun looked huge as I stared down it, thinking how woefully inadequate my pistol felt in that moment.

"Drop your weapon! Get on your knees! Put your hands on your head! Drop that goddamn gun right now!" The man barked orders at me rapid-fire without taking a second to breathe or let me comply.

I almost froze, then remembered that I was the same woman who stared down biker gangs and went toe-to-toe with demons. One cop wasn't enough to intimidate me, even if he could blow me to Kingdom Come in half a second. *Fuck this guy,* I thought. *Fortune favors the bold and all that shit.*

"So…which would you like first?" I asked, leaning against the bedroom door.

The cop looked completely baffled. "Huh?"

"Do you want me to drop the gun, get down on my knees, or put my hands over my head? In what order would you like me to do these things? Because I can't do them all at once, even if you do have a gun pointed at me. So, what should I do first?"

"Bitch, I will shoot you," he growled.

"Don't call me bitch," I said, my voice low and cold. "I don't like it." I don't, seriously. It's demeaning and dehumanizing, and I don't take that shit, even at gunpoint. I also had more than a little backup.

Apparently my backup didn't like name-calling either because Faustus reappeared right then, complete with puff of sulfurous smoke, and snatched the gun out of the cop's hands. "If you can't talk nicely, you're going to get your toys taken away," Faustus said with a smile.

The innocuous-looking man put one hand on the rifle's stock, another on the barrel, and bent it into elbow macaroni before dropping it to the floor at the police officer's feet. The cop reached across his chest for the pistol Velcroed to his tactical vest, but Faustus was faster. He snatched the gun off the man's chest and flung it aside, then punched the stunned officer right in the helmet, splitting the face shield and sending the cop to Dreamland.

The other cop turned to Faustus, who stood in front of him, hands held out wide with his palms up. "Do you really want to try that? You saw what happened to your partner, didn't you? Why don't you just run along now and let us go about our business?"

The cop stood, rifle still at his shoulder, only to catch a blow to the back of the head from Jake, who slipped up behind the man while his attention was diverted. The cop squeezed the trigger, and Faustus stepped to his left, catching a bullet square in his chest that likely would have killed me. I rushed to the demon's side, spinning him around to check on the damage, but the only evidence he was even shot was a hole in his dress shirt and a few drops of ichor oozing from a rapidly closing hole in his flesh.

"Pity," he said, smiling at me. "I liked this shirt."

"You saved my life," I said. My grasp of the obvious in stressful situations is unparalleled.

"So it seems," he replied. "Now I think you're in my debt. I rather like that." His eyes flashed yellow, and I felt a chill walk down my spine.

"What the fuck is going on in here?" A new voice came from the door, and I stepped around Faustus to see who'd joined the party now. I expected it to be another soldier type, but it couldn't have been further from that. Instead of a burly alpha male in tac gear, it was a dark-skinned woman in her forties with her hair tied back in a tight ponytail. She wore a tailored suit that looked expensive, big chunky heels, and the bulge on her left hip was the only indication that she was armed at all.

"Who are you people, and what are you doing at my crime scene?" she said, her hand drifting to the gun under her suit coat.

"I'm Gabriella Hels," I said, telling the lie that matched the Homeland Security credentials I held up in front of my face as I walked toward her. Credentials that were more useless than my Blockbuster Video card since Harker shot the head of the DHS Paranormal Division for consorting with demons and trying to destroy the world. If I was lucky, this chick was just a local PD detective, and my expired fed creds would be enough to scare her off. "And who the hell are you?"

I've never been what you call lucky. She looked at my credentials and smiled at me, pulling out a familiar-looking badge wallet. She flipped open her own Department of Homeland Security ID and said, "I'm Keya Pravesh, Regional Director for the DHS Paranormal Division. I think you and I have a few things to talk about."

Fuck.

1 2

The woman looked at me, then Faustus and Jake, then back to me. "Would you like to chat, or should we just try to kill each other now?"

I holstered my pistol and walked into the living room. "You've already tried it with one of us. What makes you think you'll be any more successful the second time around?" I sat down on the couch and propped my feet on an edge of the overturned coffee table.

Agent Pravesh, or Director Pravesh, or whatever her title was, walked into the room and sat across from me in an armchair. "Your friend here isn't on our radar. We underestimated him. You are on our radar, Ms. Van Helsing. We have an extensive dossier on you, and nothing in it mentions any supernatural abilities, much less ones that would let you avoid bullets. So we might not be able to kill your companions, but we could definitely end you, and that's really the point, isn't it?"

She had a point. I certainly didn't want Jake or his dad to end up dead on my account, but I wanted me to end up dead even less. "Okay," I said. "Let's talk. Starting with the fact that I thought Homeland's Paranormal Division was disbanded after the whole being infiltrated by demons thing."

Faustus laughed, and everyone in the room stared at him. "I'm sorry, were you serious? If being infiltrated by demons was criteria for dismantling a government agency, you people never would have gotten a Constitution. Not to mention what would happen to…oh, every government in the world."

"Ignore him," I said to Pravesh. "He thinks just because he's a super-powerful Demon Lord with an opera named after him that we should pay attention to the crap he spews." Inwardly, I was trying to figure out how I could get Dennis to figure out which members of Congress were really denizens of the Pit. I had a few ideas, but sometimes it's hard for me to tell the difference between demonic assholes and just garden-variety human assholes.

Pravesh turned from Faustus to focus on me. "There have been a lot of changes in the Division. We planned to reach out to Mr. Harker or Mr. Card soon, but your involvement in the situation last night accelerated our reveal."

"Situation?" I said. "You mean the massacre of a dozen or so people by a demon in the middle of the swankiest hotel in the Midwest? If that's your idea of a 'situation,' I'd hate to see what you call a minor annoyance."

"It usually takes high explosives or a zombie infestation to really annoy me," Pravesh said with a smile. Unlike the mocking grins and smirks I'd gotten from Faustus all morning, the agent's looked genuine. So, of course, I trusted it even less. Sincerity is way easier to fake than most people think.

"So why are you here chasing me instead of downtown looking for clues as to why a demon ripped up a black-tie fundraiser?" I asked.

"Before we were even subjected to the rubber chicken," Faustus added. "Which I suppose makes me indebted to the demon."

"Yeah, too bad you killed him," Jake said. He came into the den and sat next to me on the couch, resetting the coffee table and putting his pistol on it, then moving back from the gun slowly.

"It seemed like the thing to do at the time," Faustus said, coming over to sit on the arm of the couch by Jake. "Now, Agent Pravesh, I believe Ms. Van Helsing asked you a question?" he prodded.

Pravesh nodded. "Like I said, there were a lot of changes in the

Paranormal Division as a result of Agent Smith's betrayal, but we, as an organization, are entrusted with great responsibility, and we continue to work to protect the United States, and the world, from supernatural threats."

"Then what are you doing here?" I asked. "As you so clearly stated, I'm not supernatural." I just kinda hoped we could ignore the fact that I was running around with a pillar of the community who also happened to be a demon.

"But your companions are anything but ordinary," Pravesh replied. So much for ignoring things. She went on. "It seems that Dr. Harman is at the very least a lower-level Reaper Demon, and quite possibly some variation of a Demon Lord. That would make his son a Cambion at best, a full demon at worst."

"Nope," Faustus said. "We can't reproduce with our own kind. We don't really have the organs for it. We can only mate with humans through the use of magic. Don't you people know anything?"

"It might come as a surprise to you, sir, but most of your kind are more interested in flaying all humans alive than in conversing with them."

"Oh no, not at all," Faustus replied. "The more you speak, the more appealing flaying you becomes."

"Not helping," I said firmly. I turned my attention to Pravesh. "Okay, so you followed me because you were interested in Faustus. That makes sense. You can't have him, and it doesn't look like you brought anywhere near enough people to take him by force, so why don't you just leave until you can call in reinforcements?"

She smiled again, warmer and more sincere than before, which, of course, made the roiling sensation in the pit of my stomach even worse. "Oh no, Ms. Van Helsing, you're quite mistaken. While we certainly have things we'd like to discuss with Dr. Harman, he's not the reason we're here. You are. What is a member of the Shadow Council doing in St. Louis? What are you looking for here, and what do you intend to do with it when you find it?"

Well, shit. I wracked my brain, trying to come up with something that wouldn't get me thrown under the jail, but before I could concoct anything resembling a decent story, Faustus stepped right in the shit for me.

"She's looking for an Archangel. Lucifer plans to restart his war on Heaven, and she needs to round up all the Archangels to stop him. For some reason, she thinks there's one here, and judging by the state of this place, someone agrees with her. Or did, at least, because they beat us to him."

I whipped my head around and glared at the grinning demon doctor, who shot me back a broad smile. Asshole. I turned to Pravesh, who just nodded. "That's what we've heard," she said. "Seems some of your Council compatriots have made quite a stir in New Orleans and Charleston. Not to mention Charlotte. Does trouble just swirl around Quincy Harker all the time?"

"Does a bear shit in the woods?" I asked.

"Excuse me?" She looked startled. I couldn't tell if it was by my profanity or the non sequitur.

"Oh, I'm sorry, was that a real question? I thought we were just asking stupid questions that everyone already knew the answer to." I was annoyed now. Not only had this woman shown up and scared the shit out of me, but Faustus had let the cat out of the bag as to my objective, and to make things worse, it seems like the feds already knew what was going on. Something was jacked up with the Council's security, and I still had an angel to hunt down.

I took a deep breath and tried to stay calm. After all, I was the one without automatic rifles or magic powers, so I needed to keep my shit together. "Yes, I'm working for the Shadow Council, which might need to look into a name change given how many people seem to know its business lately. Yes, we're hunting down Archangels in an effort to stop Lucifer from doing something nasty. I don't really know what he's got up his sleeve, but from where I was raised, it doesn't matter what the devil wants to do, you should probably do anything you can come up with to stop him.

"Our intelligence came up with three people living in St. Louis likely to be the angel. Dr. Harman here, who is obviously about as angelic as I am. Ms. McCourt, who lives here, and..." I looked at my phone. Dennis popped up, his avatar holding a little sign in his unicorn hooves. It was cute, I had to admit that. "And a man named Hector Reynolds, who lives in a condo on the north side of town. He's our next stop, but I have to admit that given the state of this place, and the shitshow at the gala last night, I don't have high hopes for finding Mr. Reynolds sitting in his La-Z-Boy with his feet up watching *Buffy* reruns."

"That's a fair guess," Pravesh said. "Especially since our team that went to Reynolds's house called in five minutes ago. The place was trashed, and empty. There were signs of a struggle, and it looks like whoever lives there was injured."

"Shit," I said.

"Maybe he's okay," Jake said.

"Oh, the angel won't be hurt," Faustus said. "At least not permanently."

Every eye in the place locked onto him, and he explained. "Divine creatures can't be destroyed on this plane. Our physical forms can be harmed, but the worst thing that happens to lesser beings is that we get sent home to reconstitute ourselves. Creatures like Archangels, or Pit Lords? They just have a little lie down and they're right as rain. If someone unpleasant has captured Raguel, the worst that will happen to him is a bit of bother."

"But the humans that got swept up in all this?" I asked.

"Oh, they're fucked," Faustus said. "No hope for them at all. In fact, that's likely how the extraction team plans to figure out who's who. Just shoot them both in the head. The one that gets up pissed? That's your angel."

"What about the other one?" I asked.

"The other what?"

"The other person, Dad," Jake said, elbowing his father in the leg.

"Oh, them. Well, I assume they won't get up at all. That's kinda how you can tell them apart." Faustus looked completely undisturbed by this concept, and I wondered how the hell this guy kept his cover as a doctor for decades with absolutely no sense of empathy. I guess sociopaths really are incredible actors.

"So what's next?" I asked Pravesh. "You going to haul me in, or you going to help me?"

She looked at me, then her gaze trailed over Jake and Faustus. "I don't know what I should do, Ms. Van Helsing. On the one hand, your friends here do have some particular abilities that could come in handy in thwarting the possible destruction of the world. On the other hand, I don't trust this one as far as I could throw him." She pointed at Faustus.

"I don't blame you," I said. "All I know is that for now, he's motivated by something much greater than a desire to save or destroy humanity."

"What's that?" she asked.

"He really hates Luke Card and wants to rub it in his face that he helped me."

"So pure pettiness?" One perfectly cultured eyebrow rose skyward as she looked at the demon in doc's clothing. Faustus just shrugged. "You know what? That makes sense to me. We can work together for now, but we're going to have some very serious conversations about those credentials you've been flashing around when this whole thing is done."

Serious conversations, my very favorite thing. Right behind mammograms and hangovers. I stood up and headed for the door. "Then let's go," I said. "We need to get over to the last victim's condo and see if we can find any clues before something really shitty happens and I have to explain to Harker how I got St. Louis blown up."

A beep came from my phone. I stopped and pulled it out of my back pocket. "What is it, Dennis?"

The unicorn face appeared, managing to look sheepish. "Um, you're not going to like this."

"The list of things I haven't liked today is long, and getting longer by the minute, so why not just pile on, little incorporeal buddy?" I said, glaring at Faustus. The demon, for his part, seemed particularly out of fucks to give about me being annoyed with him.

"I monitored the search from the other tactical team, and there's nothing in the condo. So whatever Raguel's Implement is, it's got to be in that house."

"Why can't the other team have missed it?" Jake asked. He was standing closer to me than he absolutely needed to, but I kinda liked it. I was less and less sure that I was going to sleep with him, but that was mostly because we kept getting more and more likely to die before I got the chance.

"Well, they might have," Dennis said. "But that condo doesn't have a secret safe room off the guest bedroom like this house does."

I looked at Jake, who shrugged. "I didn't see anything, but I'd just started in that room when the cops showed up."

"Federal agents," Pravesh corrected.

"Whatever," I said. "Dennis, you're saying there's a secret closet somewhere in the guest room?"

"Pretty sure that's exactly what I just said."

I pushed past Jake into the den, then turned left to head down the hall. "Well, let's go play safecracker and find out what's in there."

13

So I learned something in St. Louis. I learned that breaking into a safe room is really hard. I guess if it wasn't, it wouldn't be very safe, would it? But this thing was really damn secure. Finally Pravesh called the alarm company, who called the contractor who built the safe room, who called the company that made the custom door locks, who told us that once the door was secured, no one in the world had the codes to get in because the customer was the only person who could open the door from the outside with a double-layer biometric lock that required a fingerprint and retinal scan.

Pravesh hung up the phone and kicked the door in disgust, but not hard enough to scratch her expensive-looking shoes. I thought about that for a second, digesting the fact that I now had enough of a salary to buy expensive shoes and remembering that I hate women who wear shoes that cost more than my gun, vowed never to be caught dead in a pair of Jimmy Choos, unless he started designing shoes for Nike.

"What's wrong, Agent Pravesh?" I asked. I was needling her a little, since Dennis had eavesdropped on her call and filled me in on the details.

"No one can get us into the safe room," she said. "I'm stuck."

"I think this is why your organization keeps people like us around," I said, gesturing to Faustus and myself. I turned to the demon doc. "Faustus, would you please open the door?"

He looked at me with a little sideways smile. "What's in it for me?"

"I won't tell Harker where to find you," I said, smiling right back at him.

His face darkened, but he moved toward the door. "Not that I couldn't just hide from him all over again, but this is just much simpler." He put a hand on the door just beside where the keypad nestled into the wall and closed his eyes. A few seconds later, a loud *thunk* echoed from inside the door, and it popped slightly open. Faustus looked at me and said, "You're welcome," then stepped aside.

I hung back and let Pravesh and her men take the lead. For one thing, it was a small room, not really any bigger than an oversized walk-in closet. For another, I didn't trust it not to be boobytrapped. If this was where the angel lived, and it looked more and more likely, then I didn't trust it. Other than Glory, all the angels I've seen are douchebags.

Faustus sidled up next to me and leaned in so none of the agents could overhear him. "You want to be in there. I don't know what it looks like, but the Implement is there. I can feel it."

"You can feel magic?" I asked.

"I can feel anything that strong," he replied. "Usually I only get a vague sense of where a talisman of that kind of power is, but whatever is in there is shining like a lighthouse though a fog bank. The safe room must have some kind of shielding or scrambling magic in it."

"So does that mean this angel knows what he is?" I asked. "Harker told me most of them didn't remember they were magic."

"I have no idea," Faustus said, "but once the po-po clear out, we can get in there and make off with the goods."

"You sound like a mix between an adult trying to sound cool and a fifties gangster movie," I said. "Po-po? Make off with the goods? Who do you think is filming you?"

The demon's face fell, and for a second, I worried that I'd hurt his feelings, then I remembered he was a demon and stepped on my give-a-shit reflex. I walked over to the door and looked in. Pravesh stood in the opening, looking on as one of her men in tactical gear rummaged through a bookshelf and the assorted stuff tucked away in the bugout room. The man turned to Pravesh and shook his head.

"There's nothing in here, ma'am," the man said.

"Can I go in now?" I asked.

"Why would I let you do that?" she asked back.

"I thought we were working together," I said. "Remember, going off to save the kidnapped human, free the Archangel, and probably kill a demon?"

"There's a difference between working together and letting you have your hands on a potentially powerful magical artifact. I don't care who you're working with, you're not walking out of here with anything that can be directly linked to an Archangel."

"Well, actually, I am," I said. "It's just a matter of when I do it, and if I have to hurt any of your men to do it. You see, I've got a job to do, and it involves something a lot bigger than you or me. There's some bad shit going on, and I need that angel. The key to finding that angel is in that closet somewhere, and I'm going to get it. Now do you want to stand aside, or does Faustus have to get unreasonable?"

I jerked a thumb over at my shoulder where I remembered Faustus standing, but, of course, when I turned to him, he wasn't there. He was standing behind Pravesh, holding up a silver pendant with a big moonstone in it. "Here we go," he said, handing it over to me. "Take this thing. I think it's giving me a rash just being this close to something angelic."

I took it, and a tingle passed through my body. I felt the power radiating off the necklace, and it made all the hair on my arms stand up. This thing had some serious mojo if I could feel it, because I'm about as psychic or sensitive as the average houseplant. "Wow. That thing has some juice to it."

"It should," Faustus said. "Raguel is no shrinking violet, even among the Archangels. He's also called Metatron, the Voice of God. I'd suggest locking that thing up in a box and throwing the box into the ocean, but I doubt it would do any good. It would probably just float back to him."

"Can you use it to find him?" Pravesh asked. I gave her a questioning look, and she said, "In my predecessor's notes about Quincy Harker, he said Harker once used something belonging to a victim to track him magically. I was wondering if you could do the same thing."

I shook my head. "I'm not a wizard," I said. "Harker is…well, Harker's a lot of things, not least of which is a pain in my ass. But he's got magical mojo in spades. Me? Not so much."

"I thought all you Shadow Council people were wizards, or vampires, or monsters, or had magic toys, or something," she said.

"Most of them are," I agreed. "I just shoot people. Usually bad people."

"Usually?" Jake asked from where he sat back out in the bedroom.

"We all have our off days," I replied. "Now how are we going to use this thing to track down the angel? We need somebody with magic." I might have exaggerated the last sentence a little bit as I looked over at Faustus, who shook his head and backed away.

"Oh no." He waved his hands in front of his chest. "Not on your life. I am not screwing around with an Archangel's Implement. That's a good way for a demon to end up a pile of dust swept up by Saint Peter's cleaning crew."

"What are you afraid of?" I asked. "I thought you were supposed to be powerful. I thought you were the legendary demon Faustus, the stuff of opera and theatre, the very incarnation of evil and brilliance wrapped in a mild-mannered human disguise."

"Appealing to my vanity will get you nowhere," he grumbled, but held out his hand. "Give me that thing. I'll see if I can come up with some kind of sympathetic magic to lead you to its owner."

I handed him the pendant, and he slipped past me into the safe room. "You'd better close me in here," he said. "If this thing goes boom, it has enough magic in it to level the whole block. Maybe if I'm locked in this warded room with it, it'll only destroy the house." He shooed me out of the room and closed the door. It shut firmly, and a second later, we heard the *thunk* of the lock engaging.

I turned to Jake, feeling the blood rush from my face. "Jake, can your father do that demony thing where they pop in and out of Hell and our dimension?"

Pravesh went pale as well and shoved me out of the way, then started pounding on the door. "Harman! Open this door! Harman! If you don't open this door right this second, I'll—"

The door opened, and Faustus stood there holding the necklace by its chain. "You'll what? Nuke the room from orbit? That's probably what it would take. That thing is *solid*. If we find Raguel before he's hauled off to Hell to kiss Lucifer's ring or have his wings ripped off and shoved up his ass, or whatever the boss has planned for him, I'll have to ask who the contractor was."

"Did you get the spell cast, or did the yelling screw things up?" I asked.

"Oh, sweetie," the demon said, patting me on the head. "If a little thing like humans screaming distracted me from my work, I would never have gotten anything done in the 1300s. It's done. There was enough residual divinity in the pendant that you should be able to wear it and know which direction to go."

"Me wear it?" I asked. "I thought…I mean, you…?"

He shook his head. "Demon. I'm not putting that thing around my neck. Just holding it and enchanting it gave me a migraine."

I turned to Jake, but Faustus shook his head again. "News flash, punkin', my kid is half-demon. It would probably hurt him more than it hurts me, because he's not as strong, magically speaking."

I looked at Jake, who just shrugged. Pravesh held out her hand. "I'll take it. I'm completely human, it shouldn't bother me."

Faustus snatched his hand back and held the necklace out of reach. "I'd turn it over to Lucifer himself before I give it to a representative of the government. At least Lucifer is constant in his motives. Nope, I keyed the spell to Gabby, and Gabby alone. It won't work for anyone but her." He held out the necklace, and this time I just shut up and put it on.

As soon as I did, the room grayed, as if someone suddenly turned the world black and white. The only spot of color was a bright green glow off to my left. I turned to face it, and I could see something shining through the wall of the house, as if it were very far away. It looked like a sunset just below the horizon, but I also felt it beckoning me, calling me, wanting to be reunited with whatever was over there.

I closed my eyes and tried to imagine what else was around the light, tried to send my consciousness along the path to the light. I felt a rushing sensation, as if my being was pulled through space, while leaving my body behind. It was weird, like nothing I'd ever felt before, and I've tried a lot of hallucinogenics. I felt my drifting self stop moving, and I opened my eyes again.

The house was gone, and not gone, all at once. I could see it, but it was like a transparency laid over what I was seeing. I saw green grass, and demons. Lots of demons. Big demons, little demons, demons wearing human form, and demons wearing skin suits. Literally. Some of the human-sized ones had actual human skins stretched out in weird directions to fit their misshapen forms. A man and a woman knelt on the grass before the demons, looking like absolute hell. Somebody had beaten the shit out of them, thoroughly and with great pleasure.

Above it all, above the green grass and stretching high into the sky, over the river, was the greatest symbol of the city and of America's passage into the west. A circle of red and purple fire floated in the air in front of the St. Louis Arch, growing bigger by the second. We had to move, *now*. I opened my eyes and looked at Pravesh. "They're at the Arch."

"What?" the agent asked.

"The demons. They're at the Arch. I saw two people on the ground, and they look like shit. There's some kind of spell swirling in the middle of the sky inside the Arch."

"That'll be a Gate," Faustus said. "They can't figure out which one is the angel, so they're just going to take them both to Hell."

"They're using the Arch to anchor a Gate?" I asked.

"What do you think it really is?" the demon asked. "You couldn't believe that shit about a Gateway to the West, could you? Oh, you did. Well, that's just precious. But if they're opening a Gate, that means two things."

"Which are?" Pravesh asked.

"One, that somebody way higher up the demonic food chain than me is calling the shots on this one, and two, that you'd better move that cute ass of yours. If the Gate is opening, you have less than an hour to stop this, or Raguel is going to really be in the sauce."

"We," Jake said, standing up.

His father turned to him. "What?"

"We have less than an hour. We're helping. Now let's move."

Faustus looked baffled. "Why are we helping? I don't remember anyone saying it would be fun, or profitable. So why would I do it?"

"Because I am, and you don't want to see me get killed," his son replied, moving toward the bedroom door.

His father cut him off. "But why are you doing this? You don't care a whit for an Archangel."

"That's very true," Jake agreed, then looked over at me. "But I really want to sleep with her, and if she dies, that's not going to happen."

"So let's go save the world, and get laid," I said, linking arms with Jake.

Pravesh and Faustus followed behind us, and I could almost swear I heard Pravesh mutter something about "Worst. Heroes. Ever."

14

"I hate being right," Faustus said from the back seat of my Honda as we pulled off the road into the parking lot near the Gateway Arch.

"No, you don't," Jake fired back from the passenger seat. "Being right is literally one of your favorite things in the world."

"Well, I hate being right when it means I might get my ass kicked, and since you've never seen me in that situation, you can't exactly contradict me on that, can you?" Jake's demon dad snipped at him. We were all a little jumpy, knowing that the odds were definitely not in our favor on this one.

I parked beside a cadre of black Suburbans and idly wondered if the federal government kept that vehicle in production all on its own. As I walked around to the back of the Element, strapped on a thick leather belt with my knives in holsters, and got my pistol and holster out of a bag, I heard Jake let out a low whistle. I turned to see a dozen men in full assault gear, complete with riot helmets and a variety of rifles bristling with grenade launchers and bipods and other accoutrements, heading toward us at a brisk walk.

The hard-faced men, and as they got closer I could see a few women in their number, formed up in two straight lines alongside my car, and Pravesh walked up to where we stood. She had traded in her stylish pumps for a pair of sneakers and added a bulletproof vest over her shirt, but she still looked a lot more like a supermodel than a lethal federal agent.

"Okay, we'll take it from here," she said, gesturing to the agents at the head of the two columns of men.

"What?" I asked. "What do you mean, you'll take it from here?"

"I mean that you've led us here, so your services are no longer needed. You have the thanks of a grateful nation, now piss off." She turned to go, but I reached out and grabbed her elbow.

I turned her around and stepped up until we were nose to nose. I was really grateful she'd dumped the heels, since now we were at least mostly eye to eye. "Look, lady. I don't know what kind of bullshit game you think you're running here, but I don't work for you. I don't even really know if you are who you say you are, and I don't care one way or the other. I've got a job to do, and an angel to save, and I don't need a goon squad getting in my way. Now I'm going to—"

"You're going to what?" She cut me off, then held up a finger to my mouth as I started to speak again. "No, sweetie, the grownup is talking. That means you stand there and keep your mouth shut. Your grandfather might have been some hot-shit vampire hunter back in the day, but this isn't eighteenth century Europe, this is America, and I have the full might and power of the United States Government behind me, while you have…what, a demon doctor and his half-breed brat? Stick to bail jumpers and biker trash, honey. It's safer that way." She turned to go again, and every one of my better instincts told me to listen to her, to get in the car, drive back to Chicago, and tell Harker that the government had his angel in custody and everything was fine.

Then I told every one of my better instincts to get fucked, which is what usually happens when somebody pisses me off. And Agent High and Mighty had certainly pissed me off. "Nineteenth," I said to her back.

She stopped in mid-stride and turned to look at me over her shoulder. "Excuse me?"

"Abraham Van Helsing was my *great*-grandfather, and he hunted

Vlad Tepes in the nineteenth century. And he *was* a hot-shit vampire hunter. Just like I am. Now if you don't want to help me rescue this angel, that's fine. Just try not to get in my way. We don't have time to babysit a bunch of idiot Muggles who think their guns are going to be worth a fuck against a demon strong enough to open a literal highway to Hell in the middle of St. Louis." I gestured for Faustus and Jake to follow me. "Come on, boys. Time to save the world."

I stomped past the flummoxed agent and her gunmen, heading toward the Arch where a glowing sphere of purple and red light roiled in the air. "I hate the glowing doorway in the sky thing," I said.

"You've been around a major Gate before?" Faustus asked, stepping up alongside me.

"Atlanta," I said. "A year or so ago. Demon called Orobas tried to open a passage between Heaven and Hell, using Earth as a hub. Harker and the rest of us thought that sounded pretty bad for Earth, so we stopped him."

"We?" The doubt was heavy in Faustus's tone.

"I was there," I said. "I shot things. I didn't do any of the magical heavy lifting, but that's what I've got you here for."

"We're all doomed," he said, his voice low and somber. "I'm going to end up back in the Pits, spit-shining Beelzebub's hooves or something equally vile." He stopped walking, and Jake and I turned to look at him. As we watched, a crimson glow suffused his entire form. He grew taller, and as the red got brighter and brighter, the man in the center of it got darker and darker. In a few seconds, the glow faded, and instead of the mild-looking middle-aged doctor that rode in with us, the demon Faustus stood there. His skin was so black it almost seemed to absorb light, and his eyes gleamed a golden yellow with narrow vertical irises.

He was taller and so much more muscular that his shirt shredded around him. He tore the collar from his neck and tossed the rag to the ground. The demon Faustus rolled his head from side to side, then interlaced his thick fingers and cracked his knuckles. Each finger ended in a razor-sharp claw, and narrow fangs peeked out from behind his thin lips. "That's better. Now I feel like a fight."

I turned to Jake. "You want to hulk out before we get over there, too?" I asked.

"Nah, I take after my mom a little more." I laughed, and we turned our attention to the mess developing ahead of us.

Pravesh's men had broken into a jog and were advancing on the park at the bottom of the Arch in formation. Because that's what you do when you're staging an attack on a magical entity of unknown and possibly phenomenal power—you run headlong at it. That works out well every time, I hear.

The parking lot where we stashed the Toaster was to the southwest of the Arch, and the jogging shock troopers peeled off onto a footpath that had them approaching the Arch directly from the south. I veered left to come out a bit west of the Arch so I could get a better view of the area, and what I saw wasn't pretty.

It was midday, so there were a couple of families picnicking and playing frisbee in the park, completely ignoring the six men in dark robes standing at the base of the Arch chanting and summoning a big ball of glowing magic in midair. A couple of college kids were lying back on a blanket looking up at the growing portal, maybe thinking it was a light show or something. All in all, there were probably a dozen civilians scattered around the park.

I turned to Jake. "You gotta get the civilians out of here. Your dad and I will take care of the spellslingers, but I need you to get those people to safety."

"What if they won't go?" he asked.

"I didn't say you should ask nicely. You've still got my .357, right?"

"Yeah." He didn't look like he quite understood what I was saying.

"Shoot one of them. Pick one that looks old or sick if you can. But after you shoot the first one, the rest will nope right the fuck out of here."

Faustus patted me on the shoulder. "I like this one, Jake. You should keep her. That plan was positively demonic." He said it like it was a compliment. I guess it probably was, coming from him.

"Thanks, I think," I said. "Hang around Quincy Harker for any length of time and your moral compass no longer has any idea where north is." Not that Harker really had anything to do with my moral flexibility, but he was a convenient scapegoat. "Come on, Pops. Let's go save the world."

We started moving toward the hooded figures, and for the first time, I saw that they had hostages. It made sense, of course. I knew Raguel was here, in his (her? their? Angelic genders confuse me) human form of Ms. Sheelagh McCourt, and I figured Hector Reynolds, my third suspect for who was the Archangel, was also here, but it still surprised me a little to see a pair of humans trussed up like Christmas geese sitting with their backs pressed to the back of the Arch.

We were about thirty yards out when Agent Pravesh's voice rang out across the park. "Stop what you're doing in the name of the U.S. Government!"

It worked. Well, it kinda worked, for about half a second. The six figures, who I could now hear were chanting in some language that I didn't recognize but sounded a lot like a Rammstein album played backward at top volume from inside a running cement mixer, paused in their chanting, which caused the glowing swirly thing of magic to bobble for an instant. But then five of the six refocused on their task and everything in the sky stabilized.

The sixth robed dude turned to face Pravesh and pulled back his hood, revealing a long pair of horns curving around in a tight spiral from his forehead. A broad grin split his crimson face, and a long black ponytail fell down over his shoulder. He basically looked like a miniature version of Hellboy, without the one big hand and with a better hairstylist. He looked from side to side, taking in the double row of cops advancing on him, and rolled his shoulders.

The demon didn't grow; it's more like he *swelled* to twice his size. In a matter of seconds, he was nearly twelve feet tall, and the arms sticking out of his now ridiculously small robe had textbook-sized hands with four clawed fingers. "I'm sorry, Agent," he said, and his voice boomed like thunder. "I can't stop in the name of your government. Because I don't give a fuck about your government!"

Then he held out his hands and bathed the oncoming agents in streams of purple-black fire. Those weird eldritch flames engulfed the first two men in each row, and they fell to the ground, their mouths open in a wordless scream. The men and women behind them in line scattered, bringing their rifles to bear on the demon and opening fire.

Bullets ripped through the child-sized robe, tearing holes in the demon's flesh and the cloth as the automatic rifles spat lead through the air in an amazing hail of gunfire.

For all the good it did them. The demon took every shot they threw at him, and just stood there grinning. After a few seconds, the guns all clicked empty, and before they could reload, the demon held up one massive hand and flicked his fingers in their general direction. Bullets tore back out of his chest and stomach, then flung themselves back along their path, shredding a dozen government agents in a lethal rain of their own gunfire.

Less than thirty seconds after a dozen highly trained assault troops entered the park, the only people left standing were me, Agent Pravesh, Faustus, and the demon trying to rip open a portal to Hell in the middle of St. Louis. This was not how I wanted to spend my weekend.

15

The demon's voice boomed across the grass. "Faustus? Is that you? I haven't seen you since Macedonia! What was that girl's name? The one whose liver we ate while she watched, you remember! That was nice piece of spellcraft, keeping her alive without a liver. I've never quite figured out how to keep them from dying long enough to take more than a bite or two before they expire. You'll have to teach me that trick some day."

"You know this guy?" I asked Faustus.

"It's a small Hell," he muttered. Then he turned his attention to the decidedly not small demon stomping toward us across the grass. "Ginthraxis! Old chum, how the Hells are you? What have you been up to? Still a lieutenant in Bar'ruk's Tenth Legion?"

"I'm a colonel now," the demon bragged, puffing his chest out as he came to a stop in front of us. "The boss sent me up here on a quest for Lucifer himself."

"Wow." Faustus's eyes went wide as he feigned surprise. I thought he was laying it on a bit thick, but apparently demons aren't big on subtlety because Big Red seemed to buy it. "What's the mission? Anything I can do to help? Not that you need it, obviously." Faustus waved a hand at the dead agents on the grass. "You handled those idiots without even breaking a sweat."

"Stupid humans," Ginthraxis sneered. "Always relying on their stupid guns. Like a weapon of steel and lead can hurt a demon!" The big demon's brow furrowed, and he took in Pravesh and me for the first time. "Speaking of stupid humans, did you bring these along for a picnic? The brown one's pretty, but they're both too skinny, and the pale one looks like she'll give you gas. I suppose you could make them fight, then fuck the winner and eat the loser, but honestly, I'd rather bugger a Reaver."

I didn't know whether to be offended or relieved that the giant demon wasn't attracted to me, so I just filed it away for my next meeting with my therapist and concentrated on not getting dead. Faustus ducked his head, like he was embarrassed or something, then said, "I need a favor, Gin."

"Anything for you, Faust! You know I still owe you for getting me out of that jam with that Torment Demon's parents when I got caught with my dick in an orifice not specifically designed for that."

"I've literally been trying to forget about that very thing for centuries, Gin. But no amount of brandy will get the job done. I need the angel."

The demon's head snapped back, eyes wide. "What do you want with the angel, Faust? Are you trying to get back into Lucifer's favor? I think he's forgiven you for that Marlowe debacle by now. You don't need to swipe my catch to get in his good graces. Besides, if I bring the angel down to Lucifer, Bar'ruk promised me a general's berth. You know what that means for a demon like me."

"I know, Gin, and I wouldn't ask if it wasn't important. But I have to have the angel. Well, it's not so much that *I* need the angel, I just need for Lucifer not to get her." Faustus looked genuinely contrite, like he felt bad about crapping all over his buddy's gig. I just wished he'd get on with it.

"What? Are you working with the other side now, Faust? I knew that Marlowe shit screwed you up, but I never imagined that it had sent you off the deep end." Ginthraxis waved a hand, and a huge curved sword appeared in his right hand. "You can't have the angel, Faust. If you try to take her, I'm going to have to hurt you."

Faustus snapped his fingers, and a rapier appeared in one hand with a shorter, thicker sword in his off hand. He assumed a defensive pose and looked up at the bigger demon. "You know I'm faster than you, and better with a blade, Gin. Don't make this painful."

"I know you were better with a blade, Faust, but you've lived up here a long time, getting slow and eating bon-bons while I've been down in the Pits fighting for my life every day. I'd bet we're a lot more even now." He rushed Faustus, and the battle was on.

I grabbed Pravesh and yanked her off to the side. "You get the male hostage and get the hell out of here. I'll handle the angel."

She glared at me. "You are not leaving here with that Archangel, Ms. Van Helsing. I don't care who you are, or who you're working with, I'm not—"

"You're not having a debate, is what you're not fucking doing," I snapped. "You didn't listen to me when we got here, and that got every agent you brought with you killed. Now if you want to fuck around some more, maybe you can increase your body count, but I'm going to take this necklace over to that Archangel, put it around her neck, and see what happens. I suggest you be somewhere else when all that happening starts."

She pulled her pistol and aimed it at my chest. "I can't let you do that. I told you, that angel is going into the custody of the United States Department of Homeland Security, and I meant it."

"Then shoot me," I said, staring her in the eye. It wasn't much of a bluff. I knew she wasn't going to shoot me. She thought of herself as one of the good guys, and she thought of me that way, too. In her world, the good guys didn't shoot the good guys, so I was safe as a babe in its mother's arms. After glaring at me for several seconds, she lowered her pistol. I knew she wasn't going to shoot me.

I don't really sweat the sharp lines like "good" and "bad," so I pulled out my Sig and shot her twice in the chest. She fell back, her gun flying from her hand. She wasn't going to die, her bulletproof vest saw to that, but it sure got her out of my way for a few minutes. I leaned down, picked up her gun, ejected the magazine, and threw it as far as I could across the park. Then I flung the pistol in the other direction.

"Sorry about your ribs," I said, then turned and walked off to where the Archangel and some poor bastard with a spotty employment record were sitting trussed up under a national monument. I broke into a run as the sounds of demon battle behind me grew louder, reaching the pair of trussed-up hostages a few seconds later. I knelt behind the man, a portly Irish-looking guy with a patchy red beard.

"Hector Reynolds?" I asked as I drew one of my daggers and sliced the bonds at his feet.

"Yeah, that's me," he said. "What the fuck is going on? Who is that asshole that took me? What does he want?"

"Well," I said. "Let's take a quick look. He's twelve feet tall, red skin, horns, pointy teeth…yup, probably a fucking demon. Now why would a demon be interested in you, Mr. Reynolds? And before you give me some bullshit answer, remember that I am kneeling behind you with a very sharp knife and it's just as easy for me to stab you as it is for me to free you."

I could almost feel him digging around for the lie, but his shoulders sagged, and he said, "There's a lot of people after me, but until about ten minutes ago, I didn't believe demons were even a real thing. That's the God's honest truth. I swear on my mother's grave."

I believed him. "Who's after you?"

"A couple of made guys from Boston. I wasn't always named Reynolds, and I used to have some connections with men that have less than legal occupations. But I'm out of that now. I just do my job, follow protocol, and keep my head down."

Witness Protection. That explains why he just popped into existence. It made sense. "What was your name before you ratted out the Boston mob?"

He stiffened. "I can't—"

I reached around his neck, pressing the tip of the knife into the side of his throat. "Save me the time and don't bullshit me, please. I have important things to discuss with Ms. McCourt here, and I just need to check you out before I let you go."

"Kieran. Kieran O'Grady," he whispered. I pulled my phone out and tapped the screen.

"Dennis, did you get that?"

The unicorn wore a shamrock on his forehead. I couldn't help it, I laughed. Dennis might have been a disembodied soul trapped in the internet, but he had a grasp of the ridiculous that was unparalleled. "I got it, lassie. Kieran O'Grady was a mid-level leg breaker for the Irish back in the 80s. He fell off the radar right around the time that Mr. Reynolds appeared in St. Louis. The dates line up, and the pictures match enough. He's telling the truth, Gabby."

I cut Reynolds/O'Grady's hands free. "Get out of here. Go back to keeping your head down and believing that demons aren't real. It's way safer that way."

The former mobster turned shit-scared Midwestern suburban taxpayer scrambled to his feet and sprinted away. I didn't know if he was going to run straight to the *National Enquirer,* YouTube, or the nearest bar, and I didn't care. I had bigger fish to fry. Winged fish, to be exact.

"Now, Ms. McCourt," I said to the middle-aged woman tied up on the grass. "Do we have to pretend that you're really human, or can we cut the shit?"

She looked at me with some of the purest disdain I've seen since middle school when I showed up with last year's cool sneakers on. "I think we can dispense with any subterfuge. Did you bring my Implement?"

I pulled the pendant from beneath my shirt and showed it to her. "It's right here. Safe and sound."

The woman's eyes widened for an instant. "I'm surprised you can abide that much contact. Most humans would have been driven mad by that level of exposure to pure divinity."

"There are plenty of people who'd say it's a little late for me to be driven mad. They're probably right."

"Give it to me."

I shook my head. "Hold up there, Speed Racer. We've got some things to talk about before I just go handing over this super-powerful artifact and letting you out of my grip."

"I really think you want to give me my necklace now," she said, and something in her words told me that I wasn't getting the whole story. I noticed that her attention was fixed firmly on something over my shoulder, so I turned to where I'd left Faustus scrapping with Ginthraxis to buy me time.

And promptly ran out of all that time. Faustus was looking a whole lot the worse for wear, bleeding dark ichor from wounds all over his arms and torso, while Ginthraxis didn't appear to have a scratch on him. The big red demon raised his curved blade overhead, and Faustus drove his rapier into Ginthraxis's exposed gut.

Ginthraxis just smiled at him, bringing his huge blade down on Faustus's shoulder. He cleaved the smaller demon diagonally in two pieces, and Faustus fell to the ground with a pair of wet *thumps* that I heard from fifty yards away. I heard Jake scream for his dad across the park and watched as Ginthraxis flicked the blood and entrails from his blade and turned his attention to us.

"I think I mentioned that you should give me my necklace," McCourt/Raguel said.

Without a word, I slipped the pendant from around my neck and dropped it over the bound woman's head. As soon as the chain made contact with her flesh, a brilliant white light engulfed her, driving me back onto my butt on the grass.

When my vision cleared, the thirtysomething Latina woman tied hand and foot was gone, replaced by a statuesque form wreathed in white, standing over me with wings spread and a staff in hand. Raguel looked down at me and held out a hand.

"Rise up, child. I am not yet at my full strength. I have need of you to send this fiend back to the Pits."

The angel needed my help? Oh, we were really fucked now.

16

I stood up and drew my blades, glancing over at the glowing angel standing next to me. "Um, what is it exactly that you wanted me to do against that thing?"

The demon stomped toward us, its hooves leaving deep impressions in the turf as it broke into a run. A pair of black bat-like wings sprang from its shoulders, and the checklist of demonic characteristics was complete. It still held that big-ass curved sword in one hand, and its other was curled into a fist, ready to pound me into the ground like a tent stake with its crimson knuckles.

"This would be a good time for you to use your magic, human," Raguel said to me.

I turned to the angel, my mouth hanging open. "Magic? What magic? I don't have any magic. I'm just supposed to find you and bring you back to my...okay, friends might be too strong a word, but coworkers doesn't really cover it, so let's go with friends. I'm supposed to convince you to go back with me to my friends so they can stop Lucifer from, I don't know, taking over the world, or Heaven, or some such shit I only about half believe in. But I don't *have* any magic, so what the fuck do you expect me to do now!" My words got faster and faster as the demon got closer until I was basically shrieking at the angel while I waved my knives around really fast in the air.

I talk with my hands. When I'm holding my knives, that can be hazardous for the furniture. Fortunately, we were outside. Unfortunately, Raguel really looked like they needed my help. Then the angel raised their hands over their head, and a gleaming staff of pure light appeared.

They stepped forward, which coincided with me ducking behind them, and planted the staff right in the onrushing demon's gut. Ginthraxis stopped short, doubling over with a *whoof!* Raguel stepped to one side and brought the staff around to crack into the back of the demon's right knee. Ginthraxis dropped to one knee, and Raguel looked at me.

"Attack, child!"

I stared for a second, but who the hell am I to disobey a direct order from an angel? I charged the kneeling demon, burying my knives up to the hilt in the monster's shoulders right where they joined its neck. I stabbed and twisted, kicking Ginthraxis in the nuts for good measure. And where angels might be neuter, or gender-flexible, when he swelled up to twelve feet tall and burst out of all his clothes, Ginthraxis showed off the fact that he was very much a boy demon. So I kicked him in his demonic boy parts, just like I did Kyle Farnwell at my junior prom when he grabbed my ass on the dance floor.

The demon raised one arm to swat me away, but Raguel's gleaming staff cracked him on the elbow. I yanked my knives free, black blood streaming from the wounds, and slashed across Ginthraxis's face, trying to blind him. His horns got in the way, and all I managed to do was open a long cut across his forehead, but he started bleeding like a stuck pig, so I hoped I'd, at least, obscured his vision. For some reason, the wounds left by my daggers weren't healing like the bullet holes had earlier, so I pressed what little advantage I had and looped around to the left of the creature.

Ginthraxis swung his sword in my direction, but the blood in his eyes and being down on one knee screwed with his stroke, and I managed to dive flat on my belly on the grass and avoid getting cut in half. I heard another solid *crack* as Raguel laid in with their staff again, and Ginthraxis bellowed in pain. I rolled over onto my back, but found myself somewhere I never wanted to be—under a demon's ass.

Look, I've done some things in my life that weren't fun. High school trigonometry sucked. Losing my virginity in the back of a 1999 Chevy Cavalier convertible wasn't just messy and awkward, it was also far more gymnastic than it needed to be. Fighting a shitload of demons in downtown Atlanta was scary as fuck and pretty painful, but nothing, and I do mean *nothing*, in my life ever prepared me for the horror of having my face less than a foot from a kneeling demon's taint. I thought for half a second about just rolling back out of there, then I remembered that my knives actually seemed to have an effect on this bastard. So I took a deep breath, held it, and stabbed upward with both hands, burying both blades to the hilt right in Ginthraxis's tenderest bits.

One blade went in right behind his ball sack, and the other slid between his butt cheeks like they were greased. I heard the most unholy shriek from above me, and *then* I rolled out from under the demon and didn't stop rolling until I was several feet away. I scrambled to my hands and knees and turned around, certain that twelve feet of red-skinned death would be upon me in a blink, but the demon was spinning around in a circle grabbing beneath its nuts trying to get the knife out of its asshole.

Raguel looked stunned by the turn of events, but they quickly gathered themselves together and went to work with that glowing staff. A sharp rap to one knee dropped Ginthraxis back to the turf, which judging from the way he flailed at his groin, the landing jarred something farther up inside him to where it really, *really* shouldn't have been. While Ginthraxis tried to dig the foot-long blades out of its scrotum and rectum, Raguel struck again and again with their staff.

Every time the angel struck a blow, a flash of white light seared the demon's flesh, and Ginthraxis screamed. A shot to the other knee, another scream. A strike with the butt of the staff to the demon's ribs, another scream. Finally, Raguel raised the staff high above their head and brought the end down into Ginthraxis skull, shattering the demon's head in a blinding flash of light and bathing the entire park in a suffocating blast of sulfur.

When the smoke cleared, Raguel stood alone on the grass, their staff glowing purest white. There was a small pile of reddish dust in the grass at their feet, which blew away to mix with the rest of the cloud of funk Ginthraxis left behind. The portal glowing in the air above us winked out, and there was nothing left of the whole mess but a bunch of dead government agents, a sobbing Jake, a cursing Agent Pravesh, and a pair of knives that I was never touching again under any circumstances.

***

An hour later, the bodies were cleared away, Raguel was back wearing their Sheelagh McCourt form, Pravesh was screaming at someone on her cell phone, and Jake was sitting with his back against the Arch, tears drying on his cheeks. I walked over and sat next to him.

"Sorry about your dad," I said.

"Thanks." He didn't turn to look at me, just stared out over the river.

"You know he's not, like, really dead, right?"

"Yeah, I know. But he's back in Hell, and he hasn't been back there in centuries. I think he got in a bunch of trouble over something with Marlowe back in Shakespeare's time. Something about Marlowe getting out of his deal, and Dad being in the shit over it. I don't know, but whenever he talked about Hell, he seemed really scared."

"Not for nothing," I said. "But most people are really scared of going to Hell."

He chuckled, and I took that as about as good as I was going to get out of him. I mean, even that was pretty good for a dude who just saw his dad get cut in half in front of him. "Yeah, I guess you're right. Besides, you and your people can just bring him out, right?"

I paused for a minute and thought about what he was saying. Thought it through again. Nope, still didn't make sense. "Huh?"

"Well, you said you had to go rescue some Archangel that Lucifer dragged into Hell. That means some of your people are going down there, maybe even you. Just bring Dad back when you come back. I'll help."

I looked over at Jake, and there were no real signs of a head injury, so I approached it like a psychotic break. "I don't think you quite know what you're asking. It's not like whoever goes can just buy you an extra ticket. And I'm pretty sure I'm not going. I mean, I don't have any magic. I'd be useless."

"You may not be able to cast spells, Gabriella Van Helsing, but you certainly have some form of magic. How else would you be able to absorb the divinity of my Implement and pass it along to your own?" Raguel/McCourt stood over us. I didn't hear her come up. Sneaky angel bitch. She smiled down at me, then held out my knives for me to take.

"Um…no thanks," I said. "I know where those things have been."

"I cleaned them for you," McCourt said.

"So not the point," I muttered, but I took them so I wouldn't have an angel standing over me with daggers pointed at my face. "Are you ready to go?"

"Yes," she said. "I would like to go home now."

"Not so much, sweet cheeks," I said. "You're going to Chicago with me, then we're packing up my clothes and heading to North Carolina. I've got a buddy there who needs your mojo to get a pair of wings back for his guardian angel. And maybe save the world. I'm not real clear about that last part."

"No," McCourt said, and turned to walk away.

I sprang up and grabbed her arm, pulling the angel woman around to face me. "What do you mean, no? You're a frigging Archangel. This kind of shit is what you were made for. You *have* to help us!"

"That's the problem with living so long down here among you meat puppets. Free will feels good. And you're right, I'm an Archangel. That means I don't have to do a damn thing I don't want to do." Her eyes glowed, and I snatched my hand off her arm, unsure if I was about to get smited or something.

"Have a nice life, Gabriella Van Helsing. I appreciate your assistance in dispatching Ginthraxis. I certainly could have managed it without you, but it would have taken more of my energy than I wished to expend." She turned to go again.

I ran around and stood in front of her. "Then you owe me. I helped you, now you help me. That way we're even."

"You say that as though I care if the scales are balanced between us. You are a human; I am of the Host. You are to me as an ant is to you—irrelevant. I care not a bit if you feel that I am indebted to you because how you feel doesn't matter to me. I don't owe you anything, Gabriella. Goodbye."

She stepped around me and started walking away. I watched her go and let out a howl of frustration. "Dammit, Ragu! If I don't bring you back, then I don't know how the fuck we're going to get Uriel out of Hell! Harker says we need every other Archangel to rescue him! Or her! Or whatever I'm supposed to call you fuckers!"

Raguel froze in mid-step, then turned back to me. "Uriel is in Hell?"

"Yes, that's the whole point of this bullshit mission! We're not just trying to get Glory's wings back, now we've got to get all of you Arch-dickheads together, dive into Hell, and rescue Uriel before Lucifer does something with a whip and fucks the whole world up or something!"

"And we have to get my dad," Jake said, his voice almost inaudible, but not quite. I held up one finger to him in the universal "shut the fuck up" symbol.

Raguel walked back to me, her eyes glowing a little. "Is this true, what you say?"

"I might be dumb enough to stab a demon in the nuts, but no way am I lying right to an Archangel's face."

"Uriel has been taken to Hell by Lucifer?"

"That's what Harker told me."

"You can take me to this Harker?"

"That's kinda been the plan all along."

"I will go with you. Uriel is my friend, and one of the Host. Lucifer must not be allowed to harm them."

"So it's them? That's the right pronoun for angels?" This was bugging me, and after the day I'd had, I really felt an urge to nail *something* down.

"They is fine. Or whatever form we take. Right now I choose to appear as a woman, so you may refer to me as a woman. Or you may call me Raguel, if that is easier. Now can we go? If Uriel is Lucifer's captive, we should not waste time."

"Let's go. We can get back to my place before the sun sets, and Dennis can get us on a plane tonight." I turned to head back to my car, only to find Agent Pravesh standing in front of me, arms crossed over her probably very sore chest.

"I'll do you one better, Van Helsing," she said, giving me one of those smiles that said she was neither happy nor amused. "I have a jet fueled and waiting. We can be in the air in thirty minutes and in Charlotte by nightfall. I've been meaning to meet this Quincy Harker and have a little chat with him about the demise of Agent Smith."

"I'm coming, too," Jake said.

"The fuck you are," I shot back. "Look, I'll try to get Harker to bring your dad out, but there is no way you're coming with us."

"Actually, there's no way I'm not," he said with a grin. "Whose plane do you think we're taking? My father was a centuries-old demon, remember? I'm stupid rich." With that, he turned and walked toward the parking lot, whistling.

"Stupid rich, huh?" I muttered. "Well, you're at least half right."

"I heard that!" Jake called back over his shoulder. I let out a long sigh, then a millionaire half-demon, an Archangel, a government agent, and a woman who not an hour before stared right up a demon's pooper, all rode off to save the world.

TO BE CONTINUED

105

Did you enjoy She Talks to Angels? Do you want to know when the next adventure in Quest for Glory will be? Would you like a free short story from one of my other series?

Go to the address below to sign up for my email list and you can have all those things, as well as updates on appearances, new releases, and sales!

https://www.subscribepage.com/g8d0a9

SHOUT AT THE DEVIL

1

Spoiler alert—tattoos are painful. Somebody is jabbing a needle into your flesh a few thousand times a minute, and that shit doesn't feel good. I don't care how many endorphins your body produces, or how into pain you claim to be, after the fourth hour in the chair, that shit has stopped being interesting a long time ago, and now it just *hurts*.

Second spoiler—magical tattoos hurt even more. Because not only are you marking your flesh with permanent ink, you're pouring mystical energy into the ink at the same time it goes into said flesh, bonding the magic to the ink and the skin in a complicated process that requires a fuckton of concentration, a mountain of magical power, and a practitioner who knows their shit.

Now, my tattoo artist is a friggin' wizard, which helps. I know, everybody that likes their ink says their artist is a magician of some sort, but most of them aren't firing up the gun in the middle of a protective circle and tapping leylines to power the enchantments they're pumping into the Sailor Jerry heart and roses on your bicep with "Mom" written on a ribbon in nice serif letters. No, my artist is a legitimate wizard, with a robe and everything.

He's also a goddamn giant of a man, with ink stretching from his finger all the way up his arms, across his chest, scrolling up the back of his neck and bald head, and down both legs. That proves that he knows how much it hurts. He's also had all that work done on his own body, so when he tells me to stop wriggling around like a whiny little brat, I just suck it up and sit still.

"Now, this is going to hurt a little bit," Tuck said, his blue eyes dancing as he grinned at me through his bushy goatee.

"What? Like the last four hours of this shit was a tickle fest?"

"That was the warmup," he said, not giving a single fuck about my pain level. "Those were some minor wards, some additional physical enhancements, real basic shit. This next hour is going to be more complex spell- and ink-slinging, designed to let you store more energy in your tattoos than you can usually handle in your body, and call upon it in an instant. The designs are more complex, and the power I'm pouring into these is very different from what you're used to taking in. If you need a break, this is a place where we can stop for today and you can go off and whimper in a corner for a little bit."

"Are you good to keep at it?" I asked. I could see a few beads of sweat dotting his forehead, but Georgia in July is stupid hot no matter how much air conditioning you have, so it might have been the weather instead of the strain of the magic.

"I guess I've got another hour or two in me, but it's gonna leave me pretty drained."

I thought about it, then shook my head. "Let's call it here for today. No point in you getting laid up for a week because you channeled too much power through yourself on my account. I don't think I'm gonna be running into a big bad in the next few days, so just a little extra oomph will be fine."

Tuck nodded, then set his tattoo gun down and capped his inks. He spritzed some water on a paper towel and wiped down my left arm, cleaning off the excess ink. He dabbed a little Tattoo Goo on his fingers and rubbed it into my arm. He wrapped my arm in cling wrap and peeled off his black latex gloves, pitching them into a wastebasket as he started to neaten up his workspace. "You know the drill. Keep your shit clean, keep it moist with the Goo until it heals. For you, I expect this will heal up in a day or two. Between whatever you've got going on and the magic in the ink, it'll speed the process a lot."

"Thanks, brother. I appreciate you working me in."

"Now what's this all about, Q? I keep hearing a bunch of weird shit about you hanging out with angels, pissing off the devil himself, and trying to find God. Something tells me that's not metaphorical."

I sat up in the chair and slipped my long-sleeve shirt on over my newly tattooed arms. As I buttoned the cuffs on the black shirt, I shook my head. "I wish it was, old friend. Somebody gave up something important to save my ass last year, and I have to get some divine intervention to help her out."

"But angels, Harker? That's a little out of your league, isn't it?"

"My league has gotten pretty expansive since we were closing down strip clubs together, old friend." Tuck and I had raised our fair share of hell in and around Atlanta a couple decades ago, but in the years since, he'd gotten mostly out of the mystical shitshow that I called my life and focused on becoming one of Georgia's preeminent tattoo artists. Me, I just took my hell-raising to more literal fronts these days. "I don't want to drag you back into this world, buddy. Just trust me that I know what I'm getting myself into."

"Oh, I don't doubt that you know what you're getting into," Tuck said, taking a long swig from a plastic bottle of spring water sitting on his station. A part of me flashed back to our wilder days, when there almost certainly would have been a bottle of whiskey on top of his rolling toolbox and another one in my hand the whole time he was inking me up. "What worries me, Quincy Harker, is that you usually don't give a fuck what you're getting into. Is this something you have to do, or is it just more of your bullshit death wish?"

I started a little and looked up to meet his eyes. There was no condemnation in the blue, just honest concern. "I don't have a death wish. No, don't give me that look. I probably did. Okay, I definitely did, I just couldn't find anything bad enough to actually kill me. But I don't anymore. I'm not over Anna, I'll never be over Anna, but I don't want to go chasing her into death. I've got something to live for, man. Somebody to live for."

"Your detective?"

"Yeah, Rebecca Flynn. She reminds me why I'm fighting all these big nasties, Tuck. She's worth fighting for. She's worth *living* for."

"Fuck, I'll drink to that." He slid open the bottom drawer of his toolbox and pulled out a bottle of Wild Turkey. He spun the cap off the bottle, took a long pull, and handed it over to me. I put it to my lips and let the amber fire pour down my throat. For a second, it was the nineties again, and I was ready to go out on the town looking for trouble with my old buddy Tuck.

Tuck erased the magical circle around us with his foot, and my cell phone got signal again. As soon as that happened, the notifications on my phone blew up, and trouble found me.

Tuck grinned at me, his eyes crinkling as I let out a huge sigh. "That's why I never got a real job, Q. Too many people looking for you, and you can't even enjoy a beer with an old friend after he brutalizes you for half a day."

"Kiss my ass," I said, smiling. We bumped fists, I slid him four hundred-dollar bills, and went outside to see what the hell was wrong now.

The Atlanta heat wrapped around my face like a warm towel the second I stepped out of the air-conditioned shop. It wasn't cold inside, but it was so hot, and so muggy, that I swear I felt my eyeballs fog up. My tank top instantly adhered to my skin under the long-sleeve shirt, and I felt a row of sweat pop out on my forehead in the twenty feet it took me to get to my car. I opened the door of the Toyota, leaned in, and cranked the engine. I stepped away and leaned on the back bumper to let the AC kick in before I sat down. The car was dark blue, with gray interior, which meant it would be more like a sauna for the next five minutes anyway. Hell, the way the sun was beating down on the asphalt, I couldn't touch the steering wheel without giving myself second-degree burns.

I looked at my phone, and Dennis Bolton's rainbow-horned unicorn face stared back at me. "What's up, Dennis?"

"Where the fuck have you been, Harker? Don't you know we're trying to save the world up here?"

"You know exactly where I've been, asshole. You track my phone everywhere I go." He did, too. Dennis was an old friend, a computer whiz who'd been murdered by a corrupt half-demon police detective some years ago. I saved his consciousness by shoving his soul into my cell phone, but thanks to the wonders of the nation's largest network, he leapt right out of my phone and onto the internet.

Now there was a smartass twenty-something with questionable decision-making skills and a moral compass that just spun in circles that had unlimited access to every piece of digital data in the world. It made it real convenient when I was short on cash because he could just reroute some Congress douche's latest lobbyist bribe into my account. It was less convenient when I wanted to disappear for a day or two because not only did he track my phone better than the NSA, he also had access to every traffic cam and networked security camera in the world. All that meant that he never had to wonder where I was. As long as I was in this dimension, Dennis could find me.

Which meant… "Oh shit, Dennis. The circle. I'm sorry, dude. James casts a circle whenever he's doing magical tattoos and works off a battery-powered gun so nothing breaches the barrier. Including cell signal."

"Yeah, as far as any of us know, you vanished from the face of the earth fifteen minutes after you walked into your buddy's shop. Which, by the way, has no internet security system, so I couldn't peek inside, either."

"I'm pretty sure that's exactly why he doesn't have an internet-linked security system. He knows about you, and he's got some clients now and then that he'd rather I not ask him any questions about."

"You're saying your tattoo artist also tattoos bad guys?"

"Dennis, depending on who you ask, I *am* the bad guy. But that's not the point. The point is that James is very private and doesn't want anyone snooping on him. I'd be surprised if he used anything more recent than a flip phone."

"He doesn't. I checked. Not even a burner smartphone. This dude wants to vanish, he's *gone.*"

I wasn't surprised. Tuck and I had been in some sketchy places and had to make ourselves scarce from those places more than once. I was surprised to find him operating a shop under his real name, or at least the name I've always known him by. If anyone would have an escape plan in place, it was Tuck.

"What's got you so freaked out, Sparkles?" If he hated the nickname, he could stop appearing as a unicorn.

"There's a woman in San Francisco who's been looking for you since this morning. Says it's urgent, and she was super pissed that I couldn't find you. Ask me what kind of tech ops guy I called myself, if I couldn't find one wizard in North Carolina. I didn't bother to tell her that you were currently one wizard in Georgia because her point was just as valid."

"Who is it?" I asked. I knew a few people in San Francisco, but nobody with a particularly bad temper.

"I'll patch her through. You can deal with her. I'm out of this shit. And next time you decide to vanish for half a day without telling anyone anything more than 'I'm getting new tattoos,' *you* get to be the one to talk Flynn down off the ledge."

Oh shit. I didn't explain everything I was doing to Becks before I left the apartment at the crack of dawn this morning. That was not going to go well. I sent a tentative sliver of thought down the psychic link that I shared with my fiancée, but all I got back was a general sense of pissed off, with the tiniest hint of relief that I wasn't dead. But mostly pissed off.

That was not going to be a good conversation when I got home. Just the thought of it made me dread the four-hour trip back to Charlotte. I sighed. "Okay, Dennis, put the mystery woman on the phone."

The screen went dark, then an unfamiliar face popped into view. She was a dark-haired woman in her late thirties, with strong cheeks and jawline, dark eyes, and the dark skin of a Latina. Her eyes were red-rimmed from crying, and her nose was red, like she'd been blowing it a lot. "Are you Quincy Harker? The sorcerer?"

"I usually just answer to Harker, but yeah, I've been known to cast a spell or two. I don't think we've met. How did you know where to call?" If my identity was out in the world, it could get very uncomfortable for some folks I cared about, so I tried to stay somewhat below the radar. As much as possible, given the fact that I do hunt demons and work with not only the Department of Homeland Security but also a secret organization working for the greater good called The Shadow Council.

"My name is Arlena Meneses. Lena for short. I found your contact information in my wife's phone, under her emergency contacts."

I cocked my head to the side. "I'm sorry, miss. Who is your wife? And why would she have you call me in case of an emergency?"

"I don't know. But your name was in her emergency list, with a note to call you if anything weird ever happened to her. Well, she was murdered last night, and I think it's because she was a witch. Is that weird enough?"

I wracked my brain trying to come up with a witch in California who would have me in her phone. I couldn't come up with anyone, then it hit me like a bag of bricks. "Faye?" The name came out of me in a strangled gasp. "Faye Spataro?"

The woman on the screen nodded, sniffling a little. "Yes, Mr. Harker. Faye Spataro. My wife. She was found mutilated in a deserted apartment this morning, with all kinds of magical shit strewn around the room. Is that weird enough to get you out here?"

I was already in the car, slamming the door and punching in Hartsfield-Jackson Airport into the GPS on my dash. "I'll be on the next flight out. If there are local cops there, tell them that this is now a Homeland Security case and to get the fuck out of my crime scene. I'll be there as soon as I can."

I clicked off the call, dialing another number out of my speed dial list. As Becks' phone rang, I remembered Faye Spataro, a fiery witch I'd worked a couple of summonings with out of California more than a decade ago. She was one of the good ones, and whoever hurt her was going to pay. They were going to pay dearly.

2

"Okay, but call me as soon as you land."

"Will do. I love you."

"Love you, too. And you're still taking me out when you get home. Somewhere nice, not just a food truck this time."

"Deal," I said, then pressed the button to end the call. I could feel Rebecca's concern across our mental link, but it was faint, given the distance. Without concentrating on it, the link would be almost imperceptible when I landed in California, as long as nothing too tragic happened to either of us.

I sat in the Delta lounge at Hartsfield-Jackson International Airport, the busiest airport in the United States, waiting for my flight west to board. Dennis had worked his magic and gotten me not only onto the next flight, but in first class. Somewhere there was a middle manager who was having a bad day. When I got tired of people-watching, which took about a minute and a half, I pulled out my iPad and surfed the web, looking for any news about Faye. There was nothing on the major sites, which wasn't surprising. Most witches keep a low profile, and Faye was no exception. She worked in a florist's shop doing wedding arrangements, mostly, and dabbled in the occult on the side.

Now her side hustle got her killed. Faye was always more than just the standard crystal ball and Tarot cards BS medium or prognosticator. Faye was a legit water witch, with the ability to make her primary element bend to her will. I've never met an elemental practitioner as powerful as Faye, so the fact that she was murdered concerned me, more so that it happened in San Francisco, a city with water all around. She wasn't short on resources, so what found her that took her so by surprise that she couldn't fight back? Or worse, what was powerful enough to overwhelm her?

These were thoughts that normally would have me flagging down a bartender to get another double vodka cranberry, but if something was hunting practitioners in California, I was going to need all my faculties. Plus, I hate having to piss on airplanes.

I managed to get through the flight sober, a wonder in and of itself, then I rented a pretty swanky BMW SUV at the airport and headed into town to meet Arlena Meneses. I hooked my phone into the Beamer's dashboard computer and called Dennis.

His horsey image appeared on the screen, grinning a ridiculously human grin. "How do you like the wheels, boss?"

"Pretty good, Boltron, pretty good. Not as much as I liked the first-class plane ticket, but a close second."

"What's the use of having an almost digitally omnipotent friend if you're going to fly coach?"

"I agree," I said. "Now, what can you tell me about Arlena Meneses?"

"You mean Marine Gunnery Sergeant Meneses? She of the Navy and Marine Corps Achievement Medal for her work in Afghanistan? Or do you mean Sergeant Meneses, of the San Francisco Personal Crimes Division, who is the current city pistol champion?"

"Well, smartass, I guess I mean both of them since they're probably the same person."

His computerized horse image jumped up and clicked its heels, making a shower of rainbow sparks. Sometimes, he was so cute it made me want to barf. Instead, I just suffered in silence. "You got it, boss-man! Sergeant Meneses has been with the SFPD for five years since receiving her undergraduate degree in criminal justice from San Francisco State University. She minored in art history. She's been with the Personal Crimes Division, assigned to homicide, for the past year. She's considered a rising star by the brass, a 'diversity hire' by the racist asshole desk sergeant, and a solid investigator who's a little green and carries a chip on her shoulder, but is overall worth the investment by her CO."

"You hacked her personnel files," I said. I didn't approve, but I was going into this mess blind, so I wasn't going to condemn him for doing what I would have asked him to do eventually anyway.

"Is it really hacking, though? For me, it's more like walking through the front door. Besides, you were going to tell me to do it anyway. I just got ahead of the curve."

Yeah, he got me. We spent another few minutes going over Meneses's service record (spotless), her employment record (decent), and everything Dennis could find about her relationship to Faye Spataro (blissful). I pulled up in front of a warehouse-turned-brewpub in the Mission District and tossed the keys to a pimply-faced valet with a crew cut and a red vest.

Southern Pacific Brewery is the kind of industrial chic joint that the hipsters love, with overpriced burgers, apps like garbanzo beans, but good beer brewed on premises, and reasonably priced. I scanned the room for Sergeant Meneses but didn't see anyone who looked like the woman I video called with six hours before. I grabbed a barstool, ordered the house porter, and leaned back on the bar to watch the room until she showed up.

Which was about two minutes later as a woman bulled her way through a clump of dudes by the bathrooms, making her way over to me with all the subtlety of, well, a Marine Gunnery Sergeant. I guess you don't ever get rid of some things. I stood up as she approached and held out my hand.

"Mr. Harker," she said, giving me a firm handshake.

"Sergeant Meneses," I replied with a nod. "Beer?"

"Not for me," she said. "Did you drive here?"

"Yeah, I rented a car at the airport."

"Good. Our...*my* apartment isn't far from here, so I walked. You can drive us to the scene."

"Now? It's a little late, isn't it?" It was only about nine-thirty, but that was still later than most cops wanted to be out looking over a crime scene. Especially one that's a day or two old.

"You need your beauty sleep, Demon Hunter? Shit, from what Faye told me, I thought you were a badass."

"From what your file told me, I thought you gave more a shit about protocol."

"My wife is dead, Mr. Harker. If it gets us closer to finding the motherfucker that killed her, I'll go over that crime scene with a toothbrush at midnight." The fire in her eyes was real, and I saw some of what her Marine evaluators saw in her to promote her all the way to E-7 before she decided to get out.

"Fair enough, Gunny. You drive, though." I downed the rest of my beer, tossed seven bucks on the bar, and walked out to the valet stand.

A couple of minutes later, another crewcut pimpled valet pulled up front in my rental, and Meneses looked up at me. "You rollin' like that, buddy, you damn skippy I'll drive." She slid in behind the wheel while I tipped the valet and walked around the SUV.

"Don't be too impressed," I said as I fastened my seatbelt. "I got hooked up at the rental car place. Now where are we going?"

"Hope you wore good shoes," she said. "'Cause we're going for a hike."

She wasn't bullshitting me, either. An hour after I walked into the brewery, I was following Sergeant Meneses up a dirt trail on the side on Mt. Sutro, a giant hill in a city made of giant hills. This one was also a nature preserve, with one-hundred-foot trees and fog rolling in as the night grew dark. We'd been walking about fifteen minutes when the glow from her flashlight flickered, then died.

"Shit," Meneses muttered, slapping the flashlight with the heel of her hand.

"I got this," I said, reaching for the light. She obliged, and I focused my will on the tiny bulb. "*Lumos,*" I whispered, almost a breath of a word, and released a tiny sliver of power into the bulb. It lit up at least three times as bright as before, and I handed it back to the sergeant while I tried to blink the spots out of my eyes.

"Nice," she said. "I guess Faye was right when she said you threw around magic like white girls drink pumpkin spice."

I managed not to laugh out loud but couldn't hold back a snort. "How much farther to…where she was found." I was trying to both treat this like a normal murder scene, and be respectful of Lena's feelings, but I was tired as fuck, my new tattoos hurt, my back still hadn't forgiven me for driving four hours to Atlanta, then jamming myself into an airplane for another six hours, and I was more than a little unnerved that someone had the balls, and the talent, to catch Faye Spataro off guard. She was one of the best fortunetellers I'd ever met, so whoever got the drop on her had some serious juice.

"You can call it the crime scene," Lena replied, her voice small and tight. "It helps me, too."

"I'm sorry," I said. "I know that doesn't help worth a damn, but I feel like I should say it."

"Thanks," she replied, forging ahead with the new super-flashlight carving a wide path through the growing darkness. "It does help, a little. I think I'm still in shock, to be honest. It happened…they just found her this morning."

I stopped in the middle of the trail. "What?"

"What do you mean, what?"

"You mean to tell me your wife died this morning, and you've already gotten your shit together enough to call me in and walk me to the crime scene? Holy shit, Marines are tougher than fuck."

She laughed then, and it was a brittle thing that sounded like the slightest touch could shatter it, and her, into a million pieces. "You think I've got my shit together? Mr. Harker—"

"Call me Q. Or just Harker. Mr. Harker makes me think you're going to try to sell me something."

"Okay, Harker. I'm focusing on this because the longer I'm out here with you, the longer I can avoid going home to a house with no Faye in it. The longer I hunt for the bastard who took my baby away, the longer I don't have to deal with telling our dog that Mommy isn't coming home, and I don't have to look in the closet, which is almost all her clothes, by the way, and figure out which one of her flowy hippie dresses I'm going to bury her in. The longer I'm out here, the longer I can avoid lying in bed with the awful goddamn silence I know is waiting on me...*goddammit!*" She veered off the trail, stomping a few feet into the woods, and slammed her hand into the trunk of a towering eucalyptus. She hammered the tree with palm strikes once, twice, three times, then leaned her head against the trunk and let out a scream so primal I knew I'd heard it before.

I knew I'd screamed it before, more than seventy years ago in France when the woman I loved was taken from me. I knew that pain, and knew that Lena Meneses was dancing on the razor's edge to madness. I knew, because when I danced on that edge, I fell over and lost myself for four years. I stood by, waiting and watching, ready to bind her if she looked like she was going to do herself any serious harm. She was done, though, and after another minute or two, she came back to the trail, reached down to her hip, and handed me a pistol in a holster.

"Hang on to that for me. For a little while."

I didn't say a word, just clipped the Sig onto my belt and nodded. Nothing else needed to be said.

She took a deep breath, then said, "Okay, now that we've had our moment, let's go start the real work."

It was another twenty minutes of walking before we came to the crime scene tape, but I saw the light from the portable floodlamps long before that. The scene was lit up like a movie set, with crime scene techs buzzing around the place, snapping pictures and taking samples of dirt and other trace evidence. A burly uniform came over to us as we ducked under the yellow tape, his hand out, but he froze when he saw Lena.

"Sergeant Meneses...um...I...you can't..." He looked around, desperately searching for anyone higher up the food chain than him.

I took pity on the poor bastard and pulled out my badge holder. "Quincy Harker, Homeland Security," I said, handing over the ID. He didn't need to know that my relationship with DHS ended not long after I put a bullet in the head of one of their regional supervisors. I mean, he was half-demon and a multiple murderer who was trying to bring about the end of the world, so he totally deserved it, but they still got a little pissy about me shooting their agent.

The badge had the desired result, though. It immediately got the local LEO's panties in a twist about the feds coming to take their case away, all the worse because it was the spouse of one of their own. No way was he going to let me in there without a fight. Except, I was with Lena, so...

I watched all those thoughts flicker across his face in the span of two heartbeats and held up a placating hand. "I'm not here to step on anybody's dick, Officer..." I leaned in to read his nameplate.

"Burleson," he said.

"Officer Burleson. I promise, I'm here to help. Sergeant Meneses and I served together, and I have some resources that local police departments don't, so she called in a favor. It's not like I don't owe her enough."

Burleson let out a breath as some of the tension eased from him. "Oh, okay then. Let me call this in, and I'll..."

I wasn't listening. I'd opened my third eye to the scene and was scanning the area in the mystical spectrum. I rocked back a little on my heels at the ferocity of the energy in the small clearing. There was more anger and pain in a fifty-foot circle than I'd seen since I had a rogue angel serial killer loose in Charlotte. Only the magical footprints this creature left behind were even more vibrant, meaning whatever had killed Faye had more juice than one of the Host.

I started to think I might be fucked.

3

The clearing was circular, about fifty feet across, with a couple of little hiking trails leading in and out. The ground was littered with dozens of little yellow evidence tags, every one near an area of blood spatter. There were a lot of them. Like, more than I thought most forensic teams carried in their cars.

"Are you sure you want to be here?" I asked Lena.

"I want to be any fucking place *but* here, man. Are you stupid? I'm sorry, that was…"

"It's fine. It was a stupid question."

"But the real answer is I *have* to be here. I have to work the case. Even if I can't work the case, I have to."

"I get it."

"Okay. What do I do?" She looked up at me, barely hanging on to her sanity through her grief, and she was looking to me for coping advice. I didn't have much for her. My reaction to loss was half a decade of blackout insanity and a body count that made Jim Jones look like an amateur.

I took a deep breath. She was not going to like my answer. "You run interference with Burleson for me, make sure nobody screws with me while I do my thing, and generally stay out of the way." I braced for the inevitable explosion.

None came. I raised an eyebrow at her. "I get it, man. I'm not a magical type. I don't have the juice to do what you do. If I did, I would have let you stay on the east coast with all the other uptight wizards. So, go do your thing. I'll keep Burly off your back. But as soon as you're done, I get the full debrief. None of this bullshit where you hide stuff because of some Wizard's First Rule or something."

"I'm pretty sure that's just the title of a book," I said. Actually, I knew it was the title of a book. I love Terry Brooks.

"I don't give a fuck if it's the Latin translation of those tattoos you've got on your arms, I want to know every fucking thing you find out about the son of a bitch who killed my wife. *Comprende?*"

"*Comprendo,*" I replied. "But one question first."

"Go for it."

"Were you a badass, then a Marine? Or did the Marines turn you into a badass?"

"The Corps doesn't make you anything. It takes what's inside you and makes you into the best you possible, but if you don't have it, you're not gonna get it just because you put on a uniform. Now get to work."

I resisted the urge to snap off a salute, mostly because my salutes have always been sloppy and usually disrespectful, and said, "Yes, ma'am." I got to work. I started walking the scene by looking around in the mundane spectrum. I knew the crime scene techs were better than me, there was little to no chance I was going to find anything they missed, but I wasn't looking for footprints, or dropped cigarettes, or a discarded condom full of the killer's DNA. I was looking for signs that a ritual was performed here, scratchings in the dirt that appeared random to folks who had never actually summoned a demon but looked like magic to me.

The soil was thick, dark, and rich. The kind of dirt where you could drop an apple on the ground and come back five years later to find an orchard. Leaves and twigs dotted the clearing between the blood spatter and landscape of yellow plastic evidence tents but nothing arcane in nature. There were scuffed patches in the dirt and a couple of long drag marks, but no evidence of a casting circle, or wax from candles, or anything to indicate that a ritual was performed here.

I waved Lena over. She patted Officer Burleson on a shoulder and came over to where I knelt on the ground. She crouched beside me, averting her gaze from the patch of bloody earth three feet away from my knee. "What's up? Did you find something?"

"Not yet, but I need to talk through what I'm seeing with someone. It helps me process, and sometimes can get me to logic leaps I can't make on my own. I need you to tell me the truth, can you be objective enough to be that person, or do I need to call my people back home?"

To her credit, she didn't answer right away. Her mouth opened, then she closed it again after a second or two. "I don't know. I want to say yes because telling you I can't feels like weakness. It feels like I'm not doing everything I can, but…"

"But it's your wife."

"Yeah. It's my wife. And I don't know if…"

"Then don't. I'll call my people back East. If we do this right, there's going to come a time in the next day or two that I'm going to need you to dig deep and maybe pull my ass out of some bad mojo. If I break you today, there's no damn way that can happen. Now go back to keeping your buddy Burleson company, and I'll Skype with my consultants in Charlotte."

"You mean your girlfriend," Lena said.

"Oh, hell no," I replied. "It's almost one in the morning back there. If I wake her up, she'll march all the way to San Francisco to kick my ass. No, I'll call Luke. He knows more about this stuff than Rebecca anyway."

She chuckled. "Sounds fair. And thanks."

"Don't thank me until we get through whatever this shit is. If we're still alive when whatever killed Faye is dead, then you can thank me."

She nodded at me, dashed away a tear from one eye, and walked back over to where Burleson watched us. I pulled out my phone and pressed the home button.

Dennis's human face popped up, looking like he did the last time I saw him alive. He'd been a round-faced twenty-something with curly hair and a feeble attempt at a beard, and seeing that face rocked me a little. It was way more comfortable talking to a digitized unicorn than the actual face of a friend who died because I got him involved in something over his head. I hoped I wasn't repeating history in the west coast in this case.

"What's up, boss?" Dennis asked.

"How much do you know about what's going on out here?"

"I know that Faye Spataro, regarded as one of the most skilled practitioners of elemental magic in the Council's experience, was found horribly mutilated in the clearing where you're currently standing. I know her body is currently at the San Francisco City Morgue, where Dr. Jacob Yao is scheduled to begin her autopsy first thing in the morning. The investigation has been assigned to one Harold Rinol, the most senior detective in the Mission District Station. His partner, Arlena Meneses, has been placed on light duty and officially ordered not to have anything to do with the case, due to her personal connection with the victim."

"Lena's partner is the lead detective on the case?"

"Yep."

"That explains why we haven't had much trouble with the cops on the scene. Lena probably got the nod from her partner to be up here, even if she didn't mention me specifically."

"Yeah, about that," Dennis said. "How did you manage to not get thrown out the second you got there?"

"I'm still carrying around a Department of Homeland Security badge. It's not like they called anybody to check up on me."

"Yeah, that never blows up in your face at all."

"Have a little faith. Is Luke around?"

"Yeah. I'll buzz him."

A few seconds later, the aristocratic features of Lucas Card, real name Vlad Tepes, my "uncle," popped onto the screen. "Quincy, how are you? Rebecca told me of the death of your friend. My condolences."

"Thanks. Comes with the longevity, I guess."

"How well I know," Luke said. He did, too. He'd buried more people than I'd met, and I'm a lot older than I look. "What can I do to help?"

"I need to run the camera around the scene. Tell me if anything looks weird to you." I held up the phone and pressed a button to transmit the camera view from the back of the phone to Luke's screen. I slowly turned in a circle, trying to make sure he got a good view of the entire scene. I pressed the button on the screen again, and his face came back into view.

"What do you think?" I asked.

"I couldn't see much, but I am sure that Dennis was recording everything you transmitted, so we can go over it in greater detail at our leisure. I do not know what did this, but there are some things we can eliminate fairly easily."

"Like what?" I had my own ideas, but I wanted to see if Luke's matched mine.

"This obviously was not a vampire kill. Even the youngest of my kind would not waste such blood. The body would have been equally exsanguinated, but there would not be such a wealth of overspray. I sincerely doubt it was a were-beast of any type because there does not seem to be enough scattered viscera. Even assuming that the police removed all the remains, some indication of dismemberment and disembowelment would remain. I saw nothing of the sort."

"No," I agree. "There's nothing like that here. Just a lot of blood spatter."

"There does not seem to be a pattern to the blood, either. And no mud. Was it particularly hot there today?"

"I don't think so," I replied. "It's foggy now, and everyone I've met has been dressed for warm, but not crazy hot weather. Why?"

"Your friend Faye was a water witch, correct?"

Son of a *bitch*. He was right. "If she had called water to defend herself, there would be mud."

"Or if she drew water from one part of the nearby earth, there would be arid soil in that area, and an excess of water somewhere else."

"That means whatever killed her either caught her by surprise or dampened her power somehow. Shit, that's even more power than I thought I was dealing with."

"Yes, Quincy. I fear your foe in this escapade may be more than you can safely handle on your own."

"There's nobody else to call," I said. "I mean, there's Norton, but he was crazy the first time he was alive. I sure as fuck don't trust him now. I have to take care of this, Luke. She was one of us."

"So is Glory, Quincy. Do not forget that there are many who depend on you now." His words hit me like a sledgehammer between the eyes. Because he was right. Glory gave up her divinity to save me, and I was supposed to be helping hunt down angels to get it back for her. But I couldn't leave Faye's killer to run free. She'd been a friend, and she deserved better.

"I'll try to wrap it up fast so I can get back on the hunt for Implements and Archangels," I said.

"I might be able to help with that," Dennis said. "I think the two might be connected." He was wearing his unicorn face again as he made a split screen with Luke.

"You wanna tell us about it, or just look smug?" I asked.

"I think you have bigger fish to fry right now," he replied. "Look behind you."

I turned to see a fortyish Asian man walking my way, one hand clamped on Lena's upper arm. He carried an air of authority and wore a gold badge on a chain around his neck. Everything about him, from his neat haircut to the pissed-off look on his face, said that he was the man in charge, and no matter what Lena's partner thought about her being up here, he had some serious issues with it.

"Quincy Harker," he said, stopping about two feet in front of me.

"That's me." I swiped the phone off and slid it into my pocket.

"I'm Captain Paul Chou. This is my District. And, therefore, my crime scene."

"Pleasure to meet you," I said, stepping forward and holding out my hand.

"I'm not very goddamn pleased," he snarled, taking my hand and slapping a metal band around my wrist. He was angry, and fast. Before

I could pull away, he spun me around and cuffed my hands behind my back. "You are interfering with a police investigation, and you are under arrest."

Goddammit. Not again.

4

The Park District Station of the San Francisco Police Department has better interview rooms than the Charlotte-Mecklenburg Police Department. I decided while waiting for Captain Chou to return that I'd bring that up with Flynn's boss the next time I was home. It would be a terrible idea, but that's never stopped me before, so why let it now?

They had me settled into a standard metal chair, one leg slightly shorter than the other, with shackles on my ankles and handcuffs on my wrists. The cuffs were fastened to a large ring mounted in the table, which was bolted to the floor. For some reason, they were treating me like Public Enemy #1 instead of some nosy asshole with an expired badge from a federal agency. I wasn't sure what was going on, but the minute the stocky patrolman finished securing me and left the room, I set to work on getting out of that shit.

First, I closed my eyes, summoned up a little energy, and whispered, "*Nigreos.*" I breathed the word, blowing air out of my lungs in a cloud of darkness that spread through the room. My breath mixed with the air in the room, plunging the room into inky blackness. I pushed the darkness into place with my will, shoving it against the mirrored wall, the window in the door, and covering the camera in the corner of the room. When I was pretty sure I couldn't be seen, I peeled the spell away from the ceiling so I could see what I was doing.

I sent a sliver of power into the lock of each cuff, snapping them open. That done, I did the same thing to the shackles on my ankles, stood up, and sat on the edge of the table. I picked up the chair, flipped it over, and started to screw the loose foot in so it would sit level. That's what I was doing when the door burst open and three people charged in, one with a drawn pistol.

I released my darkness spell, and the haze over the walls vanished like smoke in a tornado. I turned to Captain Chou, the burly cop who'd settled me into the room, and a woman I didn't recognize. Most of my attention went to her, not only because she was the stranger in the room, but also because she might as well have been wearing a neon sign around her neck saying "Federal Agent." She was an athletic woman of Indian descent, with her black hair pulled back in a severe ponytail. With cheekbones like razors and a Roman nose, she would have been pretty in a bar, but with the expression on her face, I was more than a little afraid that she was going to cut her losses and send me to Gitmo without even a conversation. I'm about fifty percent sure Gitmo wouldn't hold me, but those aren't exactly great odds.

Regardless, I kept my cool and smiled as they charged in. "Hi, Captain. Your chair was a little wobbly. I fixed it for you."

"I swear to God, Captain. The prisoner was secure when I left the room. You saw on the monitor, didn't you?" The burly cop was sweating bullets.

"Oh, that? Yeah, he locked me up good and tight," I confirmed.

"And yet you aren't locked up good and tight now," the woman said.

"No, I'm not." I stood up, set the chair down on its feet, and stepped forward, my hand out. "Quincy Harker. And you are?"

"Keya Pravesh, with Homeland Security. You remember them? The agency you *used* to be a consultant for?"

Well, shit. This was going to get awkward fast. More awkward, that is. "I've heard of them." I sat down, gesturing toward the chair.

Pravesh turned to the patrolman and Captain Chou. "Give us the room, please. And kill the surveillance. This is not an interrogation. I just need to have a conversation with Mr. Harker."

They stared at her, and Chou looked like he was about to say something, but a glance from the steely-eyed woman in earth tones stilled his protest before it ever left his lips. I was impressed. The captain didn't look like the kind of man who was silenced easily, especially not on his home turf. He nodded at the agent, shot me a dirty look, and walked out. The patrolman followed, obviously confused at seeing his boss shut down like that, but smart enough not to open his mouth. Hell, I was wondering if *I* was going to have the stones to stand up to this chick. She made Agent John Smith look like a cupcake, and he was half-demon.

She watched the men leave and looked up at the camera. When the red light winked out, she turned to me. "What the ever-loving fuck do you think you are doing, Harker? Masquerading as a federal agent is a felony. You could have ended up in prison, or worse."

I gestured to the cuffs on the table. "They could have tried." No matter how intimidating this woman was at first glance, threatening me with jail wasn't going to do her any favors. "Now who are you, and what are you doing here?"

"I'm the Midwest Regional Director for the DHS Paranormal Division."

"We're not in the Midwest," I pointed out in my most helpful voice.

"She told me you were a huge pain in the ass," Pravesh said, walking to the chair and sitting down. "I'd have to say she understated your charm, such as it is."

"Who exactly is the she in question?" I asked, a glimmer of an idea forming in the back of my head, but still nebulous enough for me to hope it wasn't true.

"Gabriella Van Helsing."

So much for hope. "You know Gabby?"

"We met a few days ago in St. Louis, when she was working on a project. For you, as I understand."

"Was the project a success?" I hadn't been keeping tabs on Gabby since she was a little nuts and kinda wanted to rip my face off on alternate Tuesdays.

"We managed to locate the antique you were looking for." I was glad she was keeping things circumspect. I didn't *think* Captain Chou would go against her instructions and leave the recording equipment on, but you never can tell what people will "forget" to turn off.

"So why are you here? It not being in the Midwest and all."

"My superiors decided, given your previous history with our organization, that your activities should be monitored. Closely."

I didn't like the sound of that. The last "monitor" from Homeland that I'd dealt with ended up murdering one of my best friends, among others, in an effort to open up a doorway to Hell in downtown Atlanta. I'm still not sure if anyone would have noticed if he succeeded, but we stopped him anyway.

"What exactly does that mean?"

"It means that I'm your case agent, Mr. Harker. I've been reassigned from my very nice, calm post in St. Louis, where the worst thing I ever had to worry about was a MoMo sighting on camera, or a rogue gowrow in some backwoods chunk of Missouri. Now I'm supposed to follow you wherever you go and make sure you and your cohorts don't destroy too much of whatever city you're in at the time. Thanks to you, I'm going to rack up the frequent flyer miles, and my cat is going to forget what I look like."

"You could move to North Carolina."

"I was going there to look at apartments when you booked a flight for San Francisco. I wasn't happy to put my realtor off. Again."

I didn't mention that I owned a building in Charlotte. I had enough weirdos living with me. The last thing I needed was to add a fed to Chez Harker. "Sorry about that. But I got this. If you hop a redeye, maybe you can hit up some showings tomorrow."

"Not that easy. I'm here now, and you're stuck with me. Now, what's going on?"

Yeah, like I was going to tell the whole sordid story to a woman I just met. "You're gonna need to let me have my phone so I can check you out first. Then we'll see if we can work together."

"You don't get to make demands, Harker. I'm the actual federal agent here; you're the one impersonating a federal agent. If you think you get to dictate the terms, then we can continue this conversation after I—"

"After you what, Agent Pravesh?" I asked, standing up and raising my hands in front of my chest. They glowed crimson in the fluorescents of the room. "Do you think I opened those shackles by pulling a pick out from under my tongue? I'm not anything you're used to dealing with, lady. I'm not a charlatan, a swindler, or a low-level illusionist with visions of David Copperfield money dancing in his head. I'm Quincy fucking Harker, Demon Hunter, part vampire, and general badass son of a bitch. I'm going to find the thing that killed my friend, and I'm going to ruin its fucking week. If you want to help, get me the fuck out of here and stay out of the way. But if you think I work for you, or with you, or generally give a good goddamn what you have to say about anything, then we're going to have a fucking problem. And I don't think you want to have a problem with me, do you?"

Pravesh stood up, her face stony. "We don't need to have a problem, Mr. Harker. But we are going to work together, and you are going to keep me looped in on what is going on because I am charged with the defense of this country against supernatural threats, and the jury is still very much out on whether or not you are one of those threats, or one of our allies." She drew her sidearm and pointed it at my face from five feet away. "Now if you want to throw fireballs, or lightning bolts, or whatever the hell you think I'm supposed to be afraid of with your little light show, you go ahead. But you'd damn sure better ask yourself—"

"Do you feel lucky, punk?" I gave her my best Clint Eastwood impression, and she stopped cold. "Dirty Harry was from San Francisco, remember?" I let the glow around my hands dissipate and sat back down. She holstered her pistol and did likewise.

"Are we good now? Did I pass whatever test you were putting me through?" she asked.

"That wasn't a test," I said. "I wasn't sure whether or not I was going to kill you and everybody in my way, but you made a valid point. I can kill you. I can kill every cop in this station. But I can't kill every Homeland Security puke in the United States, and there are people I care about who wouldn't do well in prison."

"Detective Flynn," Pravesh said.

"Among others." I was actually thinking more about Luke. His aversion to sunlight would be a challenge with yard time, and I don't think that was going to be negotiable with prison officials. "Let's back up a step. I'll make a couple calls, check you out, then you can get me out of here and tag along while I hunt down whatever killed my friend Faye."

"That's a little condescending, don't you think? I am a federal agent, and I did just work with your friend Gabby on stopping a demon."

"No offense, but I wouldn't send Gabby after anything I thought needed much in the way of supernatural mojo. She doesn't have any talents in that arena. She was just supposed to chase down a missing person."

"She ended up dealing with a demon that tried to open a gateway to Hell in the middle of the St. Louis Arch."

I thought for a second. "I might've underestimated the shitshow I was sending her into."

"Looks like you underestimated her as well."

"That happens sometimes. When you get to be as old as I am, you think anyone younger than you is young and stupid. The real problem there is almost everybody is younger than me. Makes shit complicated." I held out my hand, and she put a phone in it.

I sent a quick text to Dennis, who popped back immediately with, "Gabby says Pravesh is legit. Gabby also showed up at the apartment with a dickhead Archangel and a half-demon hunk in tow. I'm not sure if she's going to kill the angel or screw the Cambion first, but pretty sure neither option is off the table."

I looked up at Pravesh and sighed. "Okay, you're in. Let's go hunt a big bad. If we get lucky, maybe it'll eat us both and solve all my problems."

She nodded, but before we could formulate a plan, the door to the room opened and Lena walked in, followed by Captain Chou. They didn't look happy, and not the normal kind of unhappy that I tend to inspire in law enforcement. This was the unhappy that said, "Shit just got worse."

I looked to Lena. "There's another one, isn't there?"

"Yeah."

"Where? Still in the city?"

"The Sutro Baths," Chou said, his face grim. "That's a national park, which means that—"

"It means that it's now my jurisdiction," Pravesh said. "I had our local field office contact all the other agencies that would normally look into this and told them that we suspected a terrorist plot going awry. That means it's mine, and I'm bringing in Captain Chou and Detective Meneses to liaise with the local police."

"Richmond District is the closest, and I've already talked to Captain Vanderschmidt over there. He's got the scene secured and has forensic techs already out there. They'll process the scene, then we'll get in there and you can do whatever it is that you do."

"That's all great, but what makes you think this is the same guy?" I asked. "I mean, you might be right, but I'm pretty sure there's more than one murder a week in San Francisco."

"But there aren't two in as many days that are this vicious, and not two back to back that seem to target members of the supernatural community," Pravesh said.

"So you're saying that the victim—" I started, but she silenced me with a word.

"Victims."

"Fuck," I said. "How many?"

"Four. All members of the same coven. They seem to have been performing a sunset ritual. Diners at The Cliff House saw flames and called it in. The responding officer found the bodies and called it into the local park rangers. My division scans all incoming reports of unusual crimes, and they alerted me. As soon as someone said the word 'ritual,' I took over the case. I got a look at the first crime scene photos...it's the same guy."

"One killer, four victims. Captain, I hope you believe in monsters because I'm afraid your eyes are going to be opened."

"Mr. Harker, I live in San Francisco. You can't swing a dead cat without hitting a coven of witches here. It's one of the most supernatural major cities in the country, right behind New Orleans. It's not that I believe in them, I've seen them. Now can we stop talking about what I do or don't believe and go find the son of a bitch?"

5

Chou rode ahead of us in his official car. Pravesh followed in her black Suburban, which made her look tiny in the massive SUV. Lena rode in the passenger seat, her face pale at the thought of visiting another crime scene from the same man who murdered her wife. I took the back seat and slipped in my headphones before I swiped open my phone and called Dennis.

"What's up, boss? I see you're moving, which I guess means you and Agent Pravesh must have come to some understanding. That's good because Gabby seems to think she's pretty tough, if a little green to our world."

"There's been another murder. Looks like the same guy. Somewhere called the Sutro Baths. Get me everything you can on it."

"Will do. That's...pretty fast, isn't it? I mean, if he killed your friend Faye yesterday, this is pretty quick if it's a compulsion."

"Yeah, it is. If it's a compulsion, it could be he's unraveling and heading into the end stages of his nutjob-ness. Or if it's a demon, maybe it just got loose yesterday and is killing as many people as it can before it gets sent back downstairs. The full moon was last week, so this isn't a baby were going nuts, and Luke said there was too much blood left behind for it to be a vampire, even a fledgling."

"That makes sense," Dennis said. "It's probably a demon. Maybe it's hunting the Spear, too."

"What Spear?" I asked.

"Oh shit, that's right," Dennis said. "You got arrested before I could tell you. I think I figured out what you're hunting."

I sat up in the seat. "I'm all ears."

"I'm pretty sure you're looking for Azrael's Implement, which was the tip of his Spear."

"Azrael was the Angel of Death, right?" I tried to dredge up more than that on the Archangel, but I kept getting my theology and my *Batman* comics mixed up. After a while, I gave up and let Dennis explain it to me.

"Yeah, he was basically God's enforcer. Michael was the Sword of Heaven, the righteous avenger who smite down God's enemies. Azrael was…more like an assassin. He took out the people God wanted taken out."

"Why didn't God do His own dirty work? I mean, He's God, right? Couldn't He make people do what He wanted? Or make them not suck? Or whatever He needed to do to keep from feeling like He needed to kill them?"

Dennis stared at me, his big blue horsey eyes looking out at me from the screen. "That's some pretty advanced philosophical shit you're posing to a guy who basically dresses up like a My Little Pony for kicks, Q. In short, I don't know, and I don't give a shit. Leave all that crap to the theologians. What I do know is that Azrael's Implement was the head of his Spear, which has been used throughout history in some pretty famous murders, including one at Calvary."

"Wait, you're saying…"

"I'm saying that the Implement you're looking for is the Spear of Destiny that pierced Christ's side while he hung on the cross."

"Shit."

"Yeah, not only is it powerful as shit, it's got some serious mojo."

"And you think it's in San Francisco?" I asked.

"I kinda do. More and more now that I'm tracking similar murders over the past seventy years."

"Seventy…what the hell are you talking about, Dennis?"

"I'll get back to you on that. I've got some more shit I need to look at."

"You're essentially a super-computer. You process information faster than any ten humans."

"True. That doesn't mean that I make intuitive leaps any faster. My lizard brain might be digitized, but it still works the same way, Harker. It's part of my soul, not part of the internet."

I don't pretend to understand how Dennis works as part of the internet, and part of me likes it better that way. Less guilt. I changed the subject. "Tell me about the Spear and why you think it's here."

"You remember that Hitler was obsessed with the occult, and with magic, right?"

"Yeah. That was one of the things Luke was doing back then, making sure that items of power didn't fall into Nazi hands, or if they did, recovering them."

"Well, he missed one. A big one."

"I remember there were talks about Hitler getting his hands on the Spear, and what a bad thing that would be, but I never heard why."

"Nobody knows why," Dennis said. "The Spear has never done anything particularly impressive to its bearer, but Hitler may have had a ritual in mind for it. Whatever it was, it died when the *Führer* put a bullet in his head because there's no record of him sharing that information with anyone."

"So Hitler had the Spear. How did it get to San Francisco? Why isn't it still in Europe?"

"Well, after Hitler and Eva Braun's joint suicide, Braun's kid sister Gretl survived. Like a lot of Nazis and sympathizers after the war, she fled to South America, where she lived out her days in comfort."

"With the Spear."

"Yup. She died in 2002, and pieces of her estate passed through a bunch of hands until finally the Spear was purchased early this year by a collector of obscure mystical objects."

"In San Francisco."

"Yup," Dennis confirmed. "A Wyatt Earl Hunnicutt, age seventy-one, currently living in Pacific Heights, one of the swankier neighborhoods in the City by the Bay."

"Okay," I said. "I go check out this crime scene, see what I can find out about what's killing magical practitioners in what should be a haven for them, and tomorrow maybe I go see Mr. Hunnicutt and ask to see his new toy."

"Sounds like a plan. In the meantime, I'll do some research and see if there's a pattern to the deaths of practitioners and if there's anything else I can dig up." Dennis's face vanished, and I leaned back in my seat, closing my eyes as I tried to process this new information. Maybe everything was connected. If Lucifer was marshaling his forces here on Earth to keep us from gathering the rest of the Archangels and reuniting them with their Implements, then maybe whoever was killing magic users here was connected to the Spear. Or maybe it was some random psycho, who happened to end up in San Francisco the same time as an angelic Implement.

Yeah, because my life has always been prone to coincidence. No, the two things had to be related. We can assume that whatever murdered Faye was also sent by Lucifer to get its hands on the Spear, which meant a demon, and a strong one. That fit with the level of magic that had been thrown around at the scene of Faye's murder and with something being able to overpower her with so much water at her disposal.

But where was Azrael? There was no chance that he was far from his Implement, but so far we hadn't found any Archangels that knew what they were, except for Raguel, and apparently they were just an asshole who knew exactly what they were, didn't want to go back to work and didn't give a single solitary fuck what happened to the world and all the humans in it.

Sometimes I fucking hate angels. Not Glory, of course, because even though she nags me and kicks my ass, she's also saved my ass more times than I can count, and she did give up her wings to save my life. Glory's cool. But the rest of The Host? Nah, fuck those guys.

"We're here," Pravesh said, rolling down her window. "Homeland Security," she said to a uniform outside. We got out of the SUV at a parking lot looking down over the ruins of what was, at one time, the largest indoor swimming pool in the United States. Nowadays it was a national park and tourist spot, where people wandered around taking pictures of the few rocks still standing and the admittedly impressive view of the Pacific Ocean.

It was a long hike down to the beach, and I felt a little pity for the crime scene techs who had to haul all the battery-powered lights around. This made two remote crime scenes in as many days, a lot for a city police department. There was a uniform standing at the bottom of the trail to head off any onlookers, since there was no way to string crime scene tape across the hundreds of yards of open space.

He held up a hand at us, but Parvesh flashed her badge at the young officer and strode right by, never slowing down. Lena and I followed suit, but Captain Chou stopped to clue the poor guy in on what was going on.

What was going on was a goddamn mess. I've seen some horrible crime scenes, and some even more horrible things that the police never knew about, but this was like something out of my nightmares. The only way I figured out there were four people strewn around the beach was by counting legs, and even then, it took me a couple of times because I got confused and lost count, the limbs were scattered in so many different directions.

The last scene had been cleared by SFPD before we got there, so the only hint I had at the savagery this guy had unleashed was by looking in the magical spectrum and the blood spatter. This was a lot more gruesome, and it was evident by the fact that the sand was turned to rust-colored mud by the carnage exactly how much blood had been shed here.

"Holy…" Pravesh stood stock-still for a few seconds, then spun around, her hand clapped over her mouth. She pushed past me back to the trailhead and dropped to her knees in the grass, sending her stomach contents back to nature.

Lena looked worse, but not nauseous. She looked like she'd been punched in the gut, and I realized that she was replacing every one of these victims with a mental image of her wife. She didn't see the remains of a coven of witches, their white robes shredded and torn to ribbons, she saw the woman she loved with her entrails strung across the sand like Christmas garland.

I put a hand on her shoulder. "Don't," she said.

I moved my hand. She didn't look at me. Didn't look anywhere but at the dead bodies before us. "Don't comfort me. Don't tell me I don't have to be here. Don't tell me I should be at home. I know all that. But I can't. I *have* to do this. I have to find the son of a bitch and bring him in, then I have to watch him go to prison. Then if I'm 'lucky,' someday I'll get to watch a prison doctor put a needle in his arm and watch him die. So whatever comfort you want to offer, save it."

"Okay."

"Okay?"

"You're a grown-ass woman, Detective. You know what you need better than I do. Besides, I suck at comfort. I'm way better at hunting and killing, and this looks like it's got my name written all over it."

"Then get to hunting, Harker. You hunt this motherfucker down, and if it's human, we arrest it. If it's not, we get to kill it."

If we can, I thought. I wasn't going to say it to Lena, but whatever did this was incredibly strong, and judging by what I saw up on the mountain earlier, had an immense amount of magical power. I had every faith that we could find the demon that did this, and after looking at what it did to those witches on the coast, there was no doubt in my mind that it was a demon.

I knew we could find it. I just didn't know what the hell we were going to do with it when we did.

6

<hr>

I looked around the scene. It didn't get any better. There were four people, or rather, the component parts of four people, strewn around the beach like discarded Legos covered in ketchup. Lena stepped up to my side, pale but with her jaw set.

"What do you see?" I asked.

"You're the expert, why are you asking me?"

"I'm a sorcerer, Detective. You're a cop. We look at things a little differently. I want to know what *you* see."

She took a deep breath. "Okay. I see rage. Incredible rage. I don't know what could motivate somebody to do this to other human beings. It was also fast. There were four people killed here, and no matter how peaceable you are, you're not going to stand still and let someone get butchered in front of you."

"How can you tell that's what happened here? How do you know they didn't fight back?"

"They almost certainly did, but not in any effective way. They also didn't make a serious effort to run, which means this guy took them all out before they could react. Look at the footprints." She pointed to the sand, but all I saw was a jumbled mess, and I said as much.

"Come closer." We walked closer, to where the forensics team had

144

managed to put up knee-high stakes with yellow tape strung between them. It looked like a morbid archeological dig site. "Now look at the footprints inside the circle of tape. See the four sets of bare feet?"

I nodded, then looked back to the end of the trail where four pairs of shoes were surrounded by another tape circle. "Those are the victims' shoes." She pointed over to a calf with a foot still attached that lay in the sand about three feet to my left. "They're all barefoot, and those tracks move from the trailhead, where they left their shoes, in a nice, neat line down here, then they branch out and take their places around the circle."

"To the cardinal points," I said.

"Probably," Lena agreed. "I don't have a compass with me, but I know from living with Faye for a decade that a lot of rituals use that as grounding points. Now look at the prints with shoes." She pointed to a single set of footprints. "You can see from the trail that these prints were at a run, judging by the distance. Unless this guy was over ten feet tall."

"None of the monsters I know that are that tall wear shoes, and certainly nothing that small, so let's assume at least humanoid, and running."

Her head snapped around at me, and I could almost see the anger in her eyes as she readied a retort. She relaxed as she saw the absolute sincerity on my face. "You're not fucking with me, are you?"

"I wish I was. I've fought several things that were more than ten feet tall, and they've never worn shoes."

"I'm going to focus on my piece of the world, and you take care of the supernatural shit."

"Don't know how well that's gonna work out for you, but we'll give it a shot." I waved at the tracks. "What else can you tell me about the attacker?"

"It was one guy, unless he had somebody who could step exactly in his footprints, and not only is that impossible at a dead run, it also shows up in the details of the print. This was one person. One really fast, really strong, insanely rage-filled person."

"I think you got most of that right," I said. "Except the 'person' part. No human could do this. Look at the bodies. What do you notice about the limbs?"

"You mean aside from the fact that they've been ripped from the bodies and flung around the beach?"

"No, I mean exactly that. They were *ripped* off. Do you have any idea how much strength that takes? I can't do it, and I'm stronger than any human I've ever met."

"What are you talking about? You're human, just…magic. Like Faye."

"Yeah…not exactly." I explained about Uncle Luke, and who he really is, and his relationship with my parents, and how being the firstborn son of two people who were bitten by a vampire and almost turned did something to my DNA. She didn't take a step back, but she did look a little spooked.

"That's…new information."

"It's not listed on my Facebook page, no."

"You have a Facebook page?"

"Well, no. I mean, I've got an excuse. I'm *really* old. I get a pass on not being up on the latest tech."

"If you think Facebook is the latest tech, you *are* old." She shook her head. "Whatever. I'm a Latina lesbian cop who was married to a witch. I don't get to be all judgy. The killer isn't human. Where does that put us?"

"That puts this right back where we started, with the ball firmly in my court. Can you make sure nobody disturbs me for a couple of minutes? I need to try a few things." I settled down in the sand cross-legged and breathed deeply to center myself. When my mind was relatively clear, I opened up my third eye and peered around the beach, examining my surroundings in the magical spectrum. Like the clearing in the woods earlier, this place was covered in magical trace energy. It looked like a Jackson Pollack painting, only with mystical energy in reds, oranges, and purples splattered all over the place. I focused on the killer's tracks where I could see them, trying to get an energy signature from any residue he may have left.

Once I was able to isolate his trail from the investigators coming down from the parking lot above, I noticed something strange—he never went back up the hill. His tracks led off down the beach, past the Cliff House and disappearing into the water. I stood up and ran down the beach, ignoring the shouts from Meneses and Pravesh as I poured on the speed. I ran parallel to the killer's trail, then clambered over rocks at the base of the cliffs until I saw the trail turn left up the hill to the highway and disappear.

I let my vision slip back into the normal and sat down on the rocks, all the energy of the hunt disappearing in a rush.

"Goddammit, Harker, these were decent shoes," Pravesh called from behind me. "Do you know what saltwater does to leather?"

"Don't give a shit, Agent P.," I shouted back. "I had a trail, so I followed it. You weren't part of that process." I didn't mind using her to get through the local cops, but damned if I wanted her to start thinking we were partners. We weren't partners. I had a partner. She was a continent away, but I could feel her presence through the mental bond we shared. It was faint. But she was still there, sleeping quietly back in Charlotte.

"I'm not climbing that shit," the angry fed yelled to me. "But I've got a lead, so if you're done chasing ghosts, maybe we can go hunt vampires for a little while."

I stood up fast, almost toppling over into the sea. "What did you say?" I bounded down the rocky cliffside and stood in front of Pravesh a few seconds later.

"I said that there were reports in my system of this coven's leader having issues with a local vampire nest. I'm heading over to check it out, and I thought you might want to come with me."

"You might want me there," I said. "Walking into a vampire den this close to sunrise could be viewed as a threat, an attempt to catch them when they're weakened."

"Is that a thing? The whole sleeping during the daytime bit?"

"They sleep, but not like humans. And since they can't go outside, they do usually sleep during daytime hours, but they don't all slip into a coma the second the sun comes up. They can feel it, no matter how far inside they are, but I don't know if that's a magical thing or a subconscious survival instinct."

"What did you see?" she asked as we walked back to where Lena was talking with the crime scene photographer.

"There was a trail. The killer's essence was still faint on the sand and rocks, but I lost him when he climbed the hill. I don't know if he had a car up there or if he ran off, but smart money is on a car or van."

"A panel van, like all good serial killers?" Pravesh said with a smirk.

"Make fun if you like, but something with a closed back so people passing by couldn't see the bloody clothes would be important. Whoever this asshole is, he's *covered* in blood and gore. He'd have to have a vehicle he could wash out, or a change of clothes and some-place to stash his messy stuff."

"I'll have the techs go up there and check the side of the road. Maybe they can pull a tire track." That was a pretty good idea. Maybe this agent wouldn't be a total waste of space after all.

Lena looked up from her conversation when we walked up. "Anything?"

"Nothing solid," I said. I turned to the tech. "You guys should haul ass and see if he left any trace when he was running along the beach. The tide is coming in, and anything still there will be gone in a couple of hours."

The tech, a skinny black guy with close-cropped hair and an earring, gave me a tight smile. "Thanks. We'll jump right on the suggestion from the civilian from a couple thousand miles away. Let me drop everything I'm doing at the actual crime scene to go see how badly you fucked up any evidence that might have ever been over there."

"When you're done with that, check the side of the road past the Cliff House for tire tracks. We think the killer parked up there." She completely ignored the guy's sarcasm, and I decided that even with as tired and grumpy as I was, breaking his nose was a bad idea. The tech gave me another grumpy look and walked off muttering to himself about assholes from back East.

"You look like you've got something," Lena said to Pravesh.

"The coven leader here has had run-ins over the past few months with a local vampire group. We're heading over to have a chat with them. You in?"

Lena's face was pale in the LED lights from the crime scene crew. "Vampires? Do you have a name for the guy they had beef with?"

Pravesh pulled out her phone and tapped the screen. "Yeah, I do. The vampire in question is Doctor Joseph Scolari. According to our records, he's been in California for at least a century, since before the Division existed."

"Oh yeah, Dr. Joe has been here since the gold rush days. He came out right after the Mexican-American War looking to make his mark as the region's first doctor, got turned sometime around the beginning of the rush, and never left."

"Sounds like you know the guy," I observed.

"Oh yeah, I know him. Faye did business with him. Until about a month ago when they had a big falling out. Seems he's been making new vampires, and she didn't like how he was recruiting. He was in the shop a couple weeks ago, and they had a big argument. Scolari said he'd make her regret she ever laid eyes on him. She called up water out of the air and doused him right in the middle of her store, with his top lieutenants watching. Told him to cool off. He was *furious.*"

"Mad enough to kill?" I asked.

"Dude, I don't know," Lena replied. "All the normal rules go out the window when you're trying to read vampires. You can't get shit off them as far as getting flushed, and their nostrils don't have to flare when they don't need to breathe. If he was human, I'd say sure, he was mad as hell. But a vamp? I don't know how long they stay mad about stuff. I'd think grudges would seem petty when you basically live forever, but who knows?"

I did. I knew exactly how long vampires could hold a grudge, having seen Luke's original Renfield try to kill him more than a century after they last saw each other. Vampires don't let shit go, ever. And loss of face is the gravest insult one of the undead can suffer. Dr. Joseph Scolari just went to the top of our suspect list. Admittedly, he was the only one on the list so far, but that's all I had to work with.

"Let's go talk to a vampire about a murder or five," I said. "Maybe we stop for Italian takeout on the way. I could go with some garlic bread."

"That's not real is it?" Lena asked.

"Nah, I'm messing with you. But it's been a while since dinner. I could go for a bite for real."

"After this?" Pravesh gestured toward the crime scene. "Harker, you're disgusting."

"Agent Pravesh, when you've seen the shit I've seen, four dead people aren't nearly enough to put you off your feed."

"Then I sincerely hope I never see all the shit you've seen," she said, turning to head up the trail back to the Suburban.

"Amen, sister," Lena agreed, following her.

I hope neither of you do, either, I thought, knowing deep in my gut that they were going to see a lot worse shit than was on the beach behind me before we got to the end of this case.

7

The deserted pre-dawn streets made the drive from Cliff House to the Pacific Heights neighborhood where Dr. Scolari kept his main home uneventful. I got my Italian takeout, after a fashion. Pravesh decreed that there was no way in hell I was eating chicken marsala in her Suburban, so I had to make do with a footlong meatball sub from a 24-hour Subway. It was mediocre, but filling, and I took solace in wiping my hands on the upholstery. What can I say? I'm petty.

We passed Scolari's address and turned onto a side street. I balled the sub wrapper up and tossed it into the floor, then opened the door.

"You planning to leave that in my car, Harker?" Pravesh said.

"Yep."

"Get your trash," Pravesh ordered.

I turned to her. "Look, lady. I don't want you tagging along with me, but I can't kill you. I've killed a DHS agent before, and it made life very difficult for someone close to me. So, you live. That doesn't mean I can't be a passive-aggressive prick and do everything I can do to make you want to leave of your own volition. If that means leaving garbage in your ride and making it smell like marinara, that's a sacrifice I'm willing to make."

"You're an asshole."

"Not the first time I'm hearing that."

She glared at me for another moment, then turned and fished the wrapper out of the car. She pitched it into a wastebasket on the street and shot me another dirty look. I remained unimpressed. I've gotten dirty looks from *Dracula*. Maybe in a few centuries, Pravesh will be close to Luke's level, but I doubt it. He's got a pretty significant head start.

The three of us walked up the sidewalk to the house, Pravesh and Lena whipping their heads this way and that at the slightest sound. After the third time one of them jumped in half a block, I couldn't hold my laughter inside any longer. "What the hell is wrong with you two? You look like a pair of guilty teenagers sneaking in after curfew."

"In case you missed it, we're trying to get the drop on a nest of vampires, Harker," Pravesh grumbled.

"Oh, you are? Then we should have either waited for six hours until the sentries are asleep, or maybe not driven a vehicle with government plates right past the front door. I guarantee that Scolari's security, if they're worth any fraction of what he's paying them, have already logged your plate, found out who the vehicle was signed out by, researched you and everyone you've ever known, and identified me and Detective Meneses using facial recognition software or some other tech mojo. We've been in the line of a camera ever since we got within two blocks of the house, and it would be naïve to assume the badass head vampire wouldn't have access to all the feeds."

"What would you suggest, since you're the expert?" Pravesh asked in a tone that clearly showed she thought whatever I suggested would be stupid.

"Well, I suppose where vampires are concerned, I am the expert, given my bloodline. So I was going to walk up to the front door and knock." Then I left them standing in the middle of the sidewalk, covered the last twenty yards to the door, and did just that.

The door to the well-appointed house swung open almost immediately, and a woman in jeans and a pressed shirt greeted me. "Mr. Harker, a pleasure to meet you. I am Jacqueline, Dr. Scolari's current

Renfield. Please come in. Will your companions be joining us, or would they prefer to stay outside?"

I couldn't answer her for a second. It took me back a little, her casual use of the term "Renfield" as a vampire's personal assistant. I knew the original Renfield, helped kill him, as a matter of fact, but that wasn't the thing that choked me up a little. No, that was the memory of Uncle Luke's last Renfield, a man named Sylvester Thomas Efor IV, who died a year ago.

He was killed by the half-demon asshole that set all my current problems in motion, a Homeland Security agent named John Smith. That Renfield had been my friend, and Luke and I both swore after his passing that no one else would ever bear the title. I guess the rest of the world either didn't get the memo or didn't care what we thought.

More likely the latter, as the short, brown-haired woman continued to stare up at me with her kind eyes and friendly smile. "I'm not sure," I said. "I think they'll be joining us, but Agent Pravesh is having a rectal issue at the moment."

Jacqueline blanched, then stammered, "A-a rectal problem?"

"Yeah," I said. "Her head is currently lodged too far up her ass for her to find the door." I raised my voice a little and beckoned the others to follow. "Come on up here, you two. I told you they had spotters."

Pravesh and Meneses covered the distance to the door, the federal agent scowling the whole way while Lena tried unsuccessfully to smother a grin. We entered the foyer of the house, and Jacqueline locked the door behind us. The deadbolt gave a solid *thunk* when she locked it, and I knew that nothing was getting through that door without an invitation, or a tank.

"Steel frame?" I asked.

"Reinforced, welded into the floor and ramset into the concrete slab. That door can withstand a bazooka," she replied, stepping past us to lead us into the house.

"What about the wall beside the door?" Lena asked.

Jacqueline froze in mid-stride, then turned slowly to look at the cop. "What?"

"The walls are just drywall and studs, right? The door might stand up to a bazooka, but if the wall isn't made of the same stuff, it's worthless. Any breaching team worth their salt will test the door, but after that they'll blow a hole in the wall."

"You've done that kind of thing before, haven't you?" Jacqueline asked.

"I'm a Marine. We're the first ones through the door. If there's not a door, we make one."

"I think I may have to re-evaluate our security measures." The slightly less confident Renfield motioned for us to precede her through an open door into a well-appointed study. "Please wait here. Dr. Scolari will be with you momentarily. He was having a snack when you drove up."

"He needn't stop on our account," Pravesh said. "We can speak with him in the dining room."

Jacqueline looked at me, and I gave the slightest shake of my head. I turned to Pravesh. "I'm pretty sure that Dr. Scolari's dinner date would prefer to be dined on in privacy."

The agent looked confused for a moment, then a slight blush crept across her dark cheeks. "Oh! I…um…"

"It takes a little getting used to," I said, then nodded at Jacqueline. "We'll wait here." Of course, it didn't take any getting used to for me, but my upbringing was a little unusual, to say the least.

Jacqueline nodded and walked out, closing the door behind her. I, of course, took the opportunity to snoop around the room. The study was laid out with a couple of small sitting areas around coffee tables, and one large armchair with an ottoman in a corner by the fireplace. Guessing that this was the doctor's favorite chair, based on the wear of the arms of the chair and the stack of books on the side table, I walked over for a closer look.

The armchair was a rich brown leather, plush with a spot in the seat worn smooth from years of use. The stack of books ranged from a couple of Jonathan Maberry novels, to a Walter Cronkite biography, to a history book on Japanese tea ceremonies.

"What are you doing, Harker?" Pravesh asked once she had recovered herself a little.

"I'm doing exactly what I was brought here to do. I'm snooping."

"I did not bring you here to snoop. I brought you here to help me question a suspect in a string of murders and to cover my back if he tries anything hinky."

"I know that. You weren't who I was talking about. The doc could have left us cooling our heels in the foyer, or brought us someplace with coffee, but he stuck us in this room. Why? There's something here that he wants us to know about, and I—"

"This," Lena interrupted from the other side of the room. While I'd been explaining my snooping, she had continued with her own scan of the room. Now she stood in front of a wall covered in framed photographs. "He wanted us, me, to see this."

I walked over, Pravesh in tow, to see what she was pointing at. It was a photograph of a tall man with hair slicked straight back from his forehead in a tuxedo, grinning at the camera with a woman on his arm. The woman was in profile, laughing at something the man said, but she was unmistakable. It was Faye Spataro, her dark hair slipping loose from its bun and curling around her ear like it always did after she had a couple drinks.

"They knew each other. Well. I mean, I knew that much. But this picture, it…" Lena's voice trailed off.

"This looks like a couple of good friends having a good time at some formal function," I said. "Nothing more."

Lena looked up at me, a grateful look on her face. "I knew Faye was bi from the moment we met. It wasn't a big deal to me. I knew she'd had boyfriends before we met, and other girlfriends, too. I didn't know…"

"That one of them wasn't completely human?" I kept my voice mild, but it stung a little more than I wanted it to.

"Yeah, I guess. We didn't talk about our exes, either of us. That was something we agreed to early on. But still…"

"I guess it explains why they got in such a big argument about the doc's recruitment methods," I said. "If they were close, then it would have been a bone of contention in the past, too."

I opened my mouth to say something else, but the door opened to admit the same trim man from the picture into the study. Obviously, he hadn't aged a day, since he was dead more than a hundred years before the photo was taken, but it still made for a second of cognitive dissonance, even for me, and I live with Luke.

"In fact, that was the reason Faye left me," Dr. Scolari said, walking over to where we stood. "That very night, as a matter of fact. Ten years ago. That was the San Francisco Opera's annual fundraising gala, and I had Golden Circle tickets. I am a significant patron of the arts, as was Faye. You must be Arlena. I am terribly sorry for your loss." He held out a hand, and Lena took it. "If there is anything I can do to help you in your time of grief, please let me know. I loved Faye, and even as strained as our relationship was, losing her takes much of the light out of my world."

He looked sincere, but that was the tough part about vampires, they didn't give off the little clues that humans do. Their micro-expressions are very different, and like Pravesh said earlier, they don't show the variations in breathing or coloring that normal people do when they lie. But there are ways to tell when a vampire is lying to you, if you know what to look for.

"Dr. Scolari, I'm Quincy Harker," I said, holding out my hand.

"I know you, young man. I know your uncle, as well. A good man, if a little archaic in some of his beliefs."

"Like?"

"His view that we need to remain hidden from the humans. It's silly. We could easily learn to live alongside humans, if we manage the reveal in the right way."

"Sure," I said. "Because humans do such a good job of living along-side themselves."

"That is a valid point," Scolari agreed. "But please, sit. Would you like a drink?"

"No sir," Pravesh said. "We need to talk to you about Faye Spataro's death, and the murder of a group of witches out at the Sutro Baths tonight."

Scolari blanched, and if he could have gone pale, he would have. "The Baths? A coven was murdered tonight?"

"Yes, sir," Pravesh replied. "Do you know something about this?"

But Scolari was already on his feet, heading for the door to the study. "Renfield!" he shouted, and Jacqueline came running.

I caught up to him in the foyer as he was slipping on a jacket. The look on his face was one of pure murder. I grabbed him by the arm and turned him to face me. He resisted, but I'm a lot stronger than I look.

"Let go of me, Mr. Harker. This does not concern you."

"The fuck it doesn't," I growled. "This has something to do with Faye's death, and you have an idea what's going on. That makes it concern the fuck out of me."

"Why? What do you care about a California water witch?"

"Faye was my friend," I said. "I don't have a lot of those, and I take it personally when somebody hurts one. Now tell me what you know."

"Let go of me, or I will have to hurt you." His eyes were inching closer and closer to the full black of a raging vampire, but I held on to him.

"You want to step it down a notch and remember who you're talking to, pal. You might be King Shit of Turd Mountain out here, but I learned to fight by having Dracula himself kick my ass, and I've got magic to back up my haymakers. Now, we can stand here all night measuring our dicks, or you can tell me what you think is going on, and why you suddenly went from grieving friend to avenging fucking angel." I let enough power leak through to make my eyes glow red, and I felt Scolari try to draw back.

He took a deep breath, then closed his eyes and let it out in a *whoosh*. "You're right. I'm sorry. You and your friends may prove helpful, and Mrs. Meneses certainly has a right to be with me when I confront the bastard responsible for this."

"Responsible for what, Scolari?" I asked. "Loop me in, man. What the fuck do you think is going on?"

"It's a turf war. It's a stupid, petty, magical turf war, and it's gotten out of hand. It was silly and funny when it was vandalism and spell slinging, but now people are getting killed, and I'm the only one who can put a stop to it."

"Well, then lead on, Macduff," Pravesh said, jingling the keys to her SUV. "I'll drive."

We stood there in the foyer for a few seconds as Scolari looked from me, to the federal agent, to Lena, and back around the circle.

After what felt like ten minutes, but was probably more like fifteen seconds, he nodded. "Fine. We can all go together. But in my car. It's got better UV protection, I guarantee it." He opened the front door and hurried down the steps, the three of us in tow. I gave Jacqueline a nod as I pulled the door closed and followed the motley crew out into the gray predawn light.

"And it's lay on, Macduff," Lena said to Pravesh as I caught up to them on the sidewalk. Lovely. I was rushing into a supernatural street fight with the world's most literary Marine.

8

———

We hadn't even made it to the car when a trio of black luxury sedans pulled up in front of Scolari's house, disgorging nearly a dozen very angry, very muscular men and women onto the street and sidewalk in front of the vampire's home.

Scolari whirled around and stalked toward the new arrivals, his body language screaming that a fight was about to break out with every step. Jacqueline put a hand on his shoulder, but he shrugged her off with a growl. She stepped back and pulled out a cell phone, tapping the screen and pressing the phone to her ear.

I muttered, "Goddammit," and went after the vampire. Along the way, I pitched my phone to Lena and said, "Dennis, get me some intel."

I didn't slow down as Lena looked at me in confusion and asked, "Who's Dennis?"

I caught up to Scolari as he squared off with a big black dude with dreadlocks and more muscles than I'd ever seen on a human. He stood easily six and a half feet tall and wore a sleeveless shirt more out of practicality than pride, because I couldn't see how fabric was going to holster those guns without ripping. His upper lip was peeled back in a snarl, and I could tell it was taking everything these two had not to throw down right in the street.

Scolari pulled up before he dove right at the guy and somehow composed himself enough to say, in a voice as smooth as lake water, "Darius, I was on my way to see you. How nice of you to save me the trip. Shall we take this inside? To my gym, perhaps?"

"I would love nothing more, Joseph. My seconds here will accompany me, unless you have an objection, of course?" The veneer of civility was thin, but it was all that was keeping these two from coming to blows. I couldn't put my finger on what type of supernatural being this giant was, but if he wasn't afraid to go toe to toe with an elder vampire, he was either packing some serious juice of his own, or he was brutally stupid.

"Then let us adjourn." Scolari executed a sharp turn to the left and stalked over to his front door, where Jacqueline met him at the top of the three steps and unlocked the door. The behemoth followed him, along with his entourage, leaving a quartet of Jaguars half-parked and double-parked on the street. I looked from Lena to Pravesh, then back, and when I got blank looks from both of them, I followed the party back into Scolari's house. It seemed as though the good doctor's quest for justice was put on hold until he kicked this guy's ass, and since there was definitely something weird going on, I thought I'd better stick around.

I followed Scolari and the new arrivals down the long main hall of the house, then down a curving flight of stairs. *Underground lairs, great. I love underground lairs. They always work out well for me*, I thought as I looked around for something I could use as a weapon. I was underground, outnumbered, and I had two humans to protect from becoming collateral damage in a throw down between an angry vampire and whatever this Darius dude was. My gun was under the seat of my car in the Atlanta airport parking lot, and something told me that Lena and Pravesh would need all the firepower they had before the sun rose.

I needn't have worried about weapons since the steel door at the bottom of the stairs opened up into a gym loaded with weapon racks. There were swords, axes, staves, chains, knives, shields, and all sorts of things for people to beat the shit out of each other with. Now I had an entirely different problem. It was no longer worrisome that I didn't have a weapon, but I was certainly concerned that I was hugely outnumbered and *surrounded* by weapons.

I sped up and stepped between the two men, holding out my hands. "Hold up, kids. I hate to be the voice of reason in a room, but would somebody tell me what the actual fuck is going on here?"

"Get out of the way, little man," the dreadlocked man growled. And when I say growled, I mean he literally growled, low in the back of his throat. *Shit*, I thought. *He's a were. A tiger, from the look of him.*

"Mr. Harker, I would hate for you to come to harm under my roof, but if you do not remove yourself from this conflict, I cannot ensure your safety," Scolari said, the threat heavy in his voice, too.

That was it. I was tired as shit, my arms hurt from hours of tattooing, I hadn't slept in about thirty-six hours, and a good friend was dead. I needed a shower, a nap, a good meal, and a fresh set of clothes. What I didn't need was a pair of macho assclowns flexing on me. I called up power, feeling it rush into my body way more easily than usual thanks to the new ink focusing my personal energy.

Surrounding my hands in disks of pure kinetic energy, I shoved them outward from my body like Samson toppling the pillars, and slammed Scolari and his were-buddy about ten feet backward. I called up even more energy and wrapped myself in a cocoon of magical flame. "Stop!" I bellowed, glaring at each of them in turn. My voice was magically amplified and lowered a full octave by the amount of power I was channeling, so I sounded even more commanding than normal. And let's face it, a full-grown man wrapped in fire was pretty goddamned commanding.

I turned to the minions who rode in with the were-boss and stilled them with a look. "Move, fuckers. I dare you." They didn't take my dare.

Motioning for the guy called Darius to step over beside Scolari, I gave them a stink-eye learned at the feet of the master himself. Nobody throws side-eye like Vlad Tepes, so when I gave the vampire boss and the were-asshole the hairy eyeball, they knew that teacher was *pissed.* "Now do you two want to tell me what this is about, or should I just fucking incinerate everyone in the room and go about hunting down Faye's murderer myself?"

"There is no need to hunt anyone, Mr. Harker," Scolari said. "Darius has been kind enough to deliver himself up to us for his just punishment. Now stop being foolish and let me kill this overgrown housecat."

Darius turned to Scolari, and if looks could kill, the vampire would have died all over again. "This pompous piece of shit murdered my niece, and I'm here to rip his heart out and eat it over her grave. Now turn off your fireworks and get out of here before I show you what power looks like, human." When he turned back to me, his eyes were the yellow of a big cat, and I could see the tips of fangs protruding past his upper lip.

I did drop my flames, but only to walk over and level the were-cat with an uppercut that would have shattered the neck, jaw, and skull of a normal human. I put everything I had into the punch and drew in some power from my surroundings as well. He floated a good six inches off the floor before flying back about four feet and stretching out to his full length on the floor. I walked forward, standing with my feet on either side of his head. "You want to threaten me again, motherfucker? I'm not human, you dipshit. I'm Quincy Motherfucking Harker, and I've gutted more weres than you've scratched fleas. Now you lay there like a good kitty and I won't have to hit you again."

I very much wanted him to lay there like a good kitty because that meant that I could give all the broken bones in my fist time to heal. I wasn't going to let either of them see it, but my hand fucking *hurt*. Pro tip: the jaw is fucking *hard*. Try not to punch it without brass knuckles. Mine were back in Georgia. With my pistol. If this cross-country shit kept up, Luke and I were totally going to look into chartering planes.

I looked back at Scolari, who was covering his mouth with his hand. "Don't you look fucking smug, Doc. I will beat your ass, too. Now what makes you think this asshole killed Faye?"

Darius started to speak, and I whirled around, holding up one finger. "Don't. I asked Scolari a question. He gets to answer it. When I want any shit out of you, I'll squeeze your head." The big were growled but kept otherwise quiet. I hazarded a glance around at his pack. They were all looking at each other, completely confused. If he wasn't a psychotic murderer, I owed Darius some help in rebuilding status with his pack when this was over.

Back to Scolari. "Go ahead."

"His niece was almost certainly in the coven that was murdered tonight. Well, last night, now. The sun just came up." It's a little creepy how vampires *always* know when the sun comes up, no matter how light-tight the room they're in might be. "Darius hated the idea of any of his family practicing magic. He wants them all to live normal lives, to be productive members of society, to *fit in*." The last bit was said with a pretty hefty sneer, and I flashed back to his disapproval of Luke's idea that vampires and other supernatural folk should stay hidden from the humans.

"I would never hurt Tanya," Darius snarled. "You killed her whole coven because Faye was mentoring them, and you were pissed that she went off and got married. You couldn't stand the thought that she was happier without you, you jealous fuck." Darius was up on one knee now, but he showed no desire to dive in and start throwing punches, so I didn't give him any shit for it.

"I was thrilled that Faye found some measure of happiness, you idiot. She could never be happy with me. I will outlive any human that I consort with, and she would never allow me to turn her. We were doomed from the beginning; why shouldn't she find happiness with someone more like her? Someone she could actually walk in the sunlight with?"

"Faye loved the sunrise," Lena said from behind me. I caught a flicker of movement from the corner of my eye and saw Scolari dash away a reddish tear.

"I did not hurt Faye. I did not harm Tanya. *You* are the one who got in a very public screaming match with your niece several months ago when she told you she wanted to join a coven," Scolari said, pointing a finger at Darius.

"Tanya was my family," Darius protested. "She was like my own cub. I would never hurt her. I didn't want her to be a witch, no. But I wouldn't hurt her. And I *liked* Faye. She helped our people. Made poultices for us when we got hurt on hunts and gave us readings when we had big decisions."

I sighed. "Oh, for fuck's sake, can we all sit down now? Obviously neither one of you had a goddamned thing to do with the murders, or you wouldn't be this upset over them. But you had to go after each other to show off who's got the biggest dick, didn't you?" They both looked reasonably ashamed at that.

"Darius," I said. "Can you have a couple of your guys go park their cars in reasonable spaces. And maybe send most of them off to...I don't know, wherever cats go. Have them chase a laser pointer or molest a milkman or something. The rest of us need to talk about this and see if we can actually come up with a clue or a plan, instead of running off half-cocked to bash somebody's head in."

Darius nodded and stood up to walk over to his people. Scolari came over to me. "I'm sorry, Quincy. I lost myself for a moment when I was certain that Darius was responsible. You're right, we need to pool all our resources to find the killer. I will have Jacqueline prepare some breakfast. We can meet in the study and discuss our options."

"Have her bring a bowl of ice, too?" I asked. He didn't say anything, just gave me a quizzical look. "My hand hurts. Were-cats have hard heads."

"Oh, you have no idea," Scolari said with a mild chuckle. "You have no idea."

9

Twenty minutes later, we were seated in Scolari's ornate dining room with plates of food in front of us, and I had my hand soaking in a bowl of ice. Scolari offered a few drops of his blood to speed my healing, but I demurred. I tried not to use that method of boosting my recovery unless it was absolutely critical, and it would have felt a little bit like cheating on Luke. Which was weird in its own way, but my relationship with my "uncle" has never been what any sane person would consider normal.

Jacqueline set us all up with a decent if hastily assembled spread of scrambled eggs and bacon, with orange juice, and milk for the kitties. I didn't make a single crack to Darius about him wanting a saucer, and he didn't sharpen his claws on my face. I felt like that was a fair trade. There was even toast, with a couple of kinds of jam.

"This is a lot of food for a vampire to keep around, Doc," I said around a mouthful of bacon. "You got something you're not telling us? A bevy of humans chained up as blood donors in the basement?"

Scolari looked embarrassed, but after giving me a plaintive look that I completely ignored, he sighed and said, "My breakfast book club meets tomorrow. It is my turn to host, and now Jacqueline will have to go shopping again."

"You have a book club?" Lena asked, a thin smile playing across her lips.

"I am very old, Detective," Scolari replied. "Reading is one of the pleasures that I still have afforded to me. One that doesn't require seducing or assaulting humans, that is."

"What's the book?" Darius asked. Scolari looked over at him, a look of surprise on his face. "What? I read."

"This month's selection is *Lost Boy*, by Christina Henry," Scolari said. "It is a retelling of—"

"Yeah, it's the Peter Pan story," Darius said. "I liked it. Listened to the audiobook a few months ago when I took a trip down the coast. Can I come?"

"Come?"

"To the book club. I've been looking for more people to talk books with. My pack doesn't read a whole lot."

"Color me surprised," Pravesh muttered.

Darius glowered at her, but let it slide. "They're good kits, but way more interested in hiking and music than sitting still reading. I can't blame them. They're all pretty young, and you know how kittens are —all energy, no focus."

Scolari seemed genuinely pleased, and surprised. "You certainly may join us, Darius. I do feel like I should warn you, though. Many of the members are human, and not everyone knows about my true nature. They think I have an odd skin condition that makes me extremely sensitive to ultraviolet light, thus never leaving the house during daylight hours."

"Well, that's technically true," I said.

"Exactly," the vampire agreed. "And if the members of my book club don't know the full details about my condition, well, that's something that doesn't harm anyone."

"Whatever," Darius said, snatching the last scrap of bacon from the plate and shoving it into his mouth. "I just want to talk to some people who like good books, and I really liked *Lost Boy*."

"Be back here tomorrow morning at eight a.m."

"If we're still alive, I'll be here."

That was my cue. The food was gone, and Jacqueline cleared the table while I patched Dennis into Scolari's wall-mounted smart TV. And by "patched him in," I mean I called him and told him to hop onto the screen and make himself look like a grown-up human. I had to clarify that, because even as an adult, Dennis had one of those round faces that kept him getting carded at R-rated movies well into his twenties. Not that he had a problem with that now, what with being a disembodied soul trapped in the internet, but at least he could watch anything he wanted while it floated around in the digital sphere. Look on the bright side, right?

"Dennis, what do you have for me?" I asked.

Dennis actually conjured up an image of a dress shirt and tie to make himself look more official. I was impressed. There weren't even any zombies having sex on the tie, which was a thing that happened once. I never knew there was a zombie Kama Sutra, but apparently there is, and there are neckties.

"I looked into other cities along the west coast that may have had murders with similar MO's in recent months, but the only thing I came up with was a ghoul attack in Portland back in November."

"There is no way this is the first time this guy has killed," Pravesh said. "The level of savagery at the Baths was more than any first-time murderer could manage without extreme provocation, and certainly not without getting caught. This guy has done this before."

"Give the lady extra bacon!" Dennis exclaimed, a grin breaking across his face.

"I keep kosher," Pravesh said. "Harker can have my bacon."

"There's no more bacon," I said. "Eating breakfast with a were-tiger will do that. What do you mean, Dennis? You said there weren't any similar murders."

"No, I said there were no similar murders *on the west coast*. There have been killings of occult practitioners all over the country in an unbroken string dating back almost twenty years. The murders start in New York City, go down the Eastern seaboard all the way to Atlanta, turn across the country and zig-zag up and down from Nash-ville, to Alabama, to St. Louis, to Dallas, to Denver, to Phoenix, then finally through Vegas, LA, then here to San Francisco."

"Why hasn't anyone from the FBI looked into this?" Lena asked. "If you found the pattern, shouldn't they be able to?"

"I have…certain advantages that the FBI doesn't have," Dennis said.

Like a moral compass that just spins in empty space and the ability to hack into any computer network with a thought. I managed to keep my statement to myself, but it was a struggle.

"For example," he explained, "I was looking specifically for the deaths of people with a Talent, or practitioners of one sort or another. The FBI didn't know to look for that. Also, I could go back thirty-five years without a real stretch. For the feds, that would take weeks of research."

"How did you manage that, young man?" Scolari asked, his curiosity obviously piqued.

"I have my resources," Dennis said. "And yeah, before you ask, Harker, I did exclude any mass murders that happened when you were in a city, or any of the other Council members."

"We don't murder people," I said. *Anymore*, I added silently, thinking back to a few dark times in my travels with Luke.

"Right, but the authorities don't know the difference between a bunch of guys playing RPGs, and an evil den of necromancers harnessing the power of a cemetery to enslave all the women of a small Nebraska town."

He had a point. That particular adventure had left a half dozen dead farmers laid out in a field surrounded by calf's blood and a strangled cat. We took the trappings of their half-baked ritual and added a few twenty-sided dice and *Monster Manuals* to the scene. *Viola!* Instant Satanic panic in the heartland, and nobody knows how much panic they very nearly saw.

"Is there a pattern to the killings?" Lena asked. "Anything traceable?"

"At first I didn't think so," Dennis said. "But I worked the murders backward, and I saw it."

He paused, and I gave it to him so we could get on with the show. Dennis was performing for an audience, and if I had to play Vanna to his Pat Sajak, fine. "Saw what?" I asked.

"I saw that the killings in each area stopped when a specific trigger happened."

"Are you going to tell us what that trigger is, or do I have to beg?" I was getting less and less interested in feeding Dennis's performance and more interested in tracking down whoever murdered Faye.

"The Spear." Just before he said the words, it clicked in my head, and I spoke in unison with his digitized image.

"You guessed it. That's why they put your name on the door," Dennis said with a grin. "The Spear of Destiny was in each city before a string of witches, sorcerers, or otherwise Talented people were killed."

"What's the difference?" Darius asked.

I turned to look at the big were-cat. "What?"

"Witches and sorcerers. What's the difference?"

"None," I said. "It's just a preference of terms. We all manipulate energy to do things that humans can't do. Often witches will use objects as their focus, or work with plants and potions, infusing them with magic to do specific things. And usually sorcerers just fling fireballs around."

"Faye always said that sorcerers are more showoffs, and witches get shit done," Lena chimed in with a sad smile.

"She said that for years," Scolari said with a nod.

"And it's pretty much true. The focus of a witch's training is more internal, and they can perform a lot finer workings than most sorcerers. Witches are a scalpel, where sorcerers are more of a shotgun."

"What are you?" The alpha were's tone was mild, but I could hear the meaning under his words. He wanted to know how much splash damage there would be when I went after the murderer.

"I'm the guy you call when it's time to nuke the site from orbit. Let's be clear, guys. I'm not here to keep the peace and make things comfortable in good ol' San Fran. I'm here to find out who killed my friend and fuck them up in new and creative ways, then tear them apart and fuck up the pieces. This information about the Spear, that complicates shit, and that means it's going to get even messier before I leave. I'm sorry for that. I really am. It won't stop me, or even slow me down, but I promise to add it to the list of things I regret when I can't sleep at night. If that helps."

"Something tells me it won't." The alpha cat met my eyes, and in his yellow irises, I saw a man who had fought, and lost, and gotten back up to fight again. Darius knew what the deal was.

"No, it won't. But it will help us win this fight. If whatever is killing mages is tracking the Spear, then it's here to do one of two things, neither of which I can allow."

"What are those things, Mr. Harker?" Scolari asked.

"It's either here to destroy the Spear, or to kill the Spear's rightful owner. Both of those options are unacceptable to me, so there's going to be a fight."

"Who is the Spear's rightful owner?" Darius asked.

Dennis and I shared a look, but just as I drew breath to answer, Pravesh stood up. "I'm sorry, gentlemen. That information is classified. It is a matter of national security, and Mr. Harker faces significant consequences should he reveal the identity of the person we feel is the rightful owner of the Spear."

"Well, since the centurion Longinus has been dead for several millennia, I don't think he will mind Quincy telling us his thoughts on the current owner of the Spear." Scolari's tone was mild, but I could see in the tightening around his eyes that the boss vamp was not accustomed to being told what he could and could not know, particularly in his own dining room.

"I'm sorry, I truly am, but—"

"Azrael." I cut Pravesh off before she started to spin more bureaucratic bullshit about why I shouldn't tell everyone exactly what we were dealing with. I'd seen this kind of "operational compartmentalization" before, and all it ever did was get people killed. "The Spear is actually the Implement of the Archangel Azrael, also known as the Angel of Death. At the end of the War in Heaven, the Archangels ended up on Earth, without their Implements or their memories. Now the Spear is in San Francisco, and whatever demon is chasing it has followed it here. We need to find the Spear, kill the demon, and hunt down Azrael so that I can find God and have a little chat with Him."

Darius looked at me, his eyes wide. "You are either the bravest or craziest white boy I have ever met, and that is a high bar, Mr. Harker. You mean to tell me that there's an angel in San Francisco, and now there's a demon in the city trying to kill it?"

"Yeah, pretty much," I said.

"Fuuuuuck," he said, leaning back in his chair.

"Yeah, pretty much," I repeated.

"You're standing there acting like this shit is normal."

"I wish it weren't, if that helps."

"It doesn't."

"Didn't figure it would."

The big were-tiger let out another long breath. "Okay. We gonna hunt down a magical Spear and kill a demon so we can save the Angel of Death. Got it. I've got one question before we start on Pee-Wee's Big Adventure."

"Shoot," I said.

"Can we go back to when I just wanted to strangle the vampire? That shit sounds way easier."

10

"Okay, the first thing is to find the Spear," I said. "Dennis, you said you had a line on its location?"

"Oh yeah," he said. "The Spear is owned by a gentleman named Wyatt Earl Hunnicutt, a third-generation millionaire who seems…eccentric, to use a less insulting term."

"Or batshit crazy, to be honest," Darius snarled, his lip curling to show a canine that seemed to have more of a point to it than it did a few minutes ago.

"Care to enlighten the out-of-towners?" I asked.

"Sure," the big cat said, leaning forward and placing his elbows on the table. "Wyatt thinks he's the reincarnation of Wyatt Earp, right down to buying the old lawman's Colt for a quarter of a million bucks. He walks around in a cowboy getup, with a big ten-gallon hat on his five-quart head, that big old Peacemaker on his hip, and says shit like 'pardner.' It's like talking to a parody of a John Wayne movie, only in a five-foot tall body."

"Little man with a big pistol?" I asked.

"Oh yeah, with all the scrappy attitude that comes from being a short dude with a buttload of money in a tall man's world."

"What does this have to do with the Spear?" Pravesh chimed in.

"He sounds charming, but not all that out of line for San Francisco. Your fine city did have the United States' only emperor, after all."

"If only Norton would stay in the past tense, we would have far fewer problems," Scolari muttered. I raised an eyebrow at him, but he waved me off, and I didn't have time to ask about his time-traveling Emperor Norton. That sounded like a story better left for another time.

"Yeah, but at least Norton wasn't an asshole," Darius said. "Hunnicutt throws money around like it's confetti and expects any supernatural in the area to do whatever he wants. He's got mediums on staff to let him talk to Wyatt Earp's ghost whenever he feels like it, a wizard that he keeps in the house to glamour him to look taller, and a curator for his personal museum. That's probably why he wanted the Spear— to put it on display in his house and have it for the party tonight."

"Oh shit, that is tonight, isn't it?" Scolari's eyes went wide. "I need to make sure my tuxedo is back from the cleaners."

"It is," Jacqueline said. "I had to order a new shirt, though. You were messy and got blood on the collar. That stuff never comes out."

"Would you like to explain to the folks who don't run in your social circles exactly what the hell you're talking about?" I asked, raising my voice to get over the vampire and the were-tiger complaining about some soirée.

Scolari and Darius both swung their heads to look at me, then Scolari chuckled and shook his head. "I'm sorry," he said. "Hunnicutt throws a big party on the fall equinox every year, kind of his beginning of the Halloween season bash. It's a smaller affair than his Halloween party or his solstice celebrations, but it does get most of the city's powerful practitioners and high-ranking supernatural beings in attendance."

"Tonight is the equinox?" I asked. "I thought it was in about a week."

"It's next Tuesday," Lena said. "Faye had the shop scheduled to be closed."

"Yes," Scolari said with a nod. "But today is Saturday, and Hunnicutt is far more interested in having a big party and getting people to look at his newest toys than he is with actually observing a holiday."

"That tells me that most of the city's Talented will be in his house tonight," I said.

"Yep," Darius said.

"And the Spear is there."

"Also yep," Dennis chimed in.

"Does the fact that this party looks like a beacon in the dark to exactly the demon we're chasing occur to anyone else?"

"Oh yeah," Pravesh said. "I'd better get in touch with our local field office. We're going to need a bigger boat." She got up and walked to a corner of the room, her phone already out.

"Dennis, does the Council have anyone close enough to get here?" I asked, already knowing the answer.

"Not in the time we have," he said. "It's already eleven on the east coast, and one by the time I can get anyone scrambled to an airport, if we're being realistic. Even if I could charter something that can make it nonstop, by the time they get here and get to us, it'll be too late."

I did some quick mental math and nodded. "Yeah, if this mess is going to happen at sundown, then we're going at it solo. Not to mention Luke can't move around in the daytime."

"And Adam can't fly commercial." He was right. The metal detectors in airports had issues with certain of Adam's components, and if he went through one of the full-body scanners…well, let's just say it was a good thing it looked like I was back in the good graces of Homeland Security, at least for the moment. That left us with the human members of the Shadow Council, and while they were great in a gunfight, I had the sneaking suspicion this demon might be a little more than they could tackle.

"Okay, then let's get our shit together and reconvene here at four to go crash a party. I guess I have to go rent a tux," I said, standing up and walking toward the door. Nobody else moved. I stared at them all. "What are you waiting for?"

"That's it?" Darius asked. "Just…go get your affairs in order because we have to take on a demon who wants to steal the Spear of Destiny? That's all you've got to say?"

"What do you want, the fucking St. Crispin's Day speech? Fine, fine." I hopped up on the table and surveyed them all. "We few, we merry few, we band of brothers. We are truly fucked. We are probably all going to die, and if we don't, we'll see some shit that we can't ever un-see and will wake us up gasping and sweating until finally we don't wake up anymore. We're rushing headlong into a confrontation with a demon that I don't know a goddamn thing about except that yesterday it murdered one of the most powerful witches I've ever met, and that scares the fuck outta me. So we're going in without a plan, without enough backup, and without nearly enough mojo, but we're going in anyway because this son of a bitch killed our friends, and I cannot, *will not*, let that shit stand. Now go get your pack, and get your ammo, and meet me back here at four o'clock to go demon hunting."

I jumped down off the table, and this time when I headed for the door, I heard the scrape of every chair pushing back from the table as they all followed me. Not for the first time in my life, I wished they wouldn't.

W hen the going gets tough, the tough go shopping. And shop we did. With time of the essence, we had to go for the places that could hem a tux and make any alterations in a matter of hours, and that didn't come cheap. After a little whining about explaining things to her boss, Pravesh broke out the DHS company card. Two hours later, she was rocking a black Diane von Furstenberg pant suit, while Lena and I both sported Dolce & Gabbana tuxedos. We didn't have enough time to get either of them tailored enough to hide a shoulder holster, so I had Lena's backup .380 in an ankle holster while she could stash her service Sig at the back of her waist. I didn't ask Pravesh where her sidearm would go, but looking at the lines of her suit, I assumed it was in the small shoulder bag she carried.

After picking out our respective ensembles, we changed back into our street clothes and made a stop by the magic store Faye had run. The door was shrouded in black fabric, and the place was obviously closed in mourning, but Lena gave me the key. I didn't say a word when she stayed behind in Pravesh's SUV, but there were some things I needed to pick up. I grabbed a small bag of sea salt, some holy water, a silver *athame* in case I needed a little of my blood for a working, and a couple of other herbs and spices that might come in handy.

I sat down on a stool behind the counter and opened up my Sight. The shop, a warm, homey kind of place with a vaguely hippie vibe in the daylight, blossomed into a rainbow of colors in my Othersight. Every surface swirled with color, trace energy from the good people that Faye served. And they must have been good people, too, because there was hardly any black or red energy mixed in with the blues, yellows, oranges, and greens of the trace the customers left behind.

I could see Faye's essence, too, which was the whole point, and why I was happy that Pravesh and Lena let me have a moment in here alone. Her silvery lavender streaks were everywhere around me, and it felt like having my friend back, just for a moment. I remembered the fun Faye and I had working together on a couple of cases in San Francisco, like when we laid a revenant to rest at Alcatraz so the tourist boats could resume unmolested. Or the time a junkie was possessed in the Tenderloin, and we got stuck in a strip club trying to cast an exorcism while strung-out bottle blondes kept offering lap dances to both of us, but mostly to Faye.

I dropped my Sight, surprised to see my vision foggy, but when I felt my face, I realized that I was crying. "I'm sorry, Faye," I whispered to the empty room. "This is on me. I've been trying to do too much, deal with too much shit at home, and I didn't start looking for this goddamn Spear soon enough. Now you're gone, and there's a fucking demon murdering Talents in San Francisco, and I don't know if I can stop it. It took you out and slaughtered a whole coven in the middle of a circle. That's some serious power, and I don't know if I've got the mojo to pull this off. And if I don't? Well, then I don't have to worry about it because I'll be dead, but Glory is stuck as a human, and Dennis is already stuck in some kind of awful *Tron* remake, and Lucifer takes over the world.

"I don't know if I can do it, kiddo. I just don't know. I try to keep my shit together while the rest of the crew can see me, but this might be too much. I mean, it's fucking *Lucifer*, Faye. The goddamn devil himself. And I'm supposed to take him out? Me, an aberration from London, with the help of my two-hundred-year-old golem and the king of the goddamn vampires. If we aren't the sorriest excuse for a bunch of heroes the world has ever seen, I don't know what is. Fuck. I don't even know why I'm doing this. Sitting in your store, laying this all out on the universe when I know you're not even here." I sat there with my eyes closed for a while, trying to soak in some of Faye's leftover positive energy, hoping it would somehow give me the backbone to get up off that stool and charge into another unwinnable fight. Again.

I heard someone clear their throat behind me, and I spun around. Pravesh stood in the doorway that led back into the storeroom, looking more than a little embarrassed. "Sorry to intrude. I came in through the back, so the door didn't chime. We had to move the car into the alley to keep from attracting too much attention, and I wanted to let you know where we were."

I looked at her, this woman I'd never met before the previous morning, as I stood there with tears coating my cheeks and my eyes redder than a drunkard on Monday morning.

"I'm sorry to intrude—"

"You said that."

"I know."

"Say what you want to say." I heard how my voice sounded. Curt, clipped, frankly rude. But I didn't care. She caught me off guard, something not many people get to do.

"I just wanted to say I get it." There was more following that, I could see it hanging in her eyes, but she stopped herself.

"You get what?"

"The doubt. The fear. The guilt. I get it. You're wrong, though. We can do this. Lucifer is powerful, but so are we."

"Because our cause is just and our heart is pure?" I could hear the bitterness in my words, but I couldn't keep it out. She'd caught me in a moment of weakness, and that gifted her with the dubious pleasure of seeing a piece of Harker that only Luke and Becks had seen in a long, long time.

"No." She shook her head with a smile. "Because we are His chosen children. That's why The Host hates humanity, you know. They're jealous. They want to be more like us."

"Frail, fragile, mortal?"

"Free." I didn't respond, so she went on. "We have free will, Harker. That's is His greatest gift to us, and our greatest burden. But it gives us *everything*. It makes us unpredictable, and a little crazy, and more powerful than even Lucifer himself. So yes, we can do this. We *will* do this. Now let's go. We've got a party to crash."

Pravesh turned to go back into the storeroom and out through the back door, but as she spun, a hip caught the corner of the counter, and a medallion fell off a rack by the cash register. I picked it up and looked at it. A little silver medallion, like you see everywhere, except it felt a little out of place to have a rack of saints' medallions in a magic shop.

"Whose is it?" Pravesh asked, looking to my hand.

It was a silver medallion depicting a man with a club or staff in one hand and a corona of light around his head. I chuckled, and moved to put it back on the rack, then paused. "It's St. Jude."

"The patron saint of lost causes."

"I thought you said you were Jewish?"

"I'm Jewish, I'm not uneducated. You should keep it. Maybe someone here wants you to have it." This time when she turned to leave, she made it through the doorway without incident.

I looked around the shop, wiped my eyes and cheeks, and nodded. "Okay, kiddo. I can take a hint." I put the necklace around my neck and went off to chase my lost cause.

11

And crash we did, in spectacular fashion. Admittedly, the party was pretty spectacular even before we got there, with magicians throwing around illusions like sparklers at a kid's birthday party. The house was more of an estate, with a long circular driveway pulling up in front of a huge three-story main house. Magic flowed down the marble steps on the front of the house like a waterfall in jewel tones, pooling around our ankles as we made our way to the front doors, glamoured to look like the front doors of Hogwarts. The grand foyer was exactly that, grand. Chandeliers floated around the room, from barely above head height to twenty feet in the air, casting flickering shadows in brilliant color into every corner.

"This guy isn't into subtle, is he?" I said, looking around. The entire place was a mishmash of fantasy novels, science fiction movies, and magical tomes brought to life. A faun straight out of a Narnia book carried a tray of drinks, and I took a flute of glowing blue champagne with a nod. At least it tasted like champagne. Good stuff, too.

"Subtle is not a word that has ever been associated with Wyatt," Scolari said, the disdain dripping off his words like venom. He had that look of moral and intellectual superiority on his face that old money always trots out whenever they deal with someone they think is beneath them somehow. It wasn't a good look, but I expected it to come out at some point.

"Yeah, well, we can't all be old-money vampires," I said, fully aware that I was at least tangentially related to the oldest-money vampire in the world. Scolari shot me a look but didn't say anything more. I needed him, but I didn't have to like him. He was snotty, and condescending, and I wanted to punch him, just a little. Well, I really wanted to punch him, but I didn't want to punch him too much.

We walked farther into the house, me, Lena, and Pravesh with our heads on a swivel trying to catch all the razzle-dazzle flying around. As we stepped through into the great hall, which was bigger than some ballrooms I've been in, I was rendered speechless by the enormity of the illusion in front of me. The entire roof of the room, which was bigger than a basketball court, had been enchanted to appear like the night sky. But not the night sky as it actually appears over San Francisco, which would have been a large but relatively simple working. No, this was a mystical tapestry of shooting stars, constellations whizzing by, aurora borealis ringing the horizons, and a few very familiar spacecraft making a lazy trek across the sky.

"Is that the *Millennium Falcon*?" I asked, pointing up. I couldn't help staring and pointing. I felt like a kid on his first trip to Disneyland. Or at least what I felt like a kid would feel like at Disneyland. I was nearly ninety the first time I visited the house that Mickey built.

"Hunnicutt is a huge *Star Wars* fan. Don't get him going about Jar-Jar Binks," Darius warned. "You'll think George Lucas invented a time machine just so he could go back and shit all over little Wyatt's seven-year-old head."

Down on the ground, the illusions were at least as amazing, if not as grand in scope. All the catering staff were glamoured to look like mystical creatures, from unicorns and fauns, to an ogre that was realistic enough to have me reaching for my gun, to a very disturbing little man in a red flat cap walking around with a tray of canapés and a chilling smile. I passed on the taking a baby quiche from the murderous redcap and kept my fingers close to the grip of my gun.

The action in the room centered around a huge sculpture seemingly made of spun gold, platinum, and harnessed light. It was a huge tree, reaching from deep within the floor all the way up to the vaulted ceiling, with branches spindling up and out some dozen yards in all directions.

"That's—" Scolari began, but Pravesh cut him off.

"*Yggdrasil*," she said, a tone of pure wonder in her voice. "The world tree of Norse myth. I've never seen a more beautiful representation of it. It's truly astonishing, and beautiful."

"You know your Norse," I said, seeing another layer of the Homeland Security agent. If she wasn't careful, I was going to stop hating her on principle and actually think of her as a human being. Dangerous thing to do with a government agent.

"I spent some time in Norse Studies at UW," she said, not taking her eyes off the sculpture. "This is remarkable. I can almost feel the other realms pressing against the barriers here, as if the tree is an actual conduit between dimensions."

I opened my Sight, and what I saw was, in addition to being almost overwhelming in the sheer amount of magical energy around me, was a little terrifying. Pravesh was pretty much spot on. The tree, or image of a tree, was actually woven into the barrier between dimensions, and everything was a little closer to our world here. It wasn't exactly *Yggdrasil*, but it wasn't exactly not, either. It was some kind of manifestation of the world tree bound to this spot by a fuckton of magic. I could feel the distant touch of the Divine, and sense the malevolent attention of Hell, among other dimensions. There was enough extra-dimensional magic seeping through along the seams to feed the magic of the tree, and keep it firmly anchored in our world. But if anything ever happened to that tree, we were going to have big problems. Like, world-ending, dimension-shattering problems.

I dropped my Sight and looked at Scolari and Darius. "Does this Hunnicutt guy know what he's doing? Because there is a flaming fuckton of energy harnessed in that tree, and if it ever went down..."

"Then the entirety of San Francisco would be nothing but a much larger bay?" Scolari said.

"Yeah, he knows. All of us know," Darius agreed. "It's part of our job. To protect Yggdrasil, and to make sure that it's fed with enough magical energy from this side to keep the boundary intact."

A lightbulb went off for me. "That's why he throws the parties. He uses a shitload of magic on the quarter-year holidays, and when the party's over, he funnels it into the tree to reinforce it. Like mystical fertilizer."

Darius nodded. "Yeah, Hunnicutt definitely throws around plenty of manure, but once a quarter, his parties keep the World Tree growing strong."

Scolari sniffed, his sneer growing every second we talked about Hunnicutt.

"What's your problem with this guy, Doc?" Lena asked. "It sounds like he's one of the good guys."

The old vampire looked slightly abashed, but after a few seconds, he finally said, "It's so...*gauche*. I can't bring myself to approve. In my time, we fed the Tree as well, but our ceremonies were much more restrained, much more—"

"Boring," said the short man in a bespoke tuxedo and a giant cowboy hat from behind Scolari. "Your ceremonies were boring, Joseph, and when I took over as the Tree's Guardian, I decided to liven things up a little. Now we feed Yggdrasil every few months, and everyone gets together and has a good time. It's what I call a win-win. Now, please introduce me to your friends." He turned to us and bent down into a florid bow, sweeping the hat off his head with a smooth motion and exposing the yellow smiley face painted in the huge bald spot atop his round dome.

I couldn't help it, I kinda liked the little guy. I started to hope I didn't have to punch him too many times to get him to hand over the Implement.

"Keya Pravesh, Department of Homeland Security Paranormal Division," Pravesh said, stepping forward and holding out her hand.

"Whoa, little lady!" Hunnicutt stepped back, holding up both his hands with a big grin. "Ah didn't know we was gonna have no gubmint types at this here shindig!"

"Hunnicutt, your family has been in California since Scolari last had a suntan. You can drop the accent," Lena said.

The little man's big grin fell away, and he stepped over to her, holding out his arms. She nodded, and he hugged her tight for a moment. "I'm real sorry to hear about Faye. I thought a lot of her, and she was a hell of a power. She will certainly be missed. Now who's this tall drink of water with you?" He turned to me and cast an appraising eye. "He smells like power and trouble in equal parts."

"Nah," I said, holding out a hand to shake. "I'm more like two parts trouble to one part power. Quincy Harker. I hunt bad things."

He put his hat back on and shook my hand, grip firm but not over-bearing. "I've heard of you, Reaper. There's a lot of folks here who won't like you just for who you are. Or who your uncle is. I don't want no trouble at my party, you understand me?"

"I don't want any trouble, either," I said, thinking at the same time, *Trouble seems to find me whether I want it or not.* "But we need to talk to you. Preferably somewhere private."

Hunnicutt looked around the room and laughed. "Son, if you're looking for private, we'll have to relocate this party to my mountain house! There's people everywhere, all over the estate. The only place I can go to get some peace and quiet between now and sunrise is my panic room, and not only am I not interested in showing all y'all where it is, it ain't big enough to hold more than two or three folks. So, anything you need to talk to me about, it's gonna have to be right out here in the open, not in the shadows where you usually operate."

The weight he put on the word "shadows" told me that he had some dealings with the Council in his history, and it didn't sound like they were good ones. But whatever, that wasn't my problem tonight. Tonight, I needed him to give me the Spear before the demon arrived and turned his party into an all-you-can-eat magical murder buffet.

"You recently came into possession of an extremely powerful magical artifact," I began.

"The Spear of Longinus," he said with a nod. "I've been hunting that thing for most of my life, all over the world. When that old biddy down in the jungle died, I thought I could get it then, but I had to chase it down the last fifteen years or so through a bunch of other collectors until I could finally get my hands on it. It was worth the hunt, though. It's one of the greatest artifacts I've ever laid my eyes on, much less my hands."

"Yeah, about that…I need that Spear." I said.

He looked at me and laughed, almost losing his Stetson in the process. "Boy, you *have* studied at the feet of that old vampire, haven't you? Well, son, let me tell it to you like I told Vlad the last time we got in a bidding war over an artifact. I wanted it, and now I got it, and if you don't like it, you can kiss my ass."

I took a deep breath and silently counted to ten. I wanted to break his nose, but I've been working on my anger management issues, so I tried to explain things to him instead. "That Spear is more than the weapon that pierced Christ's side as he hung on the cross. It's—"

"One of the seven Implements. I know. It's not just holy, it's *God-touched*. It belonged to the Archangel Azrael, the literal Angel of Death, until he lost it in the War on Heaven."

I managed to hide my surprise. For all he looked like a dilettante, Hunnicutt knew his magical artifacts. I didn't sense any Talent around him, but he could have masked it somehow, I supposed. It didn't matter. Talented or not, he was going to give me that Spear. "I hate to be the heavy, Mr. Hunnicutt, but I need that Implement. I need all the Implements. The Archangels can't remember who they are unless they're in contact with them, and I need the Archangels to be their old angelic selves for one more big scrap. After that, you can take it up with Azrael. Maybe he'll let you have it back."

The smile was gone from Hunnicutt's face, and now I didn't see the genial party host, I saw the shrewd businessman and ruthless negotiator. "Mr. Harker, let me be perfectly clear. I don't give a good goddamn what you want *my* Spear for, you can't have it. I bought it, fair and square, and now it's mine. If you want it, you can wait around until I die, then you can talk to my son, Billy, about what he wants to do with it. I expect he'll sell it to you for not much more than I paid for it because he doesn't like magic. But I do, and as long as I am drawing breath, the Spear of Destiny is going to stay right here, warded by the strongest circle California's top mages can create, and guarded by two ogres, a wyvern, and a half-dozen armed human guards."

He pointed over to a case on a dais, where the Spear rested on a pair of Plexiglas arms allowing it to be observed from all angles. It didn't look like much, just a bronze spear tip on a bronze haft covered with a patina of age. But when I looked at it with my Sight, it almost blinded me. This was definitely an Implement.

"That's it, all right," I said. "That's the Spear of Destiny."

"Yep," Hunnicutt agreed. "And if you want it, you're gonna have to pry it out of my cold, dead fingers."

It was all I could do not to oblige the little man, but just as I opened my mouth to reply, the doors exploded inward, splinters followed by the corpses of the four security guys we'd seen on the front steps. I threw up a quick shield to keep us from getting pelted with debris and turned to see what the hell was going on.

Standing in the doorway, looking like ten thousand miles of bad road, was a man. Or at least, something wearing the skin of a man. He was tall, built like a powerlifter, and looked like he'd been living out of a dumpster for about a hundred years. I called up my Sight, and when the glow coming off him seared my mystical retinas, I knew we were well and truly fucked.

There was no question that this was the guy who'd torn through Faye's defenses and slaughtered the coven on the beach. There was also no question that he had enough power to level everyone at the party without breaking a sweat. The question was, now that I'd found the obviously psychotic Archangel Azrael, what the fuck was I supposed to do with him?

I stepped in front of Lena to keep her from charging in after the angel. "Change of plans. Lena, get yourself and all the human waiters and servers the fuck out of here. Scolari, get ready for a fight. Darius, time to let the dogs out."

The big Alpha gave me a dirty look. "Seriously, man? Now? And we're not dogs!"

"I know, but I might not get another chance to make jokes, and I really wanted to work that in somehow tonight."

"What about me?" Pravesh asked, stepping up beside me with her gun in hand.

"Can you call in an airstrike? Drones? Tanks? Small nuclear weapons?"

"Ummm, no."

"Then go with Lena and get the hell out of here. Don't forget Hunnicutt. He's a bit of an ass, but he doesn't deserve to get ripped to pieces for it."

"You're way too slow for Hunnicutt," she said. "He vanished before the splinters from the door stopped falling."

"Smart. He could no more stop an angel than an earthquake. Did he happen to take the Spear with him?" I wasn't taking my eyes off

Azrael, who whipped his head around like a predator with a scent. The angel wore a long coat, tattered jeans, no shoes, and no shirt. I could see bloodstains on the coat and his pants. How in the hell had this guy been wandering around San Francisco looking like a mass murderer for days?

"No." Pravesh's words broke me out of my reverie. "It's still in the case."

"Okay, then. That's the plan. We defend the Implement. I don't know how much power this asshole has right now, but it's going to be multiplied by a shitload if he gets his hands on that Spear, and there is no guarantee that it will snap him out of this rage. Scolari, will these folks listen to you?"

"To a degree."

"Then get them organized and let's throw everything we've got at this motherfucker." I shrugged out of my tux jacket and rolled up my sleeves as I walked toward the angel. I snatched up a discarded serving tray and wove magic around it, turning it into a glowing purple replica of Captain America's shield, but with a lot more magic repellant. With my other hand, I drew my pistol and aimed it at the angel.

"Hey asshole!" I shouted, squeezing off two shots that whizzed by Azrael's head. "I don't think you were on the guest list."

The angel focused on me, his eyes blazing with golden light. In a blur of motion, he was across the fifty feet of floor that separated us and in front of me. I barely got my shield up in time to block his first punch, and I felt the shock reverberate up my arm all the way to my teeth. My defenses flared to life, and his kinetic energy was amplified and returned to him by the energy repelling spell I'd spun on the shield, hitting him with three times the force that he used.

It didn't even faze him. His eyes widened ever so slightly, then he raised both hands overhead and clasped them together, preparing to bring them down in a crushing blow. I knew that even through my shield, that shot would shatter my arm, so I decided I wouldn't be there when it landed.

I darted around behind the angel, pressed my gun to the back of his head, and squeezed the trigger three times. I would have done more, but since I couldn't penetrate his skull, the bullets and gases had nowhere to go, and the gun blew to pieces in my hand. I snatched back my bleeding fingers, noticing that I was now missing the tip of my pinky finger, and swore loudly. Parts of my shirt caught fire from the gunpowder, and I patted them out, diverting my attention for a crucial second.

I swore again, much less loudly, when the angel swept his arm around and clubbed me in the gut. The only thing saving me from broken ribs was my shield, which managed to angle his blow to the side. I still fell flat on my back, skidding a good ten feet and ripping the back of my shirt to shreds. I scrambled to my feet and readied myself to take the angel's next charge. He raised a fist and moved toward me, but a huge black blur slammed into him from the side.

The panther was big. Like seriously big. It was taller than my waist at the shoulder, and when it crashed into Azrael, the psycho angel went flying. They rolled across the marble floor all elbows and fur, then slid apart and got to their feet. I let the magic around my shield dissipate, and it dropped to the floor with a clatter, once again just a serving tray. Raising my hands above my head, I summoned up a flood of raw energy from the room. The entertainers had been flinging magic around the party for a couple hours already, so there was plenty of extra mojo to grab hold of, and I sucked it in.

The hair on my arms stood up as I channeled energy, then released it in a crimson ball of eldritch fire straight for Azrael's chest. I guess I felt a little encouraged by the fact that he didn't laugh, but just a very little. His coat burned off, and he staggered back another couple of feet, but otherwise the dirty Archangel was completely unharmed by a blast of power that would have sent most demons home to Lucifer in a pizza box.

"Shit," I said.

"No kidding." I turned to my right and saw Lena standing there, her Sig in hand.

"What the fuck are you doing here?" I asked. "I told you to get to cover."

"Last time I checked, I didn't take orders from skinny-ass east coast white boys. That motherfucker killed my wife, and I'm going to kill him or die trying." She raised her pistol and fired three times, all striking the angel right in the middle of his approaching torso. None of them broke the skin or slowed his steady walk across the remains of the scattered door even the slightest.

By this point, the great hall was total chaos. Darius was in his half-tiger form, a towering seven-foot beast clad in orange fur and bad attitude. I watched as the rest of his crew converged on him, some on four legs, some on two, but all of them exuding menace. They came at the angel from behind as Lena and I backed away, her shooting him in the chest every few steps and me calling up bolts of power and throwing them as fast as I could. Nothing slowed the monster down, and nothing seemed to draw his attention until Darius stepped in front of him and laid down a huge punch that shook the entire room.

The angel staggered, and the weres swarmed. Darius slammed another punch into the side of Azrael's head, knocking him back another couple of steps. Pack members in big cat form darted in to rip and bite at the angel's hamstrings, but their teeth found no purchase. Still, they harried the demented bastard enough for me to catch a little bit of a breather. My shoulder throbbed, my gun was a mess of twisted metal and plastic, and my finger hurt like a son of a bitch.

Lena and I took refuge behind an overturned buffet table. I looked over at her. "You've got to get out of here."

"Kiss my ass."

"Seriously, Lena, get the fuck out of here. You can't do anything against him."

"Neither can you, but I don't see you going anywhere."

"It's my job."

She held up the badge that now hung around her neck, the gold shield a stark contrast to the eveningwear she wore. "Mine too. Now how are we going to stop that thing?"

"I have no fucking idea."

"Then it's a good thing we have backup, isn't it?" Scolari's voice surprised me a little, but when I looked up, he'd brought the whole goddamned cavalry. Spread out behind the dapper vampire were supernaturals of all shapes and sizes. Vampires, witches, ogres, creatures of the Fae—you name it. If it was a Talent with enough juice to be at Hunnicutt's now-ruined party, they were standing in front of me, a phalanx of freaks the likes I'd never seen. And I've gone drinking with Frankenstein's monster.

A loud yelp from behind me told me that we'd better get our shit together, and fast. I stood up and looked over the assembled troops. "Okay. Scolari, you and the vampires are going in close. Hit like cavalry—in and out fast. Don't stay too long within reach because if he gets his hands on you..."

As if to punctuate the idea, another yelp sounded, and a mountain lion's head flew across the room to splatter against the far wall. "Yeah, that happens."

Scolari nodded, then he and the vampires were off, headed into the fray like streaks of very well-dressed death. I looked at the others, a mix of humans and Fae. "Who here is a wizard, witch, warlock, or other kind of spellslinger?"

About a dozen hands went up. "Okay. I need four of you to work together to make sure the building doesn't fall down on us. Until I tell it to."

"You're going to destroy the house?" a slight woman with long blond hair asked.

"If it stops the pissed-off Archangel, yes. Now the rest of you, take up positions around the room and hit that motherfucker with everything you've got."

I looked at the others. "Faeries—sprinkle faerie dust on him, or fuck with him somehow." I had a chilling thought. "Can Fae magic touch divine beings?"

They looked from one to another, apparently not knowing the answer. I couldn't blame them. After all, how many Archangels is a person going to run into in their life? A person who isn't me, that is.

The redcap I'd seen serving canapés earlier cleared his throat. "I don't think so. Our magic can only touch someone from Faerie or one of the lands that touches ours. Those planes are far from ours, and since I know our magic doesn't work on demons, I doubt it will do anything against that thing."

I hazarded a glance back over my shoulder at the thing in questions. The cats and vampires were holding it in place, but they weren't doing any harm to Azrael. Every few seconds, he would throw a punch or a kick and someone would go flying, but he'd stopped coming at me and was kinda looking around the room, like he was looking for something. Then the mission, the part of it that was bigger than just "don't die" slammed back into my head.

"Shit. I forgot about the Spear. We've got to keep him from getting it."

"On it," Lena said.

"I'll help," Pravesh said, stepping forward from the line of humans that still stood assembled in front of me.

"I thought I told you to leave," I said.

She gave me a smile and said, "That's cute, Harker. You actually thought I'd listen, too. I don't work for you. I work for the United States government, and those are my citizens that thing is killing. That means it's my job to stop it." She turned and followed Lena into what was very quickly becoming an absolutely destroyed great hall.

I watched them go for a few seconds, then turned to the others. "What are you guys?"

"Psychics and mediums." One guy with curly brown hair and big eyes stepped forward.

"Get the fuck out of here. Go help the mundanes and try to keep the cops out of here. I don't need more deaths on my conscience." A scream from the battle in the center of the room reminded me that I didn't have a choice.

"What are you going to do?" the curly-haired boy asked.

I ripped my tattered shirt apart and threw the pieces to the ground, displaying the ornate and now glowing tattoos that covered my entire chest, back, and arms. "Me? I'm going to call down the motherfucking thunder."

13

I strode through the wreckage of the room, Azrael in my sights. As I walked in his direction, I watched him literally rip the arms off a half-transformed weretiger and bludgeon a vampire with them. He was still in human form, but he moved faster and stronger than any human, vampire, or were that I'd ever encountered. Hell, he was stronger than a lot of demons I'd met.

How the hell was he so powerful without his Implement? None of the rest of the Archangels had this kind of power. Was it because of his gig? Was the Angel of Death mojo so potent that he was a badass even in human form? Or did the rest of them have the same juice, they were just too sane to tap into it? I gave my head a shake and banished the contemplation for another time. If there was another time. But now? Now it was time to fight.

"Hey, dickhead!" I shouted, using a trickle of the ambient energy in the room to amplify my voice. The angel's head whipped around, and he grinned at me through a mask of blood. "Yeah, you," I said, a lot more confident than I felt. "You ruined a perfectly good party. And a bunch of perfectly good weres. That's not cool. Now why don't we all sit down and talk about this before somebody, and I mean me, gets seriously hurt?"

"MINE!" the angel bellowed, loud enough that I almost felt the sound waves from twenty feet away. "MIIIIINNNNE!"

"Okay," I muttered. "Guess talking it out is off the table." I pointed my hands at a pair of four-foot tall stone planters on either side of the grand staircase. *"Wingardium Leviosa!"* I shouted. The planters flew through the air and crashed into Azrael's shoulders, exploding into dust, potting soil, and expensive greenery.

Oh, that? Sue me, I love Harry Potter. I didn't expect the assault by fauna to do a whole lot more than distract Azrael, but that's all I wanted. I ran across the room and jumped up onto one of the remaining tables to get a better vantage point and started calling up power. Scolari gathered his vampires and lined them up for an assault from the front and sides, while Darius got the few surviving weres set to try for Azrael's unprotected rear. We had barely ten seconds before the pile of dirt and stone fragments shifted, then exploded upward with a Hulk-worthy roar.

Azrael looked around the room, and his eyes lit first on the Plexiglas case with the Spear in it, then on me. I could see the indecision in his eyes. Did he kill the annoying wizard, or get his precious back? While he took two seconds to think about it, I acted, channeling more power through myself and casting green and yellow strands of magic into the plant parts that surrounded his ankles. *"Adalligare!"* At my words, the plants grew into vines, thickening to the size of fingers, then more until they twined around Azrael's legs all the way up to the knees, trapping him in place. He jerked against his bonds, but I kept pouring energy into them, replacing the strands almost as quickly as he could snap them. But only almost. He was getting ahead of me, and I felt like I only had a few seconds left before he was loose again.

"Now!" I shouted, and the vampires, weres, and other supernaturals sprang into action. Scolari led the charge, darting in and ripping out a huge chunk of the angel's throat with his bare hands. I thought for a second, *It can't be that easy,* and then the universe proved me right again, as the wound closed in seconds. Scolari dashed away from a clubbing fist as two of Darius's cats came in behind their prey, ripping at him with claw and fang alike. It did a little more than the last time, since this time I actually saw long scratches open up before healing immediately. Azrael reached around behind him, caught a tiger by the tail, and effortlessly swung the half-ton cat around in front of himself, knocking down two vampires and the redcap, who tumbled ass over teakettle back before sprawling on the marble, unconscious.

The angel lifted the huge cat overhead, then slammed it to the ground with a sickening *crunch*, reaching out to each side and crushing the skulls of two vamps that were too slow getting out of the way. My vines were weakening, and even with all the magic that had been thrown around earlier, I was exhausting all the spare energy in the room. Pretty soon I was either going to have to use up my own stores, or tap into the local mystical reservoir. I was pretty loathe to do that since if I drew too much, I could screw up the magical environment irrevocably, and something told me that taking out this angel was going to require more power than I'd ever used before.

"Get out of there!" I shouted, and the surviving creatures retreated. Most of them, anyway. Two remained, the largest of the half-transformed tigers, and the oldest and most dapper of the vampires. Darius and Scolari regrouped about ten feet in front of where I had Azrael pinned, stood shoulder to shoulder for just a second, nodded to each other, and dove in.

I've seen Luke fight. I've watched him pushed to his limits by the strength and speed of another vampire, and I gotta say, Scolari looked like he could certainly give my uncle a run for his money. The tuxedoed Master charged in, then leapt over the angel's head at the last second, pulling Azrael's attention away from the onrushing man-tiger and landing a thunderous punch in the angel's spine. Half a blink later, Darius closed on Azrael and threw a haymaker that came from somewhere about ten feet underground. His fist crashed into Azrael's jaw, and the force of the punch ripped him out of my plant bonds and knocked him several feet backward through the air.

Azrael landed with a clatter of overturned chair and tables, and I staggered back with the unexpected shattering of my spell. I dropped to one knee, and by the time I recovered enough to look up, everything had gone south. Again. The angel was back on his feet, and he had Scolari held off the ground, with one hand wrapped around the vampire's throat. I thought for half a second that it was going to take a lot more than choking to kill a creature that didn't need to breathe, but Azrael shoved his other hand into Scolari's chest and ripped out his heart. He held the unbeating organ up in front of Scolari's face, then tossed it back over his shoulder, letting the true-dead vampire drop to the blood-spattered floor.

Darius let out a roar that rattled the crystal chandeliers and shifted fully into his tiger form. I know they say lions are the kings of the jungle, but I think that term was coined by someone who had never seen a pissed-off Bengal tiger charging. Darius slammed into Azrael, shoving the demented angel back, then he reared up on his back legs and dug his claws into his foe's shoulders. I watched the tiger's giant jaws open wide, but Azrael didn't give him a chance to chew his face off. He stepped forward, into the tiger's grip, and wrapped his arms around the big cat's chest. I remembered with horror the story of the Nemean Lion, and watched as Azrael squeezed Darius tight, then tighter, until finally I heard a sickening *crack*, and a gout of blood fountained skyward from the dead Alpha's mouth.

Azrael tossed the pack leader to the side like he was a rag doll, and he locked eyes with me. A tiny smile crept across his face, and I could see through the madness that he *enjoyed* this. I shook my head. Of course he enjoyed killing. It's what he was made for, after all. The Host don't have free will, their only real satisfaction came from doing their job, and the Angel of Death was about to do his job all over me.

He raised one arm and pointed at me, and said, "Mine." I looked behind me and realized that he wasn't staring *at* me, he was staring *past* me. I was standing on a table ten feet in front of the case holding the Spear of Destiny. Azrael started in my direction, while I turned around and vaulted the table, hurrying to the case where Lena and Pravesh stood, their faces pale but their guns drawn and expressions resolute. "Get in close to the case," I said.

I looked to the great hall's shattered doors, where a dozen witches and other practitioners stood, their faces a mask of concentration as they kept a shield around the room that limited the casualties to those of us on the wrong side of the dome, as it were. "Get out of here!" I yelled. "I'm about to do something really, really dumb!"

As opposed to all your other great ideas tonight? I felt Becks in my head, even from a continent away.

Hey babe.

Hey. Looks like you're having a rough night.

Yeah, you know, angels. What are you gonna do?

What are *you gonna do, Harker? Do you have a plan?*

Yeah, but it's not a very good one. I love you.

Don't say that shit like you're about to die, Quincy Harker. You deal with this asshole Archangel and get your ass back to Charlotte. We've got shit to do.

I love you.

I love you, too. Now go do your job.

I felt her close down our connection, down to just a trickle so she could keep an eye on me, so to speak. *Good.* I didn't want her seeing what I was about to do. The witches dropped their shield and ran like hell. Pravesh, Lena, and I were all standing right by the case holding the Spear, so I drew in all the ambient power from the room and spun a dome of force around us. This was more than just a circle to keep out mystical threats, this was a forcefield, hopefully impenetrable, eight feet in diameter, big enough to wrap around the three of us.

With us hopefully shielded, or as shielded as I could manage, I spun out all the power Tuck had drawn on my body two days ago. Or was it yesterday? The days were starting to blend together thanks to no sleep and a shitload of stress. The tattoos were a battery, super-charging my own mystical energy and giving me at least triple the mojo I could usually call up. As I pulled in power from around me, I felt another source nearby, one with more juice than anything I'd ever touched. *Yggdrasil.* I tapped a line into the power of the world tree and spun power around me, leveling up my attack and unbinding the tree from this point in our plane at the same time. I felt the energy feeding into me from the tree vanish as it blinked out of our plane, and knew I could unleash hell without, well, unleashing Hell. I wrapped all my siphoned energy around my personal stores, drew up what I could from the earth around me, and let it all out in a huge circular maelstrom of magical power the likes of which I've never summoned before.

My vision started to get sparkly from the strain, and I could feel the lights starting to go out, but I grabbed the St. Jude's medal around my neck and felt the tiniest bit of power bleed back into me, barely enough to keep me conscious. I called up all the power I could, spun it out into the sky over the house, and slammed it down like a magical thermonuclear warhead, directly onto Azrael.

The magical sledgehammer had about exactly the effect I expected, weakening the building around us enough that it couldn't hold together anymore. So just like Dorothy all those years ago, I dropped a house on the bad guy. The whole mansion came down on us, walls, ceiling, staircases, upper floors, everything. It hit my dome and bounced off, the slight bit of repelling magic I had put on the shield keeping us from being buried.

After a few seconds, when we were the only thing standing in a clear circle of floor, and the house looked like a giant had stepped on it, I let the shield drop. I dropped with it, every bit of magic gone. I didn't even have enough juice left to light a cigarette if I wanted to do a cool John Constantine pose. Of course, I'm not as cool as Constantine, and I hate trench coats, so it wouldn't have worked anyway.

"Did that kill him?" Lena asked.

"I doubt it," I said from the floor. "Our best hope is that it knocked him unconscious and we can bind him somehow before he wakes up."

"What if it didn't?" Pravesh asked. I noticed that her gun was still pointing at the wreckage.

"Then we're fucked."

"Well, that's disappointing," she said.

"Why?"

"Because that section of roof is still moving." She pointed one long brown arm, and I turned to the area in question in time to see Azrael stand up and fling a big chunk of ceiling off himself. He was dirty, even dirtier than before I dropped a building on him, and he wobbled on his feet a little, but seemed otherwise unharmed.

"Yeah," I said, struggling to stand. "We're fucked." I turned to the crowd of partygoers and first responders scattered across the mansion's lawn. "Get out." I tried to yell, but it was more of a croak. Didn't matter. They were in full gawker mode, and nothing was going to get them to leave until the psycho angel had them strewn across the grass like Dahmer-brand Tinkertoys.

I drew my pistol and leaned on the case. Lena looked at me. "That's not going to do a goddamn thing, is it?"

"It'll make me feel less useless as he kills me."

"Fuck this." She reached over and tried to open the case. Locked. One quick 9mm bullet took care of that, and she reached in and pulled out the Spear. "He wants this thing that fucking bad, he can have it." With that, she darted around me and ran at Azrael, who was staggering a little, but walking toward us nonetheless.

"Lena, wait!" I reached for the furious detective but didn't have the speed or strength to stop her. Pravesh stepped in and caught me before I fell over. "Thanks."

"You want this, asshole?" Lena asked, standing five feet from the Angel of Death.

"Mine."

"Oh yeah? Well, here you go, motherfucker." She took one big step forward and shoved the Spear at Azrael's chest. At the last second, something under her feet gave way, and she stabbed him, not in the chest, but in the right side, right under the ribcage where that same Spear had made a lasting scar in a Jewish carpenter convicted of blasphemy two millennia ago.

"Mine?" Azrael said as the Spear pierced his side. Then he wrapped his hands around the haft of the Implement and pulled it free. "MINE!" A brilliant white and gold light shone from within him, and in seconds, all the dirt and blood of his human form burned away, and he stood before us, a resplendent divine creature reunited with the tool God Himself had given him to do his job.

Azrael looked around, then his eyes locked onto Lena. "Thank you, mortal. I have searched for this for many years, in many places." His face grew troubled. "All the...places. All those...people...none of them had it, but they had...power...I..." His words trailed off as his face grew stricken. He whirled around, surveying the wreckage of the house, the blood-splattered onlookers, the carnage in his wake. "Oh, my Father, what have I done?"

With those words, the Archangel sank to his knees and began to weep.

EPILOGUE

The red and blue lights of emergency vehicles flashed across all our faces, making us into disco-lit harlequins standing in stark contrast to the flattened house behind us. I leaned on the stone banister beside the steps. Pravesh was off dealing with Homeland Security jurisdictional stuff and making sure that the night's carnage got written off as a tragic gas main explosion or some such bullshit. Lena stood ten feet across the paving stones from me, arms folded across her chest as she glared at the final member of our little dance party, the Archangel Azrael.

He hadn't spoken a word since he came to his senses, just knelt in the wreckage sobbing until the first fire truck rolled up. Then Lena and I were able to hoist him to his feet and haul him from what was left of the three-story mansion I'd dropped on his head. We made it as far as the steps before he collapsed again, and I didn't have the strength to carry him any farther. I was spent, physically and magically. I could feel the magic trickling back in, but the area around the battle was going to be pretty much a magical wasteland for a while after all the haymakers I threw. It was kinda like the Bikini Atoll of magic—not a place you wanted to try to grow tomatoes.

"What are we going to do with him?" Lena asked, her voice tight.

"I have to take him back to Charlotte with me."

"Why?"

"I need him. There's a big fight coming, and he's got a role to play."

"He's a murderer."

"I know."

"He killed Faye."

"I know."

"He killed dozens, no, *hundreds* of Talents across the country."

"I know!" I shouted. I walked over to her, looking down at her scowling face. "You think I don't know that? You think I don't want to rip his head off and shit down his neck for what he did? Faye was my friend, and I've had damn few enough of those in the far too many years that I've been alive. If I could kill this motherfucker without unleashing perhaps literal Hell on Earth, I would. But I can't. It would fuck up things that are way bigger than either of us."

"Bigger than Faye?" Her jaw was tight. I could see the muscles twitching in her face as she tried not to break. One tear rolled down the side of her face, and I saw her shoulder twitch as she reflexively started to dash it away, then stopped herself. She held my eyes, her brown eyes on my blue ones, and in them I saw the strength, the passion, the fire that Faye must have fallen in love with. This woman was fierce. And I couldn't let that stop me.

"Yes," I said, hating the sound of my voice. "Bigger than Faye. Bigger than Faye, bigger than you, bigger than me, bigger than even this clusterfuck behind us. This is some cosmic-level shit we're dealing with, and I need every Archangel I can get my hands on to deal with it. I've already lost one, and I can't afford to lose another. And that's if I could even hurt him if I wanted to. He might have been mortal in his other form, although it sure as fuck didn't feel like it, but like this? There aren't enough magic users in America to even give him a hangnail."

Lena nodded, never taking her eyes off mine. "I know. I just wanted to hear you say it."

"Say what?"

"That the mission was more important than the individual. That we all had a part to play. That our sacrifice was important, but not as important as the objective. I've heard it before. I heard it playing sports, I heard it in the Marines, I hear it in the squad room. And it's bullshit, Harker. It's nothing more than bullshit."

I opened my mouth, but she closed it for me with an open-handed slap that turned my head to the side. "It's bullshit," she went on. "It's bullshit because the people we fight for are important. They're *why* we fight. They're how we get up when the bastards knock us down. I didn't stab this motherfucker for me, I stabbed him for Faye. You didn't drop a house on him for some abstract idea of a job, you did it for *somebody*."

As soon as she said that, I saw dark hair and coffee-colored skin in my mind's eye. I saw brown eyes full of love and a heart full of strength. Becks felt me thinking about her all the way across the country, and I felt her blush and felt the little smile purse her lips. I felt the love pulse between us, and I knew Lena was right.

"That. That right there, Harker. That look in your eye. *That's* what you're fighting for. So take him. Take him back to Charlotte, and take him along to save the world. But don't forget who you're fighting for. Because that's the important part."

We stared at each other for a moment that stretched into minutes, our eyes locked, until finally I felt like we'd communicated everything that we couldn't say, and I nodded. "Got it."

"Good. And if you both live through this, bring that son of a bitch back to me so I can figure out how to put an angel on trial for mass murder." With one more glare at Azrael, she turned and walked off into the night.

I looked down at the Archangel, once again wrapped in his human form, but without the madness in his eyes from before. He was shirtless, shoeless, and silently weeping on his knees as the chaos of firefighters, EMTs, and cops whirled around us. Now that he wasn't trying to kill me, he wasn't a bad-looking guy, which made sense with the whole divinity thing. He had long blond hair, a strong jawline, and muscles on top of muscles. On his face, he wore the mien of a broken man, one whose entire world had shattered in an instant, which I guess it had.

"What the fuck am I going to do with you?" I asked, not expecting an answer.

"I don't know, but I've arranged it so we don't have to do it here," Pravesh said, walking up beside me. Her approach was masked by the noise around me and the general ringing in my ears from the battle. I looked down and saw that thick rubber boots had replaced the designer heels she'd worn to the party, and a pair of SFPD sweats covered her legs. I was still in my tux pants and shoes, my shirt a casualty of the fight, and of my need to make a badass hero gesture by ripping it off to show my ink before I charged the boss monster. I needed to quit watching all those superhero movies.

"We're good to travel, and I have my plane waiting for us at a private airfield about twenty miles from here. If you're sure that Hannibal Lecter here won't go nuts and tear the plane apart in mid-air, we can leave immediately."

I looked down at the catatonic angel. He just sat there, on his knees, silent, tears streaming down his face. "Hey, asshole," I said, nudging him with my foot. "Let's go. You gotta walk to the car. I'm too worn out to carry you."

He looked up at me, and the pain I saw in his eyes went on forever, from tonight back to the beginning of the War on Heaven. "So many… dead." Tears ran like rivers from the corners of his eyes, and I idly wondered if angels ever ran out of tears.

"Yeah, you killed a lot of people. It was kind of your thing, being the Angel of Death and all."

"Why?"

That stopped me. This was a first for me, one of The Host questioning his purpose. But he wasn't an angel now, was he? He was in his human form, but with all his angelic memories. No wonder the poor guy went batshit. The human brain just isn't built to comprehend some things.

I knelt down in front of him, picked up the Spear from where it lay in the grass, and held it out to him. He looked at it, but didn't reach for it, so I pressed it into his chest. The second the Implement touched his skin, he flashed into his celestial form, and I had to look away for a second until he dimmed his light.

Azrael in his true form was not nearly as broken as the human version, but there was still a heaviness to his gaze that I hadn't seen in any of the other angels I'd dealt with. "What do you want, human?" His voice boomed, and I scooted back, my ears ringing. I looked up, because without ever seeming to move, the Archangel was now standing. And glowing.

"I need you to dial down the light show, turn down the volume, and make your human self able to cope with what he did, at least a little. We've got a job to do, and I can't very well haul one of The Host through airport security."

"You don't go through—" Pravesh started, but I held up a hand.

"I know. I was making a point. I turned back to Azrael. "Your brother has kidnapped...well, your other brother. Lucifer, I mean. Lucifer has kidnapped Uriel and taken him to Hell. I think he plans to kill him there, take his Implement, and Ascend."

Azrael's face grew even more grim, if that's possible from something that looks like it has a jaw made of solid gold. "He must be stopped. I cannot do it alone. I am not strong enough, and he has had much time to fortify his realm."

"Yeah, I've got help. Most of your other brothers, or sisters, or whatever you are." I gestured to his blank crotch. "Are in Charlotte with the rest of my team. We're getting ready to...did you say fortify his realm?"

"Of course. Lucifer will torture Uriel for quite a long time, but he will not attempt to Ascend without destroying the rest of us first. He knows that we can Ascend at will, and if we are in Heaven, he cannot breach the Gates."

"Then that's good. He can torture Uriel, we can keep looking for God, and a couple of you guys can go to Heaven and keep it on lockdown. Sweet, that's one less thing to worry about."

"No."

"No?"

"No. We cannot stand idly by and allow one of the Host to be tortured, especially not by our wayward brother. We must take this opportunity to do what Father should have done millennia ago. We must gather our forces, charge into Hell, and slay Lucifer. It is the only way we can end this conflict and rescue our brother."

"Did you just say charge into Hell?" I asked. I turned to Pravesh. "Did he say charge into Hell?"

"That's what I heard," she said with a nod.

"Of course, human. We must assault the gates of Hell as Lucifer stormed Heaven, and bring his realm crashing down upon him as you brought this building down upon my other form."

"Yeah, 'cause that worked out real well the last time," I muttered. "You're saying as long as I agree to go to Hell to help you fight Lucifer, you'll put your human self back together enough to get on the plane?"

He looked around the wreckage, taking in the flashing lights, the firetrucks, the parade of ambulances and coroner vans lining the road, and nodded. "Yes. I will restore some of the broken pieces of his mind."

"What happened to him, anyway?" Pravesh asked.

"These forms are not truly human," the angel said. "They are constructs, and they wear out over time. The one I inhabited began to wear thin the barrier between my divinity and this plane, and my power was too much for the construct to contain. Its mind splintered, it knew only the need for my Spear, and the need for more energy to hold itself together."

"That's why it killed Talents. It needed their mojo to keep from dying," I said.

"We cannot die in any form," Azrael corrected. "He would have simply ceased to be, and I would have created another construct to house my essence for a time."

"Yeah, that would have been better," I said, looking around and the devastation. "How long did you wear that construct, anyway?"

"I do not know," he admitted after a long pause. "Being separated from the Spear for all those centuries weakened my ability to control my shell. I am afraid that it went quite mad, and I was not strong enough to break it free and create a new form."

That explained a lot. The dotty bookseller in Charleston, the savant trumpet player in New Orleans. All these were constructs, and without frequent contact with their Implements, the Archangels trapped within them lost control, and the bodies they wore were driven insane. But why only some of them? I shelved that question for a time when I wasn't at the center of a bomb strike, and looked back to Azrael.

"Well, can you put Humpty Dumpty back together again enough for us to get him across the country? We need to hook up with the rest of my team. It looks like we've got some shopping to do."

"Shopping? For what?" Pravesh asked, as Azrael morphed back into the grief-stricken human, who for the moment was neither catatonic nor psychotic, so I grabbed his elbow and started walking to Pravesh's Suburban.

"He said we've got a trip to take, and I don't have anything suitable for a nice summer jaunt into Hell."

THE END

If you'd like to hear more about or from the author, please join my mailing list at https://www.subscribepage.com/g8d0a9.

James R. Tuck, Jr. is a real tattoo artist. I have three tattoos by him currently, with a plan to get more. He's a great friend, a hell of a writer, and an incredible tattoo artist. Look him up.

III

ANGEL OF HARLEM

1

I looked at the phone in my hand. I could feel my pulse beating behind my eyes and fought to control my temper. The last thing I needed right now was to melt the phone and have to get Dennis to reload all my contacts and apps. "What the fuck do you mean you can't make it? It wasn't a goddamned invitation, Jack. We need you to get your ass to New York and hunt down this angel."

The cultured voice coming through the speaker didn't sound nearly as apologetic as I wanted it to. "I'm sorry, mate, but your immigration folks have me flagged. I've been barred from entering the United States for a year after what happened last time I was there. That leaves another six months before I can set foot on U.S. soil. Nothing I can do."

I shook my head. It's not like we destroyed a chunk of downtown Atlanta the last time Jack Watson came to visit. Okay, we did, but I thought we covered our tracks pretty well. I looked over at Keya Pravesh, the new Department of Homeland Security liaison assigned to deal with the Shadow Council and our exploits. "Keya, can you deal with this?"

Her expression told me all I needed to know before she even opened her mouth. "I'll give it a try, Harker, but ICE has been on a tear the last few months. It's like they don't think they have to listen to anyone from any other department. I have to admit, I don't have a lot of faith in my people's ability to cut through this red tape."

"Shit." I turned back to the phone. "Okay, Jack. I guess you're off the hook. Go hunt down something creepy in England and blow it all to fuck. We'll handle this shit and hit you up if we get it sorted."

His voice sounded a lot more relieved than disappointed. "Will do, Q. Let me know if there is anything I can do from this side. At least until we get our own stupidity sorted, I can still move within Europe fairly easily. Good luck."

"Thanks." I clicked off and slipped the phone into my pocket. All the anger and frustration welled up inside me and boiled over in one giant shout. "FUUUUCCCCKKKK! Fuck fuck fuckity fuck fuck FUUUUCCCCCKKKK!"

"Eloquent," Cassandra Harrison said, walking up to me with a cup of tea in one hand. I reached for the tea, but she shook her head and held out her other hand. "Nope. Pay up first."

"Seriously, Cassie?" I stared at her, but I couldn't hold her gaze for more than a few seconds before I reached for my wallet. I pulled out a twenty and handed it over to her. "How much credit does that get me?"

"By my count, you have seven swears left out of twenty before you owe the jar again."

"You're going to bankrupt me, woman."

"I'm going to adjust your behavior, Quincy. If this doesn't work, I'm going to start rationing your whiskey when you swear." She handed me the tea and tucked the bill into her pocket.

"What is all this money going toward, anyway?" I asked.

"You'll see," was all she said. It was all she ever said, no matter how many times I asked.

I grumbled, walking over to the conference table in our "war room," actually an apartment I'd set up as the Shadow Council's base of operations. All the apartments on the floor were dedicated to our use, either as living quarters or operations. There are some benefits to owning the building, and not having to ask permission to redecorate is just one of them.

Pravesh closed her laptop and looked at me. "What's the plan now, Harker?" She'd slid right into our team after helping Gabby in St. Louis and me in San Francisco. Her government contacts did a good job of keeping me out of jail in California, and having a private plane at our disposal was pretty damned handy as well.

"I don't know. I'm going to have to go to New York, but I'm worried about the Not-So-Magnificent Five here."

"Don't be. We can handle these dorks." She gestured with a hand behind her, encompassing the general area.

"You can unless they turn into the Mighty Morphing Archangels, then what are you going to do?" I asked.

"The same thing you would do, Harker. Absolutely nothing." Glory's voice came from a sofa behind me, and I turned to see her smirking at me. "They're *Archangels*. There is not a thing on this plane that can match their power when they are in their true form. Not you, not me, not Adam, Luke, or any human military force. The good news is that none of them want to be hanging out on Earth in their angelic forms."

"The bad news is that they're all either broken, or assholes," I said. "So while they might not want to hang out around here in all their angelic glory, I don't trust them to not fuck shit up while I'm gone."

"Down to four!" Cassandra called from the kitchen.

I shook my head. That woman was turning into a hell of a Renfield and waking up a joy for life that I hadn't seen in Luke in decades, but she seemed determined to do it by driving me either insane or into a monastery.

"We'll handle it, Harker. Raguel and Gabriel have always been assholes, and Sealtiel is working on getting Azrael put back together. So, go collect Detective Flynn and get to New York. We need to find Raphael so we can devise a plan to rescue Uriel."

Uriel, right. The Archangel that was currently being tortured in Hell by a Lucifer that wanted to steal his Implement and use it to get back to Heaven. That was the boss fight this was all leading up to. Except I didn't know how I was going to rescue Uriel, I wasn't sure I could wrangle the Archangels I had into a cohesive unit to give enough of a shit to go after their brother, and I didn't know if bringing the six remaining members of the Host together would be enough to summon God himself (herself? themself?) to show up after a couple millennia of absence and deal with their wayward children.

I lowered my head to the table and closed my eyes for a moment. "I didn't sign on for this, you know?" I said, my face still aimed straight down at my knees. "I'm not the save the world guy. I'm the get loaded and kick somebody's ass in a bar guy, and maybe once in a while take out a demon that manages to sucker some frat boy into doing something awful. This cosmic-level stuff? That's Luke's scene. This shit is the whole reason he created the Shadow Council. I'm just…I don't know." I looked up at Pravesh. "It's just…a lot, you know?"

She gave me a wry smile. "Don't you think I know it? I came to work for Homeland Security to make sure that people with brown skin have some representation inside the government after some assholes flew a plane into my uncle's office on 9/11. I just wanted to make sure that my country was safe from human beings with ridiculous beliefs. I never thought I'd end up hunting monsters all over the country and doing battle with demons under the St. Louis Arch."

She took a sip of her tea. "But it's what we do, Harker. Now that we know the fight is out there, we can't just walk away from it. We at least have some of the tools we need to fight the battles. The rest of the world doesn't even have that."

"So suck it up, buttercup?" I said, feeling my own half-grin stretch across my face.

"Yeah, pretty much. You've got a job to do, and like it or not, it's a job that most people couldn't even begin to handle. Now go put on your big girl panties and get to work."

I stood up and walked over to the counter that separated the kitchen from the dining room area and picked up my holstered Glock. I clipped it to my belt and looked at the federal agent, who was fast becoming a valued member of our team. "I think you're gonna be alright, Pravesh. For a fed."

She smiled, her perfect teeth gleaming. "I think you'll be okay, too, Harker. For a half-vampire magician with a drinking problem and a potty mouth."

"That's as good an assessment of my character as anyone's made in a long time, lady." With that, I pulled out my phone and tapped the screen. "Sparkles?"

A unicorn head with a rainbow mane popped into view. "Yeah, boss?"

I sighed. "You're just wearing that face to annoy me now, aren't you?"

"That depends," he replied. "Is it working?"

I shook my head. Dennis Bolton was our resident tech wizard slash ghost in the machine, literally, since his soul had been trans-ferred into the internet some years back thanks to an unfortunate run-in with a demonspawn asshole. "Is Becks at police headquarters?"

"Yep. She's online searching wedding venues while she waits for forensics to come back from a crime scene this morning. You'd better get killed or get your shit together, Harker, because she's starting to get quotes and look for open dates next spring."

"If the world is still here next spring, I'll figure something out, Dennis. For now, send her a Lyft to the airport and tell her to bring her go bag. We're heading to New York to chase down an Archangel."

"Will do. Want me to book the flight?"

"Nah, I'll take Pravesh's plane," I said with a smile. I heard her stiffen in her chair behind me, then sigh. She knew it was useless to argue.

"I'll set it up," she said. "And you're an asshole."

"That's two from you, Agent Pravesh," Cassandra said from the kitchen.

"Use Harker's change. He's leaving town and won't remember it when he gets back," Keya replied.

I slipped the phone in my pocket and grabbed my own go bag from the closet by the door. "Cassandra, will you tell Luke what's up?"

"Will do, Quincy," the small woman came around the corner and held her arms out to me. "Now you give Mamma Cassie a hug before you go." I did as she asked, and as I bent down to her, she whispered in my ear, "You take care of that detective, Quincy Harker. She is so far out of your league it ain't even funny."

"I know, Cassie, I know." I kissed her on the cheek and straight-ened up. "You guys know how to find me if you need me. Just…try to keep the angels from blowing up anything while I'm gone. I kinda like this building."

"Harker, this building is atrocious," Pravesh said. "It's a giant pink phallus in the middle of South End."

"I know, and all the neighbors hate it," I replied. "That's why I love it."

"You're horrible."

"You're right. Keep an eye on the kiddos. I'm going to go save the world."

2

Three hours later, Rebecca Gail Flynn and I were in a black Suburban headed from Teterboro, New Jersey, into New York. "That beats the shit out of flying coach," Flynn said, motioning behind us where a government plane was disappearing in the rearview mirror.

"Beats flying commercial, no matter the seating," I said. "This way we didn't have any issues carrying our weapons." I had my Glock on my hip and a Ruger LCP strapped to one ankle, things I'd missed on my trip to San Francisco the week before. Not to mention my duffel bag in the back compartment with other things I thought would come in handy on the trip.

"Yeah," Becks agreed. "I'm pretty sure we could have badged our way through, but it would have been a hassle. We might want to think about keeping Agent Pravesh around for a while."

"I don't know as how we've got much choice in the matter," I said. "She seems pretty determined to hang around. And she was useful in San Francisco."

"Well, with the size of the crew you're running these days, one more isn't going to make much of a difference," Flynn said. "What's the plan? Where are we headed?"

"I've got a connection in Harlem that should be able to help us narrow things down," I said. I leaned forward and gave the driver the address. The man, an interchangeable government agent with a cheap suit and bad haircut, nodded and pointed the SUV toward 143rd street.

I tapped the screen built into the headrest of the driver's seat and said, "Dennis, you got anything new for us?"

A curly-haired young man with a scruffy reddish beard popped into view. "Nothing's come up that would corroborate your spellwork, if that's what you're looking for."

"Yeah, that's kinda exactly what I'm looking for. Something to let me know I'm on the right track, aside from a piece of improvised sympathetic magic on Michael's sword and the Spear of Destiny." I'd cast a ritual back at the apartment using two of the Implements we had in our possession and a globe to triangulate the location of the third. It took a few castings to narrow the focus down to Manhattan, and as soon as we headed to the airport, I set Dennis to digging for anything out of the ordinary happening in New York.

The problem with that is, *everything* out of the ordinary happens in New York. Like, all the time, so unless there was a demonic incursion in the middle of Central Park, it was going to be hard for anything to stand out. "Nothing?" I prodded. "Not even a series of mysterious deaths centered around one conveniently located church, synagogue, or mosque?"

"How about a string of grisly murders with religious symbology?" Becks asked.

"Nothing, guys. We've had the normal muggings, shootings, robberies, rapes, and other nastiness that people do to each other, but nothing with any pattern to it or anything more or less awful than every other week in the Big Apple."

"Well, shit. Okay, back to Plan A," I said.

"What is Plan A, Harker?" Flynn asked. "Or are you just going to keep me in the dark until it's time to start shooting things?"

"Oh, didn't I tell you? We're going to Catholic school."

———

The Our Lady of Eternal Hope Church and School sat on 143rd and Frederick Douglass Blvd. and was home to not only one of the city's oldest sanctuaries, but also one of the very few pieces of the True Cross to actually have ever resided on Calvary. We left our ride idling at the curb and bypassed the front entrance, walking down a narrow alley between the sanctuary and the church office building before coming to a door with a metal grate over it. I pressed a button on the intercom by the door, and a few seconds later, a metallic voice came through the speaker.

"What you want, white boy?" the box snarled at me, sounding like an octogenarian woman who smoked a pack of Camel unfiltered every day for forty years.

"I need some of that old black magic, you grouchy old biddy," I replied.

The red light on the intercom went out, and the lock on the grate buzzed. I pulled it open and turned the knob on the door. It opened freely, and we stepped into a narrow tiled hallway that led off to the right and the left. I headed right, then turned down another hall to the left, then stopped in front of a scarred wooden door marked JANITOR.

I knocked, and that same gravelly voice came from within. "It's open, cracker!"

"I love how your friends refer to you," Flynn said.

"Yeah," I said with a grin. "My enemies are way more respectful." I pushed the door open and stepped into the cluttered office, threading my way through a maze of books, manila file folders, and boxes stacked like an obstacle course.

"Don't you ever clean this place, old woman?" I said as we stepped through the last of the labyrinth and came face to face with the office's owner, Sister Lucia. Sister Lucia was an ancient black woman who might have made five feet tall if she wore heels and stood on tiptoes while you measured. Her face was a roadmap of lines and crevices, each one with a story to tell. I'd been there for some of those stories, but a fair number of them predated our acquaintance. Sister Lucia had been old when we first met, and I was constantly amazed that she was still alive.

"I been waiting on you, Quincy Harker. You said you were going to come back here one of these days and help me straighten this mess up." A grin split the wrinkles on her face as she waddled out from behind her desk with her arms outstretched, a spherical little wrinkled penguin with twinkling eyes.

I hugged her and stood up. "Sister Lucia, this is Detective Rebecca Flynn, of the Charlotte-Mecklenburg Police Department. She's helping me on this investigation."

"Helping you on more than that, if I can read the look she's giving you, Harker. Come here, child, and give me some sugar." She held out her arms to Flynn, who obediently stepped in for a hug and kiss on Lucia's wrinkled cheek. "It's good to meet you, sweetheart. I can see you done took some of the darkness off this boy's soul. That's good. He been carrying that weight too long."

"Lucia," I said, my tone warning, but she paid me no heed.

"You hush up, boy. You came here looking for my help. You get my guidance in everything, not just looking for whatever monster you're chasing this time." She turned and walked back behind her desk, then hopped up into her chair. "Now, why are you here befouling the holy spirit of my church, Quincy Harker?"

I moved a stack of papers from one of the chairs in front of the desk onto the floor and sat down, depositing the duffle I had slung over my shoulder on the floor beside me. "I'd pretend to be hurt if it wasn't completely true, Sister. We're here looking for something, but it's not a monster this time."

"Well…" Becks said.

"Not really a monster," I clarified. "But it certainly isn't human, and we definitely don't want it running around New York any longer than we can help it."

"You gonna tell me what you're after, or am I just going to have to throw cards blind and be all cryptic and shit?" Lucia asked.

"You are the only potty-mouthed nun I've ever met," I reminded her.

"You should get to know more nuns," she shot back. "No, scratch that. I wouldn't wish you on most of my sisters. They can't take the stress of knowing you and knowing that your soul is unsalvageable."

"You wound me, Sister. You wound me. We're looking for an angelic Implement. The caduceus of Raphael."

The old woman's eyes widened, and she sat back in her chair, blowing out a low whistle. "Quincy Harker, you are punching way above your weight class this time. That is the Implement of an Archangel, boy. Not something mortals need to be messing with."

"Tell me about it," I agreed.

"Then why you messing with it? Don't answer that. I know why. Because you too stupid to leave things alone that you don't understand. I bet you were the child sticking butter knives in the light sockets when you were a baby, weren't you?"

"We didn't have electricity in our house until I was old enough to know better," I replied.

Her eyes widened, then she chuckled. "Oh yes, I forget you are older than you look. That means you're old enough to know better than to mess around in the affairs of angels. This Implement does not concern you, boy! You should leave it alone."

"I wish I could, Lucia. But I can't. This is important. Worldchanging important. I need that Implement because it's the key to finding Raphael itself, and I *need* that Archangel. Maybe as much for Raphael's sake as for my own."

A calculating look came across her wizened face. "You were in San Francisco last week, weren't you? And St. Louis before that?"

"I wasn't in St. Louis, but I know what happened there. And yeah, I was in San Francisco. It's all part of this same thing, Sister. I wouldn't be here if it wasn't important. Now please, help us find this Implement."

"Not until I know what you're up to, Quincy. I'm sorry. I know you always think what you're doing is the right thing to do, but without some kind of explanation, I cannot help you meddle in the affairs of angels. That goes too far counter to my vows." Her affected accent was gone, and the cultured voice that spoke of dual doctorates in theology and anthropology took over. My teasing friend was gone, replaced by one of the brightest minds of Christian academia. I didn't mind. I needed all the big guns for this quest, and if Lucia decided to drop any pretense of being a silly old woman, it was fine with me.

"Okay, but remember that you asked to be brought all the way in on this." I reached down to the floor beside me and opened the duffel bag.

What are you doing, Harker? Becks asked across our mental link.

She needs proof. I don't have a whole lot of choice but to give it to her.

"That's rude, you know. Whispering behind somebody's back," Lucia said.

I felt more than saw Flynn's head whip around to focus on the nun. "You heard that?"

"Of course I did, child. You think I don't have my office warded against mind-magic? I couldn't tell what you were saying, just sounded like bees buzzing behind my eyes, but I knew what the score was. You really are close to him, aren't you? Be careful, child. I love this boy like he was my own, but riding with him doesn't take you down the safest roads."

Flynn's voice was warm, but firm. "I can handle myself, Sister. I appreciate your concern, but I know exactly what I'm getting into."

"Long as you know the score, you can make your own decisions. Now what are you digging out of that bag, Harker?"

I straightened up, a cloth-wrapped rectangle in my hands. I placed it in the one clear spot on Lucia's desk, then stepped back. "We're not just looking for one Implement, Lucia. We're looking for all the Implements. Raphael's caduceus is the last one we need."

"Then what's this?" She gestured to the object in front of her.

"Proof that I'm not full of shit." I unwrapped the cloth covering the thick, leather-bound book and sat back down. "Go ahead, Lucia. Open it. Read the book of the Archangel Gabriel. That's the *Tome of Heaven*, where Gabriel wrote down the true name of God. But I'd put on sunglasses before I opened it if I were you."

3

She sat there looking at the book on her desk for a long moment before wrapping it back up in cloth and pushing it toward me. "If somebody told me yesterday that Quincy Harker would walk into my office with one of the holiest relics in history, I would have called the men in white coats. But here it is."

"You believe it's really the Implement?" I asked.

"Good lord, child, can't you *feel* it? This thing radiates power like a supernova. I don't know how I didn't feel it the second you walked into my office."

"There are masking spells woven into the cloth," I explained. "That helps."

"What are you doing with this, Harker? It's not that I don't love you, child, but you are not the first person I would entrust something of this power to."

"Hell, Sister, most of us are still wondering why he doesn't burst into flames just being in the same room with it," Flynn added, her voice dry as the Sahara. That's the woman I love, my biggest fan.

"I'm collecting Archangels, Sister. It started out with me just trying to help out a friend, but it's escalated a little since then."

"This might be a first, Harker," Flynn said. "You're actually under-stating things."

"Bite me."

"Maybe later. Now go on, explain yourself to the nice nun. If I'm lucky, she'll go after your knuckles with a ruler."

"Oh, honey, we are so far beyond the ruler at this point," Lucia said, regaining some of her sense of humor, albeit at my expense.

I told her the whole story. From Glory losing her wings, to needing to find God to get her wings back, to gathering up Archangels and running afoul of Lucifer, to now needing to mount a rescue mission into Hell to save Uriel and keep Lucifer from Ascending into Heaven. Again. It took a little while, and when I was done, Lucia reached down into a drawer in her desk and pulled out a bottle of Johnny Walker Black Label and two glasses.

"You two will have to share," she said, pouring a healthy slug of liquor into each glass and passing one to Flynn.

"I'll take the bottle," I said, and did.

Lucia drank her whiskey slowly, rolling it over in her mouth with her eyes closed as she thought about everything I told her. The clock on her desk ticked, the only sound in the silent office, then she set the glass down on her desk and glared at me. "Quincy Harker, if you aren't the least likely damn savior I've ever seen, I'll eat my wimple."

I took another swig from the bottle and refilled her glass. "I'll drink to that, Sister. But will you help us?"

She didn't let up with the dirty look but after a few seconds responded. "Of course I'll help you, moron. I can't exactly let you blunder about my city like you did St. Louis and San Francisco. If I don't help you find this thing, you'll probably blow the head off the Statue of Liberty or something."

I couldn't really argue with her. The property damage in San Francisco had been pretty spectacular, with me leveling an entire mansion in a futile effort to rein in a rogue Azrael. "That reminds me, I need to get my tattoos touched up. You know a good mystical tattoo artist in town? My guy is in Atlanta, and I don't know when I'm going to get back down there."

"Do I look like somebody who knows about tattoo parlors, Harker?"

"I don't know, Lucia. For all I can tell, you could have full sleeves under that habit. Shit, you might have the Twenty-Third Psalm tattooed on a butt cheek for all I know."

"And you never will, either," she said. A little bit of the old glint was back in her eyes, which I was glad to see. As long as Lucia could banter back and forth with me, she didn't think I was too far gone. "Now put that thing away and let's see what we can find. What do you know about Raphael's Implement? And I assume you think the Archangel won't be far from his caduceus?"

"That's been what we've seen so far," Becks said while I tucked the book back into my bag. "All of the Archangels except for Azrael and Michael have been nearby their Implements, and Azrael was driven to chase the Spear until he found it."

"But Michael still has no knowledge of his true self?" Lucia asked, standing up and walking to a bookshelf.

"No," I said. "And he doesn't transform when he's brought into contact with it, either."

"Although the sword does," Becks added. "It bursts into flame whenever he touches it, but he stays human."

"I wonder…" Lucia pulled down a dusty volume and set it on top of a stack of papers on her desk. I watched the tower wobble for a few seconds before it stabilized, but it held. I reminded myself never to play Jenga with Lucia. "I've got a few ideas about that. I'll look into it while you two go chasing after Raphael. Now, let's see what the cards tell us."

"Cards? Seriously, Lucia? I thought you'd…I don't know, pray on it or something. Look for divine guidance."

"Quincy Harker, what in the world do you think I'm doing? I am asking for divine guidance. I'm just using my Tarot as the medium. It's no different than prayer, child. I'm putting something out in the universe, and the universe will respond."

"That sounds awfully pagan, old woman," I said with a smile.

"It's the twenty-first century, Quincy. I try to be more open-minded than some of my forebears." With that, she opened the center drawer of her desk and pulled out a bundle wrapped in rich black velvet. I stood up and cleared off more space on her desk. I'd seen Lucia cast the cards before, and this was going to take some real estate.

She laid out the cards face down, in a pattern I'd seen her use a dozen times or more, but something in her hands seemed different this time. Maybe it was a tiny tremor, maybe it was the speed with which she handled the cards, but it definitely felt like this was unlike the other times I'd had her do readings for me or seen her read for others.

"This card symbolizes the past," she said, reaching for one of the cards. She flipped it over, and it was blank. "What?"

"Very funny, Lucia," I said. "But we don't have time to screw around."

She looked up at me, and I saw something new in her ancient eyes —fear. "Harker, I swear I didn't do anything to the cards." She set down the deck and flipped over another card—also blank. One by one, she revealed all the cards she'd dealt out, and every one was completely featureless. Then she took the deck, turned it over in her hand, and spread the cards out on her cloth. Every image was gone, every word wiped clean. Her entire Tarot deck was nothing but blank cards.

"How could this happen? You saw it, the deck was in my hand the whole time. I've played with a little sleight of hand before, but nothing like..." Lucia stared at the cards on her desk, visibly shaken.

I opened my Sight and looked at the desk, hoping to see if there was any residual trace of the magic that had erased her cards, but found just the opposite. Instead of trace magic, the rectangles of reality where I knew the cards were in real space were voids in my Sight. They weren't just mundane objects; they were actively leeching magic from their surroundings. I could see thin streams of power, like iridescent spider silk, flowing from various objects around the room into the black hole where the cards sat. A pair of books on the shelf behind Lucia's head bled purple energy into the void, while warm yellow light streaked from her umbrella in the corner. Various tchotchkes and mementoes on her bookcases spilled light in a myriad of colors into the space where the cards should be but a pure blackness sat.

I snapped my eyes open and stood. "Wrap them up."

"What?" Lucia said, standing with me.

"The cards. Wrap them in the cloth, then put them in something. Something warded. Do you have a safe box in here?"

"Bottom drawer," the old woman snapped as she sprang into action. She swept the cards into a messy stack and wrapped them in the cloth she used as a reading layout. I hoped that would provide some insulation against the mystical vacuum the cards were producing.

I shoved a stack of papers and books out of the way of the four-drawer filing cabinet against the wall and yanked on the bottom drawer. "It's locked," I snarled, putting more force into it. The cheap lock on the file cabinet gave way with a clatter, and the drawer shot open. I pulled a small wooden box out of the drawer, about eight inches on a side, and stood.

The box was old and radiated power. It was inscribed on all sides with words of power in a dozen or more old languages. I recognized Aramaic, Arabic, Enochian, Latin, Greek, Arabic, Sumerian, and Japanese, and that's just the ones I caught at a glance. I set the box in the center of Lucia's desk and opened the lid. She dropped the cards inside and slammed the box closed, then I pressed my hands around the seam and whispered, "*Integro.*"

The lid and the body of the box fused into one solid hunk of wood, and when I checked the container in my Sight, the siphoning of power from all of Lucia's artifacts had ceased. I sat down, heaving a sigh of relief, and looked over at Flynn, who stood with her back to the wall and her pistol in her hand. "It's okay, you can relax. There was never anything to shoot, anyway."

"I figured," she said as she holstered her pistol and sat in the chair next to me. "But when mundane solutions are all you've got to offer, they're what you reach for."

"Makes sense," Lucia said, sitting down behind her desk and pouring another round of drinks. "Besides, whatever Harker was dealing with, there's nothing to say it didn't have friends in the physical realm that would pay us a visit. So, Quincy, you want to tell us exactly what the hell that was about?"

I sat and thought for a moment, taking a rare opportunity to formulate my words before spewing them out into the universe. "I'm not sure, Sister, but something bespelled your Tarot. I don't know how, and I don't know what, but it didn't just wipe your cards clean, it sucked all the magic from your deck and turned it into a black hole that was pulling all the magic from every artifact in the room."

Lucia's eyes went wide, and she looked around, first at the ornate paperweight on her desk, then at several items sitting around the office. "That...that could have been very bad. Some of these items carry a significant amount of power and are very important to the Church. Who could have done something like that?"

"Someone who doesn't want any questions being raised about Raphael's Implement," Becks said. "Either someone who wants it to remain hidden, or someone who wants to find it first would be my guess."

"Whichever it is, somebody else has a serious interest in this Implement, and we need to make sure they don't get their hands on it, or the Archangel, before we do," I said.

"What do we do now?" Lucia asked. "It seems like any scrying for the caduceus is going to result in more problems."

"We split the party," I said. "You go do some research in the Church's archives on the Implements and any unusual magical phenomena in New York over the past six months—"

"Harker, this is New York City," Lucia interrupted. "Most people's unusual is our Tuesday afternoon."

"Then narrow it down to unusual for New York. While you're playing Giles in the library, Flynn and I will go see a man about a spell."

The old nun's eyes narrowed. "Who are you going to see, Quincy. Remember, most of the practitioners in the city hate you."

"Yeah, but there's only one place to go if you're hunting a spell-slinger in New York, and you know I'm right."

"He swore he'd kill you if he ever saw you again."

"I'm sure he didn't mean it."

"Harker, I've met you," Becks said. "Whoever it is, I'm sure he did mean it. And there is no way in hell I'm letting you go alone into a meeting with someone you know wants to kill you. Now what the hell are you getting us into?"

"There's a guy," I said, trying to hedge, but Flynn's piercing glare and the fact that she was literally inside my head didn't let me avoid the question. "Okay, he's more like…a goblin. Maybe some kind of dark Fae. We don't really know what he is. But he's the guy to go to about obscure workings in New York. He knows pretty much everybody with any magical juice in the city."

"And he hates Harker's guts," Lucia added.

"And he hates my guts," I agreed. "But we need him. So we're going to go to his club and hope he's mellowed a bit since the last time I saw him."

"You almost started an interdimensional war in his place of business," Lucia reminded me.

"Maybe he's mellowed. A lot," I said.

"You know what you'll have to do to get a meeting with him," she said.

"I know."

"You know you ain't getting out of it."

"I know."

"Okay. I just hope you know what you're doing."

"That makes two of us."

"Would somebody please tell me where the fuck we're going?!?" Becks exploded. "Sorry, Sister."

"I've heard it before, sweetie. But if it makes you feel better, say ten Hail Marys."

"I'll get right on that. Now what are we getting ourselves into?"

"We're going to see a man about a cage fight," I said. "And I'm probably going to have to blow some shit up."

4

———————

Dusk was settling in as we entered Central Park off Malcolm X Boulevard and headed down to Lasker Pool. I kept my Sight open as we walked, knowing full well that my old buddy who ran the fights was pretty keen on his privacy and probably had sentries stationed all around the entrances. I spotted three pixies flying around, along with a pair of gargoyles and at least one were, but I think he was just a seal coming off lifeguard duty.

"Where the hell are we going, Harker?" Becks asked as we approached the entrance to the pool. "I'm not exactly dressed for swimming."

"Don't worry, where we're going should be pretty dry. Just follow me and look like you know where you're going."

"That would be a lot easier if I had any idea where we were going."

"Nah, it really wouldn't," I said. I walked down a hall in the main pool building and pushed open a door that read MAINTENANCE - AUTHORIZED PERSONNEL ONLY.

"Doesn't anyone in this city have an office that's actually in an office?" Flynn asked, following me through the door into a maintenance tunnel.

"If they do, I don't know them," I replied. We passed through another door and started down a narrow flight of steps. "Watch your step, it gets slippery down here sometimes." The smell of chlorine and something metallic pierced my nostrils as we descended, the last sounds of laughing children disappearing as we made our way down underground. The worn concrete steps were slick with water and algae, making our footing treacherous, and the rusted handrail rattled in its moorings, giving only the barest illusion of safety.

We'd walked down for several minutes, our steps illuminated by the flickering of lamps set into the wall beside us, when even that hint of civilization vanished, leaving us to continue our descent in complete darkness. I called up a trickle of power and whispered, "*Lumos.*" A ball of white light blossomed to life over the outstretched palm of my right hand and floated until it was about three feet over my head, casting a glow in all directions.

"You know, Harker, most people would have just turned on the flashlight on their phone," Flynn said, thumping me lightly on the shoulder.

"Most people don't have the flair for the dramatic that I do," I shot back.

"God, tell me about it."

"Hold up. We're almost there."

"You ever going to tell me where 'there' is?" she asked.

"Nah, some things are better left for you to experience all on your own. But keep close to me. The folks down here don't like me, but they like strangers even less."

"As if that's possible," Flynn muttered, but she reached out and put a hand on my shoulder all the same.

A few more steps brought us to a wide room, apparently empty to both my mundane eyes and my Sight. The only thing in the room was a door with a sickly yellow bulb over it and a pipe sticking out of the wall opposite the stairs at about waist height. A viscous green substance glowed at the end of the pipe and pooled onto the floor. I shut down my Sight and was way more disturbed when it glowed in the visible spectrum, too. I walked over to the door and banged on it with a fist.

A speakeasy window slid open a little below my chin height, and a pair of rheumy eyes with enormous bushy eyebrows appeared. "What's the password?"

"Open the fucking door before I roast your dick off, you scabrous shitweasel," I snarled.

"That was last week's password, you worthless dung-crawler," the doorman shot back.

"Then let's try 'if you don't open this door right now, I'm going to rip your head off and skullfuck your throat until your grandchildren's tonsils spontaneously combust, you rancid goat-penis,'" I said, pouring just enough power into my eyes to give them a reddish glow in the gloom around us.

"That's close enough, you bag of pubescent rat shite," the voice replied. The small door slammed shut, and I heard half a dozen locks disengage before the door opened wide and a three-foot tall man who looked like a cross between a Shar Pei and a purple-skinned Yoda dashed out and wrapped himself around my legs.

"Quincy goat-fucking Harker, how the shit have you been, you horrid old ball-sniffer?" the little man shouted into my thigh.

I knelt down and wrapped my arms around his wrinkly neck then stood, lifting the door guard high into the air as I did. "Fuck, it's good to see you again, you eggplant-skinned cockpimple! Blackie, I want you to meet somebody, and she's fucking civilized, so you keep your goddamned filthy thoughts about her to yourself, or she'll kick your giblet up around your pointy fucking earlobes, you got me?"

"I got you, Harker, you wretched twatwaffle. Now put me down so I can greet this fucking marvel of gentility all nice and proper."

I set him down and stepped back to stand beside Becks. "Detective Rebecca Gail Flynn, please allow me to introduce Thaddeus Bartholomew Filbertson Andrew Blackstone. He's the doorman here at the Fight Club and the single most foul-mouthed creature I've ever encountered. You can call him Blackie. Blackie, this is Detective Rebecca Gail Flynn, my partner. She's heavily armed and not afraid to shoot off any parts of you she doesn't consider vital."

Flynn's face read like something from an old Mary Tyler Moore skit where there's one person who's not in on the joke so the entire world just seems surreal. But dating me has made surreal kinda the default, so she just took a deep breath, bent at the waist, and held out her hand.

"Hello, Blackie. It's a pleasure to meet you. Any friend of Harker's—"

"Jesus Christ on the motherfucking cross, Harker, has she got a set of yabbos on her! Please tell me you're banging that. Please tell me you've got naked pictures. Please tell me something, buddy, please. I spend my whole life locked down here with goblins, trolls, and dark faeries. Give me something to live for!"

Flynn did him one better. She gave him something to fear. She switched from handshake to bitch slap in a thought, then grabbed one giant pointed ear in her right hand and twisted, yanking Blackie forward in the process. Hauling him up onto his tiptoes so they were face to face, she said, her voice low and threatening, "You ever say another word about my 'yabbos' and it'll be the last word that ever crosses your rotted teeth, you fucking sewer-dweller. Do you understand me?"

Blackie nodded, and Flynn released him with a shove that sent the little hobgoblin tumbling back ass over teakettle. "Sorry about that... Detective, was it?" Blackie said, his eyes firmly aimed at his toes. "I don't see many human women down here, and most of them sure aren't as pretty, or as alive, as you. I forgot myself. I swear on my hairless testicle it won't happen again."

Flynn stood up, folded her arms over her chest, and glared down at the purple little monster. "There are things in that statement that I'm not even going to begin to try to parse, so let's leave it at apology accepted, and see that you do not ever speak to me, or any other human woman, that way again. We don't like it."

"You don't?" Blackie's head snapped up and a look of sincere confusion crossed his face.

"No. We don't."

"Oh. I thought all humans were kinda the same. Harker likes it when I talk shit to him. And all those other humans tell me that I'm number one whenever I talk to them."

I stifled a grin. "Blackie, when they tell you you're number one, do they use sign language?"

"Yeah, just like this!" A grin split the mound of wrinkles that was his face as he held up both hands and shot us the bird. "You guys are number one, too!"

"Yeah…that's not what that means, buddy," I said.

"It's not?" He looked from me to Flynn as if for confirmation.

"Not even close, little guy," Becks said.

"Is there a fight tonight?" I asked.

"Does the Pope shit in the woods?" Blackie shot back.

I sighed and glanced at Flynn. "That one's my fault." I turned back to Blackie. "So that's a yes? The boss here yet?"

"He's here, but…I don't think he's gonna want to see you, Harker. He kinda hates you."

"Yeah, I remember he wasn't too fond of me that last time we talked."

"Sure, if by not fond you mean he said he'd wear your nuts on his nose ring if he ever saw your scrawny human ass again."

"He has met you," Flynn said with a grin.

"Doesn't matter," I said. "There's important shit going down, and I think your boss might be able to help me deal with it."

"Able and willing are two different things, Harker." The little hobgoblin didn't look enthused about my chances. I didn't blame him. When I last left Fight Club, it was made pretty clear to me that I wasn't going to be welcomed back with open arms.

"Either way, we're going in. Anything else we need to know?" I asked as I headed for the door.

"Cathy's working tonight."

"Fuck." I stopped in mid-stride. "That's going to complicate things."

"Who's Cathy?" Flynn asked.

"My ex-wife."

5

I didn't stop to explain myself to Flynn. In fairness to me, and I don't deserve a whole lot, it was going to take more explaining than I wanted to do in front of Blackie, and more than I wanted to do that close to the sheer number of people inside that room who wanted my spleen for an appetizer. In all honesty, I was a jumble of feelings about going back into the Club, and I wasn't sure what I wanted to, or even *could* say to Becks to explain my time there.

I swear, it's not how it sounds, and I'll explain it all when we get out of here safely. If we get out of here safely.

That's good, because it sounds like you have an ex-wife you've never told me about and are now avoiding telling me about.

Okay, maybe it's exactly how it sounds, but that still doesn't mean we can deal with it right now. Please, just follow my lead in there, and remember that no matter what comes out of my mouth, you can feel what's in my heart and mind. I love you, Becks. More than I have anybody in a long time. Just... trust me. I tried to project all the fervent hope that she'd believe me along with my words, and I felt her giant iceberg of pissed-off thaw just a touch. I knew I was still going to have a *lot* of explaining to do, and some of that explaining would require expensive chocolate, good

235

whiskey, and probably something shiny from the local gun store when we got home.

But I had to shove all that aside because Blackie opened the door into the "World Famous, Infamous, and Completely Obscure Literally Underground Supernatural Duelist's Society, Supernatural Sanctuary, Neighborhood Bar, and Social Club." At least that's what the very wordy neon sign on the wall proclaimed as soon as I pushed through the door.

The first thing that hit us was the sound—an absolute wall of noise that could only have been masked by magic. There was screeching guitar, pounding drums, a shrieking singer, and a baseline that would have given Geddy Lee heart palpitations thundering from the opening, all topped by a chant of "Kill! Kill! Kill!" in a dozen human and inhuman languages. The second thing that enveloped us as we stepped through the rusted iron portal was a rainbow glow of neon and LED in colors to make Sparkles' unicorn mane look duller than dishwater. Colored light shone from almost every surface, including the floor and ceiling, all jumbled together in a crazy-quilt of illumination like a psychedelic strip club strobe light. I stopped just inside the door, taking deep breaths to steady myself against the sensory onslaught, and reached out for Flynn's elbow.

I caught her before she went down and held her tight to my side. "Don't fall," I whispered. "If you fall, we're dead. Breathe. It'll all pass in a few seconds."

"I can't tell which way is up, Harker. What the fuck is this place? A funhouse built specifically to torture epileptics?"

"It's for security," I murmured into her ear. "The sensory overload breaks everyone's concentration and shatters any spells visitors are wearing. Nobody can keep their shit together enough to hold an illusion through this crap. It should be easing up, though. You feeling better?" Almost as if on cue, the sound and light show dialed back from an eleven to maybe a four, bringing all the flashing and thumping down to a bearable level. Flynn nodded at me and straightened up, pulling her elbow free. I stepped back, keeping an eye on her in case she face-planted, but she seemed okay.

I turned to the receptionist, a slender female vampire standing behind a low counter with a cash register on one end. "First time at the club," I explained with a shrug.

"That happens to most folks," the vamp replied. "Welcome to Baron Ludwig von Lichtenstein's World Famous, Infamous, and Completely Obscure Literally Underground Supernatural Duelist's Society, Supernatural Sanctuary, Neighborhood Bar, and Social Club. Or the Fight Club, for short."

"Baron Ludwig von Lichtenstein?" I asked with a smile I couldn't quite suppress. "Has Henry been watching *A Knight's Tale* on repeat again?"

"It's on every goddamn screen in the place," the door girl said, snarling just enough to show a hint of fang. "I can't even watch Netflix on my phone when it's slow. He's got a spell that locks every fucking device into repeating that fucking Heath Ledger wank-fest."

"I don't know, I kinda like that flick," I said.

"I did. The first three months it was on repeat. After that, it starts to wear on you. Trust me."

"I'll take your word for it. Two for the fights, please."

She straightened, and her face took on an official mien. "Do you agree to abide by the sacred rules of Sanctuary for your time here? You pledge to start no shit, to fuck up no idiot, no matter how much they deserve it, to leave all your bullshit at the door, and to save the fighting for inside the cage where it can generate entertainment for the groundlings and money for the house, on penalty of evisceration?"

"I swear," I replied, equally serious.

She looked at Becks, who gave her a blank stare. "Your turn, human," the vampire said.

"Me? The fuck am I going to do to most of the creatures in there?"

"Not a goddamn thing, but the oath is more about promising not to make the bouncers work too hard than it is about actually not hurting anything. Every creature in that room could rip your arms off and beat you to death with them, but the whole point of a Sanctuary is that no one tries. Now, do you swear to abide—"

"Yeah, I swear," Flynn said, holding up a hand. "No need to go through all that shit again."

"Thanks," the undead woman said. "That'll be two hundred."

"Two hundred?" I exclaimed. "Jesus fuck, what's wrong with that scrawny bastard? Has he forgotten how to make fucking book and now he needs to charge people an arm and a leg to get in?"

The vampire grinned at me. "Nah, admission's still free. The cover charge is just how I check to see if people know the score. Anything they pay me, I split with Blackie, and I let the bouncers know they might be too stupid to play by the rules. Anybody who raises a stink, they know what's going on and get in free. Hand over your weapons and any magical items, then you're good to go." She spun a dial set into the countertop and opened a twelve by twelve hole in the surface. "Just put all your shit in there. It'll be there when you get back."

"And if we don't come out, Henry gets to sell it all at the Faire?" I said, pulling my Glock and reaching into the hole with it. I stretched my arm down but didn't feel a bottom, and when I waved my hand around, I couldn't find the sides, either. "This is new. What is it?"

"It's an interdimensional lock box. Your items are keyed to your aura, so nobody, not even Henry, can take your shit. If you die inside, your gear is lost forever. On the other hand, it's all completely safe while you're inside. When you come out, you just put your hand in, and your stuff flows to you. Hank got the idea playing *D&D* with some nerdy TV guy last year."

I let my Glock go, then placed my ankle piece, a pair of belt knives, a mildly enchanted ring, my wristwatch, an ink pen, and my cellphone in the box.

"Your phone?" Flynn asked.

"I enchanted the case to make the screen indestructible. I break a lot of phones."

"Have you ever heard of an Otter Box, Harker?"

"Their warranty doesn't cover demons," I explained, stepping away and gesturing to the lock box. Flynn divested herself of two pistols and her engagement ring, then reached under her shirt and made a knife materialize from somewhere, and I took another step back. "Did I know that was there?" I asked.

"Nope. And as long as you were a gentleman, you never would have." Flynn and the vampiress behind the counter shared a nod, and she dropped the tiny blade into the hole.

The receptionist waved us toward what looked like a metal detector in front of a plain black door, and said, "Go on in. But be aware that anything magical on your person when you pass through the portal will set off the security system, and you'll be pierced by ten blades soaked in holy water, then set on fire."

I nodded, then reached into the back pocket of my jeans and pulled out a pair of silver brass knuckles and dropped them in the lock box. I thought for a few seconds, then added my pocket knife to the box, and unstrapped another small blade from my left ankle and dropped it in.

Flynn stared at me. "Are you quite done?"

"Yeah," I said. "The only thing left are the remnants of my tattoos, and they're just storage, so they don't count." It's not like there was much ink left of the sleeves I'd once had after I drained them in San Francisco. I barely had enough art on my skin left to make a tramp stamp, much less the intricate designs I'd just had redone. I didn't mention the holy Implement I carried in my shoulder bag. I just hoped that Gabriel's book was so far beyond the pale of the shit Henry usually saw that his magical detectors missed it. There was no way I was putting one of the most holy relics in the universe into Hank's homemade bag of holding, no matter the consequences.

Fortunately for me, the book didn't trigger my immolation or dissection, and we passed through the security barrier without incident. "Have fun!" the receptionist called to us as I pulled open the black door and we stepped into the Fight Club.

And, of course, the first person I saw when I crossed the threshold was the last person I wanted to see. My ex, Cathy.

"Quincy Fucking Harker," said the tall pale woman with the green mohawk and razorblade cheekbones. Her eyes were a pale blue that made you think of arctic winds and blizzards, and her breath frosted the air around her even in the steamy heat of the club. "I thought Hank said he'd rip your balls off if you ever set foot in here again. I know I did."

"Hi, Cathy. Long time, no see," I said, trying for my best disarming grin. There was a time when it actually disarmed her. A little. That time, unfortunately for me, was 1974. Cathy hadn't changed much in over forty years. She was still all punk, all the time, from her Sex

Pistols t-shirt held together with half a dozen strategically placed safety pins, to her leather pants and black combat boots. She stood an inch or two over six feet, and her arms were corded with muscle and scars. She looked like a woman equally at home walking a runway in Milan or in a knife fight in Brazil. I knew for a fact that she'd done both.

"Not long enough, you filthy cocksmoker. We had a deal. You stay the fuck out of New York, and I don't kill you."

She is not happy to see you, Harker, Flynn sent across our mental link.

Yeah...I didn't leave here on the best of terms.

Do you ever?

Good point, I replied. I held up both hands to try and forestall any violation of Sanctuary. "Come on, Cathy. You know I wouldn't break my word unless it was really important."

"Yeah, it would have to be some world-changing shit to bring you back here, Harker. Like *Hamilton* tickets, or a Guinness special at The Playwright's Tavern," the tall woman snarled. I watched as her fists clenched and unclenched, a sure sign that she wanted to put one of them down my throat.

"Come on, Cath," I said. "You know I'm not wizard enough to get *Hamilton* tickets. Besides, we're under the rules of Sanctuary. We can't start a fight here."

She rolled her head from side to side. "Fuck." Then a smile crept across her face, and I felt my breakfast start to do cartwheels in my stomach. "You're right, Harker. We can't start a fight. Out here." She pulled a walkie talkie off her belt and pressed the button on the side.

"T-Bone? Cathy. Tell Henry we've got a new main event. Quincy Harker's come back to the Club, and he's looking for trouble."

I heard through the static someone on the other end say, "Boss wants to know who gets to fight that asshole first?"

Cathy looked at me, that smile glued to her lips. "Me. Tell the boss I've got dibs."

6

I stepped into the cage, shaking my head and wondering, not for the first time, how in the hell I got myself into these things. I took off my jacket and handed it and my bag to Becks, who stood just outside the door. She shrugged my coat on and slung the bag over her head, messenger bag-style. "If I go down, get the fuck out while everything's going nuts. They'll spend a little while partying before anyone thinks to look for you, so get to Blackie and tell him I'm calling in my favor to get you safe passage to Lucia's place."

"Will the rules of Sanctuary or whatever protect me once I'm outside the doors of this joint?" she asked.

"Hank put a special rule in place to keep people from starting fights in the stairwell outside his joint. Sanctuary is in effect until you set foot on the surface again. And any place with supernatural business within twenty blocks of here has a basement entrance, including Lucia's church. You'll be safe until you get to her, and then she can call down hellfire on anything that tries to get in."

"I don't like the idea of cutting and running. That's not how I roll, Harker."

"I know, but you can't fight most of the things down here." I gestured to the crowd outside the chain link. There were werewolves, vampires, demons, cambion, nephilim, faeries of all shapes and sizes, witches of every gender, and about a dozen humans with more money than sense and an Aleister Crowley fetish. In short, even with her gun, Flynn would be at a huge disadvantage. "You can't let the Implement fall into the wrong hands. And every set of hands out here but yours and mine is wrong."

"Fine, but if that bitch cheats, I'm coming back here once I stash this book and I'm going to beat the shit out of her." I didn't bother to correct her misunderstanding of just what a badass Cathy was, just gave her a quick kiss and peeled off my shirt, leaving me in just my jeans and my Doc Martens. I wasn't trying to impress anyone with my skinny frame, but I'd sparred with Cathy before, and giving her fabric to grab and throw me around by wasn't a good idea. I tossed the shirt to Flynn and closed the cage door, turning to face my ex-wife, who was looking at me like almost every woman I've ever been with looked at me at least once. With undisguised loathing and a deep-seated desire to kick my ass. The big difference was, Cathy had the power to do just that.

She'd changed for the fight, too, losing her tattered t-shirt and jeans for a pair of athletic tights and a black sports bra. She kept her combat boots, though, and I knew how much she wanted to shove one of them sideways up my ass. I should know, she'd said so often enough when we were together.

"You look good, Cath," I called from across the sand-filled octagon. "You haven't aged a day since I left. What's your secret? Faerie magic?"

"Anger, Harker. My rage burns off all the ill effects of aging." She crouched down and rubbed her hands in the dirt, clapping them together in a big cloud of dust.

"Nice one, Lebron," I said, clapping my own hands together and letting a little magic out as I did, creating a cloud of my own, but of red and purple light that spun off into the air.

"You always were a showoff, Harker. I told you, that shit's going to get you killed one day."

"Yeah, but today won't be that day, sweetie." I grinned at her as her jaw clenched and her glare went even colder.

"You know I hate it when you call me that."

"You know I don't give a shit."

She opened her mouth, but her next threat was cut off by a booming voice. "Ladies and gentlemen, monsters of all stripe and creatures from all dimensions, welcome to our first bout of the evening!"

I looked up to the announcer's booth and saw Hank standing on a rusted metal platform about ten feet above the floor with an old-school silver microphone in his hand. The proprietor of the Fight Club, excuse me, the "World Famous, Infamous, and Completely Obscure Literally Underground Supernatural Duelist's Society, Supernatural Sanctuary, Neighborhood Bar, and Social Club" wore a sequined tailcoat the color of dried blood, with his hair styled in an elaborate pompadour a solid three feet tall. Hank himself was about six feet tall, rail thin, with preternaturally long limbs and fingers. In short, he looked like a ringmaster in Hell's own circus, which he kinda was.

I didn't know exactly what Hank was, but I knew he wasn't human. He gave off a faintly magical aura, but not like anything I'd ever encountered. I always assumed he was some kind of Fae creature, since there were so damned many variations of faerie, and it seemed rude to ask. Now he stood high above the ring, grinning down at me with a mouth that had way too many teeth in it, and announced the rules of the fight.

"We have a special grudge match for you tonight, folks. All the way from the Winterlands, please welcome Princess Catherine of the Tundra, an honest-to-badness faerie princess, here to kick ass and take names!" He gestured down, and Cathy stepped forward into a spotlight, raising her hands and sweeping her arms through the air, leaving a trail of snowflakes in her wake. The crowd, most of whom only knew her as the bitchy bouncer and had no clue she was Fae royalty, went absolutely apeshit.

"And her opponent, from the bottom of some filthy human's shoe, the man you all love to loathe, Quincy Harker. Ladies and gentlemen, the Reaper is here!" The spotlight swung over to shine in my face, and I held up both hands in a one-finger salute to Hank, then spun around as the crowd rained boos down upon me, extending my best regards to the entire audience with extended middle fingers.

My parading around the ring put me within a few feet of where Cathy stood staring daggers at me, and I whispered, "Looks like they've picked their favorite already." I turned and walked straight over to Cathy, putting us almost nose-to-nose in the stereotypical fighter stare-down and shit-talking segment.

My gorgeous and lethal opponent sneered at me and kept her voice too low to get out of the cage, especially over the curses being hurled at me. "What can I say, Harker, your reputation precedes you. You've killed or banished somebody close to almost everyone in the audience. They pretty much all want to cut your throat. You're an idiot for coming here."

"If I had a choice, I'd be in Bali," I replied. "What's the play?"

"I beat the shit out of you, then we haul you to Hank's office for medical attention. You ask him what you came here to ask him, and you and your human sneak out the bolthole Hank has hidden under his desk."

"You couldn't have come up with a solution that didn't involve me getting my ass kicked?"

"Oh yeah, I could have. We had a bunch of options that didn't have me punching you into next week, but none of those seemed like nearly as much fun." From somewhere overhead, a bell rang, and Cathy planted both hands on my chest and shoved. I flew back ten feet, crashing into the chain link of the cage and sliding down. It didn't feel exactly like running my back over a cheese grater, but pretty close.

Great. I was pretty happy to learn that she didn't really want to kill me, but somewhat less happy that she really did want to break her foot off in my ass. I didn't blame her, of course. Our last meeting had been somewhat less than affable, and then I left town for four decades.

I pushed off the wall of the cage and rolled forward underneath a big roundhouse kick that was rushing at my head. *It's okay,* I sent to Flynn. *She doesn't want to kill me, just kick my ass a little. Then she'll help us get to her boss and get out safely.*

So she only wants to kick your ass a little? I thought you said she knew you. My fiancée's career in comedy looked like a sure thing with lines like that. I couldn't take time to trade barbs with Flynn because I was busy ducking from much sharper barbs thrown my way by my grumpy ex. Cathy stood at the far side of the cage flinging ice shards at me, conjuring them out of thin air and sending the razor-sharp missiles straight at my chest.

I ducked a few, knocked a few more out of the air, barely avoided getting skewered by another, then I got annoyed. I feinted left, then spun right and drew in a trickle of magic. *"Scutum infiernus,"* I shouted, bringing to life an oval shield of pure fire that hovered in front of my left arm. I put the wall of fire between Cathy's ice daggers and my chest and started walking forward.

"Gladius infiernus," I called, focusing my will into a sword of energy and flame that appeared in my right hand. If she wanted to make it look good, I was cool with that. I advanced, spinning the sword around my wrist as I stalked the ice faerie.

"You finally put on your big boy pants and decided to make it interesting?" Cathy said with a grin. "Let's dance, lover." She waved her hands over her head and thrust both palms at me. A wave of pure ice magic blasted me, turning my shield and sword into blocks of ice in an instant. I threw both useless hunks of ice at Cathy, distracting her long enough to make her attack stutter for a second, then I threw a blast of purple energy at her chest and knocked her back into the cage.

The crowd let out a chorus of hisses and boos, and I'm pretty sure their disdain had a lot more to do with the fact that it was me than any sense of chivalry. Besides, Cathy had probably punched out half the people watching at some point. But they still liked her better. I couldn't blame them. They called me Reaper for a reason back in the day.

Cathy popped back up, her mohawk not even drooping from the attack. She wrapped her fists in huge blocks of ice and leapt at me, swinging haymakers that I dodged easily. "I thought you were going to make it look good," I hissed, throwing a pair of kicks at her midsection that drove her backward. "A toddler could dodge those punches."

"Yeah, but a toddler wouldn't be dumb enough to walk right into my circle," she said with a grin. I looked down, and sure enough I was standing smack in the center of a perfect ring of ice growing out of the sand beneath my feet. I stepped forward but smacked into the invisible wall of will she'd surrounded me with. I leaned my shoulder into the unseen barrier, pushing with all my might. I tried to draw up power from the earth, but I was cut off from anything outside the circle, so my reserves were pretty limited.

Cathy was using magic before she learned how to use a pencil, so there were no weak spots in her circle. Magic was as natural to her as breathing, but brute force came naturally to me. I drilled down all my power into a tight area, wrapping my fist in a glowing nebula of blue and red swirling force. I didn't need to make the power visible, but it made the crowd happy and didn't cost me anything, so why not make a spectacle? Cathy followed suit, bathing the circle in a patina of green and lavender light to make my struggle more spectacular.

I'd seen this trick used in real fights, and it was pretty effective. The trapped creature would often punch itself out, using up the very last dregs of its power trying to escape, leaving it easy prey for whatever cast the circle. I didn't think that would make a very good show, so I decided to change the narrative a little. And, being the asshole that I am, I didn't bother to give Cathy any hint that I was rewriting the script on the fly. I held my glowing fist in front of my face, trying for my very best douchey Iron Fist impersonation, and focused the power in a narrow, needle-like spike that stuck out, invisible, from the center of my fist. Then I reared back and punched right through Cathy's circle like it wasn't even there.

Because it wasn't there. The crafty bitch figured out that I was up to something and dropped the circle right as I threw the punch, leaving nothing hanging in the air but her light show. I punched air as hard as I could and staggered forward, completely off balance and totally defenseless.

Cathy, never one to look a gift horse in the mouth, stepped forward and laid a kick onto my jaw that lifted me off my feet, spun me in midair, and dropped me flat onto my back in the center of the ring. The last thing I saw before I slipped into unconsciousness was Cathy smiling down at me.

"I owed you that one, Harker," she said, then the lights went out.

7

"I think he's coming around," someone screamed behind a blinding light, shattering the comfortable darkness that enveloped me. I closed my eyes and tried to take stock of my situation, but everything hurt too much.

Fuck.

I take that to mean you are *awake,* Flynn said in my head. I appreciated the mind-to-mind speech. It was a lot quieter than whoever was yelling out there.

I'm awake. And I have a motherfucker of a headache, so please put a muzzle on whoever is screaming.

Yeah...that's Cathy. And she's speaking softly. You're just concussed.

Then everything came back to me. The cage, the fight, the kick to my head. *No shit I'm concussed. She kicked the shit out of me.*

Well, apparently you deserved it.

I couldn't argue with her. I did deserve it. Kinda. Time to face the music. I opened my eyes, squinting against the hum and flicker of the fluorescent lights. "Goddammit, why does anybody use those fucking things?" I asked, pointing at the tubes in the ceiling.

"Because they're cheap as fuck, last forever, and because this is my goddamn office, not a fucking lounge, Harker."

"Hi, Hank," I grunted. I sat up, grabbing onto the cracked pleather of the couch I was laying on to keep from falling over, then grabbing it tighter as the room threatened to spin out of control underneath me. "Did you have to kick me that fucking hard, Cathy?"

My ex's voice came from somewhere behind me, slightly amused and without even the slightest hint of concern for my well-being. "Yeah, I'm pretty sure I did. You're lucky I've cooled down a little since you bailed on me. Otherwise, I would have really fucked you up."

"You would have tried," I said, trying to turn and shoot her a nasty look but being thwarted by the sloshing of my brain inside my skull. "Is there a trashcan or something around here?"

"Here," Flynn said, stepping in front of me with a bucket. "If you've got to puke, use the bucket."

"Yeah, I wouldn't want to fuck up Hank's high-dollar upholstery." I rubbed my hand back and forth across the cracked and stained seat of the couch.

"What do you want, Harker? I'm pretty sure you didn't come back to my place just to let Cathy beat your ass, and I believe I promised to wear your balls for earrings if I ever saw you again, so this had better be important." I looked over at Hank, who had discarded his sequined coat from earlier and sat behind his desk in a big leather office chair in tuxedo pants, suspenders, and a tank top stained with at least two meals. His desk was about the size of a small fishing boat and was covered with stacks of paper, most held down by a knife, pistol, or magical implement of some sort. On the wall behind him was a collection of photos, every one showing Hank smiling and shaking hands with a different species. I saw vampires, half-transformed weres, at least one faerie, and a yellowed photo of Luke dressed in one of his favorite suits. One of his favorite suits from the era of the Great Depression.

"I'm looking for somebody," I said. "I don't have a lot of time to fuck around, so I came here. This is still the place to go for information on the magical and mysterious in New York, right?"

"Yeah," Hank said, leaning back and lacing his preternaturally long fingers behind his head. "This is the place to find the vanished, decipher the incomprehensible, and unravel the mysteries of the world. *If* you've got the coin or other tender. Which I doubt you do, Quincy Harker, because your sorry ass is going to pay a premium the likes of which you've never seen."

"Jesus Christ, what did you do to these people, Harker? Screw their sister? Kill their dog? Kill their sister and screw their dog? Or are they just assholes, and this is how they are with everybody?" All eyes swung over to Flynn, who sat on a barstool along one of the walls of Hank's office. "I mean, come the fuck on, y'all. Harker's a prick, but you obviously knew that already. What is with this treating him like he's the devil himself?"

"It's complicated," Cathy said after a moment's silence.

"I'm pretty goddamn smart," Flynn snapped. "Why don't you try to explain it for me? If I don't get it, I'll ask you to use smaller words."

Hank and Cathy looked at each other, then they looked over at me. I raised my hands. "Don't look at me. I'm the asshole, remember? Any explanation I give, you won't accept."

Cathy walked past Flynn to the wet bar on the wall and poured herself a drink of something brown and more viscous than any liquor made for humans. She knocked back a healthy slug, then poured another drink and walked back to Hank's desk. She shoved a stack of papers to the side and set her drink on top of it.

"Hey, that shit's important!" Hank protested.

"You're such a fucking poseur, Hank. The same invoice has been sitting on this same stack of paper since 1992."

"I just haven't gotten around to paying the bill yet."

"That cleaning service went out of business in 2002. I think you're clear." Cathy turned to Flynn. "Okay, you want the story of why we want to kill Harker?"

"Just the Cliff Notes," Becks said. "If I let everybody list every reason they have for wanting to kill my fiancé, I'd never do anything but listen to people bitch about Harker."

"Fair enough. He told you we were a thing?"

"Yeah, he sprang that one on me right before we walked through the door."

"Sounds like our boy. So…yeah, I used to be married to the guy you're gonna marry. But it wasn't that kind of thing. A love thing, I mean. It wasn't like that. I mean, we went out, and we hooked up a time or two, but it was just for kicks, you know? I mean, he's not bad to look at, and he's okay in the sack, but—"

"I don't need the play-by-play," Flynn said, holding up a hand.

"Okay?" I asked. "Don't try to make me feel good or anything, Cath."

"Don't worry," she replied, her tone colder than the icicles she threw at me in the ring. She turned to Becks and said, "Here's the short version. I was born a princess of the Winter Court. Not in line to the throne or anything like that. My father is a Duke, and I was betrothed to a mid-level Winter Court noble that the King and Queen wanted to reward for bravery or some such shit. He was several hundred years older than me, and I wasn't exactly enthusiastic about the match. So I did what any fifty-year-old child does when she gets mad at her parents—I ran away from home."

"Most human children run to a friend's house down the block," Flynn said. "I'm guessing that your trip was a little more in-depth?"

"There might have been a dimensional portal involved. I left the Winter Court and landed in New York City, planning to get lost in the mass of humanity. My family always resembled humans very closely, just a glamour here and there to mask my ears and make my skin look a little pinker."

"There are humans of other colors," Flynn said, holding up her milk chocolate-colored arm.

"Yes, but since this is what I started with," Cathy said, waving a hand in front of her face. The glamours she usually wore fell away, and her true face came into view. She was right, she looked mostly human, just a pair of lobeless ears that swept up into two-inch points, even more pronounced nose and cheekbones, and a pale blue tint to her skin marked her as Fae. "I decided to keep the amount of magic required simple and just take the blue tinge off.

"I showed up in New York in February of 1979, with no idea how to live among humans. It was a good thing the cold didn't bother me since I didn't conjure any money and slept in Central Park for the first week I was here. I was mostly unmolested, until a group of idiots decided that an apparently defenseless young woman walking through the park at night was 'looking for it,' and surrounded me. That's when a skinny savior wandered in, hands blazing fire and throwing magic around like a fireworks display."

"Harker," Flynn said.

"Quincy gods-damned Harker. He was walking home from a club, drunk as a skunk, and came upon me fighting off half a dozen human youths. I didn't need his help, but it was chivalrous nonetheless. He scorched a few of the idiots, and when he saw me conjure an ice fist to bludgeon the last one with, he knew I was something more than human. He took me in and showed me the city."

"And showed you his apartment, I'm sure." My girlfriend always thinks the worst of me. She was right, but that doesn't change the fact that she always thinks the worst of me.

"Yes, he did. He was a perfect gentleman, though. He gave me his bed and slept on the couch for several nights. It was much later that I realized that the linens on the couch were significantly cleaner than those on the bed, so his sacrifice wasn't all it appeared to be at first blush."

"What can I say?" I asked. "I was a bachelor in New York City in the late 70s. I had much better things to do than laundry."

"And he sucked me into those better things like this mad Pied Piper. Before I knew what was happening, I was at Studio 54 every night, experimenting with every substance under the sun, dancing myself giddy, then partying until the sun came up. We lived like vampires, sleeping all day and hunting at night, but our prey was the elusive good time. We chased it with pills, powders, drinks, spells, potions, rituals, and lots of energetic and creative sex. Sorry."

"No, it's okay," Flynn said. "I've heard about Studio 54."

"Whatever you've heard, double it. We lived the life of the immortal and hedonistic for most of a year before it all came crashing down." Cathy looked over at me for the first time since she started her story.

I nodded for her to go on. "In for a penny and all that, love," I said with a slight smile.

"What happened?" Becks asked.

"What happens to all naughty children? My parents showed up, with my betrothed. They appeared right in the middle of the dance floor one night with a squadron of twenty faerie knights, all armed and armored for battle, ready to rescue their kidnapped princess."

"Who was at the moment dancing topless on a table wearing fake angel wings, hot pants, and six-inch silver platform shoes," I said. Flynn at least gave me a grin for that one.

"To say they were not pleased would be to stretch the boundaries of understatement," Cathy went on. "They ordered me to return home with them, and when I refused, they tried to use force."

"That didn't go over well with the patrons of the club, who had all grown to love Cathy, particularly in that outfit," Hank said from behind his desk. "I was the DJ that night, and when the faeries made a move toward the girl we'd come to think of as our faerie princess, things went south in a hurry."

"There might have been a fireball or two involved," I added.

"Can't imagine such a thing," Flynn said. "It's not like it's your default answer to most situations."

"Well, in 1979, I'd just gotten really good at it, so I was even more prone to fling fire at every problem than I am now. Today I'll at least think about talking my way out of a problem first."

"Then you burn it all down," Becks said.

"No," I said, aggrieved. "Then I punch the shit out of it. If that doesn't work, I burn it all down."

"There we were, with about three dozen various supernaturals in disco apparel, squared off against twenty of my father's highly-trained house guards, and throwing spells, punches, and swords at each other, when I get the message across to Harker that I'd really prefer that no one kill my parents."

"So I stopped the fight. With prejudice," I said. "I cast a spell to overload all the subwoofers in the building at once, creating a sonic boom equal to half a dozen supersonic jets. It had most of the desired effect. Everybody stopped fighting."

"It's hard to throw haymakers when you're bleeding from the ears," Hank tossed in.

"When the room calmed down a little bit, I got my parents off to one side and told them that there was no way in hell I was going home with them, and no way that I was marrying Prince Xarin. They pressed me to do my duty as a princess and a daughter, and I could see that they were moving closer and closer to taking me by force."

"And that wasn't going to happen without a lot of bloodshed," Hank said, a smile stretching his wide face into a terrifying rictus.

"So I told her parents the one thing that would guarantee they wouldn't try to take her home to marry Prince Humperdink," I said.

"You told them she was already married to you," Becks said.

"Got it in one," I agreed.

"Harker, in his terribly finite wisdom, thought that telling my mother I was already married would send her running back to the Winter Court, all thought of taking me home set aside," Cathy said. "He forgot one important thing—the desire of a mother to see her daughter's wedding. Mother didn't break down into tears and rush off home, she transformed into a psychotic wedding planner and decreed that we would renew our vows, immediately if not sooner, in a ceremony befitting a princess of the Winter Court. An hour of spell-spinning later, and Studio 54 was transformed into a wedding hall."

"And an hour after that," I said, "the wedding was underway."

"Yep," Cathy said, looking at me with an expression somewhere between amused annoyance and loathing. "We were married. Then things went really sideways."

8

———

"You're saying that marrying Harker wasn't the point at which things hit the high-water mark for fucked up?" Flynn asked, shooting me a grin. I showed her the hangnail I was sporting on my middle fingernail, just to make sure she understood that she was number one in my heart.

"No, because really, there wasn't a lot different in being married to him and not being married to him. We were never legally wed in New York City, only in the eyes of the Winter Court, so nothing about our lives here changed. We already lived together, so we just kept on as we had been, clubbing every night, sleeping every day, and consuming copious amounts of drugs."

"In my defense, it was 1983 by this point. Cocaine was a bigger Columbian import than coffee back then," I said.

"Everyone else is doing it has never been an acceptable defense, Harker," Flynn replied.

"Well, nothing really changed until the spring, when Henry opened this place."

"What can I say?" the gaunt ringmaster said. "That Palahniuk guy wasn't as original as everybody thinks. Fucker was a regular here back in the day. He got the rules wrong, of course, but that's no surprise, given how blasted he was most of the time he was here. The first rule of fight club isn't 'don't talk about fight club,' it's 'fuck shit up, get paid.' I don't give a fuck who talks about the club. Nobody with the juice to shut me down is ever going to believe there's a supernatural fight club hidden in the sewers under Central Park. It's why the were-gators don't give a fuck about the urban legends about them. Nobody who can do anything about it ever believes the truth when they hear it."

Flynn shot Henry a skeptical look. "You're telling me there's a nest of were-alligators under New York City?"

"See!" Hank spread his skeletal fingers and grinned that over-toothy grin at her. "Nobody believes the truth when it's right in front of their face."

"Anyway," Cathy went on. "Hank opened this place, and I took a gig as one of his featured fighters and security. Harker even helped out once in a while, even if his idea of helping included drinking up most of my pay in top shelf whiskey. That lasted for a few months, until Theodren showed up."

"Theodren?" Flynn asked.

"My brother. My older brother, and heir to my parents' estate and title. Unfortunately, that's all he inherited, because just as with many of the mortal nobility, my parents' title didn't come with any money. Prince Xarin, on the contrary, was very, *very* wealthy, and still very interested in marrying me, even sullied as I was by mortal hands. So Theodren came to this world to drag me home and force me to marry Prince Xarin."

"I objected, on the grounds that she was already married," I said.

"You objected on the grounds that you were shitfaced and looking for a fight, and none of the regulars would set foot in the ring with you," Hank butted in.

"Regardless, Harker objected," Cathy said. "And he objected with his normal degree of subtlety, which is to say none whatsoever."

"Fireballs. Lots of them." I smiled when I said it. Prince Teddy had been an asshole, and when I was done with him, he was a flaming asshole.

"Theodren challenged Harker to a duel, in the ring, no holds barred, with the winner holding rights to my hand in matrimony. Harker, against all my urging, accepted. They squared off, and after a pitched battle, Harker killed my brother in front of my face."

"Saving you from a life of virtual slavery at the hands of the nasty Prince Whatever his name was," I protested. "I am sorry, though. I didn't want to kill him. He gave me no choice."

Cathy whirled on me, the ice in her eyes leaking out to chill the air around her face. "You always have a choice, Harker! You didn't have to kill him. You could have injured him, or just beaten him so badly he would never return. He didn't have to die."

Aw, fuck. Suddenly I saw it. Years of pain and anger all rolled up in one package, all because she didn't see what I saw in her brother. "No, Cath. I couldn't. Never used your Sight on Theodren, did you?"

"No. He was my brother. I knew his aura like my own. I didn't need to see him that way."

"I did. When he hit me with the first blast of ice, something felt off. We'd sparred enough by that point for me to know what faerie magic felt like, and this was different. I opened my Sight and saw what was really driving Theodren. It wasn't greed, or honor, or any of that shit. It was a demon. A bad one. Ninth Circle shit. It was riding your brother's soul like a quarter horse, and it wasn't there to take you back to Faerie, it was there to take you, period."

"You're wrong," Cathy growled, her lip curling in a snarl. "I would have known if my brother was possessed."

"Would you? Now, probably, but thirty-five years ago? When you'd only been in this world a couple of years? When you hadn't seen nearly the amount of shit that you've seen now? Would you, really?"

She stared at me, anger and pain warring on her face as she thought about what I was saying. She turned to Hank. "Henry? Could he be telling the truth? Could Theo have been possessed?"

Henry looked puzzled. "Of course he was possessed. I thought you knew the whole time."

"How would I have known? Why would I have hated Harker if I'd known? What the fuck, Hank? Why wouldn't you tell me something like that?"

"Oh goddammit," I said. "Hank, you're a prick."

"Well, yes," he admitted with an unctuous smile. "But why am I a prick *this* time?"

I looked at Cathy. "He never told you because he's a Rage Demon. He lives on bloodlust and anger, and you being pissed off at me has kept a boiling cauldron of stew for him to feed off of for decades. I'll bet you spent the first couple of years after I left town fighting almost every night, pissed as hell."

"Yeah," she said, turning her glare to Hank. I'll admit, it felt good to see that anger directed somewhere else. "I beat up a *lot* of people who were my Harker by proxy. You're to blame for a couple million dollars in healer charges in the eighties."

"So Harker killed your demon-possessed brother, you didn't realize there was a demon involved, and wanted to kill Harker? Is that pretty much it?" Flynn asked.

"Yeah, that covers it pretty well," Cathy said. "Except for the deception the person I thought was my boss and best friend perpetrated upon me for decades, that is."

Hank spread his hands and grinned. "Demon, love. It's what I do. Does this mean I'm going to need a new bouncer?"

"Yes, asshole, it means you're going to need a new bouncer. It also means I need to return to my ancestral lands to see if the demon taint has spread there and destroy it if it has." Cathy turned to me, then dropped to one knee in front of me and bowed her head. "I am sorry for the injuries I have caused you, Quincy Harker. I have hated you unfairly and brought harm to you through no fault of your own. I apologize and would like to make amends." She looked up at me and grinned. "But I would like a divorce."

I struggled to my feet, the room still spinning, albeit with a little less vehemence than earlier. "You are forgiven of any slights you may have done or intended me, Catherine of Winter. All hurts are forgotten, and all debts are paid. I release you from our wedding vows. Be free."

She stood in front of me and smiled, a genuine smile this time, not the grin of someone who enjoyed beating my ass. "I release you from our wedding vows, Quincy Harker. Be free." Then she gave me a hug, and as she wrapped her arms around me, I felt a chill run through my whole body, cooling the inflamed bruises and cuts she'd left on my body and healing all my injuries.

"A going away present," she said, stepping back to look at my healed body. "Not bad. I'm a little out of practice with the healing. Been a lot more punching for the past three decades. Goodbye, Harker. I'm sorry I hated you for so long."

"I'm sorry I didn't tell you everything about Teddy sooner. Would have saved me a concussion." I pulled her to me in another hug and kissed her on the cheek. "Be careful over there in Fairyland. If you need my help, you know where to find me."

She stepped back and smiled at me. "Thank you, Quincy." She turned to Flynn. "Be careful, Rebecca Flynn. He is a good man, but trouble follows him like a cloud."

"I can handle his trouble," Flynn said, holding out her hand. My ex-wife and fiancée shook hands, then Cathy waved her hands in the air and vanished, heading back to Faerie to see what kind of shitshow the demon that possessed her brother had wrought on her family's lands.

"That's it?" Flynn asked. "That's all it takes to get divorced in Faerie? You just say, 'I quit,' and you're done?"

"Yeah, pretty much," I said. "The Fae don't have lawyers because faeries can't lie to you directly. They may not tell you the whole truth, but they can't actually lie. That doesn't work for a lawyer, so they just don't have them. Plus, when you live forever, you don't want someone tied to you that doesn't want to be there. So marriages are serious, and divorces are easy."

"Unlike humans, who are the other way around," Hank said. "The faerie way is much simpler but doesn't create nearly enough anger for my taste. I much prefer the human method. Make marriage easy, but make divorce hard. Much more rage that way." He grinned at me, then said, "Well, all's well that ends well, I suppose. Your fight is done, your wounds are healed, your marriage is over. Now you can leave. Have a nice day!"

"Hold up, assclown," I said. "We haven't even gotten to the real reason we're here. Dealing with Cathy was just a side quest. I'm glad to have all that resolved, and even more glad that one more person no longer wants me dead, but it wasn't why I risked my life setting foot back in here."

"Then why are you here, Harker, if not to settle things with your wife?"

"Ex-wife," I said. "And we were never legally married in this dimension."

"Don't think I've forgotten about that," Flynn said. "That's a conversation we'll be having when we get home."

I flinched. I'd really hoped she missed that bit. I saw jewelry and flowers in my future. And dishes. I was going to end up doing a *lot* of dishes. I turned back to Hank and a battle I had a chance of winning. I walked over and sat down in one of the chairs in front of his desk. "We need information, Hank, and you're the only person I could think of that might have it."

He leaned forward onto his desk, steepling his fingers and letting a slow smile creep across his face. "Well, why didn't you say so, Harker? You tell me what you're looking for, and I'll tell you what that information will cost you. After all, anything worth risking your life for must be worth a pretty penny, and if there's one thing my kind appreciates, it's making a deal."

I fucking hate demons.

9

Now that my head was clear, and my ex-wife was out of the room (and no longer wanted to murder me), I could focus on what brought me to New York in the first place. "I need to find Raphael, Hank."

"Well, the sewers are probably a good place to start, if he's not lounging around a pizza joint. But I hear he's been spending a lot of time with Michelangelo, Donatello, and Leonardo, and those guys are just trouble on the half-shell, if you ask me."

I stared at him. "What the fuck are you babbling about, Henry?"

"I'm talking about the Teenage Mutant Ninja Turtles. What are you talking about? The painter? He's dead, Harker, and as far as I know, he was just a human, so he's probably staying that way."

"Jesus Christ, Hank, cut the shit. I'm looking for the Archangel Raphael. He's somewhere in New York City, and I need to find him."

"Have you tried prayer, my dear boy? And why would I know where to find an Archangel? In case you didn't notice, we're not exactly on the same side."

"Well, I didn't know you were a demon when I came here, now did I?"

"I don't know. I've never made a big secret out of my origin."

"You've also never talked about it," I shot back.

"Do you go around bragging about being…whatever you are?"

He had a point. There was a kind of unspoken rule among supernaturals that we don't advertise what we are, and we don't really ask, either. It's just kind of assumed that if you work in the business, so to speak, that you'll recognize another being and its origins. It's not really on them to tell you what they are. But still, Hank being a demon is something I should have noticed. "You use a masking charm, don't you?"

"That's almost as rude as asking a woman how much she weighs," Hank replied.

"One sixty-five," Flynn chimed in. "There. I showed you mine, now you show me yours."

Hank looked her up and down, taking in her muscled arms. "Sounds about right. Fine, yes, I use a masking charm to cover my aura. We get people from every side of the street in here, and I don't want anyone starting shit just because I'm a demon. I haven't been to Hell in centuries and have no interest in tormenting souls. I just want to run my fights and feed off all the sweet, sweet rage that my cage generates. So I keep my true nature under wraps. Most people assume I'm Fae of some sort, and I don't do anything to dissuade them. Cathy knew, at least part of it. I might have left out the whole Rage Demon part, and Blackie. Most of the employees know the score. They need to be aware that if any of the Host show up, it's probably going to be our last night in business."

"So you try to keep the Host from finding out about your location?" I asked.

"I don't have to," Hank replied. "One, I haven't seen any of those assholes down here the whole time I've lived on Earth. They don't like humans much, so they don't hang out with you. No offense."

"None taken," Flynn said, making a "get on with it" gesture.

"And even if they were around, none of those douchecanoes would ever pull the stick out of their ass enough to darken the door of a fight club."

I didn't bother to tell Hank that we'd found the Archangel Michael in human form working as a cage fighter in Phoenix. No point in disillusioning the poor guy. "So if there was an Archangel anywhere around here, you'd make it a point to keep tabs on him."

"I keep tabs on everything with any real power on the island, Harker. You know that."

"Exactly why we're here, Henry, old chum." I picked up my bag from the floor next to Becks' feet and plopped Gabriel's book down on Hank's desk. "Does this look familiar?"

"It's a book, Harker. I might have read one or two." He reached out a hand to open the tome, but froze with his fingers barely an inch from the surface. He looked up at me, his eyes gone wide. "What the fuck is this, Harker, and how the fuck did you get it past my security?"

"So you recognize it?" I asked.

"Recognize it? Fuck yes, I recognize it. That's the Tome of Gabriel. It's one of the fucking Implements of the Archangels. What the fuck are you doing with it and why the fuck did you bring it into my place of business?"

"I'm trying to collect the set. Right now, I'm missing Raphael and his caduceus, and rumor has it that they're in New York."

"The set? You have the other Implements? The Spear? The Sword?"

"The Implements and the Archangels are in a safe place. Well, except for Uriel. He's in Hell, along with your boss. But the rest of them are secure."

"Except for Raphael's trinket, and this book, you mean."

"No, the book is pretty secure," I said, letting a little power bleed out through my eyes in a red glow. "Unless you want to fight me for it?"

Henry held up both hands, palms toward me. "No, no. I don't need to challenge the Reaper. Either you kill me and I'm stuck back in the Fourth Circle, or I kill the two of you and I have to replace the carpet in my office again. It's not easy getting a contractor who'll work two hundred feet underground, you know. So let's keep it civilized. You're looking for Raphael, and somebody told you he was in New York with his Implement. Okay, I don't know anything about that. You can go now."

I'd never seen Henry this nervous. I'd seen him stare down angry vampires, coked-out werewolves on the full moon, and an invading army of faerie warriors in the middle of a dance club, but he was way more rattled now than I'd ever seen. "What's wrong, Hank? You seem awfully skittish."

"Who else has been asking about angels, Henry?" Flynn jumped in, her detective instincts cutting right through the bullshit, as usual. Of course that's why Hank was dodging my questions—he was more afraid of whoever was asking about the angels than he was of me. I might need to remind him why that's a bad idea.

"Henry," I said, drawing out the word to half a dozen syllables. "Has someone else been interested in angels in New York recently? Don't make the nice lady ask again." I leaned forward, shoving a pile of papers onto the floor to make room for my elbows. I pushed a little bit of magic through my eyes to give them that "kill you and grin" glow, just to remind Henry that there's a reason demons call me the Reaper. "Talk."

"Okay, there were a couple of demons through here the other day. They were asking about divine visitations, holy relics, that kind of shit. Nothing specific about angels, but they wanted to know where God-touched artifacts might be stored in the city. I told them to check the museums, St. Patrick's, the Statue of Liberty. You know, the usual spots."

"Wait a minute," Flynn said, coming over to sit in the chair next to mine. "There are holy religious items at the Statue of Liberty?"

"There's a few trinkets buried in the base, and a piece of the True Cross in her crown, but nothing with any real power. She was built to serve as an early warning system for magical threats, so she's gotta have something powering her up, you know?"

"No," Becks replied. "I didn't know."

"What else did they ask?" I pushed. "What else did you tell them?"

"I gave them a bunch of places to look, but none of the stuff there has any real mojo. These were bad dudes, Harker. They were high-level soldiers from the Seventh or Eighth Circle. I didn't want them getting their hands on anything too potent, you feel me?"

"Your sense of discretion never ceases to impress, Henry," I said. "Now, what do you know about that you didn't tell them?"

"Why do you think this Implement is in New York, Harker? I mean, wouldn't I have heard something about it if it was here?"

"I don't know, Hank. Would you? Did you?"

Flynn leaned in. "Tell us more about these demons that came by. You said they were upper-level bad guys?"

Hank looked relieved to be able to answer somebody's questions that weren't mine. "Yeah, they were serious muscle. They weren't Reavers or any of the normal guys like me that end up here. These were the kind of guys who torture other demons for not doing their jobs. Whatever they were looking for, somebody with some real juice sent them here after it."

"Yeah," I said. "That would be Lucifer."

"The Morningstar is involved in this shit?" Hank said. "Fuck that. I'm out of here." He stood up and walked over to a safe sitting against a wall, then knelt down. He opened the safe and started pulling out stacks of cash. "Gimme that duffel bag, will ya, Harker?"

I tossed him a dusty Gold's Gym bag that looked like it had been in the office since he first opened the club. "You and Lucifer got beef, Hank?" I asked.

"Nah. Like I said, I ain't seen him in about twelve hundred years. And I want to keep it that way." He turned to me, still kneeling in front of the safe. "Look, Harker. I'm a demon. I'm not a good guy. But I'm not really a *bad* guy, either. I provide a valuable service. People have anger issues; I give them a place to work it out. They get their mad on; I get fed."

"While you get paid." I pointed to the thousands of dollars he was throwing into the duffel bag.

"Nothing wrong with getting paid for your talents. I never heard about your uncle living in a cardboard box."

He had a point. Hank continued. "I just don't want to get mixed up in anything Lucifer's got going on. I like it here, and I remember Hell. I did not like it there. It's hot, there's a lot of screaming, and there isn't a decent frozen daiquiri in the whole fucking dimension. So if it's all the same with you, I'll stick around up here. Just not...right here. Especially if Lucifer's got his eyes on this place."

"Where will you go?" Flynn asked.

"I've heard good things about Thailand," Hank said. "Sandy beaches, foreign gangs running drugs, ladyboys beating the fuck out of people who try to stiff them on money. My kind of place. I should be able to have this joint up and running in Bangkok within a month. Maybe I'll franchise this place out to Blackie. Let him run the joint."

"That would be a terrible idea," I said. "Blackie would piss off all the customers. Get the door chick to run the place. She's pretty and doesn't make you want to rip her throat out ten seconds after meeting her."

"Good idea. Thanks. Hey sweetie, do you see a box on my desk labeled 'Passports?'" he asked Flynn. She passed him a shoebox and he pulled half a dozen sets of ID out of it and tossed them into the bag. Hank stood up, slung the bag over his shoulder, and started to walk past me to his office door. "Thanks for the heads up about Lucifer. Gotta go."

He took three steps and tripped. That might have something to do with the fact that I stuck my foot out and tangled it between his gangly legs, but who can really say? I stood up and hauled Hank to his feet, then pitched him over to the couch where I'd woken up. "Don't rush off, Hank. We're not done yet."

"You still need to tell us where to find the Implement," Flynn said, standing up and moving to block the door.

"I told you, I don't have any idea," Hank protested.

"But you know what parts of the city are more holy than most," I said. "Those would be the parts of the city that you stay the fuck out of. Not churches. We'd know about those. And not museums. Places that humans just *feel better* in."

"Particularly places that may have seen an uptick in that feeling or unexplained activity within the past year," Flynn added.

I looked over at her.

"It stands to reason," she said. "That's when we started gathering the Implements and the Archangels together. It's when several of the things we've recovered became more active. I'm willing to bet this caduceus amped up whatever it's been doing then, too."

"Good point," I said. I turned back to Hank. "Okay, Henry. Give us a list, then we'll let you charter a plan to Kuala Lampur if that's what you want to do. But know that if you fuck us on this, and we don't get this Implement, that Lucifer's going to storm Heaven again. If that happens, there's no place on Earth you can go to escape the shitstorm that's going to rain down on us all."

Hank looked from Flynn to me, as if guessing how likely he was to make it past us both. Becks pushed her jacket back to reveal her pistol, and I cracked my knuckles. The dejected demon let out a sigh and sat forward on the couch. "Gimme a pen. I've got a couple of ideas."

"This is where your buddy thought we might find an Archangel?" Flynn asked as we got out of the Uber Dennis had called for us. Gotta tell you, having a buddy that's an incorporeal soul that can manipulate anything connected to the internet is pretty handy.

I looked out at the crowd skating in the late afternoon sun, thankful that for once my work was taking place in the daytime. Rockefeller Center was busy, but not anywhere near the level of packed it would be in the prime evening hours, and nothing like it would be in a month or so when the holiday rush started. Now it was just crowded, a couple dozen folks skating for exercise, twenty or thirty kids at varying levels of balance, and maybe ten or fifteen little clumps of tourist families gawking while they made slow laps around one of the most famous public ice rinks in the world.

"I don't know if he really thinks we'll find anything here, or if he just wanted us out of his office," I said. I opened my Sight and scanned the crowd, looking for any hint of divine magic or celestial beings, but nothing popped in my vision. There were a few faeries with glamours making them look human, and several people wearing jewelry with minor enchantments, but nothing too out of the ordinary. Until I swept the crowd of spectators around the upper levels of the rink, and that's when four demons popped into my view.

"We've got company," I muttered to Becks. "And it's not the kind that brings its own wine and leaves after they help with the dishes."

"Is it the kind that spills red wine on the white tablecloth and uses your good cloth napkins to mop it up?"

"More like the kind that rips the other guests to shreds and reads the future in their entrails," I said. "I've clocked four demons on street level, one at each corner of the rink."

"Are they looking for the same thing we are?"

"I don't know, but whatever they want here, I'm pretty sure it won't be milk and cookies."

"What's the play? What do they look like in the real world?"

I dropped my Sight and opened the link between me and Flynn wide, so she could see through my eyes. Then I focused on each of the demons in turn, letting her get a good look at all of them. In human form, they were pretty nondescript: an Asian man in a long coat who looked to be about sixty, a thin black woman about thirty dressed in an expensive suit, a white guy who looked like a pudgy balding accountant, and a young athletic-looking blond guy who could have been the villain in every 80s teen movie. Under their disguises, they all looked like trouble.

These weren't the heavy hitters Hank described coming by the club, but they weren't the kind of low-level Vice demons that I often saw hiding in human form. These were Lieutenants, rank and file officers in Hell's armies, with some fairly strong magic, but no creativity or authority to trade for souls. These weren't the demons you met at midnight at the crossroads; these were the errand boys the crossroads demon sent to drag your soul to Hell after you died.

"We can either make a huge scene and hope to kill them all without any of the dozen or more NYPD cops getting hurt or any of the hundreds of innocent bystanders getting killed, or we can keep an eye on them and hope to take them down if they move on anyone," I said. "If we were anywhere except the middle of fucking Manhattan,

I'd lean toward Plan A. Since we *are* in the middle of Manhattan, I think we should try to keep this on the down low as much as possible."

"Okay, then we do it my way. I'll get close to the Asian guy and keep an eye on him. You follow Brad the Super-Douche," Flynn said. "Keep our connection open wide so I know if something goes sideways."

"There are demons at the skating rink at Rockefeller Center. I think you mean *more* sideways." I flipped up the collar on my jacket and started weaving through the crowd toward the blond guy. He was taller than most of the humans around him, which helped me keep an eye on him. Unfortunately, he was taller than most of the humans around him, which meant he saw me coming from fifty yards away.

Most days I enjoy my reputation among the hellspawn. It makes interrogations go faster when they already think I use demon tendons as dental floss, and the overblown descriptions of my magical ability means that I get out of a lot of confrontations without a fight. When I'm trying to sneak through a crowd to get the drop on a demon, being infamous in the supernatural community just sucks.

Blondie did a double-take when he saw me, then started pushing his way through the crowd in the opposite direction. He got to the stairs leading down and headed into the lower levels of the plaza, toward the Concourse and the shops under the ice rink, looking over his shoulder with about every other step.

I've got a runner, I sent to Flynn. *If he gets to the subway, we're fucked.*

Yeah, I see. My target is eyeballing you guys pretty hard, but doesn't look like he wants to rabbit yet.

Keep an eye on the others, too. I don't want you getting surrounded while I chase this idiot.

Good call. I'll try to put my back to something solid. Be careful down there. If you get in deep shit, it won't be easy for me to get to you.

If I get in over my head, the last place I want you to be is anywhere near me.

I lessened the intensity of our link to allow me to concentrate on chasing the demon in front of me. The crowd thinned out significantly once he got away from the spectators, and he had to slow down to not arouse suspicion. I watched him pass the Starbucks and head off down the Concourse toward the subway. I cut across in front of the Swarovski Crystal store and trailed him from the other side of the plaza. He cut in and out of view between stores, but I kept him in sight all the way down, and I was waiting when he turned the corner, positioning myself between him and the subway station. He saw me, and his eyes widened, then he sprinted for the stairs leading up to Sixth Avenue.

"Shit," I muttered, then dashed toward him. My enhanced speed made me faster than the human form he'd adopted, and I caught him in the midsection with a tackle before he made it to the first step. We sprawled across the slick floor, sliding through the glaze of muck from the day's pedestrian traffic. Nothing like rolling around on the ground in New York City to give you that full Big Apple experience.

"Get off me! Help! Mugger!" the demon shouted as I tried to wrestle him to his feet.

"NYPD!" I shouted. "Stop resisting!" I figured if it was okay for him to impersonate a human, it was okay for me to impersonate a cop. I twisted around until I could grab him in a hammerlock and hauled the struggling faux man to his feet. I leaned down to his ear and said, "Chill the fuck out, I'm not here for you."

"I know why you're here, Reaper, and if you want it, you're going to have to go through us to get it." Then he dropped his human guise and transformed into a seven-foot tall demon right there in the mall. My first thought when that happened was, *There's no way this doesn't end up on YouTube.*

Instead of holding a two hundred pound man in a baby blue sweater, now I was holding a massive demon complete with horns, hooves that split his sneakers, and a tail snaking out of his designer jeans. The baby-blue sweater ripped as the demon's chest expanded, and he flung me off like he was a dog shaking off water. He turned to me, his indigo skin looking almost black in the fluorescent lights, and grinned. "Let's see how tough you really are, Quincy Harker. You don't look like much, for a guy with such a badass reputation."

I do have a badass reputation. I'm a hundred-thirty-year-old wizard with vampire blood and a bad attitude. I've fought monsters of every stripe from human to were-everything, killed more demons than sincere prayer, and saved the world at least once. So I've got nothing to prove to some shithead Lieutenant with ideas toward career advancement.

Therefore, I shot the son of a bitch three times in the face and left him lying in a pool of black blood and green brain matter. Most of the time, bullets don't do a whole lot against demons. But most of the time I hadn't stopped off to visit my old friend Sister Lucia the same day I tangled with a demon, so I didn't have bullets freshly dipped in holy water in my guns. Today I did, and they did an impressive job on the formerly blond assclown.

There's a lot of great things about killing demons. First, it means there's one less demon. At least, one less demon here. You can't actually kill a demon on Earth, but destroying the bits of it that are here sends it home to Hell, so at the very least, it takes it a while to return. Second, it usually fucks up the plans of whoever summoned or sent the demon. In this case, that someone was Lucifer, and fucking with Lucifer's plans for humanity is pretty much always on the side of the angels, no pun intended.

But it's not all sunshine and rose petals. Especially when killing a demon means firing off three rounds from a handgun underneath a bunch of very popular tourist attractions in New York City. For some reason, that makes people nervous. Particularly people in blue suits with badges that don't take kindly to people shooting people in their city, not even people who turn into blue giants with fangs and tails. That's why I very quickly found myself surrounded by half a dozen of New York's finest, all pointing guns at yours truly and shouting things that were all variations on "drop it" and "get down on the ground."

So...we've got a problem down here, I said to Becks.

Let me guess. You had to shoot something and now you're getting arrested.

It's like you know me.

I'll be there in a minute. Oh, shit.

Oh shit, what? I asked.

You're about to have company.
More cops? I don't know how that's all that bad. I'm already surrounded.
Not more cops. More demons. The other three are headed down to you.
Fuck. It's going to be a bloodbath.
Ten seconds later, the screaming started.

11

The cops surrounding me turned to the sound of shrieking behind them, and I took the opportunity to summon up a shield of pure energy and hold it out in front of me, Captain America-style, as I picked up my pistol and sprinted toward the noise. I learned immediately what a salmon felt like as I tried to shove my way through the tide of humanity flowing toward me. For some reason, the sight of three seven-foot blue monsters complete with fangs, tails, and claws sends people into a frenzy, even in New York City.

Can you get to them? Flynn asked in my head.

Fighting through the crowd. Stay back.

Kiss my ass. Then she shut down the link, and I heard the flat crack of a familiar .40 Smith & Wesson handgun.

Fuck, they aren't going down, Becks said.

Use the bullets we dipped at Lucia's.

Right. Fuck.

As she closed down the connection again, I broke free of the crowd and into the open area between the ice rink and the Starbucks. Sure enough, there were three demons waiting for me, all fully transformed, all fully pissed off.

"Quincy Harker," the demon who had been masquerading as a businesswoman, her expensive suit in tatters around her expanded form, hissed at me. "You killed my mate. For that I'll wear your guts as a necklace!" She breathed fire at me, a new one in my demon-fighting experience, and I ducked behind my shield.

Magical shields are great, especially the ones created from pure energy. They don't weigh anything, and they don't take up any room in your closet. You don't have to worry about carrying them in your suitcase, and they'll pretty much deflect whatever you design them for. But unlike traditional shields made from metal or wood, they aren't much good against things you didn't think of when you cast them. All that to say that a metal shield that deflects bullets will also provide some protection from fiery demon breath, but a magical shield might not do a goddamn thing.

Mine was definitely one of the "don't do a goddamn thing" variety. Flames washed over my arm, passing right through the shield and setting my coat ablaze. My hair caught fire, and one of my eyebrows was scorched off in an instant. I dropped to my stomach and rolled over several times, rolling over my arm and putting out the fire on my head and jacket. My shield vanished with my concentration, and my pistol went flying. I've been set on fire before, and it remains one of my least favorite things.

I scrambled to my feet just as the demoness was drawing in a breath for another blast. I held out my left hand toward her and shouted, *"Glacies!"* A spike of ice flew from my palm and skewered the demon right in her open mouth. She went down, but that wasn't enough to kill her, just take her out of the fight for a few precious seconds.

I needed those seconds, too, because her buddies were converging on my position with their claws out and mouths open like they wanted to see what barbecued Reaper smelled like. I charged the first one, pouring on all of my supernatural speed to close the distance between us much faster than he expected. I leapt into the air when I was about five feet from him, landing a Superman punch right in his horned forehead. His eyes crossed, and he dropped to his knees as I came down right in front of him, so I decided he looked like an excellent bludgeon.

I picked the demon up by the horns and swung around in a circle like a drunken Scot prepping for a hammer throw. I managed two revolutions, then let go of the demon, flinging him through the air like a giant blue missile, taking down his oncoming partner in a tangle of horns, tails, and limbs.

"Behind you!" came a voice I didn't recognize, but I dove flat instead of looking around. Another jet of flame shot over my head, and I rolled over onto my back, scrabbling at the holster on my ankle. The demoness was on me before I could draw my weapon, stabbing down at my chest with her claws. I rolled to the left, scrambling to my feet and headbutting her in the gut as I came up.

She staggered back, but not before she raked her claws up my back, shredding the remains of my jacket, my shirt, and my skin. I howled as her fingers left trails of fiery pain the entire length of my torso and straightened up delivering a kick to the point of the demon's dark blue jaw. She took three steps back, then charged me again, but now I had a little separation and could maneuver. I offered up a fleeting prayer to anyone paying attention that I could take her down before the other two assholes got to their feet, then spun off to my right to get away from outstretched talons.

I kicked her in the side of the knee as she went past me and slammed a fist into her temple when she staggered. She spun around, lashing out at me, but I dodge further right, putting myself behind her and pressing the palm of my right hand to her forehead.

in nomine Dei
Patris omnipotentis,
et in noimine Jesu Christi
Filii ejus,
Domini et Judicis nostri,
et in virtute Spiritus Sancti,
ut descedas ab hoc locus!

The ritual of exorcism wasn't exactly the wording I wanted, but I knew it off the top of my head, and when I threw enough power behind it, my hand flared with white light that grew to encompass the demon's whole body, then a huge flash of light bathed the entire Concourse, and the demon exploded into chunks of ash.

I turned to the other two, who stood side by side about a dozen feet away, held my still-glowing hand in the air, and grinned at them. "Who's next, motherfuckers?"

Of course the answer was "both of them." They sprinted in opposite directions, working to divide my focus. The one on the right ran straight for the café, where dozens of onlookers stood behind windows, most of them shooting cell phone video of the whole fight. The one on the left apparently decided that discretion was the better part of valor because he turned tail and ran down the Concourse back toward the subway and the exit to Sixth Avenue.

"Fuck," I growled, whipping my head back and forth.

"I've got the runner," Becks said, coming down the stairs to me, pistol drawn. "You get the one heading for the looky-loos."

"Got it. Be careful." I took off after the escaping demon, ripping off the scraps of my jacket and shirt. I really needed to stop ending up half-naked in these fights. People were going to start thinking I was the world's skinniest pro wrestler or something.

The demon skipped the restaurant and ran straight up out onto the ice, bowling over skaters as it went. I followed, but my feet didn't get nearly the purchase on the ice that the demon's hooves did, since it melted itself into the ice with every step, insuring it had solid footing. My feet went out from under me almost as soon as I stepped onto the rink, and I landed flat on my ass.

Sitting on my butt on the ice, I reached down and yanked my backup pistol from my ankle holster, steadied both hands, and squeezed off three shots at the fleeing demon's broad back. Two found their mark, and the creature slammed down face-first, sliding along the ice to the far wall. Taking a cue from my quarry, I pointed at my feet and said, *"Infernus,"* wrapping my boots in a layer of flame. The ice under my feet started to melt, and I was able to get up and stalk the downed demon.

My holy water-soaked bullets left steaming holes in the demon's flesh, but he wasn't dead. Not by a long shot. He was just playing possum and playing a very pissed-off possum at that. When I got to within ten feet of the beast, he flipped over, leapt to his feet, and launched himself at me. I caught a gut full of demon shoulder and slammed to the rink, breath rushing out of my lungs and my gun sliding across the ice.

The demon started punching almost before we landed, raining heavy blows down onto my face and chest. I felt something crack in my ribcage, then a stabbing pain in my side. Another broken rib. Great. I dodged one huge punch to my head, and he howled as he slammed his fist into the ice. There's literally nothing like having a demon yelling inches away from your face. The stench was almost physical, and flecks of demon spit peppered my forehead. I bucked my hips, trying to throw the beast off me, but he was too heavy.

The demon sat up, rearing back to slam both fists into my face, but the second of separation was all I needed. I reached down into my personal energy reserves and channeled pure force through my hands, blasting the blue-skinned assclown into the air and ten feet back. I rolled over and struggled to my feet, wincing with every breath as my broken rib made itself known.

"That fucking *hurt*," I panted.

The demon apparently skipped the witty repartee section of his combat training because he just charged at me again. This time I was better prepared, dropping to one knee and launching myself up just as the creature reached me. My right shoulder caught the demon right on the forehead, and as I stretched to my full height, I drew the knife from a sheath on my left ankle and stabbed upward. The blessed silver blade slid into the "V" under the monster's chin and effectively nailed its mouth shut.

The blue bastard staggered back, scrabbling at the hilt of the knife sticking out from under its chin, and I limped over to where my pistol lay on the ice. I picked up the gun, chambered a round, and drew a bead on the demon's head.

"Hey, asshole," I called out, sending a fresh wave of pain through my chest. The demon froze and looked at me, exactly the response I was hoping for. I put a bullet through its left eye, then walked over to stand over its prone body and pumped another one into its head and two in the chest for good measure. The holy water-dipped bullets created little clouds of steam as they bore through the monster, sending its soul back to Hell as its empty body began to dissolve into a puddle of black and blue sludge.

I looked around, but Flynn was nowhere to be seen. *Becks, how you doing over there?* I asked.

I've got it cornered, Harker, but it's got a kid. It's using the kid as a shield. Fuck, I think it's going to—

Hang on, I'm on my way. I pressed my hand tight to my side, trying to minimize the movement in my broken rib, and ran back toward the Concourse. The ice didn't cooperate, and I slipped, falling face-first and almost passing out from the stabbing pain in my chest. I gritted my teeth and pushed myself to my feet, walking gingerly until I got to solid ground, then breaking into a sprint.

I had just rounded the corner at the far end of the Concourse when Flynn came into view. She had her service weapon trained on the last demon, who had a little kid in a heavy coat and toboggan held up in front of its head.

"Back the fuck up, Reaper," the demon snarled as it caught sight of me. "I'll snap this brat's neck before you can say—"

"Fuck you," I said, and pointed my hands at the kid. *"Corporis Ferrum!"* I shouted, unleashing a bolt of magic right at the kid's chest. He turned to iron in the demon's hand, instantly gaining a couple hundred pounds of weight. The demon's hand dipped, and Flynn put two rounds from her Smith & Wesson right in the monster's face. The kid fell to the floor with a clang, and I shouted, *"Restiture!"* The boy turned back to flesh and blood and ran sobbing off toward a panicked-looking woman who was a month or two early with her ugly Christmas sweater.

"Nice one," Flynn said, not looking at me. That's when I noticed her face was pale, and not just from the shit lighting in the underground mall.

"You okay?" I asked.

"He…might have got me a little before I could get a shot off," she said, turning to me. Her left hand was pressed to her chest, which was covered in blood. "I think I might be more hurt than I thought…" She fell toward me, her eyes fluttering closed as she fainted from the gruesome slashes across her chest and stomach. The demon had done more than "get her a little." She looked like she'd been mauled by a tiger.

I turned to the onlookers, most of whom were pointing cell phones at me. "Somebody stop taking a goddamn video for a second and call 911!" I shouted, yanking out my pocketknife and slashing horizontally across my wrist. I pressed my arm to her lips, trying to force my blood into her. It had worked before, I could only hope she wasn't too hurt to save.

I couldn't feel her drawing on my blood. I could barely feel her through our link. I rolled her over, pulling off Becks' coat and pressing it into her wound. It soaked through with blood instantly, and I could feel her inside my head, slipping further and further away. I'd felt that before, and I didn't know if I could ever come back from it again.

Rebecca Flynn was dying, and there wasn't a goddamn thing I could do about it.

12

I think I broke the latch on the ambulance door when I shoved it open. I also gave not a single fuck, and they should count themselves lucky the door stayed attached at all. The EMT in the ambulance gaped at me but recovered in an instant and shoved me toward the opening.

"Get out of the way!" he snarled, and I hopped out of the back of the ambulance.

His partner met us at the back of the ambulance, and they unloaded the stretcher, extending the wheels and moving to the emergency room doors at a quick walk. I followed along, looking down at Flynn's pale face. She was unconscious, and I could feel her clinging to life in the back of my head, my sense of her small and surrounded by darkness, but holding on.

A doctor and pair of nurses met the stretcher as we came through the doors, taking hold of the stretcher and pulling. One nurse peeled off and took my elbow. "Come with me, sir."

I shook her off. "I'm going with her."

She grabbed my arm again. "You can't do anything for her right now. Please, just let the doctors work. I need to get you to our intake desk to answer some questions—"

I wrenched my arm free and turned her to look into my eyes. My glowing red eyes full of murder. "If you do not leave me the fuck alone and let me get back to my fiancée, I am going to bring the ceiling of this hospital down on your head. Do you fucking understand me?"

She glared up at me and fired back, poking me in the chest with a finger. "I understand you just fine. Go ahead. Go back there. Take your freaky eyes and charge back into the room where one of our doctors, who are among the best in the world at what they do, is trying to save your fiancée's life. You go back there with your anger and your attitude and you get right in the way, because I'm sure that some smartass with a British accent and glow-in-the-dark contacts will be able to contribute so much to her care. Where did you go to medical school again? Oh, that's right, you didn't. You just think that you can fix everything just by standing there and yelling at things, or by punching someone until it's all better. Well, listen here, Mr. Attitude, you can't help her back there. You can help her out here, by giving me her blood type, and everything you know about her medical history, and any allergies she has, and the things that might actually keep her alive. Would you like to do that, or would you like to stand here and argue while she bleeds to death?"

I deflated like a football in Tom Brady's hands. "I'm sorry. What do you need?"

She took my arm again and led me to a little alcove with a desk and a computer terminal. "Let's start with her name."

"Rebecca Gail Flynn."

"Age?"

"Thirty-one."

"Occupation?"

"Police detective."

"NYPD?"

"No. We're from Charlotte, North Carolina. We're...here for a work trip."

"Are you a police officer, too?"

"No. I'm...it's complicated. Let's just say I'm a consultant."

"What do you know about her medical history?"

"I can have it to you in a few seconds." I pulled out my phone and tapped the home button. "Dennis? I need you."

Dennis's face popped onto the screen, his human face this time, and he looked worried. "Yeah. I saw the whole shitshow on the Concourse security cameras. I've got her doctor's information, and I'm going into the CMPD system now. Okay, her complete medical history, along with insurance information and a listing of on the job injuries, is in the hospital's computer system."

"Do you have eyes on her through the hospital's security cameras?"

"Yeah." I could tell from his voice that I wasn't going to like the answer to my next question.

"How does it look?"

"Not good. I'm sorry, Harker. I'm not a doc, and don't even play one on TV, so I don't know what any of the shit they're doing means, but I know they're prepping an operating room, and everybody back there is moving like they've got a serious fire lit under their asses."

I felt the vise grip on my heart ratchet a little tighter. "Keep me posted."

"Will do." His face vanished, then popped back into view. "Harker?"

"Yeah."

"Um…this might sound weird, given what I am, but…I'll pray."

I couldn't breathe for a second. Dennis's face, which had been nothing but silly grins and animated unicorns for almost ten years, was somber. "Thanks, man. I…appreciate it."

I looked back to the nurse, who watched me with sympathetic eyes tinged with more than a hint of suspicion. "Did your friend just say that he was watching through our security cameras? Who the hell are you?"

I grimaced. One of these days I was really going to have to learn when to use the speakerphone. I pulled my new badge wallet out of a pocket and flipped it open. "Quincy Harker. I work with Homeland Security."

"And that gives you the right to hack our system and invade our patients' privacy?" She tapped on the keyboard in front of her, and her eyes widened. "Holy shit…"

"Everything you need is in there, right?" She nodded. I leaned forward on the desk and looked hard at the nurse, who was now staring at me with something between awe and horror. "When one of our people is injured, maybe dying, there is nothing we won't do to keep them safe. That woman bleeding on a table back there is the single most important person in my life, and if I have to burn the world to save her, then you'd better slip into your asbestos underpants because I'm going to light a motherfucker on fire."

She pushed back from the desk, her face a little pale. "I'm…going to go get her blood type information to the doctor, along with her allergy to penicillin. Doctor Tennon is one of the best we have, so she's in very good hands. Please wait in the Emergency Room waiting area. You can find a scrub shirt in the closet right behind you. Someone will be out to give you an update when we know something." She slipped past me and hurried back down the hall toward the Emergency Department.

After I ducked into the supply closet and grabbed a shirt, I followed her at a slower pace, sure that whoever came out to give me an update would not be her. Apparently having someone just waltz into their computer system, dump a metric shitload of information into their patient files, and hack their security feeds all at the same time was enough to freak her out a little. Good. I wanted everyone there working their hardest to keep Becks alive, and if that meant I put the fear of me into them, so be it.

I walked into the emergency waiting room, a little stunned by the sheer number of people sitting there. I counted something like three dozen people either sitting in the uncomfortable chairs or pacing the floor. About half of them looked like they were waiting for treatment for some ailment or another, from the woman with a bloody dishtowel wrapped around her left hand to the man mumbling incoherently in the corner with dirty clothes and bloodshot eyes.

I took a seat next to the woman and gave her a polite nod. I sat there for a moment, then asked, "Are you okay?"

She barked out a laugh that had as much humor as a Cormac McCarthy novel. "Do I look like I'm fucking okay? I've got a finger that's barely hanging on by the tendons, and I keep getting shoved to the back of the line by people like you that come in on the ambulance. If I'd known that's what it took, I would have called them, too."

"If you didn't come in on an ambulance, how did you get here? I'm guessing you didn't drive like that."

"Drive? This is New York, man. Who the hell has a car? No, I took a cab. He was pissed, talking shit about me bleeding all over his seats. Like my hand is the worst thing that's ever happened in the back seat of that cab. Fucker. Shit. I need a smoke. But I can't even smoke with my hand all fucked up. You wanna come outside and light one up for me?" She gave me a bitter smile, and I had to admit she had some stones, making jokes while she sat there with her hand mangled in her lap.

"Sorry," I said. "I quit a long time ago."

"Sucks to be you." She leaned her head back against the wall and closed her eyes. "If they ask for Friedman, give me a little nudge."

"Try not to bleed out," I said.

"I'd flip you off, but I think it would be a bit too literal." She smiled again and fell silent.

I sat there for a few minutes, sitting there with my elbows on my knees and recriminations hanging from my shoulders. I was stuck in the worst place I knew—alone in my own head. When I couldn't take it anymore, I pulled out my phone and walked out to the sidewalk.

"Dennis, what's going on?" I asked, tapping the screen.

"I don't know," he replied, still wearing his human face.

"What do you mean, you don't know? Aren't there cameras in the operating room?"

"There are, but I'm not a doctor, Harker. And it's a security camera, not a film crew. I've got one angle that covers most of the room but focuses as much on the door as it does on the table. It's not like it would help a whole lot if I had closeups of everything they were doing, anyway. I'm a super-hacker with more tech mojo than Steve Jobs' ghost, but I'm not a doctor. I don't know what I'm looking at."

"Put it on the screen," I said.

"No."

I stopped pacing and stared at the phone. "What?"

"I said no."

"Put the video on the fucking screen, Dennis."

"What are you going to do if I don't, Harker? Kill me? Too late, pal. Now cool your goddamn jets and listen to me for a minute. You aren't a doctor. You have exactly zero medical training. You can't do anything with that video except tear yourself apart worrying. There is literally nothing you can do for Flynn right now. Except maybe pray."

"Pray? When did you get religious on me, Boltron?"

"Maybe when we started consorting with Archangels trying to stop the literal Devil from blowing up the world. I've always been religious, Harker. It's not something I wave a flag about, but it's always been a part of me. I have to believe in something, Q. Otherwise, what the fuck am I doing this for? If I don't think there's something better on the other side, why am I even still alive and trying to help people?"

I didn't answer him. I couldn't. Hell, I'd spent most of my life trying hard to avoid that type of question. Now here I was, standing on the verge of a fight with one of the most powerful beings in the universe, and I was having a crisis of conscience. "I guess you're right," I said.

"Of course I am," Dennis replied. "What am I right about?"

"I can't do anything to make things better, so me tying myself into knots watching a video I don't understand isn't going to do any good."

"What are you going to do?"

"Something I haven't done for a very long time," I said, heading back inside and looking at the directory on the wall. I found the place on the map I was looking for and turned down the hall. "I'm going to go pray."

13

"Well, this is kinda awkward," I said, putting my bag down and sitting on the front pew in the little hospital chapel. It wasn't a bad-looking room. Nice, muted lighting, padded pews, pretty solid sound-proofing on the walls that kept most of the hospital beeps and alarms from being distracting. It was non-denominational, but representational of a lot of faiths. There was a wall with a set of votive candles in a small rack, a few sticks of incense in a holder, and a low bookcase with a few Bibles, copies of the *Torah*, *Qu'ran*, and several other books that I assumed were central to one faith or another that I wasn't familiar with. Along the top of the bookcase was a row of statues like Jesus, Buddha, the Virgin Mary, and small box with a few yarmulkes in it.

There was a pleasant backlit stained-glass window at the front of the room and maybe eight short pews in two rows flanking a center aisle. I was alone in the chapel, ergo my willingness to speak out loud to a deity that I hadn't talked to seriously in a long time. One that I wasn't sure was listening to anyone anymore, much less a half-vampire spellslinger with more blood on his hands than in his veins.

I knew the big guy wasn't sitting on some big throne up in the clouds. That much had been made pretty clear to me by Glory and other angels I'd had contact with. Apparently God went on walkabout not long after they tossed Lucifer into Hell at the end of his failed coup. No one had seen or heard from the boss since.

That didn't mean they weren't listening. Just not in the office. And hell, there might be a useful angel hanging around just waiting for a sincere prayer to come across on the hotline. Or maybe I just wanted to sit somewhere quiet and try to hold my shit together.

Either way, I wasn't sure how to start talking to a religious figure that I didn't think gave a shit about me. "Okay, here goes," I said. "I don't know if you're listening or paying any attention to anything that's happening down here since you went on your little vacation, but it's all pretty fucked up."

I stood up and started to pace back and forth in front of the first pew. "All your Archangels are down here. Except for Lucifer, who you banished, and now Uriel, who Lucifer's kidnapped and is probably torturing. I assume Raphael is around here somewhere, but we haven't found him yet. But if we don't find him soon, Lucifer is going to get tired of beating the shit out of Uriel, and storm Heaven. With no one there to hold him back. Because all your Archangels are down here.

"Some of them are crazy, by the way. Azrael has pretty much gone completely fucking around the bend, and then there's Gabriel. I guess he's not crazy. He's just a dick."

I sat back down. "But that's not why I'm in this windowless little room talking to myself and hoping you'll hear it. I'm trying to get a line to you because Becks is hurt. She got ripped to shreds by a demon trying to save a bunch of innocent mortals, and now she's somewhere in this building trying real hard not to die. I can feel her, feel her tied to my soul, but her grip is pretty fucking tenuous, man. And if she dies…well, if she dies, I don't know if that's something I can come back from. I managed it once, and it was as much Luke's doing as it was mine, and a lot of people died before I came back to myself. They were bad people, at least I think they were bad people. Luke tells me I only killed Nazis, that he steered me away from places where I would hurt innocents, but my uncle is not above lying like a motherfucker if it suits his purposes."

I had a moment of moral self-examination about saying "mother-fucker" to God, but then I decided He'd probably heard it before, so I gave myself a pass. I looked up at the stained glass, patterned in soothing blues, greens, and lavenders. "I need a little help, man. I don't know if I can handle this one on my own, so…if you could see fit to intervene a little, just enough to keep Flynn alive, I'd…well, shit, I'm not going to make any kind of lame promises about going to church or helping little old ladies cross the street. I'm trying to save the fucking world. That oughta be good enough. I guess this is when I'm glad there's not a priest here because if I heard some smug asshole talking about your grand fucking plan for all this, and Becks' life was in your hands…yeah, I'd probably strangle the son of a bitch. And I guess you frown on that.

"So yeah. I need a little help. I can't save your creation if you can't save the woman I love. It's not that I'll be all pissy and sit in the corner pouting, it's more that I'll be too busy trying to burn the whole goddamned place to slag myself. If you're listening, if you're even still out there and haven't flitted away to some other grand experiment, I'm asking you to save Rebecca's life. You do that, and I'll try my damndest to kick Lucifer's ass for you and keep your pearly gates pristine. Don't have a fucking clue how I'm going to do that, but I'll give it my best shot."

I bowed my head and said, "Amen," more because it felt like something I should do than any sense of actually having prayed. Then I sat there, head bowed, leaning forward with my elbows on my knees, feeling Flynn cling to life by her fingertips through our link.

"Wow," a voice from the back of the room came, oozing like molten tar, slow and unctuous. "That was eloquent, Harker. Seems like there's more to you than your reputation lets on."

I shot off the pew and spun around to see who was speaking. I hadn't heard the door to the chapel open and hadn't seen anyone when I walked in, so I was immediately on my guard. It's not like there were a lot of hiding places in the little room, so where had this asshole come from?

The man standing at the very rear of the center aisle grinned at me. He was tall, a solid six and a half feet, and rail thin. His wide Joker grin gave his whole face a stretched look, like the skin was pulled almost to snapping over a frame too large for the flesh. He wore a pinstriped charcoal suit that wouldn't look out of place on a mortician, but this was not a man built to comfort the grieving. I could tell by the glee in his beady eyes that this was a man made to cause pain, to get into the nooks and crannies of a person's psyche and rip them apart from the inside out.

I flickered into my Sight, and the man in front of me almost vanished. His aura was a magical siphon, leeching the life from everything around him, like a black hole of pain and anguish. His human guise stripped away, I could see the elongated jaw, the sloped fleshless skull narrowing down to a mouthful of vicious teeth. His long fingers were more like flowing stalks, each tipped with a suction cup on the end. I dropped my Sight as the demon stepped forward, and I slipped a knife out of my belt into my hand.

"A Gloom, huh?" I said, wracking my brain for information on the creature in front of me. "This is good. I've never killed one of you before. I can check you off my list."

"No, Mr. Harker, I think you will not," the demon said, his smile stretching even wider. The illusion was starting to fray at the edges, and I could see a hint of pointed teeth at the corners of his mouth. "I think I will siphon out all the magic from your body, and then as I am digesting that delicious morsel, I'll slit your throat and leave you to drown in your own blood. Then you can go meet my master without any of your protections. I think we'll do that instead."

"I think you should fuck right off with that bullshit," I said, and flung the knife in an underhand throw. It streaked through the air and plunged into his midsection, prompting a smile from the demon.

He pulled the knife out of his gut and held it up in front of his face. "Nice. Silvered edges. I bet the vampires and weres just hate that. I don't really care, though." Then he raised his arm and flung the knife back at me. Not having a demon's resilience, I chose to duck behind a pew as the knife whizzed over my head. It clunked into the drywall next to the stained-glass window and clattered to the floor. I stood up, another knife in my hand, and flung that one in a much stronger overhead throw. It tumbled end over end, burying itself into the creature's belly inches from where the first one landed.

"Don't you learn, Harker? It's going to take more than mere physical trauma…what?" He plucked at his stomach, yanking his hand back from the hilt of the knife, then dropping to one knee. "What did you do to this blade?"

"Oh that?" I asked. "I dipped that one in holy water and had it blessed by a nun this afternoon. Is it a little more effective than the other knife?"

"You…*bastard*!" He took a deep breath, gritted his teeth, and yanked the knife out, letting it drop to the floor at his feet. The demon stood, not as straight this time and certainly not smiling anymore. "I was going to kill you quickly. Just suck the magic out of you, slit your throat and send you on your merry way. But you had to go and be an asshole. So now I'm going to drain you of every drop of magic you've got, then I'm going to haul you back to your bitch nun friend, and I'm going to suck out every ounce of power in every artifact she's ever touched. Then I'm going to make you watch while I defile her on the altar of her church, and finally, once you're reduced to a gibbering pile of human excrement sobbing on the floor, I'll cut open your throat and piss in your neck as you lay bleeding, staring up and me wishing you'd never heard the name of Lachliss, Demon Lord of Despair!"

"Wow," I said, pointing my Ruger LCP at the demon's head. "You've put way too much thought into this shit. You should see a therapist. Maybe Lucifer knows somebody." I squeezed the trigger on the little .380 twice, sending two holy water-tipped bullets streaking toward the demon. He was expecting them to be something that could actually hurt him this time, so he made sure not to have his head where I was putting bullets. He dove to the left, letting out a cry of pain as his guts reacted to the impact, but my shots passed harmlessly overhead.

I stalked down the center aisle, my pistol moving ahead of me, but when I got to the aisle where the demon dove, he was already gone. "Fuck," I muttered, then dove forward into a roll as I felt the air shift behind me. The demon's arms clasped shut on empty air, and I came up on one knee and spun around. I fired twice, starting low and sweeping my arm up as I went. The first bullet went between the creature's legs, but the second caught him square in the chest.

The demon staggered back, clutching its chest and snarling at me, then sank to one knee in the center aisle. I stood but didn't approach the dying monster. The last thing I needed was to get within arm's reach of a demon that could literally suck the magic out of me with a touch.

At least that's what I thought. It turns out the literal last thing I needed was for a pair of well-meaning but doomed security guards to blunder into the chapel right at that moment and point guns at my face. Because that's exactly what happened.

Then my day got even worse.

1 4

"Put your hands up!" One of the guards, a smooth-cheeked black man with a face like Denzel and a voice like Chris Tucker said, aiming his pistol right at my chest.

I did so, summoning up my will and letting energy flow through me as I whispered, *"Tergora inpenetrabiles."* I felt my skin harden to the consistency of diamond as the magic coursed over my body. It was going to make it hard as hell to maneuver until I released the spell, but hopefully it would keep me from getting any new orifices blown into me by an overzealous youngster.

"Let's stay calm, officers. I can explain everything," I said. My interior monologue was running at a hundred miles an hour, screaming, *How the fuck are you going to explain this in a way that doesn't get you committed, incarcerated, or committed AND incarcerated?*

"I said put your hands up, motherfucker!" the kid yelled again, his gun starting to wobble. That's the thing about guns. They're not exactly light. After you hold one pointed at someone for a while, especially with your arms extended and your elbows locked, like this kid, your arms start to get tired. Then your gun wobbles off target, then you fight harder to bring it back on target. Then your finger twitches, and if you're like this kid and have your hands wrapped around the grip so tight your knuckles have gone white, the odds of you shooting something you don't want to shoot go up. A lot. Thus the magical shielding.

"My hands are up, dipshit." I knew as soon as it left my lips that I probably should have left off the "dipshit." I am not known for my poise and decorum when people are pointing guns at me, though. I'm more known for kicking ass and killing demons.

"What did you just call me, asshole?" The kid stepped forward, his face going red. Now that he was pissed off, he wasn't terrified anymore. Good. Angry I could deal with. Scared was going to get somebody hurt. Probably me.

When the guard stepped forward, I reached out with my left hand and swatted his gun to the side. Then I reminded him of the giant tactical error he made when telling me to put my hands up. He never instructed me to drop my gun. So I lowered my right hand and pressed the barrel of my Ruger to his forehead.

"Drop your weapon, officer." I kept my voice low and calm, and my finger off the trigger. The kid was in the aisle in front of his older partner, a rotund man who looked a lot like a fatter Wilforn Brimley. This was the kind of hospital security guard I could get behind. The kind that has a gun, but it might as well be glued into his holster for as often as he's drawn it. The kind of guard who can tell you how to get to the hospital cafeteria, probably in three languages, and give you recommendations for takeout, but isn't going to be the first guy on the scene if some psycho starts shooting up the ER. This fat old white dude was exactly the type of guard I wanted to deal with. Hell, I had a pistol pressed up against his partner's face and he still hadn't drawn his sidearm.

"Hey there, let's calm down," Wilford Brimley said, stepping forward and a little to one side.

"Not another step, Quaker Oats," I said, glaring at him. "Or you're wearing your partner's brains as mascara." Wilford froze and held both his hands up where I could see them.

"Okay, boys," I said, returning my gaze to baby Denzel. "Here's what's going to happen. You're going to both put your weapons on the pew beside you, then you're going to go sit down in the back for ten minutes. In that time, the body of what you think was a man will dissolve into nothing but ash, or maybe goop. It really depends on what kind of demon. But either way, in the next ten minutes, you'll realize that something really fucked up has happened, and you have no clue what it was, but it wasn't a homicide, and while you saw me shoot *something*, it wasn't human, and therefore, not your goddamn problem. When you've seen everything you need to see to convince you I'm neither a murderer nor experiencing a psychotic break, you can retrieve your weapons and go to the nearest bar, where I suggest you drink yourselves blind while trying very hard to forget that we ever met. How does that sound?"

Chris Tucker didn't say anything, but Wilford looked past me and spoke up. "That would sound fine if the guy you shot wasn't on his feet and standing right behind you."

I could almost feel the Gloom's breath on the back of my neck. "Well, goddamn."

That was all I had time to say before the asshole demon snatched me up by the collar and flung me into the far wall. I hit the rack of votive candles with a crash and fell to the floor in a cascade of broken glass and melted wax. Lucky for me there were only a few candles burning, and I didn't catch fire. Yeah, lucky.

I scrambled to my knees and looked around for my pistol. Two shots left, and then I'd have to fight this bastard with magic. And he sucked magic out of the air for funsies. Fuck. I grabbed my gun and stood, whipping my head from side to side looking for the demon.

Then I froze as I saw him, his hands pressed to the side of little Denzel's once-pretty face. The Gloom had dropped his human guise completely, and the suckers on the ends of his fingers were buried into the guard's temples and jawline, little rivulets of blood streaming down his face where the demon pierced him. The guard's face was ashen, a sickly gray color that does not exists as a natural skin tone. The man's mouth was open wide, and his eyes bulged in agony as the Gloom literally sucked the life force out of him.

There is some speculation that the first vampire came into being when a Gloom mated with a human and created a new type of Cambion. There was another theory that Luke was the first vampire and he got his powers by making a deal with a Gloom to feed it more life than it could ever desire in exchange for granting him a portion of its abilities. Luke always calls the first theory stupid and laughs at the second, but there's something in his eyes when he does that tells me there's a grain of truth in there somewhere. Luke wasn't the first vampire, but he damn sure was one of the earliest, and what he knows about his origins and what he tells are two very different things.

A muffled *thump* from the aisle snapped me out of my reverie, and I looked up to see the young guard's body drop to the floor, his life completely drained. When he fell, he didn't look like the hale and hearty man of twenty-five or so that pointed a gun at me. He looked a lot more like an octogenarian suffering from extreme starvation. His face was sunken and withered, his skin gray, and his hair completely white. I heard a soft crackling sound when his face hit the ground, like stepping on dry leaves in autumn, but it was the guard's skin splitting open, all his vitality leeched from him by the Gloom.

The older guard slapped at his holster frantically, jerking up on the butt of his gun but forgetting to unsnap the holster. His gun rode up on his thigh, but the more he pulled, the more his holster and his uniform pants got twisted until he finally pulled hard enough to shift himself completely off-balance and fall back on a diagonal, careening off a pew and plopping down on his butt in the aisle with one foot laying across his dead partner's back.

"Stay the fuck away from me!" the guard cried, his voice high and thin with terror. I saw tears leaking from the corners of his eyes as I rose to my feet, steadying the pistol with my left hand. The Gloom spun to me, ducking down and snatching up the dead guard's body with preternatural speed. It flung the corpse at me, and I barely side-stepped the poor boy's body. I heard a crash from behind me as it destroyed the shelf, and I squeezed off my last two rounds.

The Gloom, unfettered by its human guise, moved so fast it looked like nothing but a blur. It spun out of the way of my bullets and charged at me through the narrow aisle. "Run!" I yelled at the surviving guard, who nodded and got to his feet. He staggered, tripping over the end of a pew and almost going down, but he managed to right himself and charge out of the chapel.

The demon slammed into me, its tentacle fingers waving in front of my face. It latched onto my head but couldn't penetrate my spell-hardened flesh. "That won't save you, Harker. It will just prolong your ordeal," the demon hissed in my face. Its mouth yawned wide in front of me, and I got a good look at the triple row of pointed teeth just inches from my nose.

"Prolong this, fuckwit," I snarled, slamming my forehead down into the creature's mouth. I heard a sickening *crunch* as my flesh, now harder than diamond, shattered fangs and cut the monster's lips to ribbons. It yanked back from me, planting both hands in my chest and shoving me back into the wall as it went.

I hit the drywall and felt it give beneath my back. Impervious or not, the impact knocked the breath from me, and my arms flew out to the sides. My pistol flew from my grip, and I slid to the ground, landing in a pile of shattered candle holders, splintered shelves, and toppled religious statues. I reached out with my right hand and felt it wrap around something heavy. I pushed off from the floor with my left and swung my makeshift club around without even looking to see what it was.

The statue of the Virgin Mary slammed into the demon's head, whipping its jaw around and leaving a burn like I'd pressed a hot iron to the Gloom's flesh. It let out a shriek like a thousand bats screaming, and my vision went white from the pain in my eardrums. I wobbled, but didn't go down, and I drew the statue back for another swing. Mary slammed into the demon's head again, and again its skin seared like it was being branded.

I pressed the advantage, literally, shoving my way forward and smashing the demon in the head again and again with the Blessed Mother's effigy. It got an arm up, but I heard the bone snap like a twig when I cracked the statue into it and saw the arm sizzle and start to burn as I kept in contact with the creature's flesh.

"I don't know what you're doing, but I really hope you'll keep it up for another thirty seconds or so," I muttered to whatever higher power was lending a hand. The statue began to glow with a pure white light, so clean and so crisp that it made my eyes water, but I didn't let up. Again and again I swung, battering the demon with Mary's head, until finally I got enough room to plant my feet and get a solid grip on the foot-and-a-half statue with both hands. I swung at the staggering Gloom like I was Babe Ruth calling my shot, and I slammed the holy relic into the demon's face with every ounce of strength I could manage. I felt more than heard the statue crack in half right above my grip, and blazing white light poured from the effigy, engulfing the demon.

The demon's face disintegrated. It didn't crack, it didn't burn, it literally turned to ash. The statue caught the Gloom right at the hinge of its jaw and buried the head of the Mother of Christ into the monster's face. It stared at me, its yellow eyes wide, and opened its bloody mouth one last time. Then, as I stood there holding the statue of the Virgin Mary pressed to its head, the demon turned to dust from its head to its toes. The glow of the statue winked out, and the top half of it fell to the floor, snapped off clean at the point of impact.

The end came so suddenly I lost my balance and pitched forward between two pews. The end of the pew caught me right in the gut, reminding me that I had a half-healed broken rib and bringing stars of pain to my eyes. I dropped the bottom half of the statue, which thumped to the carpet right under my face as I doubled over the pew. The statue, which mere seconds before was the holiest weapon I had ever laid my hands on, was now just a hollow chunk of antique painted plaster rolling around on the floor. I stared at it, baffled, as a golden ring tumbled from inside the statue to lie on the floor.

I picked up the ring, feeling its warmth in my hand. It wasn't the statue at all, it was this thing, *inside* the statue, that turned a demon to dust. I turned it over in my fingers, trying to see what was so special about this chunk of metal. I looked at the face of the ring, where a symbol was emblazoned in the gold, and everything came clear all at once. There on the ring, was a pair of snakes twined around a healer's staff—the symbol of doctors and healers for centuries. This ring was the Implement. This was Raphael's caduceus.

If recent history served, that meant that somewhere in this

hospital was an unwitting angel who was missing his class ring. If I found it, I'd have the last Archangel I was looking for. I'd also have the greatest magical healer the world had ever known, and if the onrushing darkness I felt through our soul bond was any indication, that's what it was going to take to save the woman I loved.

15

I stood up, holding the ring in the palm of my hand, and pulled my phone out of my pocket. The screen was shattered, but all I needed to do was turn it on and Dennis could find me. "Hey, Sparkles?" I said, looking around the room at the devastation in the chapel.

"Yeah, Harker. I'm monitoring Flynn's vitals, but—"

"Why would the Implement be hidden in a statue of Mary?" I asked.

"What?"

I looked around. No surveillance cameras in the chapel. I guess some things really are still sacred. "I found the caduceus, Dennis. It was in a statue of the Virgin Mary. There was a fight with a demon, and…it doesn't matter. I need to find Raphael."

"Yeah, that's kinda the whole point of the trip, Harker, but what are you going to do, hand a stick with snakes wrapped around it to everyone in Manhattan?"

"It's a ring," I said. "And no. I think he's going to be close. All the other Archangels have been drawn to their Implements, ever since we took Michael his sword and started this whole ball rolling. It seems like the connections between the Host and their tools has been growing stronger this whole time."

"That would explain how Azrael was separated from his sword for years and years, but only started really closing in on it a few months ago," Dennis replied. "Maybe their connection has been getting stronger as more of the Archangels found themselves again."

"If that's the case, I wonder…" I let my voice trail off as I opened my Sight and glanced down at the ring in my hand. In the supernatural spectrum I couldn't even look directly at it, the thing was glowing so bright. And it wasn't just the light. It *sang*, for lack of a better word. It gave off a sound in the supernatural aural spectra that was unlike anything I'd ever heard. Hell, any sound that I picked up in that end of things was unusual. "Yeah, this thing is giving off a *lot* more magic than any of the other Implements did. It's got to have something to do with the fact that it's the last one."

"Do you think you can use it to find Raphael?" Dennis asked.

"I don't know." I closed my fist around the ring, cutting off most of its aura except for what leaked out between my fingers, and looked around. I turned slowly in a circle, holding the ring at my waist and watching the magical currents ebb and flow around us. After a couple of long revolutions, there it was. "I think I've got a trail, Dennis."

I opened the door of the chapel, peeking out into the hall to make sure there wasn't a riot squad bearing down on me. I was leaving the scene of one of the weirdest murders even I had ever seen. "Hey, Sparkles?"

"Yeah?"

"Can you get Agent Pravesh to get some of her cleaners over here? I…well, I kinda made a huge mess in the chapel, and there's a dead security guard to deal with."

"You mean cover up."

"To-may-to, to-mah-to. Just make the call, unicorn boy." An idea struck. "Hey, Dennis?"

"Jesus, what now?"

"Most of the Archangels have taken on disguises that tied to their angelic roles, right? Michael was a fighter, Azrael was a murderer, Gabriel was a bookseller, that kind of thing, right?"

"What are you getting at, Harker?"

"Raphael was the healer. I'm going to follow the trail of magic, but while I do, I want you to look through the hospital's records."

"Easy enough," the disembodied man with the head of a unicorn replied. "What am I looking for?"

"The best doctor here," I said. "Not a specialist, necessarily, but the person that gets called in when there's a case that's totally fucked. The person who saves the ones who should be dead before they get here, but sometimes once they're done with the patient, they go on to live long and healthy lives, against all odds."

"You think that's going to be our Archangel?"

"I don't know," I admitted. "But it's worth a shot. At least I think it's worth a shot. I'm going to see where this trail leads me. You get in touch with Pravesh and get back to me about whoever the super-doc is."

"Pravesh is taking care of it. I'll have your doc's name, if they exist, in a couple of minutes."

I slipped the phone in my pocket and walked to the front of the chapel. I picked up my messenger bag and slung it over my shoulder. I turned to go, then turned back and looked at the stained-glass window. "I gotta tell you, big guy. If that's your idea of a sign, I have no fucking idea what it meant." Then I followed the silver thread of power up the aisle and out the back door of the chapel. I had an angel to find.

I walked up the aisle and pushed through the door into the hall, looking both ways in my normal vision before reopening my Sight to follow the thread of magic that flowed from my hand. I can see the mundane world while my Sight is active, but it's kinda weird, like trying to watch a 3-D movie without the glasses. This was even worse because of the constant music that seemed to come from everywhere. There wasn't a SWAT team in the hall, so I called that a win.

There was a single thread of white light flowing from the ring, kinda like a very thin ribbon just floating in midair, coming from between my fingers and snaking its way down the hall and taking a left back the way I'd come. I followed the trail around the corner, managing to avoid a pair of onrushing NYPD officers leading a quartet of highly equipped and very serious-looking men in black tactical gear at a fast walk.

The lead SWAT guy looked at me and gave me a nod. "We've got this, sir."

I nodded back and kept tracing the magic back to what was hopefully its source, or its wielder...hell, I hoped I was following this thread to an angel. I was encouraged that Pravesh had jumped on the cleanup of my little scuffle before some grieving family decided to take a moment in quiet reflection and found a scene out of a horror movie.

The farther I walked, the thicker the ribbon of light became, growing from barely more than a thread to a strong rope of light that seemed to almost vibrate in the air. I walked past the turn to the Emergency Department and through a door marked AUTHORIZED PERSONNEL ONLY. I didn't even pause, just gave myself authorization and went right on in.

On the other side of the official-looking door, much to my chagrin, was just more corridor. There was less beeping and chatter back here, and the one nurse who saw me did a double-take but returned to whatever she was doing when I didn't stick out as a threat. I followed the magical trail around a corner to the left and got a sinking feeling in my stomach. Above the "T" hallway, pointing in the same direction my trail led me, was a big sign labeled "Operating Theatre."

I stepped into a room marked "Staff Restroom" and pulled out my phone. "Dennis, do you have anything on our possible angels?"

"I have three possibilities."

"Three? How does that work?"

"I ran an analysis of the national hospital mortality rate for each department, then compared that against developed countries around the world to get a sense of how the numbers were. Mediocre, by the way. American healthcare isn't all that great compared to the rest of the world."

"Not exactly something you or I are that worried about, pal. Your hacking gave you three names?"

"There was a lot of other math and analysis involved. Do you actually give a shit, or do you trust that I poked around in a lot of places I wasn't supposed to be, dicked with a bunch of numbers I wasn't supposed to see, and compared all that data to a pile of other data that I also wasn't supposed to have?"

"I trust you. Who are the three?"

"The first one is a pediatrics nurse. She's got a much higher survival rate in NICU cases than the norm."

"Where is the pediatric unit?" I asked.

"Third floor."

"Let's push her down the list. The trail seems to be getting warmer, so I don't think there are two floors between me and Raphael."

"Okay, then that is also going to eliminate our second option. He's the heard of cardiovascular surgery, and he's on vacation in Aruba for three weeks."

"Yeah, probably not him. Who's left?"

"Dr. Ralph Tennon a trauma surgeon with the best survival rate of any doctor on the East Coast. This guy doesn't lose patients. He's the guy they call when somebody is well and truly fucked, and better than half the time, he saves them."

"That kinda sounds like somebody who's rocking a little bit of a gift from God, doesn't it?"

"Yeah," Dennis said. "You don't get those kind of numbers just by making sure your OR is super-clean and nobody makes any avoidable errors on the table."

"Where can I find Dr. Styles?" I asked. "I think I've got a piece of jewelry for him."

Dennis was quiet for longer than I was used to. Frankly, three seconds was more quiet than I was accustomed to with him. "What's wrong, Dennis? Is Dr. Styles in Aruba, too?"

"No, he's here."

"Great. Tell me where and I'll go give him his ring. Then we can get Flynn patched up and head home."

"Remember when I said that Styles doesn't lose patients?"

"Yeah," I said. "That's another reason to think he's probably our guy. Or our...they, since angels don't really have a gender unless they want to."

"Well, it looks like his streak is about to get shot to shit. His patient just coded. They're trying to bring her back right now."

"That sucks. Well, maybe finding out he's an angel will make up for losing a patient."

"That's not the part that's got me upset, Harker."

"What…Dennis?"

His voice was quiet, barely more than a whisper through the phone's speaker. "Yeah."

"Who is Styles' patient?"

"You know."

"Tell me, Dennis."

"Listen."

"I can't hear a goddamn thing over this fucking ring singing angelic hymns in my fucking ears. Tell me, Dennis." I dropped my Sight, and the ring's magical glow shut off. The song it was blaring through my head stopped, too, leaving me in a deafening silence.

The kind of silence I hadn't felt in a couple of years. The kind of silence I thought I'd never feel again. The silence that said I was alone in my head. My link to Becks was gone. *Becks* was gone. I reached out, but she wasn't there. This wasn't like when I couldn't feel her because she was too far away, or when something was interfering. She was *gone.*

"What room?" I asked, my voice thick and almost incomprehensible even to me.

"OR 3. But you don't want to—"

"Shut the fuck up, Dennis. That's Flynn back there. And the man operating on her is a goddamn Archangel and he doesn't even know it. So you better fucking believe I want to. And nothing had better try to stop me." I turned the knob on the bathroom and pushed. The door opened inward. I didn't care. I pushed, and the door blew out into the hall in a rain of splinters. I stepped through the destruction, ignoring the gasps and stares as I emerged.

I turned down the hall toward the operating rooms, stopping at the one marked "3." I turned the handle, but it was locked. I turned it again, this time pouring power through my hand. The handle snapped off and the door swung open into a scene like every shitty TV medical drama ever created. Except this one was worse, because in the middle of the chaos, the yelling, and the swearing, lay my fiancée, and as I stepped into the room, the only sound coming from her monitors was a steady *BEEEEEEEEEEP*.

nurse in scrubs turned to me and shouted," You can't be in here!"

There was a cluster of people surrounding the table. Nurses, doctors, anesthesiologist—all of them moving at a frantic pace. Two nurses were working with a doctor at the lower part of the patient's torso, while a tall black man with a shaved head and a goatee reached behind him for a set of paddles.

"Charging," a nurse said, then, "ready."

"Clear," the doctor said, and everyone stepped back. That was the first time I could see her, and even then it was just a glimpse, and almost impossible to recognize. But I saw the little birthmark at the corner of her left eye, and the mole on her forehead that she almost always kept her hair down over, and it hit me like a hammer to the gut. It was Rebecca, *my* Rebecca, laying there, and she was dying.

The doctor pressed the paddles to her chest, and she jerked as the current poured into her body. The steady cry of the monitor blipped once, twice, the fell back to an uninterrupted electronic scream. The doctor turned his head and babbled something to the nurse about charging something to something, then his eyes locked on mine.

"Who the hell is that and what is he doing there? Somebody get that man the fuck out of my operating room!" he barked, and a burly male nurse peeled off from where Becks lay and started toward me.

"Sir, you're going to have to—"

I never found out what I was going to have to do. He had to take a nap because I laid a right cross on the corner of his jaw and dropped him like a sack of potatoes. Then I was at the table, not knowing exactly how I got there. I slipped into my Sight, and the ribbon of magic had turned into a thick braided rope running from my hand to the black doctor's chest. This was our guy. I found him, now he needed to do his part.

He looked up at me, and I could tell by the way his face changed that he knew I was with her. "Sir, you can't be here. I'm doing everything I can, but—"

"Put this on," I said, holding out the ring.

He looked confused, like I'd just asked him a calculus question in the middle of my physical. "What? No! I'm trying to—"

I held up my left hand and growled out one word, *"Infierno."* My hand burst into flames, extending a good foot past my fingers. "Take the fucking ring or I'm going to burn your fucking eyebrows off."

"I don't care what you do to me. I am not going to let you kill this woman." He turned back to Flynn. I still had my Sight open, and I could see her in two places. Flynn was lying on the table in front of me and standing about eight feet away looking at me. There was a thread of magic, of *her*, tying Soul-Flynn to the real Flynn, but it was very faint, and I could see it fraying.

But she wasn't gone. I could see her, and that meant I could save her. I dropped my Sight and extinguished the flame on my hand. I reached across Flynn's lifeless body and grabbed Styles' hand, pulling him toward me. He struggled, looking down at Becks' open chest cavity in horror as I stretched his whole body across her. It was awful, but if I was right, it wouldn't matter because he was about to turn into an angel and he could heal her. If I was wrong, well, it still wouldn't matter.

I ripped the glove off his right hand and slapped the caduceus ring into his palm, then stepped back. There was a flash of light, and I clapped my hands over my ears as the angelic chorus I'd been hearing ever since I picked up the ring crescendoed into something almost deafening.

When I could look at him again, Dr. Ralph Styles was gone. In his place was a six-foot-tall Archangel, in all his angelic glory. Which I'll admit was a lot more impressive before I started basically running a dormitory for wayward celestial beings. "Raphael, I presume?" I asked.

"Yes," he said, and I swear it felt like there were trumpets heralding his every word. "Thank you. I have missed my ring. Now I can resume my work." He looked confused, then looked around. "Where am I? What place is this?"

"That's a long story," I said. "But for now, can you put a little of your angel mojo into healing her?" I pointed at Flynn, lying ignored on the table. Every other doctor and nurse had backed away or fallen to the floor when Raphael transformed. Like I said, I'm a little less impressed these days.

He looked at Flynn. "This is a human," he said, confusion knitting his brow. "I don't heal humans. I heal the Host. Humans are built to die. It's what they do. Die and breed."

"Well, this one was injured fighting demons trying to find your ring so we could wake you up from the nap you've been taking for the last couple of millennia, so how about showing a little fucking gratitude and saving her goddamned life?" I asked, my voice edging nearer and nearer to hysteria as the thread tying Soul-Flynn to her body frayed every second.

"She was attacked by the Fallen? They have made it to this plane?" This seemed to strike a nerve with doctor angel because he now looked genuinely upset. "Of course I will heal her. No human should ever encounter the Fallen. That is the job of the Host. Where is Michael? Keeping the gates closed is his responsibility. This is all very distressing."

Great, from super-surgeon to nebbishy Angel C-3PO in half a minute. "Heal her," I said, pointing to Flynn. "She doesn't have much time."

"Oh, of course." He looked at her body, her stomach cavity held open so the doctors could try to repair the damage done by the demon's claws. Shaking his head, he released the clamps and pressed her flesh together, then his hands were wreathed in the same white light that I'd followed all the way from the chapel.

The light pulsed at first, weak, then stronger and stronger, like he was exercising a muscle he hadn't used in a long time. Which he was, come to think of it. But the longer he held his hands pressed to her stomach, the brighter and steadier the light became, until finally there was a glow around the whole table. I watched through my Sight as the thread between Becks' soul and her body grew thicker and thicker, then Soul-Rebecca vanished as she was pulled back into herself. And back into me, as the Rebecca-shaped hole in my own soul was filled once again. She was back, and I could feel her, once more a part of me. The very best part.

Raphael's hands faded to the "normal" level of angelic glow, and I let go of my Sight so I could take a look at him in the mundane world. Yeah, definitely an angel. He was rocking the wings and everything.

"Thank you," I said.

"Of course," he replied with a nod. "She was injured doing the work we were tasked with. It is, of course, only proper that I should restore her."

I snorted a little. "Yeah, you might want to give some of your 'brothers' lessons on the proper."

"You know where the others are?"

I opened my mouth to answer, but a noise from the table drew my attention. Flynn was still out, but her eyelids were fluttering. I looked at her chest and stomach, but there was no hint of the damage she'd sustained. Her skin looked as smooth and unmarked as it had the night before in Charlotte. I reached down to her, brushing her cheek with the back of my knuckles, and her eyes fluttered open.

"Hey, babe," I said, pushing calming thoughts through our link. "You gave us a scare there for a minute, but you're going to be fine. Let me just get this shit off you." I pulled the tube from her mouth and freed her from the tangle of tubes and wires.

"I feel...great, actually." She looked at me in confusion. "Why do I feel so good? I got my ass kicked by a demon. And I think I kinda died. What the fuck, Harker?"

I laughed. I couldn't help it, it just burst out of me. "That should be our fucking motto. 'What the fuck, Harker?' It's gotta be the single most oft-uttered sentence that's ever been directed at me. It's a long story, with a bunch of demons, a big fight in the hospital chapel, and ring in a statue, and that guy." I pointed to Raphael.

He nodded to Becks. "Hello, mortal. I have healed your injuries sustained in your confrontation with the Fallen. In the future, I would strongly recommend you not dabble in the affairs of the divine. Our conflicts are not for such as yourself. I may not be here to save you in the future."

Flynn looked at the officious angel then at me. Then back to Raphael, then back to me. And we both burst out laughing. I pulled her upright on the table and swung her legs off, ripping the shitty gown and remnants of the shit they had her covered with off and throwing it to the floor. Then I pulled her to me and wrapped my arms around her. I held her like that for a long time, then after a while I realized that her shoulder was wet, and it was my tears running down her back. I pulled back and kissed her.

I looked her in the eyes and said, "Don't ever do that to me again. You scared the fuck out of me, Becks. I don't know what I'd do if I lost you. I..."

She reached up and laid her index finger across my lips. "Shhh. I know, baby. I know. Don't worry. I'm fine. We're fine. I'm alive, we've got the last angel we needed, now we can go save the world. Again. But sweetheart, there's one thing I'm going to need before we do that."

"Anything, babe. You just let me know and I'll make it happen for you."

"Can you get me some clothes? Mine were kinda shredded by a demon, and now I'm fucking freezing." I pulled her back to my chest, laughing hysterically again. After at least a minute of this, we pulled apart. This time I looked down at her, completely naked except for her panties, covered in antiseptic swab and her hair tucked up in a pale blue cap.

"Goddamn, you're beautiful," I said. "Now let me go get you some clothes. We've got a universe to save."

"What do you mean, mortal?" Raphael asked. "How is the world in danger, and what can you do about it?"

I looked at him, standing there butt naked in the middle of the operating room wearing nothing but his wings and a puzzled look on his face. I shook my head and said, "Can you…tone down the angelic look a little?"

"Of course," he said, and with a wave of his hand he was dressed in a set of dark blue surgical scrubs. With giant white wings sticking through the back, because when you're an angel, your magical clothing comes with wing holes, apparently. "Now, I had asked you a question."

"Yeah," I said. "About that. You remember your brother Lucifer, right? Good-looking guy, but kind of a dick? Yeah, well he's decided that since your dad's gone on a walkabout and nobody's minding the store, that it's time to revisit his whole 'war on Heaven' idea. We're going to stop him."

"Who is we?" Raphael asked.

"Me, my friends, and all the Archangels. Well, except for Uriel. Lucifer dragged him to Hell and is currently torturing him until the time is right to storm the pearly gates."

For the first time, I saw something approaching emotion on Raphael's face. "Uriel? Lucifer has Uriel? In Hell?"

"Yep," I said.

"We must rescue him."

"That's what you're here for, buddy. We're gonna go to Hell and save Uriel. Or, failing that, we're just going to kick the shit out of Lucifer and keep him from using Uriel's Implement to ascend back into Heaven."

"How do you intend to vanquish Lucifer? He was second only to Michael as one of Heaven's generals, and he is much more powerful than any human. You would not stand a chance against him."

I took a deep breath, then let it out. "Yeah. I know."

"And yet you intend to enter into battle with him anyway, knowing that you will likely fail and die a horrible death."

"That pretty much sums it up."

"Why?" He cocked his head to the side, as if examining some strange new species.

"Why what?" I asked.

"Why would you willingly sacrifice yourself in a hopeless cause? You know there is practically no chance you will emerge victorious, or even survive. So why do it?"

I looked back at Flynn and smiled. "Buddy, some things are worth fighting for. Some things are worth dying for. Pretty much every one of those things I've ever found is right here on earth. Shit, most of them are right here in this room. So yeah, I'm gonna go to Hell with a bunch of half-crazy angels, some monsters right out of the movies, and a couple of humans with more guts than sense, and we're going to kick Lucifer's ass. Do I know how? Fuck no. That's the best part about being human, dude. We make shit up as we go along. It's what makes us unpredictable, and to creatures like Lucifer, it's what makes us dangerous.

"You know what else makes us dangerous?" I asked, looking back at Flynn sitting there with the scraps of a sheet wrapped around her. "Having something to fight for. Thanks to your healing mojo, I've got something worth saving. Lucifer might be this badass divine general and a warrior the likes of which the world has never seen, but I'm Quincy fucking Harker. And he ain't ready for me."

<hr>

THE QUEST FOR GLORY CONCLUDES IN *SYMPATHY FOR THE DEVIL.*

IV

SYMPATHY FOR THE DEVIL

1

"What the hell do you mean only Harker can go with you?" Flynn asked, her voice climbing already. I really hoped Glory was still bulletproof, because if she wasn't, I had a feeling I was going to be short a guardian angel here in a minute.

"Harker can go because of what he is. He's not fully human, and not exactly mortal, so the transition won't kill him. I still have enough divinity in me to make the crossing, and obviously the Archangels won't have any problems."

Looking at them when she said that, I felt like there might be a lot of problems with the Archangels. We were in the apartment I'd converted into a "war room" with all the interior walls that could be removed taken out to make it mostly one big open space. I was sitting at the head of the conference table I'd rented for the duration of the current crisis, or until the world ended, whichever came first. Flynn had been sitting in the chair to my left, but now she was on her feet, leaning over the polished wood surface and glaring daggers at Glory, who sat diagonally across the table from her.

I looked over at Jo Henry, who sat next to Flynn, giving her a pleading glance. Jo shook her head and rolled her chair back from the table a little, making sure she wasn't in the splash zone of whatever came next.

Please don't beat the shit out of my guardian angel, honey, I sent along the mental link I shared with Flynn.

Becks dropped her head to communicate with me. *Did you know about this?* The thought that came back to me had tinges of accusation to it, but I let it go. Flynn was pissed, and when cops get pissed off, they lean toward accusing people of things. Especially when that someone is their almost-always-guilty fiancé.

No, I swear to...well, whatever you want me to swear to. I didn't know shit about this ritual until just now. I thought worrying about it before we caught all the Pokémon would be stupid. Because if the world ended, I didn't need to care how to get to Hell, I'd already be there.

I hate it when you're the practical one. She looked up at Glory. "Explain it all to me, angel. Tell me why I should send my fiancé into literal Hell with a depowered guardian angel and a bunch of half-insane Archangels, one of which is a fucking psychopath, and another that won't even come out of his human suit."

"Hey, cut me a little slack," Mitchell Carson protested from where he sat at the far end of the conference table.

"Nothing from you right now, wingless wonder," Flynn snapped at him. "I'm dealing with this problem right now. We'll get to your angelic dysfunction in a minute." She turned back to Glory. "Tell me exactly why you think you're benching me and going off to fight the devil with my man, and I'll explain to you in no uncertain terms that nothing of the sort is actually happening."

"Because you'll die." Glory didn't beat around the bush, didn't try to sugarcoat anything, just dropped that turd right onto the table and let us all stare at it. "Hell is another dimension, another plane of existence. It's not like taking a day trip to the mall—you can't just waltz in like you're supposed to be there. Because you don't. You're a living, breathing human being, with a soul that you'd like to hang onto. Passing into one of the Divine planes means leaving your body behind and traveling as pure soul. Humans can do that, but they don't usually get to go back into their bodies when they're done. If you passed through the Gate with us, there would be nothing to tether you back to your body when it was time to go home."

"Then why can Harker go? He's human," Flynn said, straightening up and folding her arms over her chest. I recognized that pose. It was her determined look. Before she decided that I wasn't the biggest threat to the well-being of the city that Charlotte had ever seen, I got to see that look in the interview rooms at the Charlotte-Mecklenburg Police Department headquarters on multiple occasions. To say that Flynn and I had a relationship built on the most bizarre of foundations would be the understatement of the century.

Glory shook her head, blond curls bouncing around her face. "What in the world makes you think Harker's human? He's *never* been human."

"Well, I know he's part vampire, but what does that have to do with anything?" Flynn asked. I raised my eyebrow because I was pretty interested in the answer to this myself. I glanced over to where Luke sat at my right elbow, but his face was an unmoving mask.

"Do you even know what a vampire is, Detective?" Glory asked, then looked around the room. "Do any of you really know what a vampire is?" She glanced to her left, leaning forward to look Luke in the eye around Adam's massive form. "Do *you* even know what you are?"

Luke's face remained impassive. "I have my thoughts on the matter, but I have never had the opportunity to delve too deeply into the mechanics of my...endowment."

"That's a better phrase than you know, Luke. Far better. What happened when you became a vampire? Or, more to the point, when you became *the* vampire?" Glory asked. Her voice was gentle, like she knew she was going to say something hurtful but had to say it anyway.

"When my wife was killed..." He blinked quickly, several times, as if to bat away tears. Even after centuries, the pain he felt at the loss of his family still tortured him. "When she was murdered, I found a wise man, one knowledgeable in the dark arts. He cast a spell to give me strength, speed, stamina—the things I would need to remain alive until every one of the men who harmed my beautiful Ilona were dead, in the most painful ways I could imagine. What he did instead…made me the man I am today." Luke spread his hands with a wry smile that didn't even come close to his eyes.

"That's almost what happened," Glory said. "Or, at least, that's what it looked like from your side. There's another piece of the puzzle, however."

"Isn't there always?"

"The man you met. He wasn't a man. Not really. He was actually a demon named Skyffrax, a tinkerer from the Middle Circles. He wasn't a particularly powerful demon, but he had some frightening and potent ideas. Chief among them was that if he could enhance the human body sufficiently, demons could possess vessels on this plane that didn't die so easily."

"Makes sense," I said. "Especially back when Luke was turned, humans were pretty damned fragile."

"Exactly. Skyffrax conducted a lot of experiments over the millennia, some of them resulting in horrifically strong Cambion, but most doing nothing more than destroying the human and the demon he was trying to meld together. The Host tasked a group of us with keeping an eye on him, but we were not to interfere. As long as his experiments were destroying his demonic volunteers rather than strengthening them, we didn't really care. Then something happened."

"I happened," Luke said.

"Yes. You happened. A human with such a fire, such an indomitable will that he would allow his body to succumb to the strain of the fusing of his human body with a demonic soul. Skyffrax fused a part of his soul with your flesh, and his intent was to subvert your will with his own, to strengthen your flesh with his essence, and to take over your enhanced body."

"But only part of his plan worked," Luke said. I had to give him credit, he looked pretty calm for a dude who just found out that he existed because of a demonic science fair project.

"Yes. Your body was transformed according to plan, but he couldn't subvert your will."

"I've always said you're the most stubborn man I ever met," Cassie said, walking in from the kitchen to stand behind Luke's chair. Luke gave a soft smile at this, an unfamiliar expression on his face. Was that…tenderness? On *Dracula*?

"What happened to the demon?" I asked. "If he couldn't meld his soul with Luke, did he just pop back down to Hell?"

"No," Glory said. "He was…dispatched. Like I said, we were monitoring the situation closely, so when Skyffrax got close to his goal, we…eliminated the threat."

"But he was not entirely destroyed," Luke said. His face was still as unmoving as normal, but he had reached up to take Cassandra's hand where it lay on his shoulder.

Glory's face was almost as grim. "No. A part of Skyffrax remained melded with your soul, and a sliver of his essence was passed down whenever you turned someone."

"What about the others?" Jo asked.

"What others?"

"Other vampires. If Luke made a vampire, and that vampire made a vampire, do they all have pieces of demon in them?"

"No," Glory said. "It seems that the demon's life force dilutes too much after one generation from the source, so only the vampires that Luke has sired over the years have Skyffrax's essence in them."

"That explains why my progeny have always seemed stronger than most other vampires, I suppose," Luke said.

"But what's so special about me?" I asked.

"Many of us ask that same question, Harker, but in a different context." This shot at my self-esteem brought to you by Adam, Frankenstein's monster, who sat at the table between Glory and Luke. He gave me a lopsided grin, and I decided that I definitely liked him better when he didn't have a sense of humor.

"Harker is the son of two vampires that are of Dracula's line," Glory said. "And not even fully vampires, but humans bitten by vampires. He is an anomaly, something unique in all of history. We believe that is why he is…well, special."

"But wait a minute," I protested. "If the demonic essence faded within one generation of Luke, how did it affect my father? He was bitten by Luke's…lady friends." I had made the mistake once of referring to the trio of vampires that chewed on dear old Dad as Luke's "brides" once, and he corrected me with the back of his hand. I never called them brides again, and even forgave Luke once the bruise faded.

"The sisters and I were…close," Luke said. "They partook of my blood often, many more times than any other vampire I turned. It is likely that is the reason the demonic taint was able to carry through to your father."

"It may also be that the slivers of Skyffrax that lived within those female vampires latched on to Jonathan Harker's living soul and reacted differently to him than to another vampire. We will never know, but we do know that Harker is unique in his heritage, and the touch of demon in his nature will allow him to pass through the planes without harm."

"That also explains why I must not accompany you," Luke said.

"Exactly," Glory agreed, nodding. "If you go to Hell, the piece of Skyffrax that remains within you would almost certainly detach from your soul and reform the demon, leaving you a mortal."

"And a very, very old one," Luke said.

"No, you'd just turn to dust," Glory said, proving once again that no matter how much time she spends among humans, sometimes the nuances of conversation just slide right by.

"What about Adam? He's not part demon, is he?" Flynn pointed at the giant across the table from her. "Seems like if he can't take me because I'm too human, and he can't take Luke because he's too demon, he oughta at least be able to take a little extra muscle along."

"Unfortunately, I cannot pass through the planes either," Adam said, his gravelly voice rumbling deep in his chest. "I am sorry, Quincy. I do not know if I have a soul, or if I have no soul, or if whatever moves within me is a crazy quilt of fragments of the souls of all the people who went into my creation. But I…I am still afraid to find out, even after all these years."

I looked at Adam, the man who had been a rock-steady influence in my life since the very moment I met him, and could almost feel his shame. He wasn't supposed to be afraid, he was supposed to be implacable. I shook my head. "Don't apologize, pal. I wouldn't want to take you into Hell with me anyway. Not because I'm afraid you don't have a soul. No, I can't stand the thought of taking a soul as pure as yours into that place."

He gave me a grateful smile and nodded. "Thank you, Quincy."

I leaned forward a little in my chair and put my hand on top of Flynn's. She looked down at it. "That's the deal, babe," I said. "It's gotta be me. It's always had to be me, and I've always had to go alone. That's the way these things go."

She looked at me, and one tear rolled down her perfect caramel-colored cheek. "That fucking sucks, Harker."

"Yeah," I agreed, reaching up with a finger and wiping the tear away. "This hero gig sucks some days. But somebody's got to do it. So get your ritual ready, Glory. Let's go save the world. Again."

2

The ritual itself was pretty simple. A lot simpler than the arguments preceding it, at any rate. Me, Glory, and the Archangels gathered on the roof of my building at dawn. She scribed a circle some twelve feet across with Enochian writing along the outer ring, then drew a smaller circle inside that one, writing around the circumference between the two circles in Latin. Finally, she put Norse runes of protection at four points of the circle corresponding to the cardinal compass points and motioned for us all to step inside.

"Join hands," she said, and I felt Raphael's hand clasp my left.

I looked down at the hand in my right and was surprised to see Michael standing there. I raised an eyebrow, and his eyes narrowed. "I don't like you, Harker, and I haven't forgiven you for bringing my brothers and I into your fight. But we are here, and our brother is in need of us, so I will do my duty. As always."

Those last two words carried such weight, such sadness, that I almost regretted the last two years. All the traveling, all the fighting to get to this point seemed worthless in that moment. Then I caught sight of Glory. She stood facing east, and I could see how difficult it was for her to lift her arms above her head to begin the ritual. The

324

scar tissue on her back from Barachiel cutting off her wings made some movements almost impossible, and extremely painful.

Seeing her push through that pain, pain she got defending me, stiffened my spine and hardened my resolve. There was no angelic guilt trip that was going to make me let my friend down. Fuck the rest of the world. It could all go straight to Hell for all I gave a shit. But Glory? Nah. She was one of my people, and if I had to kick down the door to Heaven itself to put her back right, then Saint Peter better stock up on ice and Advil because I was going to bring the pain.

"Good," Michael murmured beside me. I glanced at him, and while he didn't look any happier, he at least looked like he didn't want to beat me senseless. "I wanted you to remember why you're really doing this. It can't be abstract, Harker. If you're going to lead an army against Lucifer, it has to be personal. It certainly was for me."

In that moment, I got it. I understood why Michael had retreated so far into Mitchell Carson's consciousness, locking himself away in a vault of memory so deep that not even the touch of his flaming sword could drag him back to the forefront. Nothing we tried would bring Michael out, until I got back to the apartment with Raphael and a still-healing Flynn in tow.

Raphael took one look at Mitch, sitting on the sofa in my apartment shooting the shit with Jo and Cassie, and rushed to his brother's side. He slipped his human form in mid-stride, crossed the room in six quick steps, and stood in front of a very confused Mitch. In full angelic glory, which admittedly was less out of place than it would have been a year ago, Raphael pressed his hands to his temples and kissed the big man on the forehead.

I remembered it like looking through a window into the past. Raphael stooping down and pressing his lips to Mitch's shaved head. A white light so bright and pure it made everything I'd ever seen feel dirty filled the room, but instead of being painful, and making us shield our eyes, it was warm, and welcoming, and drew us all in.

Raphael stood there for a long moment, then straightened, tilted

Mitch's head upward, and pulled slightly. The big man stood, his eyes never leaving Raphael's, tears streaming down his face, and the only thing any of us heard was three whispered words coming from Mitch's lips.

"No. Please, no."

Raphael looked at him, the kindness in his eyes somehow both heartbreaking and hopeful, and said, "You must. We need you."

Mitch's voice was different, fuller, more resonant, somehow other-worldly. "Please, brother. I put that aside."

"I know. But it is time. We must take up the mantle once more. It is what Father would want."

"I don't want to do it again."

"I know," Raphael repeated, and the sadness on his beautiful face was heart-rending. "But there is no one else."

"I know." Mitch, or something somehow more than Mitch, lowered his head, and when he spoke again, his voice like nothing of this world. When he spoke, I heard trumpets blare. I heard the beat of drums, the clash of steel, the screams of rage and pain. When Mitch opened his mouth again, my mind and heart were filled with the sounds of war.

"I know," he said, and he wasn't Mitch anymore. Standing in my apartment was the Archangel Michael, and if I thought I knew what an angel looked like before, all my preconceptions were shattered in a heartbeat.

Where the other Archangels were beautiful, glowing white in robes or garbed in pure white clothes of a more modern cut, Michael was the Archangel of War, and he dressed the part. Taller than the others and broader of shoulder, he stood at least six inches over Raphael, and there were no soft robes anywhere on him. He was wrapped head to toe in chain mail, leather, plate, all in variations of white and silver. His wings, which were snow-white on his brothers, started off pure white at the top, but bled into a crimson at the tips that made them look tipped in blood.

His sword, for so long a source of pain to Mitch, now hung at Michael's side like he was born wearing it. An open-faced helm sat on his head, and the face that looked out at us from under the steel brow was stern, as if chiseled from stone. His armor was white except at the wrists and the feet, where it bled the same crimson as his wingtips. This was the Archangel Michael, and he did not look like he was going to take any shit from anybody.

Raphael looked up at him, a graceful smile on his delicate lips. Raphael was the prettiest of the Archangels, with the kindest disposition. It fit with his role as the healer, I suppose, but at the time, the soft curve of his features stood in stark contrast to the razor cheekbones and square jawline of Michael looking down on him. "Welcome back, Michael," Raphael said, and held out his arms to his brother.

Michael ignored him and turned to glare at me. "Quincy Harker. I suppose this is all your fault?"

To say my first meeting with Michael in his angelic form had been a little rocky would be an understatement of biblical proportions, all puns intended. Now he stood next to me on the roof of my building, a building I might be seeing for the last time, as we stood waiting for the sun to peek over the horizon so Glory could finish her ritual.

"Do you know what we're getting into over there?" I asked.

"No. The last time I did battle with Lucifer and his legions, he was storming Heaven. Here, we are not waging a war, but a guerrilla action, in enemy territory, surrounded by powerful enemies and on unfamiliar terrain. We have no advantages. We are outnumbered by a magnitude unseen in history, and we are fighting an incredibly powerful foe in his home."

"So…you're saying there's a chance?" I quipped, looking up at the grim-faced angel with a sideways smirk.

"If there is anything that will turn the tide of this battle and tilt the odds ever so slightly in your favor, it is you, Quincy Harker. You have no idea how much it pains me to say this, but you may be the only advantage we have."

"The fuck?" The words slipped from me before I had the chance to frame them into something suitably snarky. "How the hell am I the secret weapon in a fight against all the devils of Hell and Lucifer himself?"

"Because you are what humans call the X-factor. Lucifer knows how I will mount my offensive. He knows me better than anyone in the universe save our Father. The Lightbringer and I were the closest of the Host, before…" He gave his head a very human shake and went on. "But you? No one knows what you will do from moment to moment, often not even you. While that is frequently maddening, this may be the one time it is actually a useful trait."

"So we might have the proverbial snowball's chance in Hell because I'm unpredictable?"

"If we have any chance at all, that is where it lies. Now be silent. The ritual begins."

I turned my attention back to Glory, who raised her arms to the rising sun and began to chant. The Archangels murmured along with her, and as their chorus of voices wove together into a song of praise, a song of celebration, and song of devotion, the writing of the circle began to glow. First purple, then blue, then finally a blinding white light that seared my eyes against lids pressed tightly closed. The angels chanted, then sang, and their voices danced along the wintery air, calling the sun, the air, the very fabric of the universe itself to their will.

Even with my eyes squeezed shut, I could see the brilliance beating against my lids. The sound of the Heavenly Host singing rang across the dawn in the city of Charlotte, their song a beacon cascading down upon the city streets below. As they sang, I heard the bells in the Pritchard Memorial Baptist Church bell tower across the street begin to ring, then a chorus of car horns began to blare, and all these dissonant noises wove together into a crescendo of glorious, praise-filled song of glory to God on the highest, and as the song reached its peak, just as my heart felt filled to bursting with the magic and beauty and light of it all…it stopped. The light cut off, the sound stopped in an instant, and the solid concrete beneath my feet vanished, replaced by rocky dust.

I felt the first blast of oven-dry heat on my face and opened my eyes. Charlotte was gone. Hell, my whole *world* was gone. I stood in a circle of angels in a blasted movie-Martian landscape of red rock, dust, and bleeding red light suffusing everything around me. The crisp winter chill of North Carolina was gone, replaced by a scorching heat that seemed to radiate from the very air itself.

This was Hell, just as advertised. Except, in the movies, Hell didn't have Dennis Bolton looking around with a very confused look on his face.

He looked over at me, suddenly alive and in the flesh, so to speak, after almost ten years of living in my phone, and said, "Huh. So that happened."

3

"What the fuck are you doing here?" I asked the curly-haired man standing beside me.

For the first time in the better part of a decade, Dennis Bolton looked at me and said, "Harker, I have no goddamned idea."

I stood on the rocky ground in the First Circle, the beginner level of Hell, so to speak, surrounded by Archangels, Glory, and one very confused dead hacker. Dennis Bolton died almost ten years ago at the hands of a Cambion posing as police detective Richard Sponholz. It was my fault. I wasn't fast enough, and Dennis got killed for it. I tried to find a way to bottle up his soul until I could find it a new home, and it...kinda ended up in the hard drive of my phone, which was connected to the internet, and thus Dennis became a slightly snarkier and way better animated Max Headroom.

Until now. Now he was standing right in front of me, apparently as solid as he'd ever been. Testing a theory, I reached out and poked him in his left shoulder. Yup, solid.

"How did you get here?" I asked.

"Dude, I have no idea," Dennis replied. He looked at his hands, opening and closing them, then patting himself on the chest and running his fingers through his light brown hair. He cocked his head to the side, then reached down and grabbed his crotch. "Dude, my dick's back!" He looked like a kid at Christmas who just found the toy he'd always wanted under the tree. Which, I guess he kinda had.

"Don't care about your dick, Dennis," I said. "I care a lot more about how you're here."

"You should probably care at least a little about them, too," Glory said from behind me. I turned to see what she was pointing at. Demons. Oh yeah, Hell. That's where the demons live.

These weren't the big boys. Apparently Dante had his shit pretty much right on because where we were, the fires weren't all that hot and the demons were pretty small. More like imps than anything else, but there were a lot of them. I wasn't all that worried. I brought backup.

I turned to the assembled Archangels. "You guys want to take care of this?" I gestured toward the oncoming horde of three-foot-tall demons with long spiked tails flailing the air above their heads.

Raguel looked down his nose at me, a feat made a lot simpler by the fact that in their divine form, the Archangels were all a good seven feet tall. I'm a tall dude, but NBA Center has never been on my resume. "No," the snootiest of the Archangels said with a sneer. "We do not sully our hands with rabble such as these. Feel free to dispatch them yourself."

I goggled at him. "You're seriously not going to fight the demons? The things that are kinda your biggest enemies in creation?"

"These are barely even worth our notice. They cannot harm us, no more than a swarm of mosquitoes can drain all the blood from your body."

I turned to the other Seraphim standing around looking regal and in varying degrees of snotty. "What about the rest of you? Do any of you feel like actually showing up for work today, or is the whole fucking Host still on vacation?"

Judging by the looks I got from most of them, the Host gave not a single fuck. Somedays I can't decide who are the bigger assholes, the angels or the demons. It's usually pretty close to a toss-up. At least

Azrael looked like he might be interested in killing something. Made sense. Angel of Death and all.

"What about you, Azrael? Still got a little bloodlust in you? Need an acceptable target for that big fucking Spear you're toting around?" The demons were getting closer now, barely a hundred yards away and moving fast. If I was going to get any help out of these fuckers, it needed to be quick.

"I..." He looked at the demons, looked back at Raguel, who gave a slight shake of his head. That stuffy prick was really moving up on the list of angels I wanted to shank. Yes, it's a real list. I keep it in my wallet.

"Don't look at him, look at the demons. You're the fucking Angel of Death! How about you visit a little death onto the bad guys for a change? Come on, Az, you've got some innocent deaths to atone for or some such shit!"

He looked at me then, his eyes blazing with internal fire. "Do not presume to know my sins, mortal. I will destroy this rabble, but not out of some misplaced desire for your forgiveness."

"I don't give a good goddamn why you save my ass, Az. I just care *that* you save my ass. Now let's go fuck up some demons!" I reached down for my pistol and saw that it hadn't made the trip to Hell with me. In its place was a sword, which burst into white flame as I drew it. "What the fuck?" I muttered.

"It's a manifestation, Harker," Glory said, stepping up beside me with a flaming sword of her own. "Here your weapon, and your armor, are parts of you, or your soul, rather. A gun wouldn't do anything on this plane, and since your body isn't really here, your soul manifested a weapon that would actually be useful. Now we just have to hope that you can use that thing." She gave me a fierce grin and charged into the fray, her blade held high over her head.

"Bitch, I learned from Vlad the fucking Impaler. I know where the pointy end goes," I said. I turned to Dennis. "Stand behind one of these chickenshit Archangels. You and I have some shit to discuss when I get back."

"Yeah, like your browser history," he shot back. I turned to the less lethal option, the oncoming demon horde, and followed the Angel of Death into battle.

Fighting shoulder to shoulder with an Archangel sounds cool, until you realize that Archangels are dicks, all of them kinda hate humans, and that Azrael in particular is batshit crazy. He strode into the oncoming surge of demons with his Spear in front of him and just started skewering imps right and left. When he got two or three of them on the hook, as it were, he flung them over his shoulder to land in a bloody, crumpled mess a yard or so behind him. It was a goddamn wonder to watch, for the half a second or so I had to pay attention before I was hip-deep in demon troubles of my own.

They came on me like a wave, like that really freaky scene in *World War Z* when the zombies pile up so high against the wall that they just climb up one another like a big ramp. That's kinda what happened to me. I slashed, sliced, and diced my way through about half a dozen before there was a pile of three or four demon corpses on the ground in front of me. The red-tinged terrain was treacherous enough without slipping on the viscous black sludge that passed for demon blood, and the last thing I needed was to step on a severed arm and roll an ankle, so I stood my ground.

Big. Fucking. Mistake. As soon as I stopped moving, they surrounded me. It wasn't so much that they attacked me, forming up around me like a gang bent on destruction. No, it was more like I was standing in the path of oncoming water that just flowed around me and filled in the gaps behind me, then turned around and started biting me on the hamstrings.

Okay, it's a shite metaphor, but you try to get creative when you're reminiscing about demons eating your thighs. I hacked, I slashed, and I diced. I chopped, I scattered, I chunked, but I couldn't keep them off me. In less than a minute, I had imps hanging from all my limbs, sinking their teeth into any flesh unprotected by my thick leather duster, and was slowly being dragged down to the ground so even more of them could gnaw the flesh from my bones.

I dropped to my knees, pulled my head down to my chest to protect my throat, focused all my will inward, then with a bellow of

"FUCK YOU!" at the top of my lungs, I threw my power outward in all directions.

It worked. I had no idea if it would, but apparently my magic crossed dimensional boundaries completely intact. Even a little stronger than normal, judging by the results, which were spectacular. The demons that were hanging onto me were obliterated, literally blasted to pieces from the force of my magic. Power radiated out in a circle around me, smashing demons within five feet of me into gobbets of red slimy flesh and viscous blood. The ones a little farther out just tumbled ass over teakettle in a circle away from me, which was all I'd hoped to do to any of them. Sometimes it's really nice to overdeliver.

I looked around at the surviving demons, their numbers reduced by half in just a couple of minutes, and found them all staring at me, their eyes wide and mouths hanging open. Apparently they had as little experience with half-vampire wizards coming into their neighborhood and fucking them up as I did. Azrael was about twenty feet away, ignoring me completely. He just stalked forward, jabbing demons with his Spear and dropping bodies like a sanitation worker picking up little pieces of garbage with a spiky stick.

One of the surviving demons let out a shrill roar and charged me, but he was the only one. I chopped his head off with my sword and kicked it into the crowd of imps before it hit the ground. "Now fuck off!" I yelled, and the entire horde turned tail and ran back the way they came, only a lot faster and significantly reduced in number.

I walked up to Gabriel. The keeper of divine knowledge and formerly a bugnuts-crazy bookseller in South Carolina who only spoke in Shakespeare quotes, and looked up at him. "What the fuck was that?" I asked.

"There is a certain provenance in the fall of a sparrow," he said, his face completely grave.

"Motherfucker, I know you're not crazy anymore, so don't jerk me around. Unless we want to find out what that kind of force blast does to irritating Seraphim."

He looked down into my face, smeared with the blood of a couple hundred imps. "I am but mad north-northwest. When the wind is in the east, I know a hawk from a handsaw."

I raised my glowing sword and held the point an inch below his jaw. "I will cut you, motherfucker. Now stop pissing about."

Gabriel looked down at me, superiority written on every inch of his smug face, then he smiled. "Sorry, Quincy. I was, in the parlance of you humans, just fucking with you."

Goddammit. I was in Hell chasing Lucifer him-fucking-self, with powers that suddenly acted like they were jacked up on steroids, and this was the moment one of the Heavenly goddamned Host decided to develop a sense of humor.

I fucking hate angels.

4

I looked up at Gabriel with absolutely zero humor in my tone, and said, "Let's try this again, Mr. Scribe of Heaven, repository of all divine knowledge, and whatever else you are. Why is my magic super-charged all of a sudden?"

The angel looked down at me, superiority shining in every perfect hair on his perfect head. Asshole. "You are in a plane of pure magic, Quincy. Your magic flows nearer to the surface here. Plus, there is no interference from all the noise you humans create for yourselves."

"Noise?" I asked.

"All those wavelengths of chatter you wrap the globe in. It's a wonder that you can touch the soul of the world at all with all that static."

"I don't follow," I admitted after a couple second's thought.

"He's talking about technology," Dennis chimed in. "Up until a few minutes ago, he meant me. There's a *lot* of electromagnetic energy tossed around by the everyday life of humans. It's evident even in the remotest places now. That's what he's talking about. Tech interferes with magic, and vice versa. That's why America is such a magical wasteland for the most part."

"There's tons of magic in the U.S.," I protested. "I can't swing a dead cat without hitting half a dozen witches, psychics, or demon summoners."

Dennis sighed. "If it's possible, I think you're dumber now than you were when you got me killed the first time. Of course you run into a lot of magical stuff; you're out there chasing it. But if you want to feel what magic is really like, you've got to get away from all the stuff people have created to insulate themselves from it. Head out into the Australian outback, or the Sahara, or the top of a mountain in Tibet. That's why a vision quest is a *quest*, dumbass. You've got to get away from people and the noise they bring with them to find yourself. But here, there are no humans. Just souls and demons. And demons don't give a shit about tech because they can just magic up anything they need. Souls, well, they don't need a whole lot anymore."

"But we're here. I'm not a soul. And you're…what are you, Dennis? Are you…" My voice trailed off as I started to realize what had happened to my friend.

"Yeah, Harker. That's what's up. This is my soul, unwrapped. Your phone is still in your pocket, isn't it?"

I pulled out the useless hunk of plastic and glass. "Of course. For all the good it'll do me. Needless to say, the reception here is for shit."

"Yeah, that's how I got here," he said.

"Still not understanding you, buddy. Spell it out for me."

"When I was in the internet, a piece of my soul was in every connected device. Like your phone. When you walked through the Gate, you brought me with you. Or at least the copy of me that was in your phone. Kinda like Glory was talking about the sliver of demon inside Luke that would get out and run rampant if he came with you. I don't know if there's still a me inside the internet back home, but I wouldn't hold my breath. I feel pretty complete, so I'm guessing that I made the trip with everything I've got."

"So it's not enough I got you killed, now I carried you to Hell. Goddammit." I turned around, looking for something to punch. I gave a glance to Azrael, knowing I wouldn't hurt him, but then I saw the look on his face and decided I couldn't say the same about him hurting me. My eyes lit on something round, about the size of a volleyball, so I kicked it in frustration. I'll admit, watching the demon's head flying through the air to bounce along the rocky ground twenty yards away was pretty gratifying.

I looked back at Dennis, who didn't look nearly as pissed at me as I would have expected him to, given our location. "I'm sorry, Dennis. I didn't know that could even happen, which seems to be a recurring theme with you and me. If I did, I would have left my stupid phone at home."

"Whatever, Harker. Just keep some asshole from killing my soul while we're here, and we'll figure out how to get me home after we get this chick her wings back." He smiled at Glory, who gave him a nod.

"I'll help keep you safe," she said. "If we count on Harker, you won't make it past the Third Circle."

"Speaking of Circles, are we going to have to do the whole Dante tourist shtick before we whip Lucifer's ass, or is there a shortcut?"

Glory shook her head. "Sorry, Harker. I've never been to Hell before."

"What about you guys?" I asked the other Archangels. They all shook their heads. All except one. Michael walked up to me, a grave look on his face. He hadn't spoken to me since we got here, and I got the distinct impression he was pissed at me for yanking him out of his mortal form and forcing him to come to Hell with us. I also didn't give a single fuck how pissed he was if he had the information we needed.

"Lucifer will most likely be in the Ninth Circle, with his most trusted lieutenants. We will have to fight our way there to rescue Uriel, and it is quite likely we will have to do battle with one brother to save the other. None of us want to do this. We have fought this war once before, and it rent Heaven asunder and almost destroyed the universe. You have brought us to this place again, Quincy Harker, so it is only right that you risk all alongside us to rectify the situation you helped to create."

"*I* helped?" I tried to keep my mouth shut, really I did. I don't have many cast-in-stone rules in my head, but "don't piss off incredibly powerful divine beings when they're right in front of you" is usually near the top of the list, right up there with "put the seat down."

Since I already had most of my foot in my mouth, I figured I should go ahead and swallow the whole damn thing. "How the *fuck* is any of this my fault? You motherfuckers are the ones with the divine edict to keep your asshole brother in line while Dad's off on walkabout. What the fuck were you all doing while your buddy Barachiel was going bugnuts and trying to destroy the world last year? Or when Orobas tried to murder me and steal your goddamned sword?"

Michael didn't answer me; he just backhanded me across the jaw and dropped me flat on my ass. I looked up at the stone faced Archangel as he loomed over me.

"Do not think to take my Father's name in vain with impunity, mortal. I laid down my sword millennia ago, hoping that by never taking it up again, I could cleanse myself of the blood of my brethren that covers my hands. I spent the intervening eons walking your Earth in mortal guise, trying my best to stay out of the affairs of Heaven and Earth, until you brought Raphael to me and had him restore my memories."

The look on Michael's face was something I'd never seen on one of the Host before. It was sadness. The deepest, most soul-wrenching sadness in the world. The kind of sadness that can only be borne over thousands of years. For the first time, I thought about what the first war on Heaven must have cost the angels. They were forced to fight their brothers, to *kill* other angels, and hurl the survivors down here into Hell, banishing them from God's grace and their home forever.

He caught me looking at him and must have read the pity in my eyes because in an instant any vestige of pain was gone and the general of Heaven was back in its place. Michael bent down and grabbed the front of my jacket in one hand, lifting me to my feet with no more trouble than me picking up a puppy by the scruff of its neck. "Do not presume to know the mind of the Host, Quincy Harker. We are infinite, we are eternal, we are—"

"You are a bunch of stuffy pricks who couldn't even remember where you left your favorite toys until me and my people found them for you. You were busting your knuckles in a cage fight in the desert. Azrael was racking up a body count that makes Pol Pot look like a rookie. Gabriel was one step above a gibbering idiot, and Sealtiel, who by the way is the only one of you outside of Raphael who hasn't acted like a complete asshole since getting his wings back, was living in the gutters in New Orleans dancing for tips outside a bar. So don't talk to me like you sons of bitches are so fucking superior to us lowly humans. Remember, dickhead, Daddy likes us best anyway."

That last shot hit home, and I was pretty sure I was about to end up flat on my ass again, but Glory yanked me back by my belt and pulled me out of arm's reach. "Chill out, Harker," she whispered in my ear. "You made your point; now can we get back to the part where the best strategist in Heaven's army wants to help us instead of wanting to kick your ass?"

I sucked in a breath, counted to ten, then tried it again in Latin. That didn't help, so I cycled through French, Spanish, Mandarin, and Khmer before I was calm enough to speak without almost certainly pissing off the giant warrior angel even more. "I'm sorry, Michael. I know this shit is hard for you. I didn't want this fight. But apparently something inside me woke up your sword when I picked it up, and that set this whole mess in motion. I don't know why it happened, and frankly, I don't care. I just want to get Glory her wings back and keep Lucifer from killing everyone in the world that I love. Along with about seven billion people who I don't really give a shit about, except in an abstract sense."

Azrael did something I'd never seen any of the Archangels do since I'd started messing around with them. He laughed. "I like this mortal, brother. He fights well for one of them, and his words are amusing. I have almost forgiven him for dropping a building on me."

"Well, if you hadn't been a psychopathic serial killer, I wouldn't have needed to drop a house on you," I replied.

"He does have a point, brother," Raphael said, stepping up to Michael's shoulder. "As mortals go, this one is more useful than most. He did bring us back to ourselves, something that most of us appreciate."

Michael looked at his brother, the healer, and scowled. "Don't think I've forgotten your part in this, Raphael. Your 'healing' brought me back to myself, someplace I never wanted to be. We will have a reckoning of our own once we have rescued Uriel and reminded our wayward brother Lucifer of his standing among the Host."

Raphael blanched and took a step back, his jovial round face losing a big part of its grin. It sounded like Michael was planning a serious and unpleasant conversation with his brother on letting sleeping Archangels lie in the near future.

"But that means you'll help keep Lucifer out of Heaven, right? And restore Glory's divinity?" I asked, not loving the idea of turning Michael's focus back on me but needing to know where we stood before another horde of midget demons came washing over us like a pointy-tailed tsunami.

Michael's face may as well have been carved out of marble it was so expressionless when he looked down at me. Why did these bastards have to be so tall, anyway? "Yes, Quincy Harker, we will deal with Lucifer, and given the work that Glory has done on our behalf and in the cause of keeping the planes safe from not only Lucifer's efforts, but your bumbling, once we are a complete Host again, we shall restore her wings."

I guess that was about as good as I could hope for. "So what's next?" I asked.

"Next is the Second Circle," Gabriel said. "Gird your minds, mortals, for the demons of the Second Circle are crafty."

"And probably kinda hot," Dennis said.

I turned to stare at him, confused.

"Don't you remember from Dante? The Second Circle of Hell is Lust, bro. I'm expecting a whole lot of succubus on succubus action." He looked inordinately happy about the prospect, then I realized that this was the closest he'd been to having a corporeal form in over a decade.

"Dennis, you are a disturbed human being," I said.

"Yeah, but at least I'm human again for now," he replied. "And I plan to appreciate every moment of it."

"Just try not to get yourself killed again," I cautioned.

"Okay, but there are worse ways to go out than as the meat in a sex demon sandwich," he said with a grin. I was really starting to wonder if I liked him better as a unicorn.

"Can we get a move on?" Glory asked. "Because it looks like the imps you beat the shit out of are back, and I think they brought a couple thousand friends."

5

"Huh," I said, looking at another oncoming wave of imps. "This might get tiring." I swung my arms around and rolled my head from side to side, loosening up for the fight that was rapidly rushing toward me.

"You know you don't have to fight them all, don't you?" Gabriel said from behind me.

I didn't turn around. The imps were still well over a hundred yards away, but I try not to take my eyes off an army of supernatural assholes if I don't have to. "I'm open to suggestions. I mean, I suppose me and Azrael could just keep on slaughtering imps until our arms get tired, but that's going to get old really fast."

Gabriel moved around in front of me. I looked up at him, because I didn't have any choice. He'd kept a little of the look of his human avatar when he switched to his divine form. He was tall, like the other angels, but instead of walking around in armor like Michael, or a pure white version of surgical scrubs like Raphael, Gabe wore long, flowing robes, like a scholar. Or Gandalf.

The *Lord of the Rings* imagery was further helped by the long white beard he sported, and the wizened face. I knew angels didn't age, so it must have been an affectation. I kinda liked the fact that the

Archangels let their personalities, or roles, impact their appearance. If they were all just tall, ethereal-looking winged creatures glowing with heavenly light, not only would that have been boring, but they would have been really hard to tell apart.

Gandalf/Gabriel spoke, and the lecturing tone almost put me to sleep immediately. I made myself stay awake, figuring that my life probably depended on it. "This is Purgatory, the First Circle. It was created more as a holding pattern than anything else. If you want to break out of a holding pattern, what do you do?"

"Fuck, I don't know. Call Ground Control and ask for Major Tom? I don't even know what you're talking about with holding patterns and that bullshit," I said, peering around the angel at the advancing horde. The imps were taking it a little more slowly this time, marching steadily toward us instead of running, but it looked like there were a lot more of them.

"I think I get it," Dennis said. "This is like *Groundhog Day*, only in Hell."

"Every time I've ever watched *Groundhog Day*, I thought I was in Hell," I muttered.

"Do not sully the good name of Bill Murray and his comedic genius, you Philistine," Dennis said. "If we're stuck in a loop, we have to stop doing the same thing over and over again, right?"

"That would be the logical conclusion," Gabriel said with a nod.

"So, fighting the demons didn't do anything to get us out of Purgatory, so we should try something different," Dennis continued.

"Got any bright ideas?" I asked. "Because in about twenty seconds I'm gonna be nuts-deep in demons. Again."

"Yeah," Dennis said. "But you're not going to like it."

"When do I ever like your ideas?"

"Valid. Okay, here's the plan—we run." He grabbed Glory's arm, spun her around, and took off running away from the tsunami of demons as fast as he could. I had to admit, for a dead guy, he was pretty damn spry.

I looked at Gabriel, who nodded, then at the other Archangels. "The Seraphim do not run," Michael said, his tone flat.

"Then fly, you big winged prick, but if we don't get out of the First

Circle, we don't rescue Uriel." I turned to Gabriel. "You want to convince your brothers to go for a jog?"

"Go," the scholarly Archangel said. "We will follow."

I turned and ran after Dennis and Glory. It didn't take me long to catch up. Apparently even my soul is inordinately fast and strong. We dashed over the shattered landscape, leaping over rocks and dodging outcroppings of stone and obsidian, or what passed for it in this dimension. Glory was nimble, moving like a gazelle through the savannah. Dennis…not so much. He moved more like a drunken rhinoceros trying to dance *Swan Lake*. I was somewhere in between.

We hadn't gone very far when a shout came from behind us. I spared a glance over my shoulder and saw the imps had broken into a sprint as the Archangels took to the air and flew after us.

Then flew past us. Damn, those guys were *fast*. The imps were no slouches in a footrace, either, and our lead cut to maybe twenty yards in less than half a minute. I saw Dennis stumble, and reached out to grab his upper arm. He steadied himself and gave me a grateful look.

"Got any other bright ideas?" I asked. "Because the demons are gaining on us, and I haven't seen anything that looks like an elevator yet."

"Maybe run faster?" He looked over his shoulder and stumbled again. This time Raphael swooped down out of the sky and picked him up under the arms. Dennis looked up at him, a grateful smile on his face, then his mouth fell open. "There! It's up there!"

Raphael looked where Dennis pointed, then stopped in mid-air. I looked up and froze. Floating in the air a good hundred feet above us was a portal. I couldn't tell where it went, but I was willing to bet it was the only way out of this plane.

"Well, shit," I said. "Now what?"

"Now we fly, human," a voice behind me growled, and I felt strong arms wrap around my chest. My feet left the ground as someone picked me up without a second's hesitation and left the red rocks and dirt of Purgatory far beneath us.

"Holy shit!" I yelped, then clapped my mouth shut. I didn't know if there were bugs in Hell, but I sure as fuck didn't want to swallow any of them, and whoever grabbed me was hauling ass. I tried to get a glimpse of my porter but couldn't get a good look at them. Then I looked down at the arms around my torso, and as soon as I saw the black metal bracers, I knew who had me clasped tight in his arms as we rushed through a glowing hole in the sky of Hell. I was wrapped in the arms of Azrael, the Angel of Death.

I had just enough time to process that idea when we passed through the portal, and I felt my very essence being ripped apart. I screamed, I spun wildly through the air as I was torn from Azrael's grasp, and my whole world was filled with the sound of souls shrieking as we passed into the Second Circle of Hell.

"Well, that sucked," I said with a groan as I slowly rolled over and pushed myself up to my knees. Something was definitely different. For one thing, I was in a building. For another, I was alone. "Well, goddammit." I let out a little chuckle. "I guess, by the definition of it, that's already happened to most of the things here."

I stood up and looked around. I was in a big hall, a long rectangle with a vaulted ceiling and polished marble floors. Huge polished stone pillars lined the walls, and a long red carpet ran down the center of the room, leading to a dais where there was, on a platform covered in crimson carpet...a bed?

"What the literal fuck is this?" I turned in a circle but couldn't see a door anywhere. Whatever portal I came through to get here was gone. The ceiling was an ornate mural of cherubs cavorting among the clouds. Oh, wait...that's not cavorting...oh my. Yep, that was a giant ceiling full of pictures of cherubs fucking. In every position I'd ever considered, and about a dozen that were so complicated I couldn't tell exactly where one chubby naked body stopped and the next one began.

There were missionary angels, doggy-style angels, cowgirl angels, piledriver angels, reverse cowgirl angels, human centipede angels, and something that looked a lot like they were trying to fuck themselves into a divine version of a Flying Spaghetti Monster. Every inch of the ceiling, a sweeping expanse that must have been fifty feet wide and two hundred feet long, was covered in nothing but images of clouds, wings, and intertwined cupids.

I finally tore my eyes from the bizarre and somehow entrancing spectacle and walked to the bed. Big surprise, there was someone in it. She was pretty, if overblown in practically every dimension. Lips a little too full, eyes a little too narrowed in passion, cheeks a little too flushed, breasts a little too perfectly round and perky, legs a little too perfectly muscled, toes a tone of crimson that was just a little too bright and splashy. She looked like someone's idea of the sexiest woman in the world, only turned up to eleven with the knob ripped off.

"Hey there, sailor, looking for a good time?" Her voice was sultry, seductive, and like everything about her, just a little too much.

"Nah, I'm good. Just looking for an exit, thanks." I looked past the dais to a short stretch of polished floor and then a wall covered with a tapestry embroidered with scenes of nuns and priests doing their best to mimic all the poses the cherubs were demonstrating overhead.

"What about a good time with me?" The voice was male now, and I turned back to the bed. The woman wasn't a woman anymore, but a gorgeous naked man, at least as overblown as the woman he'd replaced. His hair was just a little too perfect, falling down over one of his too-smoldering eyes in a flop that was just a little past sexy. His lips glistened with moisture, and when he ran his tongue over them, he showed just enough too much to make it not sexy at all. His abs were chiseled a little too sharply from his torso, and his biceps were just a hair too developed. He was hung like a goddamn bull moose, too. That wasn't a little overblown—that thing was fucking terrifying.

"Jesus Christ, put that thing away before you put someone's eye out!" I said before I could stop myself. My hastily concocted plan to just ignore the obvious succubus went out the window when I got a glimpse of the near foot of demonic man-meat lying across his thigh. "How do you pick these forms? Goddamn, it's like somebody took a porno and worked really hard at making it not sexy at all."

Before my eyes, the beautiful man changed form again, this time into a woman in a red silk blouse, tight jeans, and a black blazer cut a little roomier through the ribcage to hide a gun in a shoulder holster.

Dark hair spilled over her shoulders, and her caramel skin called out for my touch. Her deep eyes drew me in, and I swear as she opened her mouth, I felt my breath drawn into her like she was stealing my soul right through my libido.

With that thought, I snapped out of her spell and yanked my sword free. It burst into white flame, and I shoved it through Rebecca Gail Flynn's chest, right underneath the ribcage on the left side, angling up as I went through to shove three feet of heavenly steel through her evil, demonic heart.

"That's not my fiancée, you asshole. Now quit trying to fuck with my head and show me the way out of here," I growled as I leaned into the thrust.

"There's no escape, Quincy Harker," the demon hissed, shifting to its true form, an almost skeletally thin creature with mottled black and maroon skin stretched taut over its skeleton, with short horns on its forehead and a tongue to make Gene Simmons envious lashing the air in front of its face.

"I'm not trying to escape, you skinny fuckwit," I snarled, putting a foot on the thing's chest and shoving it back off my blade. "I'm trying to get to the center of the fucking labyrinth so I can kick David Bowie's ass once and for all." I took a step back, raised my blade, and swung. The demon's head came off and rolled down the steps, turning to dust as it did. The body stood for half a second before it, too, collapsed in a heap of ash.

"Who's next?" I yelled, raising my sword high above my head and turning around in a circle. "Who wants some of me now?"

"I do." I froze. My arms turned to jelly, and every hair on my body stood up. I knew that voice. I'd heard it speak, I'd heard it sing, I'd heard it whisper in my ear as we lay together in the deepest night.

I turned to that voice, the voice I never thought to hear again, and the blade fell from my hand to clatter on the stone. Standing not twenty feet in front of me, looking as beautiful as she had the night we'd met in a bar in Grenoble in 1939, was Anna Treves, the first woman I ever loved.

She smiled at me and held out her arms, and any shred of will I had dissolved like the demon on the floor behind me when I saw what she was wearing. Anna, my love, the woman murdered in front of my eyes, stood before me with a spray of wildflowers in her hand and a glorious white dress of lace and silk on her body.

Anna appeared before me wearing a wedding dress, and my world shattered.

"What's wrong, Quincy?" she asked, and it was like the last seventy-five years never happened. When I heard her voice again, we were walking down a sidewalk in Grenoble, with the stars just starting to peek into view, not a hint of a cloud in the sky, and the tinkling of her brother Edgar on the piano from the window of our flat above us.

I could smell the baguettes from the bakery around the corner, the thick diesel smoke of the delivery trucks making their last rounds of the day, fresh-cut flowers in a market stall along the storefront to my right elbow. Everything in the scene was perfect in my mind, the memory as clear as... "You're not Anna."

"What do you mean, Quincy?" Her voice was perfect. Goddammit, her voice was right, with just the slightest German accent to her English. Except Anna didn't speak English. She was just learning, beginning to get a grip on the language for our escape from Europe, but she never became fluent. She died too soon.

"You're not her. You're not her because we never got married, never even planned a wedding, never even fucking *discussed* it. You're not her because she never learned English, you horned fuck. You're not her because you painted this perfect fucking memory in my head, but you had me walking beside her. Walking on the inside, next to the buildings. I was born in England under the reign of Queen Victoria, you ignorant twat. No true gentleman would ever let his beloved walk on the street side. Your details suck, and that dress looks like something a porn star would wear to try and look respectable."

I snatched up my sword from the floor and charged, sweeping through the air with a huge, looping slash aimed at the demon's throat. The succubus, seeing her first ploy fall to pieces, switched gears and morphed into full-on *Spawn* movie reject form. This one was taller than the first, at least eight feet tall, but still skeletal. Her arms ended in long, hooked, sword-like hands, with serrated edges. They looked like the blade of a scythe, and I didn't want to know if they were as sharp.

They were definitely as strong though. She blocked my first cut with a flick of her wrist and whirled in place to send the other scythe-hand whirling toward my throat. I dropped backward in a really clumsy version of that badass move Keanu Reeves did in *The Matrix*, except I just flopped flat on my back instead of leaning way back and dodging a bunch of bullets. I dropped my sword, and it winked out of existence, the hilt reappearing at my hip. I guess there are some benefits to not really being in a place in your physical form.

I rolled back onto my shoulders, pressed my hands into the floor above my head, and pushed my body forward into a neat kip-up, landing on my feet just as the demon sliced toward me again with her giant blade-hands. This time I took a lesson from my old Aikido Master and stepped inside her stroke, grabbing her right arm just about where the wrist should be, and spun under her arm. I bent down as I pulled forward, then stood up into a Judo throw. The demon went over, slamming into the ground on her back, staring up at me.

I kept hold of her arm and stepped over it, spinning my body around to wrap her arm around my knee and thigh. I bent at the knee and twisted, snapping the arm with a *crack* that echoed off the marble floor. The demon threw her head back and let out a shriek that I would call unholy, except that's redundant in this case. I stepped free of the writhing creature, pulled my sword loose, and slammed it down into the thing's chest. It let out another howl of pain as the white flame of my blade pierced it, and as its shrieking faded and its contortions grew slower, it shifted back into Anna's form as one last torment.

The demon wearing my love's face lay there on the white marble floor, wrapped in the white wedding dress Anna never got to wear, crimson blood pooling out from her chest and staining the silk and lace. She looked up at me, eyes full of pain and sorrow, and said, "Why? Quincy, why would you hurt me like this?"

I felt the rage tickling behind my eyes and fought to keep the beast locked away. Letting that part of myself free in here would guarantee I never left Hell. I stuffed my fury back into a box and locked it away, putting it onto the very crowded "deal with it later" shelf in my mind. I stared down at the dying demon wearing my true love's face and said, "Because you're not her, you sick fuck. You could never be her. You couldn't even stand a moment in her presence, because her beauty and light would burn you to ash like a papier-mâché crane on the surface of the sun. Die, you sick bitch."

I stabbed down with my sword, and the flaming sword pierced the demon's face right above the bridge of her nose, destroying the mockery of Anna's face that it wore and sending it into whatever oblivion awaits demons that are well and truly killed.

I wrenched my sword free from the marble where it had buried itself, threw it aside, and dropped to my knees, falling forward on my elbows as huge, wracking sobs shook my body. I rolled over on my side, curled up in a little ball, and wept until I was empty. Then I lay there, empty of everything but hate and rage, until I could summon the strength to stand.

I don't know how long I lay there, but it doesn't matter because I don't really have a good sense of how time works in Hell. But eventually I got up, and I looked around the room again. It was much smaller now, as if somehow killing the succubus had removed the room's reason for being. There was something else new—a door. It was set into the wall behind where the bed had sat, and I was certain it hadn't been there before. What once had been a featureless stone wall now held a plain door, dark wood, with a brass handle beckoning to me.

I stood up, dried my eyes, and took stock of the room. It was completely empty. The dais was gone, the bed was gone, and the dead demons were both gone. The only thing to give evidence of anything that happened here was the ache in my chest and my red eyes. That, and my heavy soul.

I walked to the door and put my hand on the knob. Turning around, I gave the room one last glance, as if to make sure I hadn't left anything behind. I certainly felt like I had, but it wasn't anything that could be seen, only felt. I turned the knob, and as I pushed the door open, the room dissolved around me.

I stood on another desolate plane, another landscape that looked like the set of *The Martian*, only missing Matt Damon making science quips. The Archangels stood some ten yards in front of me, divided into two clusters. Raphael stood with Michael and Azrael, obviously arguing with them about something. Raguel, Gabriel, and Sealtiel stood in a circle a few feet away, all trying very hard to look like they weren't actively trying to eavesdrop on their brothers' conversation. Spoiler alert—they weren't doing a very good job.

I walked over to the trio of arguing angels because I still wanted to hit something and that looked like my best option for someone pissing me off. "What's up, guys? Where's Glory? And Dennis?" I'll admit to a little worry in the pit of my stomach when I realized Dennis wasn't with them. He had no magic to protect him in this place, and he wasn't much of a fighter the first time he was alive. I couldn't imagine that being dead all those years made him a combat expert, no matter how many kung fu movies he absorbed.

Although I'd heard worse origin stories.

Raphael turned to me, relief washing over his features. That was a nice switch. It was the first time any of the Host had been happy to see me. "Thank the Father," he said, grasping me by the elbows. "You're still with us. We were concerned that you may succumb to the trials of the Second Circle."

"You mean the fuckbunny demon, or the one that wore my dead love's face? Because they both sucked, but I killed them." Raphael's face dimmed as he picked up on the pain in my voice, but he nodded.

"The temptations will get nothing but stronger as we move

through the Circles. It seems that our brother is allowing us to pass through unmolested, but he apparently plans to make things as difficult for you mortals as possible."

"And here, in the set of his power, he can make things very difficult indeed," Michael said, his voice a low growl.

"So if he's fucking with the mortals, why isn't Glory here?" I asked.

Raphael gave me a pitying look, kinda like you do to someone who is truly stupid. "She is mortal now, Quincy. She may be the most vulnerable of you all because not only is she mortal, but she has had less experience resisting temptation."

Azrael let out a short bark of a laugh. "Do you really believe that Harker has ever resisted temptation before today? Look at him! He's an absolute hedonist, doing nothing that he doesn't want to do. He fights, he fucks, he kills, regardless of the destruction he leaves in his wake."

I felt my face go a little red. "You condemning or admiring, assclown? Because I'm pretty sure you've killed more people than cholera, so you can take your superiority and—"

"And what, human?" Azrael flared his wings out to their full seven-foot wingspan and stepped up right in front of me. His wings were so black they made the air around them darker, and he was clad in plate armor covered in sharp points and spikes. He wore no helm, and his long black hair was swept back from his imperious brow in a ponytail that curled down his neck and lay across his left shoulder. He was an impressive sight, and if I hadn't been in an astronomically shitty mood, I probably wouldn't have puffed up on him.

But I was not in a good place and throwing hands with the Angel of Death felt like a good idea. This is what happens when I go to Hell: my already suspect judgement becomes even worse. I literally didn't know that was possible.

"And your fucking attitude, you goth prick," I said, hating the fact that I had to look up to insult the angel. I always found that it was hard to be intimidating when you were giving up more than half a foot to your opponent. That's why I left the Sasquatch and other monsters to the Templars. Let them tilt at those windmills. Most demons at least wore human suits when I scrapped with them, so I felt like I was fighting someone my own size.

Angels not so much. Azrael was a big motherfucker, and I knew from past unpleasant experience that I couldn't even hope to take him down. Maybe that's what I wanted. Maybe I was spoiling for the demon hunter version of suicide by cop, just getting an Archangel to kill me so Lucifer couldn't. So I didn't have to face any more of my countless past failures in this shitty dimension.

But Azrael didn't kill me. Instead, he smiled down at me, then he patted me on the head. He patted me on the top of my fucking head, like I was a goddamn puppy or something. "I like you, Harker. You're stupid, but you are braver than any ten men should be. See that you don't point that bravery in the wrong direction." Then he turned away and looked back to Raphael. "We will remain with the mortals. They must battle through the Circles to reach Lucifer's sanctum, and we shall aid them as much as possible. In some trials, like those of this Circle, we will be useless, but in others we may lend our strength to theirs. Father decreed that they shall have dominion over their world. Who are we to run counter to his will?"

"Father never said that they should rule Heaven, Earth, and Hell, brother," Michael snarled, but Azrael held up a hand.

"You are our general, Michael, but Raphael has always been the true leader of the Host. Be the sword, let him be the heart. We will follow the heart." He nodded to Raphael and walked away to join the other trio of Archangels.

Michael glared at Azrael's back as he walked away, then turned to Raphael. "I shall do as you ask. We will aid the mortals." He folded his arms across his chest, sulking.

"Good," Raphael said. "I didn't want to have to fight you. You always get so embarrassed when you lose."

Michael's eyes blazed. "I have *never* lost!"

Raphael turned to me and smiled. "Sometimes I just like to wind him up."

I remembered my own brothers, James and Orly, and how we would often find ways to get under each others' skin just to see the reaction. I guess brotherhood is universal. I opened my mouth to speak, but as I did, Dennis appeared a few feet away.

He just stepped into the scene as if walking through a door, which I supposed he probably did. He looked disheveled, his hair tangled and his clothes twisted. He was sweaty and looked a bit dazed. I knew that look. For the first time in a very long time, Dennis had just gotten laid.

"Please tell me you did not bang a succubus," I said.

He looked at me, a slow smile stretching from ear to ear. "Okay. I did not bang a succubus." His smile widened further than I thought possible. "I banged three succubuses."

I looked at the ground and shook my head. "I…I got nothing."

"The plural of succubus is succubi," Gabriel corrected. "So you banged three succubi."

"That's great. You got your rocks off while I killed a demon wearing my first love's face. Now can we please find Glory and get the fuck out of here?"

"Glory?" Dennis asked, looking past me. "She's right behind you."

I turned to see Glory standing right where Dennis pointed. She stood with blank eyes, as if whatever she had just seen had pierced her to the very core. "Glory?" I asked. "Are you okay?"

"No. I'm not. But I made it out, and there's the door. So let's get the fuck out of here and never speak of this place again. Okay?"

I could tell she was a long way from okay, but that was certainly something I could relate to, so I just nodded and walked toward the door she was pointing at. It looked a lot like the door out of my magical room: plain, wooden, with a brass knob. I put my hand to it, and the second my fingers touched the handle, everything winked out and we were somewhere new.

Somewhere worse.

7

It didn't *look* worse. It didn't really look like much of anything at all, really. The door opened into a gray hallway with speckled gray and darker gray tile. It felt like every bland office building ever, or maybe a hospital that didn't give a single fuck about the mental health of their patients or visitors. There was the basic white drop ceiling with fluorescent lights set into it, gray walls in a shade slightly lighter than the floor, with a wide rubberized handrail in darker gray running along it. The hallway stretched as far as I could see in either direction, so I instinctively turned right and started walking.

"Where are you going, Harker?" Bolton asked.

I turned and looked at him. "I have no idea. But I know I'm not going to get there by standing in the middle of a hallway. Better to move in any direction, even if it's wrong, than to stand still."

"That sentence right there explains so many of the decisions I've watched you make over the last few years. Better to move in the wrong direction than to stand still. Why not take a second to look around, see if any more information presents itself?"

I turned around and started walking again, calling to Dennis over my shoulder, "You do that, Dennis. While you're waiting for anything that isn't a soul-shredding demon to present itself, I'm going to look for the door. Or the trial, or whatever the fuck I have to shoot, punch, or blast out of my way so I can get to Lucifer, kick his ass, and get home."

"You're an idiot," Michael said from beside me. His voice was low enough that no one but me could hear him, so apparently he wasn't looking for an argument, just stating what he thought was fact.

I didn't slow down, just turned my head to the angel and said, "Why am I an idiot now?"

"Probably a design flaw in the species, but you seem particularly affected by it. Specifically, you never take the time to evaluate a situation fully before taking action."

"This from the warrior angel whose motto is 'slice first, ask questions later,'" I grumbled.

"Do not presume to know me, mortal. I have depths that your limited intellect cannot begin to plumb. Regardless, you should listen to your friend. A more cautious approach is warranted the farther into Lucifer's domain we travel. We are all on unfamiliar ground here, and none of us knows how the lower Circles will affect us. You may find yourself without our assistance."

I thought back to the last Circle and seeing Anna's face on the succubus. "I've managed this far without any help from you. If I have to get all the way to the basement of Hell on my own, I'll do it." Now I did stop, and I looked up into Michael's eyes. "That's what you fuckers have never understood about humanity. You look at us and you just see these weak, fragile bodies that, for reasons unfathomable to you, God put in dominion over this world. What you're missing is the soul. That's what keeps us going. Yeah, we die. We bleed, we get old, we get sick, and we die. But through all of that, we still have our souls. Our unwavering, unyielding, unbending, stubborn as fuck souls. That's why we're the favorite children, idiot. It's not free will; it's determination.

"When we set our minds to something, we fucking do it. Whether it's parting the Red Sea or putting a man on the moon or walking through every circle of Hell itself to help our friends. Once we've picked a path, there's nothing in Heaven or Hell that can stop us. So yeah, I might blindly run into situations without considering every fucking potential consequence, but once I start something, I fucking well finish it. Now you gonna come with me, or you gonna stand here in this shithole hallway looking for your dick?" I turned and started back up the hall, not looking back to see if anyone followed me. Aside from my supreme confidence that they would, it would have blown the moment if I wasn't badass enough to walk away without looking behind me.

A few seconds later, my self-image was saved when I heard the unmistakable sound of a group of people walking down the hall behind me. We trooped along the featureless corridor for several minutes before coming to a set of blank institutional double doors. They looked like every set of hallway doors in every old hospital in every horror movie, the doors that always have some kind of scene of mayhem on the other side of them. No window, no handle, just a gray rectangle standing in a gray hall, with polished metal squares to push on where a knob should be.

I did just like the B-movie scriptwriter in me wanted the hero to do, and pushed the door open, fully expecting to step into the zombie apocalypse or something equally fascinating, only to stop short when I stepped into…a cafeteria. It was like something out of an elementary school movie, complete with the long institutional tables jammed end-to-end, with round, orange-topped seats attached to the bottom of the table and extending out on curved aluminum arms.

A sea of these tables stretched out across a room the size of a football field, at least three quarters of the seats filled with people sitting silent, focused on the trays in front of them, shoveling food into their faces like machines. There was no conversation, no pause, just endless eating, like an assembly line of consumption running without pause.

The men and women who sat at the tables were as gray as the walls, dressed in colorless jumpers that looked like they had just stepped off their stations on an assembly line. They all had medium-length hair, all brown, and they were all the kind of bland-skinned white people that looked like an ad for Abercrombie & Fitch. It was like they had normal skin tones when they sat down, but the longer they sat there eating, the more the color just leached out of them.

"What the literal fuck?" I asked out loud. I turned to the folks standing behind me, hoping someone would give me some idea of what kind of torture this was and how we were supposed to get through it.

"Looks like a cafeteria," Dennis said from my right shoulder. "Works for me. I haven't had anything to eat since before Obama was President." He pushed past me and peeled off to the right, grabbing an obnoxious orange plastic tray and getting in line behind a five-foot demon with a spiked tail waving in the air.

I stepped farther into the room to let the rest of the group in, then turned to Gabriel. "Is the Third Circle of Hell the employee dining room or something?"

"Close," he said. "The Third Circle is dedicated to Gluttony, another of the Seven Deadly Sins."

"I could eat," Glory said. She slipped around the Archangels to stand in line behind Dennis.

"What kind of torment is eating?" Azrael asked. "How is this torture to humans?"

"You've obviously never eaten in a public school cafeteria," I said. "I mean, neither have I, but I watched *The Wonder Years*. It seemed awful, but not exactly hellish."

"It's not hellish at all, Harker. This stuff is fantastic!" I looked around, and Dennis was already seated at a table, shoveling food into his face as fast as his hands would move. Only problem was, the stuff he was shoveling into his mouth didn't look like food, it looked more like mud. Gray, slimy muck that splattered all over his face and arms and ran down his chin to splatter on his shirt.

I walked over to him and snatched the spoon out of his hand. "Dude, that's nasty. Cut that shit out."

He looked up at me, and the rage smoldering in his eyes made me take a step back. "Give me back my spoon, Harker. You can't have my food. There's plenty for you. Get your own."

I held up both hands. "Dennis, chill out. This stuff isn't food. It looks, and smells, like ruby buttholes. Here, smell the spoon." I held it out to him, and he snatched the utensil out of my hand. Dennis plopped back down on the round plastic seat that stuck out from the underside of the cafeteria table and resumed shoveling glop into his mouth at a breakneck pace.

"Dude!" I said, louder this time. "Cut that shit out!" I snatched the spoon away again, and this time he just started shoveling the slime into his mouth with both hands. I turned back to where the Archangels stood just inside the door. "A little help, please?"

Azrael and Gabriel came over, and each took one of Dennis's arms. The angels lifted him off the seat and held him away from the table. He strained and fought them, his teeth snapping on empty air. It kinda was like a zombie apocalypse, watching the hunger consume my friend totally. Yup, definitely Gluttony.

I looked around for something appropriate to punch, and my gaze lit on a tall man standing behind the serving trays. He stood staring at me, a scowl on his vaguely French face. Maybe it was the chef's hat he wore, or maybe the narrow mustache, but something about him just looked French and, therefore, disapproving.

"Lemme guess," I said, looking over at Michael. "That's the boss demon?" I pointed at the snooty-looking bastard in the chef's hat.

"Let's find out," Michael said, drawing his sword and hopping up onto the long table beside him. The warrior angel strode down the Formica table, kicking aside the plates of the people who sat there, mindlessly shoveling slop into their mouths.

"You!" Michael called, stopping at the end of the table and pointing his sword at the man in the chef's whites. "Are you the ruler of this domain?"

"No, monsieur, I am merely the sous chef. You, I believe, would like to speak with the head chef." The snooty man waved an arm off to his left, and the whole room shook as the head chef stepped into view.

"Well, fuck," I muttered as I saw the thing I was supposed to fight through to get out of this particular corner of Hell. It looked like Jabba the Hutt, or maybe a flesh-colored Stay-Puft Marshmallow Man. Unlike the slimy *Star Wars* slaver, this demon had feet, although the only evidence that it had legs was in the twin mounds of fat rolls that cascaded down over most of its clawed feet.

The demon was at least a dozen feet tall, and easily that big around, with long arms covered in flab and dripping sweat and maybe grease with every movement. Its head looked like someone dropped an all-white beach ball onto a pair of fleshy shoulders, and from deep within its lard-covered face, I could see a triple row of teeth that had "the better to eat you with" written all over them.

"Welcome to the Buffet, Quincy Harker," it said, and when it spoke, it sounded like someone rolling a raw turkey down a flight of stairs. "What can we tempt you with today?"

"How about an exit, Tubby?" I asked.

"Of course," the fat demon said, a grin splitting its fleshy face and making it somehow even more nauseating when it smiled. Maybe it was the gobbet of meat hanging from between its teeth and jiggling against its chin. "We certainly don't want anyone here who doesn't deserve to be here. But why not have a quick snack before you go? The way to the Master is long, and you need to eat to keep your strength up." It gestured toward the serving line, where a string of half a dozen tall demons in aprons stood at attention, big spoons loaded with gray glop just waiting for someone to put a tray in front of them.

"I'll pass, thanks," I said, taking a step forward. "Is the exit over here? I'll just see myself out. No need for you to...I don't know, move, on my account."

"But you must eat," the demon said. "You wouldn't want to seem ungrateful, would you?" The demon managed an aggrieved look for at least half a minute before a vicious grin split its face. "Never mind, you obviously have no manners." It waved an arm to the souls seated at the tables. "Children! Extra dessert to the one who brings me the head of Quincy Harker!"

The second the fat bastard said "dessert," every soul in the cafeteria stood up and focused their attention on me. Looked like I found a way to get in the food fight from Hell. Yippee.

8

———

The horde of gray-skinned souls moved toward us almost as one entity, a thoughtless, emotionless wave of dead hunger. A few of them retained something of who they had been in life, but the vast majority of them were completely featureless, hunger having consumed everything they used to be, everything that made them individual, until they were nothing but a tide of starving souls. And I was their buffet.

I drew my sword and leapt up onto the nearest table to get a better position, but Raphael yanked me back down. "You can't kill them, Quincy," the angel said.

"Why not? Oh wait, they're already dead."

"That's not it. Your sword would almost certainly destroy them. But I can't, *we* can't let you do that."

I raised an eyebrow at the Archangel. "*Let* me? You motherfuckers were pretty content to stand on the sidelines and let me get tormented almost to insanity in the last Circle, but now that it's time to kick some ass, you won't *let* me? Give me one reason I don't tell you to fuck right off with that bullshit."

"They're people." He said it simply, like it should explain everything, and half a second after he uttered those words, it did explain everything.

"You mean if I kill them here, I destroy their souls."

"Yes. And these aren't demons, born for no purpose other than to unleash evil upon the world, or even of the Fallen, who made their choice and stood beside Lucifer against the Father. These are souls serving penance and deserve your pity."

"But they don't deserve to eat me," I said, reversing my grip on the hilt of my sword and slamming it into the forehead of a soul that had gotten a little close for comfort. "You wanna put a little distance between them and us while I think of a plan?" I asked Raphael.

He nodded and wrapped his arms around my chest. He hugged me tight and spread his wings. I felt my stomach drop out as we flew to the farthest end of the hellish cafeteria. I looked back at the rest of the Seraphim when we landed and noted, not without a touch of bitterness, that they all just stood there, half a dozen immobile pillars of light in a sea of gray souls streaming in my direction.

"Nice of your brothers to hop right in and make themselves useful," I grumbled. I had fifteen or twenty seconds at most before the herd reached me and I was in the soup again, so I wracked my brain for some way to shield myself and still be able to move. I didn't just need to keep from getting devoured, I also need to take the fight to the Jabba demon if I was going to stand any chance of getting out of here with my own soul intact.

I put my palms flat together in front of my chest and whispered, *"Invisibilia,"* focusing my energy inward as I did so. I didn't see or feel any different, but I guessed by the surprise on Raphael's face that he couldn't see me. "I guess it worked, huh?" I said.

"Well, you're certainly invisible, but I can still hear you, and I wouldn't assume you no longer have a scent. I don't think that's going to be enough to get you out of here. Then there is the matter of your friends." He raised an arm and pointed into the herd, where I could see Dennis's curly hair mixed in with the starved souls. Of course, he and Glory were stuck in the mob. They'd already fallen victim to the hunger this place instilled in people, so they would be trying to eat my kidneys just like everyone else.

I spared a brief thought to wonder why I wasn't hungry like my friends but shoved the thought aside. No time for that shit now. Assuming I didn't get ripped to shreds like an extra on *The Walking Dead*, I'd have plenty of time to think about the logic of Hell later.

I dug into my jeans pocket and pulled out half a dozen dimes and nickels. They weren't great, but they'd do in a pinch, and that's all I needed. I cupped my hands around the coins, brought them to my mouth, and whispered, *"Convitium tempus"* into my palms while pushing energy into the tiny disks of metal. Then I took each one in turn and whizzed them out into the room like miniature frisbees.

As the coins landed, all far from where I stood shrouded in my invisibility spell, they exploded into a cacophony of sound. Fireworks, cursing, hair metal guitar solos, and Nickelback choruses filled the cafeteria as the most obnoxious sounds I could conjure issued forth from the coins. The herd, baffled by the surround-sound barrage, spun in circles looking for the source of the noise. Different souls locked onto different coins as the closest thing to me they could find, and the formerly cohesive wave of hunger turned into a bumbling, stumbling mass of chaos, with all the starved gray forms shambling in different directions, tripping over each other, bumping into one another, and not a one of them coming after me.

Raphael looked over to where I stood, a little smile on his face. "Not bad," he said. "A novel solution, to be certain. But it doesn't solve the dual problems of your companions being among the horde, and the very large demon who does not seem to be distracted by your ruse."

I turned to where he pointed, and sure enough, Jabba the Chef was lumbering toward me, smacking his lips. From somewhere I don't even want to think about, he drew a pair of huge swords and started running them along each other like he was sharpening knives to carve a turkey. I didn't feel like playing the capon at his dinner party, but I didn't expect to have much choice in the matter.

"Well, this is the part where I do get to fuck somebody up," I said, drawing my sword and canceling the invisibility spell. My blade burst into pure white flame, and the demon's smile grew even wider.

"I love it when my meat gets exercise right before the slaughter. It makes it soooo tender." Then he put on a burst of speed that I never expected and charged me.

"Fuckfuckfuck*fuck*!" I shouted, leaping to the left and clearing a couple of tables before landing on a third. Apparently, it was more than my magic that was amped up in Hell, I was stronger, too. And faster, but not fast enough to stay clear of Jabba's reach forever. He barreled through the tables, sending aluminum and pressboard flying as he just stomped stuff to splinters as he came at me, swords waving like he wanted me for the entrée in a demented hibachi restaurant.

I sheathed my sword, pulled in power from around me and flung raw energy at him as I hopped from table to table, trying to stay far enough away from him to not get sliced and diced, while trying not to get so close to the horde of hungry souls that I became the dessert they were starving for. The spheres of purple light seared his flesh, drawing howls of rage and pain, but Tubbo the Fat Demon kept on rumbling my way.

"Any suggestions?" I called out to the assembled Archangels.

Silence. Of course, silence. Because angels are assholes. *Okay, dickheads,* I thought as I altered my course. *Let's see how you like a couple of tons of raging lard demon raining down on your pretty little heads.*

I pivoted to the left and vaulted a pair of tables, planted my palms on another, and sprung over it before leaping into the air again. This time when I landed, I sprang right and took up a position atop one long table, drew my sword, and waited for Jabba to rush me again.

But this time I waited in relative comfort behind a cluster of Archangels standing around with their thumbs up their asses watching me fight. Gabriel whirled around and gaped at me. "What are you doing?"

I gave him my very best smirk, and after living among the French for a decade or two, my smirk is pretty good. "I'm changing your rules of engagement, cockless. Now you fuckers get to decide if your worthless asses here are worth fighting for."

Jabba charged toward us, bellowing in rage. He sent more tables flying, and I started to wonder if Hell had carpenters, or at least contractors, or if this shit just manifested into whatever forms the ruler of each Circle wanted it to assume. Gabriel stood gawking up at me like a poleaxed steer, while Michael and Azrael looked at one another, nodded, and sprang forward, spreading their wings and flying right at the lard demon. Their swords manifested in their hands without them having to even draw, and as they reached the angry tub of guts, they crossed paths in midair, flaming blades flashing in the fluorescent light of the cafeteria.

The Archangels circled around to land in front of me, Michael glaring up at me. "That was uncalled for," he said with a scowl. I noticed that not only did Azrael not gripe about having to actually kick some ass for a change, but he seemed pretty happy to cut loose a little.

The emphasis there is on "cut" because as I looked over the heads of Michael the Pissy Warrior Angel, I saw chunks of Jabba fall off and slide to the floor with a sickening squelchy sound. The angelic blades had sliced him into four pieces, cutting a giant "X" across his front and somehow defying all laws of physics and blade length to pass completely through the demon and cut him into four huge chunks. The demon parts slid to the floor and splattered, oozing across the tile like a really, *really* disgusting chunky soup. The demon started to dissolve immediately, turning into nothing more than a grayish-pink sludge that oozed across the floor like a slow and nauseating tide of dead asshole.

I looked down at Azrael. "That was nasty."

"That was a demon. They are not known for their hygiene."

"Good point." I turned to the horde of starving souls. They weren't clamoring for my spare change anymore. In fact, they weren't doing anything, just standing stock still wherever they were when the boss demon was sliced apart. After a few seconds, the gray coloring that I had assumed was their skin began to slide off of them and run off onto the floor like mud washing off. Before my eyes, the featureless souls turned back into the remnants of men and women, looking around the cafeteria and blinking their eyes.

Dennis and Glory shook their heads as if to clear the cobwebs, and

I could see a little rivulet of gray dribble down from Dennis's ear and run down his neck. "You guys okay now?" I called to them.

Dennis looked up at me, then down at the cafeteria tray still in his hands. "What the hell am I doing with this thing, Harker?"

"Yeah, why am I over here?" Glory asked, grabbing Dennis's elbow and moving toward where I stood with the Archangels.

"It's a long story," I said as they got nearer. I turned to Gabriel, who had become my default source of information on Hell. "What happens to these people now?"

"That depends on them," he said, his expression bland.

"What do you mean?" I asked.

"They may decide that the demon's demise and their liberation from hunger means that their penance is paid and they can ascend."

"Or they may continue to believe that they need to be punished, in which case they will either move to a different Circle to atone for other sins, or they will remain here until Lucifer appoints another Lord of Glut," Raguel said.

"Wait a minute." I held up a hand. "Are you telling me that these folks are only in Hell until they think they have been punished enough?"

"Of course, Quincy," Sealtiel said. "Hell is the ultimate expression of the human's free will. You spend as much time in here as you feel you deserve. When you deem yourself worthy of God's holy light, you can ascend."

"So there's no eternal damnation?" I asked.

"Of course there is. If that's what you think you deserve." The angel looked up at me, standing on the table and staring down like they had all gone insane. In reality, it was my understanding of the universe that was undergoing a rapid shift in perception. Interdimensional travel, kids—it's a fucking head trip.

By the time my head stopped spinning, Glory and Dennis had rejoined the party, so I looked at Gabe and asked, "Got any idea how to leave this Circle, oh learned one?"

"I would suggest we use the door, but the choice, as always, is yours," he said, pointing to a single door in a nearby wall. A wall that had been featureless gray until that moment.

I shook my head and walked to the door, putting my hand on the knob and looking back at the Archangels and my friends. This trip through Hell was really starting to suck. I opened the door, and we stepped through to find out what joys Lucifer had waiting for us next.

9

I looked around the Hellscape, taking in the sleek chrome and glass surroundings. It felt more like a high-rise office building than a Circle of Hell. I stood there, feeling the plush carpet under my boots, and decided I was underdressed for this level of damnation.

"Well, this is nice," Glory said, looking around.

"Dude, these couches are *soft*. I haven't sat on a couch in…well, in a long time." Dennis was indeed sitting on a huge leather sofa with dark upholstery and had his feet up on a coffee table.

"Get your feet down," I told him.

"Don't worry, Mr. Harker, it's fine. We can replace it if he scuffs the surface. We can replace anything any of you…soil." I turned to see who spoke and saw a very nattily attired demoness holding a tray of drinks. She looked like a blend of horror movie and high-level executive, with a power suit, tight ponytail, and spike heels offset strangely by her crimson skin and spiked tail waving over her left shoulder. She looked at Dennis as she mentioned "soiling" things, and he shrank into the couch as if to try and hide from her gaze.

"Would you care for a drink? Mr. Mammon will be with you shortly. Please, make yourselves comfortable." She stepped forward, and I took a glass from the tray, looking at it with a certain level of suspicion.

"This isn't some kind of Persephone thing, is it?"

"Not at all, Mr. Harker. It's simply ice water."

I smiled a little at that. "Because people in Hell want ice water, right?"

"That is the rumor." She smiled right back at me, and I managed not to take a step back when her exceptionally pointed teeth came into view. Living with Luke had given me a certain level of comfort with fanged predators, but this chick had a mouth like a hammerhead shark.

I passed a glass of water to Glory, then turned to ask Gabriel what he could tell me about this Mammon guy, but he wasn't there. Nor were any of the Archangels. The only people in the room were me, the demoness, Glory, and Dennis.

"Where are the others?" I asked.

"Oh, them? Don't worry about the divine interlopers. They aren't welcome in Mr. Mammon's offices, so they are in another part of the building."

"You mean Circle," Glory pointed out. "This is the Fourth Circle of Hell, and Mammon is the Lord of Greed. This isn't an office building, and you aren't a personal assistant. You're a demon, and our sworn enemy. Now quit the shit and get your boss out here so he can tempt Harker, Harker can tell him where to shove his offer, and we can get on to the main event. All these distractions are getting old."

The demoness took a step toward Glory, and the tray of ice water was gone from her hands. She didn't drop it, she didn't toss it aside, it was just gone. No matter how many spells I cast, sometimes magic still manages to catch me by surprise, and it's always the little shit like that. Not the big summonings or the huge showy rituals, just making something conveniently vanish when you're done with it. That's where the magic lies to me, in making the extraordinary seem perfectly normal.

"Speak carefully, angel," the demoness said, looking Glory right in the eye. "You are no more powerful now than your pathetic mortal friends, and I would personally enjoy nothing more than ripping your entrails out and eating them in front of you, then watching them regenerate so I could do it over and over again, but Lord Mammon has decreed that you not be harmed until Mr. Harker has made his decision. So you live…for now. But do not press me, little cherub. I may be Lord Mammon's most trusted lieutenant, but I am still a demon, and we are not known for our obedience." She held up a hand and showed the razor-sharp claws that tipped each finger.

I held up my own hand and called power to shroud it in brilliant blue energy. "Hey look," I said. "I've got a hand, too." I carefully folded down all but the middle finger as the demoness stared at me. "And look, it's really fucking expressive. Now why don't you trot your little Devil Wears Prada ass back into the office and get your boss out here before I rip your face off and stuff it down your throat."

The demoness' face twisted into a scowl, and she turned from us to click-click her heels across the floor to a heavy wooden door. She yanked the door open and disappeared through it, and I released the power around my hand, letting out a sigh of relief as I did. "That was closer than I want to think about," I said.

"Closer to what?" Dennis asked, getting up from where he cowered behind the couch and walking over to where Glory and I stood. "You told that demon bitch exactly what she could do and where she could go! Which, I guess, is here, since we're already in Hell, but whatever. It was cool."

"It was also risky as fuck, Dennis," I replied. "I don't have any idea if I could have hurt her at all. She's obviously a high-ranking demon, and I'm on her turf. There's a chance I would have been the one with my head shoved up my ass when we were done."

"Not necessarily an unusual posture for you, Q," Glory said. When I turned to her, she tempered her snark with a smile. "But thanks. She could have torn me apart without batting an eye. I should have kept my cool. Sorry."

In all the time I'd known her, I think that was the first time Glory had ever admitted she might be wrong about anything. It was almost worth going to Hell to hear that.

We stood around for several minutes before a demon in a tailored suit came through the wooden door. "Mr. Harker, so good of you to join us! Please, have a seat. Mr. Bolton, Glory, I am pleased to make your acquaintance. I am Mammon, Lord of Greed, and I am all about the deal. Now let's sit down on these sofas and see if we can't negotiate a reasonable exit strategy for you and your companions." He breezed over to the sofa Bolton had sat on moments before, brushing off the spot Dennis had sullied with his ass before perching on the edge of the couch.

I just shrugged and walked over to the couch opposite Mammon and sat down, scooting forward on the seat so that I could sit upright and not be swallowed by the ridiculously soft leather. Glory and Dennis sat on either side of me, and I saw Glory rubbing the seat out of the corner of my eye.

"Soft, isn't it?" Mammon asked. "I had it specially made for me from the skin of virgins condemned to the Second Circle."

"Isn't that the domain of Lust?" I asked. "Why would there be virgins there, much less enough of them to make a couch."

"Two couches," the demon said, a smile splitting his obsidian face. "And there are plenty of virgins there. They all feel like they've committed the sin of impure thoughts and must be punished until they expiate their sins. Personally, I think they all read *Fifty Shades* too many times while they were alive and now they're taking the chance to experiment, but who am I to judge? Now, what can I offer you to stay in my domain? It would be quite the coup for me to get to torment the Reaper for at least a little slice of eternity." He leaned back and stretched his arms out along the back of the sofa, that plastic smile fixed firmly on his face.

I didn't respond at once. I took a moment to consider Mammon as he stared at me. His skin was glossy and black like he was chiseled from a chunk of volcanic rock and polished until all the rough edges were gone. A thin gray beard, perfectly trimmed, outlined his jawline, and his hair was just tousled enough to have required either three makeup artists and four hours of styling, or magic. My money was on magic. He wore his suit like it was a second skin, at complete ease in the expensive fabric. His wingtips were shinier than some mirrors I've seen, and his cufflinks gleamed with rubies the size of marbles.

He looked like a sharp businessman, except for the four clawed fingers on each hand, the three yellow eyes with vertical pupils arranged in a triangle on his face, and the short curved horns protruding from his forehead. Okay, he looked like the businessman from Hell, which I suppose he was, so it was a good look on him.

"If we don't come to an agreement, I just walk out of here, no harm no foul? Me and all my companions?" I didn't want to use the word "friends" because specificity is crucial when negotiating with demons, and most of the Archangels couldn't even be considered friendly acquaintances. I didn't want to get through Door Number Four only to find the Seraphim were trapped behind me.

"Of course," Mammon said, his tone breezy and light, like the mere suggestion of holding us in his realm was beneath him. "I don't want anyone here who doesn't want to be here, Quincy. May I call you Quincy?"

"Sure."

"You see, Quincy, Hell is a place of your own devising. You mortals, I mean. We arrange this place in domains, or Circles, because your buddy Dante ate some bad mushrooms, or some really good mushrooms, depending on your views on hallucinogens, and dreamt up all these Circles and the like. Left to our own devices, we are not nearly so structured. We like to torture lesser beings, cause them agony, but we aren't usually in for this kind of rigid hierarchy. But that's what you mortals want, and this place was created for you, after all. So we do as we're asked. Hopefully in a millennium or so, you people will forget all about that sop Alighieri and we can go back to the way things used to be."

"And get off your lawn?" I asked, raising an eyebrow.

"Something like that," Mammon said with a nod. "Now, how about it? What can I offer you to entice you to remain here on Team Greed? Money? Cars? Whores? Power? Chocolate? What is it that Quincy Harker desires more than anything else in the universe?" His eyes, all three of them, locked onto mine, and I felt him invade my consciousness. It felt like he was running his fingers over the folds of my brain, and I resorted to mental shielding techniques I developed in the late twentieth century.

So, tell me what you want, what you really really want.

I'll tell you what I want, what I really really want,
So, tell me what you want, what you really really want.
I wanna—, I wanna—, I wanna—,I wanna—,
I wanna really, really, really, wanna zigazig ahh!

On the third cycle through the most annoying Spice Girls chorus in the world, kept in my head for just those times when unwanted intruders are fumbling about in my skull, Mammon leaned back and narrowed his eyes at me.

"You're not a nice man, Quincy," the demon hissed.

"You're the one ruling a chunk of real estate in Hell, dickwhistle. You wanna compare asshole-ness, or you just wanna accept that you don't have anything I want bad enough to stick around this bougie shithole."

He looked offended. "Bougie? That's just mean. I hired some of the top designers in New York to decorate this waiting room. Well, tortured, really. Hired might be too strong a word. It's cold, it's impersonal, it's intimidating, certainly. But bougie?" He looked back and forth to Dennis and Glory. "What do you think?"

"I'm a terrible judge of human taste," Glory said.

"I've been trapped inside the internet like a low-rent Tron for a decade," Dennis said. "I don't think any of us are qualified to decide what is or is not bougie."

That was enough for me. I stood up from the couch, called forth energy into my fists, and said, "Can we agree that nobody gives a fuck whether or not your lobby is posh? Open the door, bring me the Archangels, and bid me fucking adieu, Mammon, before I blow this entire façade to ectoplasm."

"Well, if you wanted to leave, the door's right there," Mammon said, gesturing to the door he'd come in through. "You didn't even have to take my meeting if you were going to be so rude." He stood up, straightened his tie, sniffed an affronted little sniff, and vanished. When he did, so did the room. We were back in the same Hellscape of the First Circle, only hotter. A *lot* hotter.

The Archangels stood in a circle around us, just staring. None of them had so much as a drop of sweat on their brows, and I soaked through my shirt and even my jeans within five seconds of Mammon's departure. Yet another reason to have angels—no sweat glands.

"Are you unhurt, Harker?" Raphael asked.

"Yeah, we're fine. Mammon says the door is somewhere...oh." I swept my arm around the rocky desert scene before me, stopping at a door standing free in the middle of nothing. "I guess it's right here. Greed was pretty easy, what's next?"

"Greed has never been one of your major faults, Harker," Glory said. "The next Circle is going to be more problematic."

"Why? What's in there that I'll hate so much?"

"It's not that you'll hate it, Q. It's more that it's right in your wheel-house. So much so that this will be the most tempting plane for you. The next Circle is Rage."

Rage. Yeah, that's kinda my whole brand right there. This oughta be *fun*.

10

There was a welcoming party for me when we stepped through the door into the Circle of Rage, and they didn't even bring a cake. No, instead they brought every demon, monster, and human that I killed in the last hundred years, every one of them wanting to rip my head off and shove it up my ass. And standing in the very front of the vanguard of pissed-off dickheads was Augustus Renfield, my uncle's first manservant and the most famous butler in history.

"Well, this looks like fun," I said. "Raphael, make sure Glory and Dennis stay safe. I've got a whole lot of killing to do." I didn't bother saying anything to Michael and Azrael. They'd jump in on this one without being prompted. Most of the people in front of me really deserved a good smiting, and Azrael was still a bloodthirsty mother-fucker. I drew my sword and saw them both ready their weapons beside me.

Then Gus bellowed out a war cry built of pure rage, and it was on. Uncle Luke's former servant, confidant, best friend, and most bitter enemy charged me with his hands stretched into claws and his face pulled into a rictus of fury. I sidestepped his first wild slashes, cut through his hamstrings, and bashed him in the head with the pommel of my sword. He fell to the side, immediately replaced by a pair of waist-high imps that didn't look familiar but had daggers in each hand and bad intentions on their faces. I kicked one in the face, getting a long slash on my leg for my trouble, then chopped straight down on the other, splitting him from hairline to beltline with one huge blow.

I wrestled my sword free from the mess of demon bone and guts to my left, barely ducking under a wild grab at the exposed back of my neck by an angry dead Nazi. "I don't remember killing you the first time," I said as I spun around, cutting clean through him with my sword wreathed in white fire. "And judging by the crowd here, I won't remember killing you this time, either."

My sword continued through the Nazi's torso until it slammed into what felt like a stone wall. The vibration ran up my arms, and I stepped back, lowering the blade and looking up into the grinning face of the one man I hated more than any other to ever walk the earth. He was big and blond, smiling like the Cheshire Cat, and wearing a bizarre amalgam of Nazi uniform and medieval armor, complete with the heavy shield that blocked my strike. This was *Unterscharführer* Brittlav, the Nazi who in 1943 murdered Anna Treves in front of my face, killing the woman I loved and sending me into a fugue of rage and murder that lasted nearly half a decade.

Blondie smiled down at me, a cruel grin that held no mirth, just the promise of pain. "I have waited for you, little Jew-lover. I know what you are now, and here you are no stronger than me, no faster than me. Here I am the true son of the master race, and I will gut you just like I did that Jew bitch you were fucking."

I held on to myself, but just barely. Blondie's words brought back not just the memory of watching Anna die, but the memory of *feeling* her die, feeling the mental bond that we had cut like a thread. Red mist hovered at the edge of my vision, but I managed to focus on thoughts of Flynn and keep myself from succumbing to the rage that filled me.

"I don't have to be stronger or faster, you piece of shit," I said, fury leaking into my voice. "I'm a motherfucking wizard!" I raised my left hand and channeled my anger through my arm, engulfing it in a torrent of flame that flew from my palm in a widening cone. The fire burned white-hot, and whatever it touched, it turned to ash. Blondie got his shield up, but that just meant that he got covered in molten metal before I turned him to slag. The fire poured out of me, fueled by my anger and stoked into an inferno by the very nature of the Circle we stood upon.

The more I let my fury flow through me, the more rushed into to replace it. My fire was a white-hot weapon of justice, scorching the earth in front of me and blasting the demons and souls in its path to oblivion. I was a never-ending wellspring of anger, spurned into a burning hate by the site of Anna's killer, and it felt *good.* I burned, and I burned, and when there was nothing left in front of me to burn, I started turning in a slow circle to find more targets.

I felt, rather than saw, the Archangels and my friends drawing back from me as the heat began to radiate not just from my hand but from my whole body. Good. I didn't want to hurt them, but every other son of a bitch on this plane of existence was going to feel my righteous fury. I immolated demons and souls alike, not even paying attention to whom or what I set ablaze. I saw Nazi uniforms in my periphery, along with nightmare visions of some of the creatures I'd battled over the years.

I let my anger run free, not with the insane chaos of my mid-century madness, but with cold, calculated precision. I knew exactly what I was doing, and every goddamn thing around me deserved exactly what it got. But it wasn't enough. No matter how many demons I burned, there were even more coming. For every dead Nazi I killed, another brown-shirted fuck took his place. Every demon I blasted to nothingness was replaced by two more. *Fine,* I thought. *I'll crank this bitch up to thirteen and see how they like it.*

I tossed my sword to the ground and brought my right hand up, calling forth more rage and fire to bathe the entire landscape in flames. Demons fell, souls turned to vapor, and still more came. I drew in more power, more anger, pouring everything I had into the fire.

Then I felt a ringing slap upside the back of my head, and my hands sputtered to darkness at the shock of it all. My streams of fire vanished in a blink, and I turned to see Glory standing behind me, an irritated look on her face. "What the fuck, Glory?"

"You're a hardheaded son of a bitch, Harker. And this time, that's not a metaphor. That actually hurt my hand." She shook her right hand for emphasis.

"Why did you hit me? I was killing bad guys. See? They're…" My voice trailed off as I looked behind me. Where once maybe two hundred demons and angry souls had stood wanting a piece of me, now there were five times that many. "What the fuck?"

"Circle of Rage, Harker. Everyone you killed with your righteous fury came back twofold. You killed them again; they came back again. And every time they returned, another demon of rage was born right alongside them. You didn't kill anything with your little pyrotechnics show—you just made a shitload more demons."

"Fuck."

"Yeah, pretty much." She pointed to where the Archangels stood in a circle around Dennis, hands linked and lips moving in concert. "Those dickheads are the only thing holding back the tide of assholes right now, them and some kind of divine ritual that even I've never heard of. But as long as they keep chanting, the demons can't attack."

"So what do we do?"

Glory handed me my discarded sword. "Well, first you put this thing away. It might not do you any good here, but I'm betting we'll need it again before we make it to Lucifer. Then you talk to this guy who showed up under a flag of parley about three seconds after you went supernova." She jerked her thumb over her shoulder, and I looked past her to see one of the ugliest, most terrifying demons I've ever had the displeasure of meeting.

"Goddammit. Fucking Asmodeus?"

"Fucking Asmodeus. He says he can get you out of here. For a price."

"Do you believe him?"

"I don't believe anything the rat bastard says, but your normal method of burning shit to the ground doesn't seem to be working, so you might as well hear him out."

I walked across the blasted landscape that seemed to be made of finely ground obsidian to stand in front of Asmodeus. The Prince of Hell leaned against a glassy black outcropping of rock, a lit cigarette dangling from his lips. His hooved feet were crossed at the ankles, and he had an insolent smirk plastered on his face, but his eyes were locked on the Archangels. He didn't want me to know it, but it stirred something inside him, seeing his brothers again after all these millennia. I didn't know if it was regret or anger, but given our current location, I was willing to bet it wasn't the warm fuzzies.

"How's it hanging, As-man?" I asked as I approached. Glory hung back, I'm assuming to keep out of range of Asmodeus and not to end up as leverage against me, but she might have just been trying to avoid the secondhand smoke.

"You're a regular laugh riot, Harker. What are you doing in my back yard? I don't like you enough for you to come into my domain uninvited. And alive, no less. That's almost insulting."

"Lucifer has something I need. I came down to get it from him. I'm just passing through your realm, no need to worry about your property values. You going to let me through, or are we going to have to fight about it?"

The demon laughed, his mouth opening to show an almost infinite maw of needle-like teeth. His gaping mouth was like one of those optical illusions where the hallway of mirrors goes on forever, except it was row upon row of pointy agony, *ad infinitum*. "Do you actually think you could stand against me for half a second, Quincy Harker? Here, of all places?"

Asmodeus pushed off the rock and loomed over me. He grew to about eight feet tall, so he could do some serious looming. His voice deepened, and when he spoke, my liver sent out urgent messages about running away, with or without the rest of my organs. "Do not presume too much, Reaper. You're the stuff of nightmares to the imps and Pit-born, but I am a Prince of Hell. I fought with Lucifer at the Pearly Gates, and I stood against the very Archangels you now drag into my kingdom. You survive here by my sufferance, and only thus. Should I so choose, I could snuff you out as though you had never existed. Your pitiful little soul would barely leave a smear on my foot as I ground you into paste."

His black eyes bore into me, but I stood my ground. I learned a long time ago never to let a predator see fear, and bravado and bullshit were the only things I had going for me. "So what do you want, Asmodeus? If you came here to gloat, mission fucking accomplished. If you came here to lend a hand, then sidle up to your long-lost brothers and pitch the fuck in. But if you just came here to talk shit, I don't have time for that. Uriel is being tortured by Lucifer in the Ninth Circle, and we have to get him out before Lucifer gets his feathers back and storms the Gates of Heaven. Again."

Asmodeus looked surprised, like for the first time since our conversation began I'd said something he didn't already know. "Lucifer has Uriel? Here?"

"Yeah, he ripped his eyelids off back on Earth, so I can only imagine the shit he's doing down here."

"And you're here to save Uriel?"

"Among other side projects, yes."

Asmodeus waved his hand in a big circle, and a door appeared. "Go through here. It will skip the line, so to speak, and take you right to Lucifer's realm."

"And you just happen to have a back door into the boss's private office?"

"Think of it like the executive elevator. I'm upper management, and when the boss calls, he doesn't like to wait. Now are you going to take advantage of my momentary lapse of judgement and get the fuck out of my house, or are you going to stand here staring into the gift horse's mouth?"

I looked up at the demon. He still looked ugly as homemade shit salad, but there was something else in his face. Something almost… sad. "Why are you doing this, Asmodeus? Isn't there a big bonus for bringing Lucifer my head on a plate or something?"

"Lucifer has nothing to offer me, Harker. I'm already a prince. There's nowhere for me to go unless the king dies, and the king is fucking immortal. So what is he going to give me? *Two* Circles to rule? That's just more underlings to keep track of. I don't need the hassle. And I like Uriel. Or liked, rather. He's…he *was*…kind. We fought. When I stood with Lucifer. Uriel and I came face to face on the battlefield of Heaven, and he bested me. He could have killed me, like they did to so many of our brothers." He looked over at Michael and Azrael, and the anger on his face made me take a half step back. "But he didn't. He took my sword, and he cast me down, but he didn't kill me. I owe him for that."

He looked down at me again, and I felt the weight of the Prince of Hell's gaze upon me. "Our books are also out of balance, Quincy Harker. You rooted out a traitor in my ranks, which may have led to insurrection. You did so out of your own ridiculous mortal purposes, but the fact remains that the debt was not paid in full. I pay my debts, human. All of them. So go through this door into Lucifer's domain and save my brother from the torture my king has planned for him. Then get the hell out of Hell and don't come back until I can torment you for eternity."

I looked him up and down, but demons don't give off tells when they lie. I had to go with my gut, and my gut told me that the Archangels holding the mob of angry demons back were going to start tiring pretty damn quick, so I'd better quit fucking around and make a decision.

I nodded. "Thank you, Asmodeus. We're even."

He nodded back. "Get out of my house, Harker."

I turned to the Seraphim. "Time to go!" They ceased chanting and turned as one and bolted for the door. Raphael scooped up Dennis, Sealtiel grabbed Glory, and they all unfurled their wings, streaking toward me and the door barely in front of a tide of fury the likes of which I hoped never to see again.

I flung open the door, we tumbled through in a mass of wings and limbs, and the door slammed shut behind us, almost clipping Azrael's feathers as it did. I looked around and saw we were in an ornate foyer of what looked like a gothic castle painted by Hieronymus Bosch, complete with columns made of tormented human forms slowly writhing in agony all the way up to the ceiling some thirty feet above us.

"Well, I'll give him this much," I said, picking myself up off the floor. "Lucifer really does seem to be a man of wealth and taste. Let's find Uriel and get the fuck out of here, shall we?"

11

"This is the time that anyone with previous knowledge of the layout of Lucifer's castle should speak up and save me hours of flailing around looking for Uriel," I said, looking at the assembled angels.

"None of us have ever been here before, Quincy," Raphael said. "We won the war, remember? This is where we banished Lucifer. None of us would come down here except in the most dire of circumstances."

"Like now," I said.

"Um, yes. Like now."

"But what about you?" I asked, turning to Gabriel. "You've got your Big Book of Knowing All the Things, right? Isn't there a map in there somewhere?"

"There is," the Archangel replied, but the shifty look on his face told me he was about to get to the part of the answer I wouldn't like. "But I don't have access to it."

"You. Don't. Have. Access?" I couldn't quite believe what I was hearing, but there had been so much unbelievable shit in my day already that it was a lot more believable than normal.

"That is correct. I am the Scribe of Heaven, the keeper of all knowledge. But I don't actually *know* everything. There are some things that the Father hasn't shared with me, and knowledge of the deepest Circle is one of those things. He may have wanted to give Lucifer some privacy after the Fall."

"Well, we're a long fucking way after the Fall now, and we need to know where we're going if we're going to find Uriel before Lucifer kills him and marches right back up to the Pearly Gates."

"You need a guide." I whirled around at the voice, my sword leaping to my hand almost unbidden. But since I was in Hell, and expected everything to want to kill me, there was kind of a general bidden going on.

Leaning against a pillar in an affected posture of nonchalance was a demon. Because of course there was. He wasn't a very large demon, roughly human-sized, with a head full of curly black hair, angular, almost pointy features, and blue-black skin with an obsidian shimmer to it. Something about him felt familiar, but it wasn't until I spied the pointy tail looping over his shoulder that it clicked.

"Faustus, I presume?" I asked, the details of Gabby's encounter with the demon masquerading as a doctor coming back to me.

"At your service," the demon said with a toothy grin full of needle-sharp fangs. He pushed off the column and swept his arm out in an elegant bow. Maybe this guy really had lived through the Elizabethan era. He certainly had the manners for it.

"I've heard of you. Gabby speaks highly of you, as demons go. I'd almost say you're her favorite hellspawn, if we don't count your son."

A shadow flickered across the demon's face at the mention of his son. "How is Jake?" His tone was light, and there was nothing in his face to give away his concern, but I got an odd sense that this demon actually gave a shit about his offspring. I'd seen it before, of course. Mort went absolutely fucking insane when Orobas killed his daughter Christy, but it was pretty rare. Generally, demons are more complete fucking psychopaths than caring parents.

"He's fine. Last time I checked, he was shacking up with Gabby and her girlfriend and getting his horizons expanded daily. Your boy might be half-demon, but I don't think he's going to be a match for Gabriella Van Helsing."

He smiled, and a little of the tension in his shoulders eased. "Good. I was concerned that when I returned here, he would be set adrift. He's a good boy, but so...*human* sometimes."

"We all have our little shortcomings," I said. "What do you want, Faustus? We're kinda on a deadline here."

"I want to help."

"Help?"

"Is there an echo in here? Yes, I want to help. I want to help you stop Lucifer from getting his divinity back and getting back into Heaven."

"Why would you want to do that, demon?" Glory asked. Her face mirrored the suspicion I felt.

"You wouldn't understand."

"Try us," I prodded.

He took a deep breath, then nodded. "Okay, fine. Here's the deal. I want to get out of here. I like it on Earth. I like the people, I like the food, and I really like the climate. Do you have any idea how bad this place is for my skin? I'm also a fan of not having the higher-level demons beat the shit out of me, and Beelzebub and Mephistopheles have both been looking for me ever since the moment I got back. Something about shirking my duty and teaching me what torment really felt like, so I could earn my way back into their good graces."

"So, you took an unauthorized vacation, and now the bosses want to beat your ass for it," I said.

"Yeah, pretty much. I'm not such a fan of the part where I get my ass beat and way less a fan of the part where they dissolve my body in a vat of sulfuric acid, then skim me off the top of the vat, reconstitute me, and do it all over again. It makes what the Greeks did to Prometheus look like a picnic."

"I think it was a picnic. For the buzzards, I mean," Dennis said with a little smile.

"Not helping, Dennis," I growled.

"Not trying to help, Harker. Why are you even listening to this guy? He's a demon. You know, the bad guys?"

"Yeah, I get that, Boltron. But Gabby says he's okay. And he's got a real Joe Pesci vibe to him. You know what I mean? The weaselly little fuck that's always working an angle?"

"Pretty much exactly why I don't trust him."

"As long as you *know* he's only looking out for himself, you can work that around so that what's good for him is good for us, and that way we can work him while he works his angle."

"You do remember I'm standing right here?" Faustus asked.

I turned to the demon. "Have I said anything that isn't completely true?"

"Well, no."

"Are you working some angle for yourself?"

"Of course. I'm a demon. I'm completely in this for myself. I want to get out of Hell, get back to Earth, and keep Lucifer running things down here so that those douchebros Mephistopheles and Beelzebub and their twin asshole buddy Azazel don't come to power. If they take over Hell, there's going to be a lot of unpleasant changes, and one of them will be the amount of time they spend looking for deserters.

"Right now, Lucifer doesn't give a shit if somebody he doesn't need goes AWOL. He figures even if we're not working directly for him, we're probably stirring up some kind of shit that he'd approve of, so he just leaves us be. The other three? They have a more hands-on leadership style, with a lot less creative freedom for their underlings. That would suck for me, so I'm really invested in seeing Lucifer stay down here."

"See, Dennis?" I asked. "As long as our goals align with Faustus's goals, we can count on him to do what's best for all of us. So we use him, and we watch him like a goddamned hawk."

"Which I technically am," Faustus said. "God-damned, that is. It kinda comes with the pointy tail. So, you want me to show you the way to Lucifer's throne room, or you want to stand around out here jacking your jaws and waiting for his House Guard to come and take you there in chains? You're going to end up there either way, but with me you might still have all your limbs and organs when you get there."

"How are we supposed to get out of here when we stop him?" I asked. "I mean, up until now, I figured we'd be dead before we got this far, so I've just been kinda winging it."

"Oh, that inspires just a *fuckton* of confidence," Dennis said, his hands clapped to his head. He turned to Michael. "You see what I have to deal with? Can I just go to Heaven? Come on, you've got to know a guy, right? You can sneak me in? I don't think I can make it through another Harker adventure."

"I've got a plan," Faustus said with a smile. "I can get us out of Hell, but I need a human soul to do it. Something anchored to your dimension."

"Fortunately, we have a couple of those right here." I pointed at myself and Dennis. "Hell, I even brought along a spare, just in case one runs out of batteries before we're done."

"Okay, then," I said. "Lead on, tall, dark, and shifty. Let's go keep Lucifer out of Heaven."

"So, you were joking about not having a plan, right?" Faustus said as he started walking down the wide hallway.

I fell into step right beside him and shook my head. "Nope, not at all. That's what I brought them along for." I jerked a thumb over my shoulder at the Archangels trailing along behind us like pompous kindergarteners. "Michael kicked Lucifer's ass once, I figure he can probably do it again."

"Probably? I'm hinging my survival on a 'probably?'" Faustus stopped cold and gaped at me.

I put an arm around the demon's shoulder and gave him what I hoped was a jaunty grin. "What? You wanna live forever?"

12

We took so many twists and turns through Lucifer's castle of horrors that I was a little dizzy by the time we reached a pair of huge golden doors embossed with more writhing human forms, all being tortured by grinning demons. Above the whole scene was a host of seven angels, all caricatures of the Archangels with me plus Uriel. I was particularly amused by the depiction of Michael as a cartoonishly muscled figure with shoulders so buffed up his head was almost invisible.

"That's a pretty good likeness, Mikey," I said, pointing at the top of the doors. "Is that one you, Az?" I pointed at an angel with a psychotic grin on its face and drool running down its chin.

"We are not amused, Harker," Michael said, his voice cold.

"I don't need you to be amused, pal. I need you to be ready for a fight. Are you ready to throw down with the Lightbringer if he doesn't hand Uriel over?"

"I will do what needs be done," Michael said without looking down at me. "I have shed the blood of my brothers before. If I must, I will do so again."

That wasn't exactly the ringing endorsement for his battle readiness that I was hoping for, but it seemed that was all I was going to get. "Okay, then."

I turned to look at everyone. "Here's the plan: I don't really have one. Never have. I'm figuring this shit out as I go along, and I have not one fucking clue what's on the other side of that door. All I know is that Lucifer is in there, and he has Uriel. And apparently if he kills Uriel in Hell and takes his Implement, he's an Archangel again, and nothing can keep him out of Heaven. That sounds bad for Heaven, and probably not great for Earth."

"Or Hell," Faustus chimed in.

I shot him a dirty look, then continued. "So we have to stop him. Whatever it takes. Saving Uriel is our first priority, then kicking Lucifer's ass, then we get Uriel somewhere safe and you Archangels can do whatever you have to do to give Glory her wings back. Does that work for the rest of you?"

There were nods all around. Raphael opened his mouth like he had something else to say, but his jaw snapped shut at a glare from Gabriel.

"Okay, then. Let's get this shit over with." I turned and shoved open the giant doors leading into the devil's throne room.

If you do a Google Image Search for "Throne Room in Hell," you'll pretty much get what I walked into. It was friggin' huge, the kind of place that was obviously designed to make visitors feel small and inadequate. The Hieronymus Bosch columns were gone, replaced by twenty-foot Corinthian monstrosities clad in sheets of what looked like pure gold. They reached to the ceiling and flared out in ornate curlicues, with each pillar ringed by half a dozen souls with eyes glowing a baleful red.

Down the center of the ceiling stretched a row of chandeliers, also with the glowing eyes skull motif, eight heads glaring down at the room with crimson orbs glowing in the depths. This cast a reddish tinge over the whole room, despite the harsh white light shining straight down from the chandeliers themselves. Lucifer was a lot of things, but a master of creating subtle ambiance wasn't one of them.

The room stretched out in front of us half the length of a basketball court, with a dais at the other end. On the platform stood Lucifer, holding a gleaming obsidian sword and grinning at us like the cat who just ate the world's biggest canary. "Welcome, brothers! Welcome, Quincy Harker! I am so glad you decided to join us. Thank you, Faustus, for leading my friends to the festivities. I assure you, your assistance in this matter will not be forgotten." The devil's smile never wavered, but a chill crept into his voice as he addressed Faustus, and I definitely figured that he didn't want to be in the same dimension as a pissed-off Lucifer any longer than he had to.

"Thank you, my lord," Faustus said, with a bow, and retreated toward the doors.

"Stay, my loyal servant," Lucifer said, and Faustus froze. The look on his face said he was trying to move but couldn't find the strength.

"Release Uriel, brother," Michael said, stepping forward. "This farce has gone on long enough. You will never return to the side of the Father. You are banished to rule in this realm for all eternity. Cease your folly and let us return to our duties."

"Oh, do shut the fuck up, Michael," Lucifer said, echoing a sentiment I'd had pretty much every other time Michael had opened his mouth since he stopped being Mitch. "You always were an officious prick, and the millennia haven't changed you a bit. Now why don't you all just stand there like good little children and behave while I take back my rightful place at the left hand of the throne. Now that you're finally here, I can get on with the ceremony."

I looked to Michael, then to Gabriel, who both looked back at me in confusion. I cleared my throat. "Hey Lucifer," I said. "Isn't this the part where you explain your whole plan to us so that we can thwart it at the last possible second?"

"No, Harker. This is where you, your wingless angel, and your… whatever you are," he motioned to Dennis, "get to watch as my brothers help me regain that which was taken from me so many years ago." At his words, the chandeliers unwound themselves and dropped to the floor as full skeletons, not just skulls and random groupings of entwined bones. Two skeletons grabbed each Archangel, and one took hold of me, Glory, and Dennis.

No matter how I struggled, I couldn't break free of the bony grip on my upper arms. Looking at the others, it seemed they were no more able to wrest free than I was. I wasn't all that surprised about Dennis and Glory, but I figured at least Michael or Azrael would have been able to overpower a couple of bony dead guys. Lucifer's skinless guards wrangled the Archangels into a rough semi-circle in front of him and the kneeling Uriel, who looked a whole lot the worse for wear.

His eyelids had grown back, which I guess was a blessing, since both eyes were swollen shut. His lips were cracked and bleeding, and if his nose wasn't broken, I'd never seen one that was. Spoiler: I've seen may fair share of broken noses. Worn more than one of them myself. His hair was matted to his scalp with blood, and he still wore his human guise, but it seemed hazy, as if I were looking through a pair of eyeglasses with the wrong prescription.

"What are you playing at, Lucifer?" Michael asked, struggling against the skeletons as they held him fast.

"I am not playing at anything, *brother*," Lucifer said, and the sarcasm in that word carried centuries of hate, jealousy, and resentment in two syllables. "I'm going home, and not you, nor Father, nor these idiot humans can stop me. It's taken me millennia, but you are finally in my home, my domain, and under my authority. Father gave me free rule here, and you can't take that away from me. You will never take anything away from me again. No one will!"

He raised his sword above his head and grinned at me. I turned my head to Dennis and whispered in a rush, "When I tell you, I want you to get up there and fuck shit up. I don't know what the fuck Lucifer's planning, but I want you to get up there, grab that whip, and run like a motherfucker."

"Got it. But how am I supposed to get free of tall, bony, and ugly here?"

"I got that covered," I said. "You just be ready to move."

"It is time," Lucifer said, and every eye spun to focus on him. We were about to decide the fate of the world. Me, a wingless guardian angel, and a hacker who dressed up like a unicorn for fun. The universe was so screwed.

13

"At last, it is TIME!" the King of Hell shouted, and everything seemed to move through molasses. I know it all happened in an instant, but it felt like an eternity as I stood helpless and watched an Archangel die.

Lucifer's blade flashed down. I felt more than saw the impact as the obsidian sword sliced through Uriel's neck. The Archangel's head fell from his shoulders, rolling to a stop several feet in front of the dead Seraph. Instead of blood, light began to pour from Uriel's neck. A wail like Heaven itself was being rent asunder split the air, and the rest of the Host fell to their knees.

Light poured from each of the stricken Seraphim, swirling together with the light streaking from Uriel's body, and spun together into a rope of blinding holy light, the very mystical essence of the angels themselves. That's when it made sense. It wasn't just killing Uriel. It was killing Uriel with the rest of the Archangels present that completed the ritual. They all had to be here when Lucifer took on the mantle because they were all connected. A piece of each of them live in every other one of the Host, and it was that shared soul that made them Seraphim, that made them holy. They were all one Host, one

392

bright shining aspect of God, and Lucifer needed all of the pieces to get home.

Lucifer held up his hands to the sky as that white light cascaded forth, bathing him in the divine light that was Uriel, and shouted, "Home! I'm coming home, Father, and you can't keep me out again!"

That's when I sprang into action, trying the Hail Mary to end all Hail Marys. I called up as much power as I could hold, drawing energy from myself, from the screaming angels around, from the divinity pouring out of the fatal wound in Uriel's body, and from the very air of Hell itself. I drew in power until I felt like I was going to rip myself apart at the seams, then I yanked my arms free of the skeleton holding me and pointed both my fists at Lucifer.

"Hey, Morningstar!" I shouted.

Lucifer turned his gaze from the ceiling of his throne room, which was beginning to crumble and disintegrate as a pillar of pure white energy flowed from Uriel upward, to glare at me with those pupil-less black eyes. He turned his focus to me, and I felt the weight of his will pressing down on me, hammering me to my knees with nothing more than a look. Any mortal would have crumbled to dust under the weight of that glare.

But I'm not a mortal. I'm not human, I'm not vampire. I might be part demon, and there might be a trace of divine intent somewhere in my soul, but at the end of the day, I'm Quincy motherfucking Harker, and it's going to take a lot more than a dirty look to put me off my game. I looked the devil right in the eye, and I grinned at him.

"Back the fuck up, you son of a bitch." Then I blasted him with everything I had, everything the angels around me had, everything that sneaky fuck Faustus lurking in the shadows had, and everything I could siphon from my surroundings. I poured power through me until my nerves felt like they were electrified, and my veins felt like fire ran through them. I hammered Lucifer with the biggest bolt of energy I had ever touched, and it managed to knock him back about ten feet.

Ten feet. I hit the bastard with enough mojo to knock the moon out of orbit, and he took three steps back. Three steps. But that was all I needed. "Faustus! NOW!"

I know, I put the fate of the world in the hands of a demon. But I wasn't counting on his good nature or charitable disposition. I was counting on something that really existed—enlightened, overweening self-interest. I was counting on Faustus *really* not wanting to become Azazel's bitch for the next few millennia, and that Lucifer would be distracted enough by my best shot that his hold on the paralyzed demon would break.

So yeah, I rolled the dice with the fate of the universe on the line. But it worked. Faustus streaked across the floor, crashed into the skeleton holding Bolton's arms, and freed the unlikeliest hero the world has ever known.

Dennis Bolton, former wheelchair-bound hacker extraordinaire, former internet-locked unicorn-faced sidekick, sprinted forward like he was the second coming of Usain Bolt, snatched Uriel's whip from the ground in front of the dying Archangel, and plunged his right hand into the stream of divine essence streaking heavenward.

Goddamn, I hope this works, I thought, knowing that if I'd guessed wrong, we were well and truly fucked.

I hadn't guessed wrong. The divinity wasn't just rushing out of Uriel's body, it was looking for a home. That was Lucifer's play all along—to kill Uriel and take his spot among the Host, then walk back into Heaven through the front door. But Dennis taking up the Implement and shoving himself between Lucifer and the energy pouring from Uriel's body gave the power somewhere else to go.

Right into the soul of a twenty-something computer nerd from North Carolina. Dennis lit up like a cartoon character getting electrocuted. His entire body was bathed in white, then he began to glow from within as more and more power flowed into him. The swirling pillar of light streaking to Heaven cut off like a switch, and all that divine energy flowed into Dennis, wrapping his soul and his manifestation in the holy light of Uriel and his brothers.

Lucifer gaped at me, the shock of what was happening leaving him open-mouthed. He dropped to his knees as Dennis began to float, began to spin around and around in the air, faster and faster as he began to change. His tight curly hair vanished, replaced by a flowing reddish-blond mane. His whole body lengthened, stretched, and grew as his mortal soul was absorbed and subsumed into the soul of the Archangel Uriel. A pair of brilliant white wings burst from his shoulders, and as he held both hands over his head, the deafening shriek of agony surrounding us from the second of Uriel's passing suddenly transformed into a chorus of trumpets and angels singing.

Then, barely three seconds after I'd wagered the fate of the universe on a hunch, it was over. Dennis/Uriel floated down to the ground, looked at the empty husk of Uriel's former vessel, and sighed. He reached over and patted the dead Archangel's body on the shoulder, and it transformed into familiar rainbow-colored sparkles before my eyes. Then he looked at me, and when he spoke, it was Dennis, but it was much, much more than Dennis.

"Thank you, Quincy Harker. We are restored. Your friend has made a great sacrifice, and thus shall live forever after."

"So what do I call you? Are you Dennis? Are you Uriel?"

"We are Uriel. We are of the Host. And the Host is once more complete. We are in your debt."

Great. He went from being an annoying digital unicorn to the Borg. "Well, if you're looking for a way to balance your books, what are we going to do about him?" I asked, pointing behind the newly-restored Archangel at a very pissed off Lucifer.

"If I might make a suggestion?" Faustus said, peering around a column.

"I'm all ears," I said, my mind still reeling at what I'd just seen. Dennis Bolton, Archangel. That was going to take some getting used to.

"Run," Faustus said, his voice hoarse with fear as he took in the sight of Lucifer growing in size as his fury consumed him. The dapper, charming devil in a tailored suit was gone, replaced by what I gathered was as close to Lucifer's true form as my mind could comprehend.

And to be clear, I wasn't comprehending a whole lot right at that moment. I was more stumbling backward with Faustus dragging me as I watched Lucifer morph into the kind of devil that nightmares were made of. This wasn't the Tempter, or the Father of Lies. This was the King of Hell, and he was pissed.

He grew to ten feet tall, and where the Archangels seems wrapped in a bright white light when they manifested their true forms, Lucifer was shrouded in darkness so absolute it dimmed the very air around him for several feet. Blackness roiled through the air around him, spreading out in all directions like hungry tendrils, seeking any vestige of light to be absorbed, corrupted, destroyed.

He didn't look like any of the demons I'd ever encountered before. He was still beautiful, but where seconds before it was a seductive glint in his eyes and a pleasing line of his jaw, now it was a cruel smirk and a look that promised untold pain at his hands were he to catch me. His form was still mostly human, only really damn tall, with long, wavy hair so black it almost seemed blue. There were no horns, no spiked tail, no hooves. Just a huge man, so perfect as to be a master sculptor's grandest achievement, but every edge seemed just a hair too sharp, just a touch too rigid to be anything more than frightening in its perfection.

Except for one flaw. The giant, perfect image of dark divinity had one thing wrong with it—the wings. Where all his brothers had huge, sweeping wings that almost dragged the ground, Lucifer's wings were...destroyed. They were still there, and they weren't the bat wings of legend, but they were a charred, mangled mass of soot-stained feathers and blasted shapes that only hinted at the majesty he must have had before the War. Before he turned on his Father. Before the Fall.

"No!" Lucifer screamed, and the very air in Hell shook with his rage. I stumbled, keeping my feet only because Faustus yanked me up by my collar.

"If you fall now, you'll die here. I don't think you want that," the demon hissed at me.

"No, I'd rather not. Too many folks down here really want a piece of me."

"Including the boss," Faustus agreed.

"Quincy Harker!" Lucifer shrieked. The ground rippled, and both Faustus and I were thrown from our feet. I rolled onto my back and looked as Lucifer drew a black blade from the air with his right hand and summoned a globe of power the size of a beach ball with the other. "I will destroy you! Your very name shall be synonymous with pain! Every human who has ever looked on you with kindness shall be ripped limb from limb! I will kill you, Quincy Harker, and when you die, I will resurrect you over and over again just so I can kill you more!"

The giant devil took a step toward me, flinging the sphere of pure energy overhand at me. I took a deep breath, reaching for power to summon a shield, but before I could, a slender figure stepped in front of me, shielding me from the blast and taking the full force of Lucifer's attack straight in the chest.

"Glory!" I yelled, scrabbling to my knees and crawling over to where she lay, flat on her back some ten feet away. I yanked her up into my arms, shaking her.

"Hey, Q," she said, her voice wavering as her eyes flicked back and forth, trying to focus. "That kinda hurt."

"What the fuck are you doing? You don't have your powers anymore!"

"No, look. Wings." I looked down, and sure enough, there were wings growing out of her shoulders, just like the good old days. They seemed out of place, with the giant black blast mark in the center of her chest, but she had her wings back. "Looks like all that divine energy pouring out of Uriel gave me back some of my mojo. Just… maybe not quite enough to take on Lucifer."

"Glory!" I shouted, shaking her.

Her eyes fluttered open. "Jeez, Harker. Let a girl sleep, will ya? My…chest hurts…"

I looked down, and her flesh was blackened and cracked. I could see the light within seeping out, like she was a vessel overfilled with water and bursting at the seams. "Goddammit, Glory, what did you do that for?" I bent my head, tears falling onto her face and chest, my anguish mixing with her divinity.

"Don't cry, Q. This is what I'm here for. I'm your guardian angel. I've gotta guardian. Says so right there in the job description. It'll all be okay. I…promise…" Her eyes rolled back in her head and she slumped back, unconscious. I laid her down on the polished marble, feeling the rage within me building to a level I hadn't known in decades.

This motherfucker. This motherfucker had taken me on a two-year wild goose chase, collecting divine beings like Pokémon, scouring the entire goddamn country for artifacts and Archangels. This motherfucker was behind Orobas, behind Christy's death, behind Renfield, even behind Dennis getting killed the first fucking time. I wouldn't be surprised to find his self-satisfied, grinning face lurking in the shadows the night Flynn's father died. Now this motherfucker kills Glory right in fucking front of me. "No." I barely heard the word. It was more that I felt it cross my lips, solidify in my soul.

"No." Louder. I stood up, turning to face the smirking Lucifer.

"NO." I called power, shaped the energy of Hell itself into a gleaming purple-black blade of power in my right hand.

"NO!" I drew more power into myself, felt my form shift, grow, and expand until I was staring the devil in the face. "NO FUCKING MORE!"

I wrapped both hands around the hilt of my magicked blade and dropped into a fighting stance. "No more, Lucifer. No more tricks, no more lies, no more schemes. Just one last fight. You and me. I win, I walk right the fuck out of here. You win, you get to keep me."

Lucifer smiled. Not the casually cruel smirk he'd worn every other time I saw him, but a genuine smile. "If I win? You poor, pitiful mortal fool. Don't you mean *when* I win? When I beat you to a bloody pulp and break you once and for all, body and soul? When I win, I'm going to make you watch while I destroy everyone you've ever loved. Every single person who has ever sheltered you, given you aid, or even smiled at you on the street will burn in my fires forever, and they will know that it is your fault. They will all know that Quincy Harker put them there." He smiled, and I felt a chill run down my spine. This motherfucker meant every word. He was going to destroy everyone I ever cared about, and there wasn't shit I could do about it. Except the only thing I knew how to do—fight.

Lucifer raised his sword in a salute. "Remember, Harker. I was one of God's mightiest warriors. I lost only one battle in all my time in Heaven."

There is, of course, one other thing I'm really good at besides fighting. Cheating. When it comes to fighting, I'm pretty good. When it comes to magic, I'm decent. But cheating? I am an Olympic gold medal-level conniver, cheat, and schemer. And this time, I managed to be just half a step ahead of the devil himself. And half a step was all I needed.

I smiled at Lucifer and raised my right hand, middle finger pointed to the sky. "Fucking good thing for me I brought the guy that kicked your ass then, isn't it?" From across the room, streaking like a white-winged comet, a super-sized Archangel Michael slammed into Lucifer's side, knocking the devil to the floor and raising his flaming sword high above his head. Lucifer rolled aside as Michael shattered the marble tiles with his blade again and again.

"If you're planning to leave, Quincy, this would be a good time. I cannot best my brother in his domain, merely delay him," Michael said. The rest of the Seraphim were moving forward now, making a circle around the two combatants, their faces grim. It looked like a whole lot of family issues were about to be worked out, on a cosmic scale.

I released all the power I'd been holding, shrinking back down to my normal size and tossing aside the magical sword. It vanished the second it left my grasp, and I bent down to scoop up Glory as I started to sprint away from Lucifer. "Faustus, remember that portal? Well, now's the fucking time!"

As Michael stepped in front of Lucifer, Faustus pulled a small orb from his pocket. "I really hope that imp wasn't lying. Concentrate on something that you've got to go home to. Fix the one thing you want to see again most in the universe and concentrate on that." Then he threw the sphere to the ground. The glass shattered, and smoke billowed out. The smoke solidified into a circle in the air, hovering about a foot off the floor.

I concentrated on the most important thing in my life—Flynn. Every time she ever smiled at me, yelled at me, kissed me, slapped me...all those things ran through my mind as the smoke hovered in the circle, a haze of gray that swirled for a second, then vanished. Through the circle I saw the sweetest sight I think I've ever seen—my living room. Flynn, Luke, and Cassie were sitting on a couch with coffee cups in front of them. It all looked so mundane. I froze for a second, unsure if I wanted to bring all my baggage, all my shit back into the world with me. Would it be better if I just stayed in Hell and let them move on without me?

Then Glory stirred, and as I looked down at the bloodied angel in my arms, I realized that it might be better, but it would also be spitting in the face of what Glory had done for me, twice now. It would be ignoring Dennis's sacrifice. It would be selfish, not to mention it would be letting Lucifer win, and while I was perfectly willing to give that asshole his due, I wasn't in any real hurry to do so.

I nodded to Faustus, and with a dying angel in my arms and a demon by my side, I stepped through the portal and went home, the rage-filled screams of Lucifer and all his threats following hot on my heels.

All was right with the world. Lucifer was still in Hell, Dennis was an Archangel now, and we were back in the proper dimension. Glory had even started to heal once we passed through the portal and gotten away from Hell.

I guess we saved the world. I mean, I kinda brought a demon back with us, so that's got its own problems, but Lucifer isn't sitting next to the Throne of God, so we'll call it a win.

So why did I feel so goddamn bad? I mean, we won. We made it out. I should feel awesome. I even had most of my building back, now that the rest of the Council had gone their separate ways.

Most of them, anyway. Jo and her daughter had an apartment one floor down, where they lived with Cassie. Luke was next door to them in a suite of apartments I was having renovated for his particular sensitivity to sunlight.

Pravesh got a place in Charlotte, transferring her position to "keep a closer eye" on me. Gabby, her girlfriend Renee, Jake, and his demon dad all piled into Gabby's Honda Element and left for Chicago that morning. Adam climbed into his giant Hummer and rolled out for Destination Unknown, and Glory pooled out to wherever she went when she was an angel and not looking after me. My bet was New

Orleans. That girl had developed a soft spot for beignets when she was human. Now that she could basically teleport, she was going to have to watch it or she'd end up in a sugar coma.

And Rebecca Gail Flynn was curled up in my bed, hogging all the blankets and currently spooning with my pillow. I was sitting in a chair staring at her as the lights of Charlotte peeked in through the curtains and bathed her with a blueish blend of moonlight and city light pollution. She was so goddamned beautiful it hurt my chest to look at her, especially knowing what I had to do.

I stood up, put the note I'd spent the last hour trying to write on the dresser, and picked up a bag. I crept out of the room, easing the door shut so as not to wake her.

"You don't have to worry, son. I put a little something in that last hot chocolate I gave her. That child will sleep through a plane crash right now."

I turned to see a small, slender black woman standing in my living room giving me a kind smile. "Sit down, Quincy. Why don't you tell me why you're sneaking out on the woman you love after literally going through Hell yesterday?"

"I can't stay, Cass," I said, slinging the duffel up onto my shoulder. "I can't stay, and I can't sit. I won't let you talk me out of leaving, so there's no point sitting around talking about it."

"Boy, I learned forty years ago there ain't no point in telling none of you shadow-chasing dumbasses nothing. That don't mean I don't need to know what's going on in your head so I can talk to that child when she wakes up tomorrow and finds some half-assed note on the dresser that probably don't say nothing but 'I'm sorry' or some other weak-ass shit."

I gave her a little smile. Cassie knew me better than I did myself sometimes. "You owe the swear jar three dollars."

She didn't smile back, just looked up at me with eyes that had seen a lifetime of sadness. "What are you doing, Quincy? She loves you. Do you know how rare that is? To find somebody who will love and deal with the kind of baggage you carry?"

I thought about a girl in France with brown eyes, and the beautiful woman with caramel skin less than twenty feet from me. "Yeah, I know how rare it is. I've done it twice in over a century."

"Then you are a lucky man, Quincy Harker, and you need to turn your narrow butt around and crawl back into bed with her. You done lost one true love, boy. You gonna walk away from another one?"

I blinked hard. If I let a single tear fall, I'd break. I'd break, and I'd stay, and I'd bring doom and pain and fire down around every one of them. "I have to, Cassie. I can't stay here. I can't be anywhere he can find me. I can't be with Flynn. I can't be around Luke. I can't be part of the Council, or near any of you. Maybe ever again."

"You think we scared of old Nick Scratch, Quincy? I been telling the devil to take the hindmost since I was a little girl in Sunday School. I ain't gonna start worrying about him now. He's in Hell, and I'm on Earth, and when I die, I'm going to see my savior up in Heaven. Lucifer ain't got no hold on me, and I ain't got no time for fear."

I envied the unshakable faith of this tiny black woman with snow-white hair, but it didn't matter how much faith she had. She was wrong, and if I stayed, she would end up dead wrong. "You might not be concerned about Lucifer, Cassie, but he's damn sure interested in you. He's interested in you, and Flynn, and Luke, and Jo. Ginny, Cass. He'll come for Ginny. He'll come for her to get to me because hurting her would hurt me, and that's what he wants more than anything right now—to hurt me. He's going to come for me, and I can't let any of you be collateral damage when he does."

"What you gonna do? You just going to go off and live like a hermit? You know it don't work like that. You can try, but this life is just going to keep pulling you back in. Why not stay here, with the people that love you? People that can fight beside you."

"Because I can't watch them die. I can't do it, Cassie. As long as I'm here, everyone around me is in danger. If I leave, then Lucifer has no reason to come after any of you."

"Except he's the devil, you idiot! What makes you think he's going to follow your logic? Dammit, Quincy, don't do this. Do not throw that girl away. Don't throw Luke away. He loves you like a son."

"And I love him. Almost as much as I love Flynn. That's why I'm doing this." I walked past Cassie to the door, stopping with my hand on the knob. "Tell her...tell her I love her too much to stay."

Then I opened the door and walked out on my life. As I crossed over the threshold, I felt Becks' consciousness stir along the link we shared.

Hmmm? Her sleep-voice sounded in my head. *What's going on?*

Nothing, babe. Go back to sleep. I love you. Then I used every ounce of mental discipline I had to shut off the link between us, locking her out of my thoughts and my mind. As the elevator doors dinged open, I had one last thought to send her.

I'm sorry.

NOT THE END

Don't miss the next thrilling chapter of the Quincy Harker saga! Sign up for my newsletter and get updates on new releases, appearances, and more!
https://www.subscribepage.com/g8d0a9.

I don't usually do these. Author's Notes, Afterwords, all that isn't really my style. But I think this book is a big enough turning point that it warrants a little peek behind the curtain into what's coming next for Harker and the team.

Let's start with this - it ain't over. It ain't even close to over. I have a lot more Harker stories to tell, and at least so far, you guys have shown plenty of desire to read them, so I think we'll be together for several more years, at least.

The way I write and release Harker books will change, however. I don't know if you've noticed, but for the past four years, I've released four short novels (novellas) each year, and collected them at the end of the year. This has worked out pretty well with my writing schedule, and most folks seem to enjoy it.

But the stories have gotten too big for that. This book marks the culmination of an eight-novella, two year story arc that spanned over a quarter million words. That's a lot to ask for a novella series. So we're going to expand the Harker books into full novels from now on.

What does this mean for you, the reader? Well, it means that you will get Harker books less frequently, two or three times a year instead of four, but they'll be at least twice as long as the books have been up to this point. So you'll get the same amount of Harker, it will just be condensed a little.

This also means that the collections will stop for the near future, because each book will be long enough to justify a print and audiobook edition, so those of you who love reading in print and listening to audiobooks will be able to get more Harker more quickly.

It will also mean that the stories have more room to stretch, because I can write them as long as they need to be, without having to wrap up to fit a format. When I started writing novellas, I was transitioning from writing a ton of short stories, and my work was naturally growing longer. Now that I've been working with novellas for several years, it only makes sense that my natural storytelling length would get longer.

So Harker isn't walking out on the world, just this part of it. He'll be back, as will Luke, and Flynn, and Renfield/Cassie. There will be some more stories with Jo, and with Jake/Gabby/Faustus, and Adam, and probably even Watson, although he's a little bit of a prick. And there will absolutely be more Glory.

Thanks for coming on this ride with me for the past four years, and I hope you enjoy the trip even more with what's to come.

JGH
   12/20/18
   Charlotte, NC

ACKNOWLEDGMENTS

Thanks as always to Melissa Gilbert for all her help, and for trying in vain to teach me where the commas go.

Thanks to Natania Barron for her amazing covers, and of course to all of you for reading!

The following people help me bring this work to you by their Patreon-age. You can join them at Patreon.com/johnhartness.

Sean Fitzpatrick

Sarah J. Ashburn

Amanda J. Dwyer

Noah Sturdevant

MarkF erber

Andy Bartalone

Nick Esslinger

Sharon Moore

Wendy Taylor

Sheelagh Semper

Charlotte Henley Babb

Andreas Brücher

Shael Hawman

Aramanth Dawe
Butch Howard
Lawrence Nash
Delia Houghland
Douglas Park, Jr.
Travis & Casey Schilling
Michelle E. Botwinick
Carol Baker
Leonard Rosenthol
Lisa Hodges
Patrick Dugan
Chris Kidd
Arthur Raisfeld
Mark Wilson
Darrell Grizzle
Liberty Becker
Kimberly Richardson
Matthew Granvilke
Kristie McKinley
Melissa Cole
Leia Powell
Candice Carpenter
Theresa Glover
Salem Macknee
Jared Pierce
Leland Crawford
Wanda Harward
Vikki Perry
Valentine Wolfe
Noella Handley
Don Lynch
Jeremy Willhoit
D.R. Perry
Andrea Judy
Anthony D. Hudson
John A. McColley

Dennis Bolton
Shiloh Walker/J.C. Daniels
Andrew Torn
Sue Lambert
Emilia Agrafojo
Tracy Syrstad
Samantha Dunaway Bryant
Steven R Yanacsek
Rebecca Ledford
Ray Spitz
Lars Klander

ABOUT THE AUTHOR

John G. Hartness is a teller of tales, a righter of wrong, defender of ladies' virtues, and some people call him Maurice, for he speaks of the pompatus of love. He is also the best-selling author of EPIC-Award-winning series *The Black Knight Chronicles* from Bell Bridge Books, a comedic urban fantasy series that answers the eternal question "Why aren't there more fat vampires?" In July of 2016. John was honored with the Manly Wade Wellman Award by the NC Speculative Fiction Foundation for Best Novel by a North Carolina writer in 2015 for the first Quincy Harker novella, *Raising Hell.*

In 2016, John teamed up with a pair of other publishing industry ne'er-do-wells and founded Falstaff Books, a publishing company dedicated to pushing the boundaries of literature and entertainment.

In his copious free time John enjoys long walks on the beach, rescuing kittens from trees and getting caught in the rain. An avid *Magic: the Gathering* player, John is strong in his nerd-fu and has sometimes been referred to as "the Kevin Smith of Charlotte, NC." And not just for his girth.

Find out more about John online
www.johnhartness.com

STAY IN TOUCH!

If you enjoyed this book, please leave a review on Amazon, Goodreads, or wherever you like.

If you'd like to hear more about or from the author, please join my mailing list at https://www.subscribepage.com/g8d0a9.

You can get some free short stories just for signing up, and whenever a book gets 50 reviews, the author gets a unicorn. I need another unicorn. The ones I have are getting lonely. So please leave a review and get me another unicorn!

FALSTAFF BOOKS

**Want to know what's new
And coming soon from
Falstaff Books?**

Try This Free Ebook Sampler

https://www.instafreebie.com/free/bsZnl

**Follow the link.
Download the file.
Transfer to your e-reader, phone, tablet, watch, computer,
whatever.
Enjoy.**

9 781946 926883